Gillian Kersley was born in ___ where Sarah Grand and Glad___ that time. She started writing ___ that she left Bath for London, ___ be 'a useful wife and secret___ Switzerland and America, sh___ London as a public relations ___ joining Hutchinson Publishing Group to do publicity. She lives again now in Bath, writing fiction in the spare moments when she is not being a 'housewife, mother and employee in her husband's company'.

Discovering Gladys Singers-Bigger's diaries in the Bath Reference Library led Gillian Kersley to write this unusual and immensely readable biography. Sarah Grand, one of the 'New Woman' novelists of the late nineteenth century, became famous for her 'indelicate' and 'unwomanly' novels, amongst them *The Heavenly Twins* and *The Beth Book*. In addition to her writing, she was an indefatigable lecturer, suffrage campaigner, and defender of Rational Dress. Retiring finally to Bath, she became Mayoress — and the object of passion for Gladys Singers-Bigger, a woman thirty years younger than herself. Gladys' diaries, published here, are a record of her years of passionate devotion to 'Darling Madame'.

If you would like to know more about Virago books, write to us at Ely House, 37 Dover Street, London W1X 4HS for a full catalogue.

Please send a stamped addressed envelope

VIRAGO
Advisory Group

Andrea Adam	Zoë Fairbairns
Carol Adams	Carolyn Faulder
Sally Alexander	Germaine Greer
Rosalyn Baxandall (USA)	Jane Gregory
Anita Bennett	Suzanne Lowry
Liz Calder	Jean McCrindle
Beatrix Campbell	Cathy Porter
Angela Carter	Alison Rimmer
Mary Chamberlain	Elaine Showalter (USA)
Anna Coote	Spare Rib Collective
Jane Cousins	Mary Stott
Jill Craigie	Rosalie Swedlin
Anna Davin	Margaret Walters
Rosalind Delmar	Elizabeth Wilson
Christine Downer (Australia)	Barbara Wynn

Book Tokens

Give them the pleasure of choosing

Book Tokens can be bought and exchanged at most bookshops

Darling Madame

Sarah Grand and Devoted Friend

by

GILLIAN KERSLEY

Virago

Published by Virago Press Limited 1983
Ely House, 37 Dover Street, London W1X 4HS

Copyright © of all original material Gillian Kersley 1983
Unpublished diaries of Gladys Singers-Bigger copyright ©
Dr Kirk Bryce 1983

British Library Cataloguing in Publication Data

Kersley, Gillian
   Darling madame.
   1. Grand, Sarah
  I. Title
   823'.8   PR6013.R272Z/
   ISBN 0-86068-307-9
   ISBN 0-86068-308-7 Pbk

Printed in Great Britain by litho
at The Anchor Press, Tiptree, Essex

The illustration on the front cover is A. Woodroffe's view of
Lansdown Crescent, Bath, and is reproduced by kind permission of Avon County Library (Bath Reference Library).

Contents

❦

Illustrations

❧❧

1. Sarah in her late thirties (Avon County Library [Bath Reference Library]).
2. D.C. McFall in the late 1860s (by kind permission of Mr Gordon McFall).
3. Portrait of Sarah (1896) by Alfred Praga (Victoria Art Gallery, Bath City Council).
4. Sarah and hat reproduced from *The Lady's World*, June 1900.
5. *Sarah Grand and 'Mere Man'*, a caricature from *Harper's Weekly*, 2 November 1901.
6. The Dickens Commemoration Dinner at Fortts Restaurant, Bath, 7 February 1925 (Avon County Library [Bath Reference Library]).
7. Mrs Singers-Bigger in the Morning Room at Marlborough Buildings, Bath, 1923 (photograph by Muriel Blackborne, reproduced by kind permission of Dr Kirk Bryce).
8. Gladys aged thirty (by kind permission of Dr Kirk Bryce).
9. Sarah as Mayoress of Bath, 1925 (Avon County Library [Bath Reference Library]).
10. Alderman Cedric Chivers, JP, Mayor of Bath (c. 1925) (Avon County Library [Bath Reference Library]).
11. Crowe Hall, Widcombe Hill, Bath.
12. Sarah's eighty-third birthday party at the Royal

Chronology: Sarah Grand and David Chambers McFall

Frances Elizabeth Bellenden Clarke (Sarah Grand)

1854   Born 10 June, the fourth of five children, at Bally Castle, Donaghadee, Co. Down. Father naval coastguard, mother well-educated Yorkshire woman. After a few years the family moves to Co. Mayo.

1861   Father dies and family leaves Ireland to live near Scarborough, Yorkshire.

1868   To Royal Naval School, Twickenham and then to a finishing school, Holland Road, Kensington, London.

1871   Marries David Chambers McFall, surgeon and widower with two sons, Haldane and Albert, aged ten and eight and a half. 7 October, David Archibald Edward (Archie) McFall born at Sandgate, Kent.

1873   *Two Dear Little Feet*, her first book, published.

1873–8   Stationed with husband and Archie in Singapore, Ceylon, China, Japan and the Straits Settlements.

1879   Stationed at Norwich. Visits Malta, Normandy, Isle of Wight. Writes *Ideala* and *The Tenor and the Boy*; both rejected.

1881   To Orford Barracks, Warrington, Lancashire, where McFall retires on half-pay as Medical

Officer and Hon. Brigade Surgeon.

1888   Pays for publication of *Ideala* in Warrington; two years writing *The Heavenly Twins*.

1889   Bentley re-publishes *Ideala*.

1890   Leaves McFall and Archie. Begins three-year hunt for publisher for *The Heavenly Twins*.

1891   Blackwood publishes *A Domestic Experiment*; moves to Sidney House, 24 Sinclair Road, Kensington.

1892   Blackwood publishes *Singularly Deluded*.

1893   7 February, Heinemann publish *The Heavenly Twins* in England and Cassell's in America. Changes name to Sarah Grand.

1894   Many interviews, speeches, articles and short stories published. Moves to larger flat at 60 Wynnstay Gardens, Kensington, and convalesces at Kirkleatham Hall, Redcar and at Ramsgate from bouts of nervous exhaustion.

1895   To Villa Mignonne, Cannes, for six months' recuperation, and then to Hôtel des deux Mondes, Paris.

1896   To Burford Bridge Hotel; visits with George Meredith and Alice Meynell.

1897   *The Beth Book* published while she is in the Pyrenees.

1898   McFall dies aged sixty-six, 8 February. Sarah buys 5 Mount Ephraim, two miles from Tunbridge Wells.

1900   Joins stepson, Haldane McFall, and his family at The Grey House, Langton, Tunbridge Wells. Lecture tours begin.

1901   *Babs the Impossible* published. In October to America for four months' lecturing in New York, Pennsylvania, Chicago and San Francisco. *The Heavenly Twins* republished by Street & Smith in America at 20 cents.

1903   Six months' neurasthenia; cures and recuperation.

1903–12   A decade of lecturing all over the country on *Mere Man*, *The Art of Happiness* and *Things We Forget to Remember*. She becomes a member of the Women Writers' Suffrage League, Women Citizens' Association, Vice-President of the Women's Suffrage Society, President of the local branch of National Council of Women, President, Chairman and principal speaker of the Tunbridge Wells branch of the National Union of Women's Suffrage Societies.

1912   *Adnam's Orchard* published.

1913   Involved in the NUWSS Pilgrimage to London.

1916   *The Winged Victory* published.

1920   Moves to Bath, where she lives with Miss Tindall and her brother at Crowe Hall.

1922–29   Mayoress of Bath with Alderman Cedric Chivers, JP, a widower as Mayor, for six years (excluding 1923–4) until he dies.

1925   Gladys Singers-Bigger first meets Sarah.

1926   Fire at Crowe Hall. Moves to 7 Sion Hill Place with sister Nellie.

1927–44   Gladys writes *Ideala: The Record of a Dear Friendship*.

1936   Gladys moves to London and back.

1939   Nellie dies.

1942   Bath blitzed. Sarah moves to The Grange, Calne; Gladys stays at a local hotel to be near her.

1943   12 May, Sarah dies aged eighty-eight.

1944   Archie dies in London air raid.

1950   Gladys returns to Bath.

1970   6 January, Gladys dies aged eighty-one.

David Chambers McFall, MRCS Eng., Brigade Surgeon
Lieutenant-Colonel (RP)

1832   Born at Magherafelt, Co. Londonderry,
            Ireland, ninth child of Thomas McFall
            (1788–1850) livery and hostlery owner, and his
            wife Mary Anne McKendrick who died in about
            1862.

1854–5   Acting Assistant Surgeon, RN, HMS James
            Watt, Baltic Expedition.

1855–7   Acting Assistant Surgeon, RN, Crimean War.

1857   Assistant Surgeon with Border Regiment
            (80th/87th Royal Irish Fusiliers and 34th Foot),
            Indian Mutiny Campaign. Married Abigail, his
            Colonel's daughter; three sons born in India;
            wife and baby died en route for home.

1871   Marries Frances Bellenden-Clarke (Sarah
            Grand); Surgeon of depot, Sandgate, Kent;
            fourth son (Archie) born.

1873–8   With regiment to Ceylon, Singapore, China,
            Japan and Straits Settlements.

1879   To Norwich as MO to 5th Royal Irish Lancers,
            21st Hussars and 1st Royal Dragoons.

1880   Retires on half-pay as Hon. Brigade Surgeon,
            Medical Officer, Orford Barracks, Warrington,
            in charge of 8th and 40th depots.

1898   8 February, dies at Folly Lane, Warrington,
            aged sixty-six; buried at Warrington cemetery.

MADAME SARAH GRAND: FAMILY TREE

This chart illustrates the influence of the Bee and Raven families but omits all irrelevant siblings

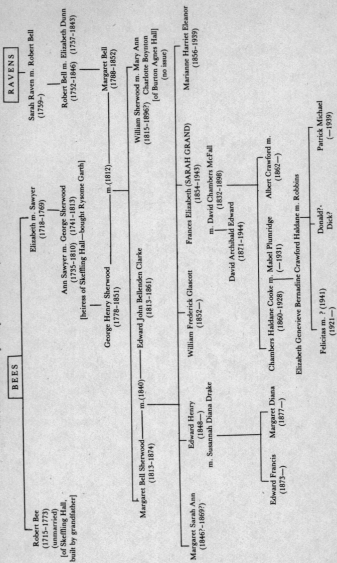

Acknowledgements

◖◗

In 1978 Virago published Elaine Showalter's book, *A Literature of Their Own*, about British women novelists and Sarah Grand's name emerged in print for the first time since her death in 1943. Carmen Callil noticed that material about Sarah was in Bath and kindly suggested that instead of writing unpublishable novels I should try more beneficial research. To Carmen and Elaine I offer my first thanks. But although it appeared that Sarah lay packaged, gift-wrapped, in my local reference library, the switch from fiction to fact was unnerving. In a novel the author has complete freedom to manipulate her characters to suit the plot, or vice versa. With fact every nuance should be justifiable. Sarah would have to be an algebra of periods and proof. How could I produce something so *numerical*? But the first step was taken without too great pain and in one month I had met Madame Sarah Grand and her acolyte Gladys Singers-Bigger through the first of Gladys' diaries. It was the perfect introduction for a non-biographer. The diaries, to me, coupled the emotion and poignancy of romance with such unimaginable and compulsive detail that fact towered above fiction. I felt so sorry for Gladys – and she had lived! Instant involvement and compassion made my hours in the library as real as those outside. I came home saturated in Gladys and Sarah, eager to return to their lives in the twenties.

Gladys first met Sarah in 1925 when, at the age of seventy-one and at the end of her career, Sarah was Mayoress of Bath. For Gladys, in her thirties and prone to hero-worship, the meeting was holy and prophetic: it led to a life-long devotion. Sarah gave meaning to her existence, as she had to many other women by her writing, and she inspired Gladys to record all the details of their relationship during her last sixteen years. These diaries, which Gladys began in 1927 under the title *Ideala's Gift: The Record of a Dear Friendship*, were written in seven volumes of minute detail as a link between herself and her Darling Madame. But they also show Sarah in the delicate role of a personal goddess when her sphere of influence had narrowed from many thousands to a handful. From the diaries I learned a great deal about Sarah's personality and also about their strange friendship and the unremitting boredom and frustration of Gladys' own life. That much was simple and enthralling.

The librarians were kind and tolerant and endlessly help-ful, unearthing all that Sarah and Gladys had left to the city. Apart from the diaries there were boxes containing some 400 letters, notes and cards, most of them still in their envelopes and tied together with ribbons; there were files of magazines and pamphlets containing many of Sarah's articles and short stories; four enormous, elegantly bound volumes containing all the press cuttings about the mayoralty of Alderman Cedric Chivers (1922–9) with whom Sarah was Mayoress, and photographs of Sarah. I owe many thanks to Mrs Joyce and Miss Wills in particular for their help and forbearance in producing all of these frequently from the vaults and, during nearly four years, for tracking down obscure books and journals and guiding me to the appropriate tomes of reference.

Elaine Showalter and Martha Vicinus (who was visit-ing England from Indiana University) advised and encouraged very early in the hunt and sent me invaluable material from America. I also had a helpful meeting with Joan Huddleston of the University of Queensland, who was compiling a bibliography of Sarah's works. Manchester Polytechnic gave me permission to read Sandra Lister's manuscript thesis on Sarah Grand which was of great assistance in leading me to other sources, and with luck I managed to obtain most of Sarah's novels and collected stories for more lengthy study at home. Suddenly it seemed that everyone I met was interested in Sarah, though some important facts about her life, notably her marriage, were for us all a matter of conjecture. However, the main jigsaw puzzle pieces were in place and it only remained to fill in the rest of the portrait of Sarah Grand.

Sarah Grand was a crusading New Woman novelist and campaigner for moral reform and sexual equality at the end of the last century: so much was abundantly clear. An immersion in New Woman novels and nineteenth-century history settled her writing and most of her preoccupations comfortably into this wider context for me. But at the same time, and the more I read, the themes of the New Women of the 1880s and 1890s appeared still relevant to today. Sarah and her peers, with their views on the education, employment, marriage and accepted role of women, could, in many ways, be describing, at the least, provincial life a whole century later. Despite so much political and economic change, so many years of agitation and awareness, despite the franchise, two world wars, and women's entry into all the 'masculine' trades and professions, there remains in this country both a suspicion about women, and a preconception of the role they can play. There remains a belief – perhaps only in the provincial middle class – that it is more necessary to educate a son than a daughter and that if a woman marries her interests and occupation should, ideally, be confined to home and hearth. Unless she contributes to the household materially, she is 'the dependent'. However well she may cook, advise, save, minister and administer, her activities outside the family

Darling Madame

can only be frivolous. Although she is now better educated, there is 'no point' in encouraging her to aim higher than to become a good secretary and a good wife. Sarah faced this problem, Mona Caird described it well (p.58), I know many women now who cope with it by conforming to the accepted nineteenth-century standard. A century of education is by no means complete.

Research into Sarah's history took as long as the background reading, but was more exciting because when a theory of date or place was confirmed another puzzle-space was filled, surrounding facts immediately took a more solid form and, as more and more accumulated, Sarah began to fatten and become more human. The pursuit was particularly exhilarating when a key supposition was verified. For example, through Major J. Kenny at the Museum of Lancashire Regiments and Mr R. Thwaites, Principal Librarian, Central Library, Warrington, I was able to establish (from an extract in the Warrington Borough Council Minutes of 1883) that Sarah's husband must have been involved with an Infectious Diseases Hospital. All that Sarah had written in her novels made this appear very likely, but to find what could be construed as proof brought that picture-piece and all that surrounded it into strong relief. I am very grateful to all who bothered to find such material for me. For their detailed knowledge of Sarah's family tree – and their efforts to explain it – I am indebted to Mr Ted Dunn and to Mrs Barbara Dando of Johannesburg. For information about Sarah's background and activities I would also like to thank all the following: the Reverend J.C. Swennarton, Rector of Donaghadee Parish, the Ulster Historical Foundation, Public Records Office, Ministry of Defence, RAMC Historical Museum, Wellcombe Institute, Dr Peter Dinnick, Mr J.C. Sharp, the Cleveland, Humberside and Cheshire County Libraries, National Library of Scotland, British Library, Fawcett Library, National Council of Women of Great Britain, Victoria Art Gallery at Bath City Council, and the

Bath & West Chronicle. For the use of many of Sarah's letters in their archives – and for the effort of selecting these for me – I am especially grateful to Mr Brooke Whiting, Curator of Rare Books and Literary Manuscripts at the Department of Special Collections, University of California, Los Angeles.

I am very much indebted to Dr Kirk Bryce for permission to quote extensively from Gladys' diaries and for most kindly supplying me with photographs of the Singers-Bigger family; also to Mr Gordon McFall for the early history of Sarah's husband – another frustrating blank – and for photographs which he found for me in the family album. Acknowledgement is also due to William Heinemann Limited for permission to quote from *The Beth Book*, *Ideala*, *The Heavenly Twins* and *The Winged Victory*.

But all the jigsaw pieces did not fall into place. I am saddened by some gaps which I cannot fill, notably about the McFalls. I have been unable at discover why Haldane McFall's wife does not appear to have been living with him during the twenty years, from 1900, that Sarah shared his house at Tunbridge Wells; nor what became of his brother Albert McFall. More important, since 1978 I have tried to discover the heirs of Sarah Grand, or whomever might now hold the copyright to her works. Letters requesting information were printed in the *Spectator*, the *Times Literary Supplement*, *Books & Bookmen* and the *Bath & West Evening Chronicle*. I have contacted the Convent where Felicitas Robbins (Sarah's youngest known heir) was educated, her retired headmistress, and Bedford College, where Gladys suggests that Felicitas was further educated. I have also corresponded with descendants of Sarah's brother-in-law. All to no avail.

Many people who live in Bath were of great help to me with their reminiscences of Gladys and Sarah and I am particularly grateful to Mrs Edna Davis, the Reverend Gordon Stringer, Mrs Doreen Radcliffe, Miss Elsie Russ, 'Destie' and Mrs Katharine Doyle. I am also indebted to

Mrs Elizabeth Turner who typed all Gladys' diaries from the manuscript and then re-typed my edition of them.

Without the support of my husband this book would not have been possible. And finally, for their belief in the project and for all their enthusiasm, I cannot effectively express my gratitude to Mary Scott Blake of Charlottesville, Virginia, Dr and Mrs Arthur Guirdham and my daughters Katherine and Caroline, to whom I dedicate this book.

PART I

Madame Sarah Grand

CHAPTER I

The New Woman

Behind Sarah Grand's story – as with most stories – we find sex and ambition. In the foreground is a proud and beautiful woman with the courage to break the mould of accepted behaviour and attempt to improve the imbalance between the sexes in Victorian England. By no means was she alone, nor was she the first. She did not leave much of an imprint on history, nor behave in any fashion that would surprise us now. But, fired by personal experience and a desire to alter the unhappy plight of women – particularly within marriage – the novels she wrote made her name notorious in the 1890s.

Many social reformers have had distinctive personalities and have exhibited unorthodox family relationships. Some drove themselves, and disturbed society, to such an extent that they cannot be forgotten or ignored; others wrestled quietly at solving apparently trivial problems. Usually, their desire to improve the world, and their belief in their message or mission, helped them survive censure and discomfort: they showed remarkable courage.

Madame Sarah Grand was such a woman. Her life spanned most of Victoria's reign and both world wars – a period of great social upheaval, particularly for women. Born before Darwin published *The Origin of Species*, at the time of Crimea, crinolines and female constraint, she lived through, and became an important figure in, the battle for sexual equality. By the time she became Mayoress of Bath in 1922, not only were women over the age of thirty allowed to vote but they had also shown themselves capable of independent thought and action – all unimaginable achievements in the years of Sarah Grand's youth.

Considering the accepted role of women in the nineteenth century – their subjection to father, husband or God – it is not surprising that an intelligent, independent-minded young woman should question this repression and, in particular, the prevailing double standard of morality for men and women. To take the next step toward open rebellion and positive action to improve the lot of women required more than shared bitter experiences. Sarah Grand possessed the necessary strength of character and drive to rebel; her medium was the printed word.

She demonstrated this strength early by marrying, at the age of sixteen, and then leaving a most unsatisfactory husband; and again later by writing 'wilfully eccentric' and 'indelicate' novels. Inspired by personal experience, she fought for moral reform at a time when women had no voice outside the drawing room and were not expected to complain. Sarah Grand's novels and articles not only defined the New Woman, they also enlightened the reading public about venereal disease: society was shocked, outraged. For a woman to have any notion of such a subject was distinctly unfeminine; for her to share and make public this knowledge was considered outrageous.

Unlike some of her equally famous contemporaries, Sarah Grand could have provided a stereotype of the 'good', silent woman in her early years. Her mother discouraged her from forming her own opinions, and from discussion in general. She was educated principally and cursorily by her widowed mother (all available funds sent her brothers to public school), and she felt herself deprived of love, concern and knowledge. Her resentment of this is reiterated again and again in her novels. Spurred on by this sense of injustice, like the heroines of her books, she set about educating herself, and discovered how easy it was for a girl to understand 'masculine' subjects such as science, mathematics, philosophy. And she was determined that other women should be aware of this ability in themselves, too. Like Olive Schreiner, she understood that 'self-development must precede social development', and so she committed herself intellectually and emotionally to improving both herself and others. Then she used that improvement as a weapon against the injustices of a male-dominated world.

She was never, I suspect, very fond of men. In all she wrote she rarely showed passion between her characters, neither did she demonstrate much compassion for any of her male creations. Possibly, her impoverished childhood, the early death of a weak but doting father, coupled with a self-sacrificing and unsympathetic mother, hardened her; certainly she was soured by her early marriage to an elderly, profligate army surgeon. Her chosen themes – 'purity' for men, and some kind of autonomy for women – are ideals pursued with more enthusiasm and verve in her novels than any sexual relationship, in however spiritual a light such a relationship is portrayed. Her heroines always suffer miserably from want of privacy or consideration, or from boredom. Her heroes are syphilitic, beat their wives, open their letters, steal their savings, flirt with barmaids and nursemaids, bring their mistresses home – or leave them to die in doss houses – drink, run Lock hospitals,[1] practise vivisection, force 'unwanted attentions'. Furthermore, if these attributes do not reduce their wives to dementia or death, these 'heroes' extract promises from their women that they will not take part in feminist activities. There is not a husband in Sarah Grand's fiction who cares for his wife's intellect or mental welfare; all her women are forced into subjection on marriage, most of them having anticipated it. Love – even the pallid sensation she allows – does not last once the banns are called.

Her characters become 'victims of holy matrimony' and
there is no joy in the relationship. Yet at the same time she
argued that 'marriage is the most sacred institution in the
world, and it is better not to interfere with it'.[2] This contra-
diction must be understood in its historical context: for
such statements helped to placate those who criticised her
'degrading' novels. But they were heartfelt too. If men
could be cured of immorality and disease and be made fit
for cohabitation with women, if the marital partner were
not from the 'sewers of society', and if he treated his wife
more fairly, then marriage was indeed good for society, she
argued. No one, after all, had yet discovered a better way
to curb 'animal' appetites. With the same reasoning,
Sarah Grand disapproved of divorce: 'Greater facility for
divorce,' she wrote in 1898, 'means more self-indulgence
for those who are that way inclined, and more misery for
the rest – especially the women and children.' And again:
'The recurrent excitement of passion is as dram-drinking
to the dipsomaniac, as dear a delight and as disastrous.'[3] In
the best of all possible worlds, she felt, marriage ought to
eliminate passion and sensuality, and free the individual
for service to the community. Her ideal was high and
perhaps uncomfortable, but certainly it was one her critics
would appreciate. Sarah Grand was one amongst many of
her contemporaries who bought sexual freedom for women
by denying her own sexuality.

Sarah Grand's upbringing was typically that of the
nineteenth-century woman: she was simply to enhance the
image of her mate and serve his needs. A narrow education
was considered not only right, but necessary for this role.
Knowledge of any subject beyond the more decorative arts
could only lead to dangerous thoughts and tendencies. The
less a girl was taught, the less she could argue; the less a
woman knew, the better (humbler, quieter) wife she would
make. Central to this notion was the belief that ignorance
was synonymous with innocence. Sexual ignorance meant
purity, chastity, and therefore 'good'; knowledge of any

kind automatically tarnished this innocence. The power to reason, or to choose, or to be responsible, could easily lead – so the argument ran – to promiscuity.

At the heart of the matter lay reproduction. For centuries women – like cattle – had been valued for their ability to breed. Their virginity was their patrimony and was exchanged for marriage. Anything that interfered with this transaction was deemed unnatural and morally wrong. To fulfil the bargain, purity was essential; contraception was considered a harlot's habit and female sexuality dangerous. Because prostitution was seen as a symbol of woman's relative (inferior) status, Josephine Butler and those like her, in their life-long work rescuing prostitutes, symbolically castrated the men who used such women. In attacking the Contagious Diseases Acts[4] so ferociously, feminists pointed out that it was male lust which created the problem. And this problem, syphilis, was a potential threat to every woman; a threat to her womb. Discussion of venereal disease for over twenty years (from the first Contagious Diseases Act in 1864 to their final repeal in 1886) and its propagandist use subsequently, in novels and on the platform in suffragette campaigns, induced apprehension, nervousness and hysteria amongst many women.

As late as 1913 Christabel and Emmeline Pankhurst were asserting that most of women's ailments and disabilities stemmed from diseases contracted from the 75 per cent – or more – of males they claimed were suffering from syphilis. Once fear of this disease had been implanted it grew with discussion, despite the indelicacy of the topic, to become a very real and personal terror for all women. The possibility of disease, which became apparent to any woman reading about the Contagious Diseases Acts in editorials or in correspondence columns in the press, was enough to create the Victorian 'virgin in the drawing room'. Sarah Grand is a prime example of such a 'virgin', but she made the outside world her 'drawing room'. In

1903 'Votes for Women – Chastity for Men', the slogan of
the Women's Social and Political Union, was to sum up
this emotion. Many women who fought for the vote
believed protection from syphilis to be as important as the
franchise: politics and purity marched together. (The suffragettes' colours included white for purity together with
green for hope and purple for dignity.) But Sarah Grand
had been writing her most outspoken novels a decade
earlier: it could be argued that she was among the founders
of the 'social purity' campaign.

The early suffragettes who fought for women's education and enlightenment found themselves in an anomalous
social position. By pursuing and advocating knowledge,
with its implications of freedom of choice and personal
responsibility, they turned their backs on the 'innocence'
of domestic passivity. All very unfeminine. The accelerat-
ing demand for female education and equality in the 1880s
brought with it open discussion of subjects formerly
considered taboo; all this talk was 'unwomanly' and
socially disruptive – and women such as Sarah Grand
appeared wicked, immoral, perverse. Independence of
thought might lead to independence of action. If a middle-
class woman could work and compete with men, what
would become of the happy home and hearth, the children,
monogamy and Christian values? And it was not only men
who felt threatened. Many women, too, foresaw chaos.
After centuries of domination and training in self-
obliteration, of being owned body and soul by father,
brother or husband, it is not surprising that the questioning of patriarchal authority appeared threatening to some
women.

Christian dogma, secular law and social custom were all
founded on the belief that woman was made for man.
Equal pay? Equal rights? Civilisation would collapse! But
revolt was in the air. At the end of the eighteenth century,
the French had effectively revolutionised their society, the
Northern and Southern states of America were at war over

the freeing of slaves, and the Industrial Revolution in England had forced social change. The Western world vibrated with the call to liberty, equality and human rights. The belief that all men are created equal, long suppressed, began to re-emerge. The idea that every man has personal, inalienable rights to freedom and justice led logically to a similar belief about woman, however much she might appear to be the chattel of her father or husband. But it was only with the transformation of marriage from a religious to a civil contract in the mid-nineteenth century that the emancipation of women really began. A number of Acts of Parliament, the first passed in 1839, gave women increasing authority over their property and person. Before these Acts women had had no legal autonomy whatever: they were the bond-servants of their husbands and 'no slave is a slave to the same lengths and in so full a sense of the word, as a wife is'.[5] In common with minors and idiots, women could not sign a contract, make a will or cast a vote – or be liable for crimes except murder or treason. They could not escape marriage as divorce was a male prerogative and, until 1858, was obtainable only by Act of Parliament – and they could be compelled to reside in their husband's house by force. They had no control over their children, who in law belonged solely to the father. As these laws were changed,[6] so the accepted behaviour of women changed too.

At the same time, the growing affluence, which resulted from industrialisation, led to the establishment of a rich middle class and many married women found themselves with nothing to do. Servants were employed to cook, clean and care for the young, and the middle-class woman was reduced to nothing more than a decorative status symbol. As Florence Nightingale wrote:

Very few people lead such an impoverishing and confusing and weakening life as the women of the richer classes . . . We do the best we can to train our women to an idle, superficial life; we teach them music and drawing, languages and poor peopling — 'resources' as they're called, and we hope if they don't marry they will at least be quiet.[7]

And when they did marry, as Mrs Sarah Ellis pointed out in one of her etiquette books: 'Depend upon it, if you were never humble and insignificant before, you will have to be so now.'[8] So the Victorian middle-class woman sat about in her drawing room, constrained by a crinoline made from twenty-five yards of silk; decorative and dumb and, according to Dr William Acton, a renowned medical practitioner, 'not much troubled with sexual feelings of any kind'[9] while her father, brothers and husband could do exactly as they wished and be as active as they liked – with or without her.

To the boredom and frustration of such a life was added a lack of purpose. In most families, no more than a generation earlier, it had been appropriate – and even necessary – for the wife to organise every detail of the household, to cook, and to care for her employees and their families in almost a feudal manner. However servile that life might have been for a woman, at least it kept her busy, and allowed little time for her to dwell on her plight or to consider the possibility of improving it. 'This consciousness of self is of recent growth . . . unknown to our mothers and grandmothers,' a critic wrote in 1897,[10] voicing the complaint of most men. But the Victorian middle-class wife, cushioned in crinoline and convention, was expected to do nothing of practical value. Even those who struggled on the fringe of this affluent society (like Sarah Grand's mother) could not envisage life without servants nor think of accepting payment for any casual creative activity. The new convention dictated that a lady did not work. Nor, as Dr Acton wrote, did 'the married woman . . . wish to be treated on the [sexual] footing of a mistress'. However, this inactive, purposeless life gave her the time to consider what she was doing and what she was not allowed to do. With the leisure to think, a sense of purpose became of supreme importance. In order to console herself that there was more to life than an animal existence – and Darwin's theory of evolution had shaken some of mankind's self confidence, as well as offering the possibility of self-improvement – she needed a role, an objective; to imagine that there was more to existence than a measuring of the days, a striving simply to survive or to pass through a vale of tears. The nullifying precepts of anodyne religion were also called into question. The object of life was no longer clear; the Age of Reason had passed with its simplistic answers. Women who had the time to look for more than delineated drudgery, took up 'causes'. They worked to improve the quality of life around them; for various reasons they so laboured. Deprived of ritualised activity, many found fulfilment in setting new patterns, fighting for new ideals. Anti-slavery, the campaign for temperance, evangelism, feminism presented themselves readily. The climate was right for the improvement of the human condition, but why had no one tried to solve these problems before? They all fell within the Christian ethic. Why, for instance, had there been so little public questioning – before Mary Wollstonecraft at the end of the eighteenth century – of the lack of opportunity for a woman to choose how she lived, and what she wanted to do?

The pattern of a woman's life seemed set, well nigh unavoidable – but why? Why should she, from the cradle to the grave, belong to a man to be ordered and ruled over as he chose? And should this be so? These questions, at first only rhetorical, became louder and more insistent. Why was the daughter not educated like the son? Why was it assumed that she could not think and act as effectively as her brother? Why should she anticipate her days as a life-long exercise in domestic economy with the production of heirs and the satisfying of a substitute father thrown in? Why? And should it be so? Once these questions were asked, Pandora's box flew open to let all the injustices tumble out, mount up and smother the questioner.

Towards the end of the nineteenth century the New Woman was born. She not only asked the questions – she demanded the answers.

These New Women wrote and talked of choice – of freedom of choice for themselves and the ability and opportunity to choose for their poorer and less fortunate sisters, too oppressed by the fight for mere survival to think about it. All they demanded was the necessary social reform that would allow a woman to live in her own right as an individual, rich or poor, married or single, from the start to the end of her life.

Sarah Grand was a New Woman – she was even credited with coining the phrase, which crystallised a mood, and captured the spirit of the age – and her crusading fiction articulated these theories and caught the popular imagination. The New Woman novels, written mainly by women, encouraged by cheaper printing methods, the growth of the popular press, and of wider literacy following the introduction of compulsory education for five- to thirteen-year-olds in 1870, achieved a temporary success greater than most books of the time that we now consider classics. They were often self-indulgent vehicles for personal affront, but they commanded a large, new readership which thrived on sensationalism. However shocked and outraged the literary critics and the establishment may have been, this new fiction sold in millions. Suddenly, it was fashionable to discuss feminine psychology and sexuality, and other 'revolting' topics such as divorce and venereal disease. Women poured out their resentments, repressions, hopes and fears to a vast and somewhat scandalised audience.

During the eighties the New Women had been reading John Stuart Mill, Flaubert, Zola, George Meredith and Olive Schreiner. But it was not until 1889 that Ibsen's *Ghosts* and *A Doll's House* were first performed in England, (a decade after they were written[11]). *Ghosts* was banned by the censor after its first performance in London because of its reference to inherited venereal disease, and reviewers described this performance as 'an open drain, a loathsome sore unbandaged' and 'as foul and filthy a concoction as has ever been allowed to disgrace the boards of an English theatre'.[12] Spurred by their own frustrations, many English women took up their pens: amongst them Mona Caird, George Egerton, Mrs Mannington Caffyn ('Iota'), Emma Frances Brooke and Menie Muriel Dowie joined Hardy, Gissing and Grant Allen in a clamour against the restrictions and narrowness of women's lives. Romanticism gave way to realism, sentiment to cynicism and, whether they pursued the 'purity' of truth and knowledge, or expounded on nervous disorders, disease and death, they were all, men and women, condemned as neurotic, self-conscious and hysterical. 'Self-sacrifice is out of fashion altogether in our modern school of novelists,' complained Hugh Stutfield in *Blackwood's Magazine*, 'and self-development has taken its place . . . their characters move about in an atmosphere of intense gloom . . . the sale of these books by thousands is not a healthy sign.'[13] A German woman of the period wrote: 'The woman writer affords excellent material for the psychological study of women . . . they all treat of the substitute which John Stuart Mill (it took an Englishman to do that) offers the modern woman in place of the right to love; they treat of woman's right to freedom.'[14] However, by the beginning of the twentieth century this theme in fiction had disappeared, and other issues took the place of female repression. But reticence on the subject of female sexuality and freedom had been broken, forever.

Sarah Grand helped to establish the concept of the New Woman. She was the first of the New Woman novelists, publishing *Ideala: A Study from Life* in 1888, and *The Heavenly Twins* in 1893, a few months before George Egerton's equally influential book, *Keynotes*. In all her novels, essays, articles and lecture tours, Sarah Grand continued her work until the subject seemed almost exhausted and women's employment during the First World War, as much as feminist activity itself, had given women many of the freedoms they demanded.

It is difficult to paint a true portrait of Sarah Grand, for her complex image is shattered by time. Unfortunately, her pride and her idea of what was right and necessary obscure some phases of her life. Through her novels, hazily, we can glimpse her feelings at particularly difficult times, but often she deliberately masks her feelings and her reactions to important and dramatic episodes, and we can only deduce the facts. Very early on she had schooled herself to suppress personal emotion and so she seldom revealed the real anguish of an often extraordinary and painful existence. She found it difficult to deal with love. Unlike most of her New Woman contemporaries, she avoids the heart-searching and the bedding: instead, she stresses the need for women to have knowledge and experience, personal integrity and freedom. Yet in spite of almost always describing marriage as intolerable, she approves of the institution in the abstract, and advocates conformity. She broke the rules of convention herself but was ever conventional.

Eighty-eight years she lived, and her body has rested high on one of Bath's hills for nearly half that time. At her death, even her obituarists had to work hard to recall her. The *Manchester Guardian* summarised the reactions:

The popularity of Sarah Grand's novels had been so completely forgotten and she herself had lived of late so secluded a life that even senior members of the firm of Heinemann, her publishers, had imagined that she died some years ago. It is hard to realise now what a shock *The Heavenly Twins* gave the reading public of 1893 or how outraged were the nineties by her conception of the new woman – one of whose characteristics was to be that she had learned about sex before marriage.

The Times gave her a firmer, though equally non-intellectual foothold in history:

In former years Ouida, Rhoda Broughton and others shocked their readers in order to amuse them, the writers of the Sarah Grand school shocked theirs in order to improve them.

And when the obituaries were over, Letitia Fairfield wrote to the *Manchester Guardian*: 'She was the real pioneer of public enlightenment on venereal disease. Participants in the Ministry of Health's campaign today can only guess dimly how much courage this took fifty years ago.'[15]

CHAPTER II

Early Life in Ireland and Yorkshire: 1854-71

In Ireland gales howl in from the sea and whip the water no
more than round other northern isles: men drown off the
shores of County Mayo perhaps no more than off the
Yorkshire coast. But to young Frances Bellenden Clarke
(Sarah Grand),[1] who grew to love the sea in all its moods,
those waves and the lowering mountains seemed as cruel as
her childhood. Corpses in the water surface in her
memories of Ireland, and again in her memories of adolescence in a Yorkshire fishing village. They first appeared in
stories repeated by her father, a coastguard, and later as
the observation of a girl with too much unoccupied time
and plenty of imagination. Because her father was a
coastguard and because her mother's family lived on the
Yorkshire coast, almost all her childhood was spent within
sight, smell and hearing of the sea. Images of waves, spray
and sea airs interweave her thoughts, actions and reactions
in her childhood and adolescence. Waves batter and break
throughout her childhood memories; later, drawing from
her experience in the Far East, her literary material dwells
upon typhoons and sea storms. And finally she always
takes her holidays beside the sea, strolling along pier and
esplanade, her eyes on the blue of the horizon.

So although the early pictures we have of her are faint
and blurred, like little sepia portraits, dark engravings seen
through murky glass, grim etchings of almost deserted
countryside, there remains a colour to her childhood – a

hint of sunlight on the sands, and a grey-green haze from the water. Although she wrote as though preoccupied with the wrongs and poverty of her youth, she could still convey the warm colour of primroses and the elegance of swans on a lake. She saw no harmony in those early years and described them as debilitating, but we can understand how at the same time they strengthened her character so that as a woman she could not only withstand tragedy, but could also observe and capitalise on her own unhappiness. From the beginning – and increasingly – she felt herself to be special, a misunderstood genius. This feeling carried her through the poverty of her childhood, the problems of her adolescence, and the very real shocks and disappointments of her early marriage.

Sarah Grand was born Frances Elizabeth Bellenden Clarke at Donaghadee, County Down, Ireland, on 10 June 1854.[2] Her father, Edward John Bellenden Clarke, a naval lieutenant then serving as coastguard in Northern Ireland, came from an East Anglian Quaker family. His father, Edward Clarke, was a London solicitor, and his sister, Harriet Ludlow Clarke, a well-known Victorian artist, designed the 'Becket' window in Canterbury Cathedral. While nothing more has been traced of the Clarkes, it is probable that Sir James Clarke Ross, who discovered the north magnetic pole, was a cousin.

On 24 March 1840, Edward John Bellenden Clarke married in Holborn, London, Margaret Bell Sherwood, daughter of George Henry Sherwood, Gentleman, of Holmpton County of York. In a letter between Margaret's cousins we learn that 'Miss Sherwood is to be married shortly to a naval officer of the name of Clarke. Mr S. gives her 6000 pounds.'[3]

Sarah's stepson, Haldane, was a keen genealogist and particularly interested in her pedigree, which he drew up on her mother's side in elaborate detail. Her mother, Margaret Bell Sherwood, was a 'well educated Yorkshire

lass', and the only sister of the last Lord of the Manor of
Rysome Garth in Holderness, whose family estates were
sold in the 1880s. Sarah's Sherwood grandparents united
in an unhappy marriage to prove and perpetuate an
ancient curse to the effect that 'the blood of the Bees put in
the same vessel with the blood of the Ravens would never
mingle'. Sarah and her stepson were both intrigued by
this.[4] (This relationship in shown in Sarah's family tree
p. vii.) When the last male Bee died in 1773, his fortunes
passed to his great-niece who married George Sherwood.
(This gentleman, incidentally, used her funds to buy
Rysome Garth, as the ancestral home at Skeffling was in
bad repair.) The last Raven, who lived nearby, was Sarah
Raven who married Robert Bell; her granddaughter
married George Henry Sherwood in 1812. This mingling
of 'bees' and 'ravens' led them into the unhappiness
predicted by the curse, according to Sarah Grand.[5] Some
belief in the continuation of this curse could explain, for
Sarah, the miserable life of her mother, her own problems
and those of her son who ended the line (as far as we know).
Haldane McFall, Sarah's stepson, in a marvellously
pompous and title-encrusted article announced:

Madame Grand is thrice in the direct descent from the
Plantagenet Kings of England, having for forefathers two sons
of Edward III, both Lionel, Duke of Clarence and John of
Gaunt. She has for ancestors the Norman Kings of England,
William the Conqueror, and the Dukes of Normandy – also
the early Kings of France, being in the direct line from Hugh
Capet and from Charlemagne; and she numbers amongst her
forefathers Alfred the Great, and amongst her foremothers the
Lady Godiva of Coventry fame, who put herself to shame to
save her people. It will thus be seen that Madame Grand's kin
have acquired a somewhat pronounced habit of making a
noise in the world.[6]

Leaving aside all that royalty, how splendid for a confirmed feminist to lay claim to descent from Lady Godiva!
Perhaps this heredity explains Sarah's ambivalence about

her birthplace which she described as little more than a hovel in *The Beth Book*, but when she became famous insisted was Bally Castle, in interviews about her background. In fact it was an ordinary house, probably called Rose Bank, a typical residence of someone acting as coastguard in the area. Sarah's facility to exaggerate, yet remain credible, grew with her, enhanced her fiction, and helped to confirm the personality she presented to the world when the world was finally forced to accept her. Who else in the turbulent yet socially correct closing years of the nineteenth century could change her name and be accepted as *Madame* Sarah Grand without better reason than that it was easier to remember than Frances McFall?

Frances – as we shall call Sarah in her youth – was the second child born in Donaghadee, the fourth youngest of five children. Both her older brothers, one very fair and one very dark, were educated as well as possible and joined the navy as commissioned officers, Edward being nick-named 'Black Clarke' and gaining a reputation for being 'rather wild'. Her elder sister died when young, leaving Frances and Nellie, two years younger, as close com-panions throughout their isolated youth and later in old age. Nellie, always in poor health with asthma, became a Queen Alexandra Sister at St Bartholomew's Hospital, London, and did much to organise probationers, and improve the nursing of diphtheria patients.

Soon after Nellie's birth, Lieutenant Bellenden Clarke moved his family to County Mayo, his last appointment. The journey from Northern Ireland to the west coast took three days of swaying down rutted lanes and across 'long lonely lands of bare brown bog', shadowed by great dark mountains, a 'nightmare of nausea' for Frances, punc-tuated by stops to change horses when she was lifted from the carriage and made to lie on a sofa, or spend nights in a strange bed. They were met at the end of the journey by her father, on horseback, who escorted them the last few miles to the mean town where they would live for the next

couple of years until he died. This town she later recalled
with childish simplicity as neatly divided into Irish and
English, Catholic and Protestant, the squalid and the
merely shabby, the immoral and the upright; divided by
the main street which acted as an invisible barrier, each
side viewing the other with distrust from its veiled windows
or shattered panes. In a predominantly Catholic district,
the Bellenden Clarkes drew together in religious hostility
with the few other Protestants, centring their lives on
Church and Sunday School. Here, at the age of six,
Frances' personality already began to make itself felt.
There had been talk, she remembers,[7] of suspending her
from Sunday School, but instead she was given a class of
twelve children and told to teach them all she knew about
God, which she did by repeating the Bible stories her
mother had told her. This sounds highly fanciful, but there
is no doubt that she was precocious – giving little Nellie
nightmares with serialised bedtime stories 'crammed with
horrors' – and that she left County Mayo when she was
seven. Certainly, too, the religious antagonism and the
poverty of Ireland impressed her as she showed later in her
largely autobiographical novel, *The Beth Book.**

The Beth Book is the only source from which we can
glimpse the young Frances, and read her observations and
memories of Ireland and of her family. She depicts a very
impressionable child, 'peculiarly sensitive, high-strung,
nervous', with surprising recall of the atmosphere of
poverty, the dour countryside and the conflict of her family
life. County Mayo is all 'great melancholy mountains',
sombre colours and turbulent seas, all of which terrified
her. Their house is 'built of stone and very damp . . . a
great deal of space in it, but little accommodation'. The
paper peels from the walls, piano strings rust despite
constant care, so that most of the notes become dull or

*All unnumbered quotations here and in subsequent chapters are from *The
Beth Book – Being a Study from the Life of Elizabeth Caldwell Maclure*, Heinemann,
1897, Virago Press, 1979.

soundless; Catholic servants from the other side of the street are sluttish, uneducated, overbrimming with Gaelic myths and superstitions, but warm and friendly with the children whose parents represent chill authority. Talk of an exhumation, a hanging and a water-distended corpse mingle with the everyday realities she witnesses: the butchering of animals in the street, a fire which guts the mill, mites in the cheese gobbled by her father. A favourite nurserymaid is sacked for 'papistical abominations' – teaching the children Catholic hymns and prayers to the Blessed Virgin. But her parents in those days showed little other interest in her development, and she was subject to her mother's inexplicable beatings:

There was no intelligent direction of her thoughts, no systematic training to form good habits. Her brothers were sent to school as soon as they were old enough, and so had the advantage of regular routine and strict discipline from the first . . . there is no doubt that [she] suffered seriously in after life from the mistakes of those in authority over her at this period.

Mrs Bellenden Clarke, for all her good breeding, found it difficult to cope with her husband, her children or their way of life. We are frequently assured that Beth's mother 'was not made for labour, but for luxury'. 'Her whole air betokened gentle birth and breeding . . . [and] she had the pluck and patience of ten men.' But all this was of little use against the damp and drink and despair:

She lived in the days when no one thought of the waste of women in this respect [a delicate woman raising too many children on too little income] and they had not begun to think for themselves . . . A woman was expected at that time to earn her livelihood by marrying a man and bringing up a family; and so long as her face was attractive, the fact that she was ignorant, foolish, and trivial did not, in the estimation of the average man, at all disqualify her for the task.

So she ordered bottles of whiskey for her husband, cooked frugal, unpalatable meals, failed to control

unsatisfactory servants and resigned herself to her duty of
childbearing. It all began happily enough when she
married: 'the daughter of a country gentleman, accustomed to luxury, but right ready to enjoy poverty with the
man of her heart.' But this – once her £6000 dowry was
spent – soured into married life which was 'one long sacrifice of herself, her health, her comfort, her every pleasure,
to what she conceived to be right and dutiful'.

   Although some sixty years later Sarah suggested that
this was not a faithful portrait of her mother, I believe that
her earlier memory was the more accurate. In two different
letters she wrote:

I can't think why you should suppose it is [autobiographical],
but I have forgotten what it is all about. I haven't looked at it,
that I can remember, since I corrected the proof sheets.[8]

That reference of Dr Whitby's to my mother which suggests it
is possible to mistake Mrs Caldwell for her displeases me. I
think Mrs Caldwell might well have the qualities of courage
and endurance I give her. Many a woman has them. But my
mother was *grande dame* to the tips of her fingers, and Mrs
Caldwell was not, if I remember myself.[9]

Grande dame she may well have been, but that does not dis-
count her inability to cope with a less than grand life, run a
house and control a family without the funds and assistance
natural to *grandes dames*.

   In her earlier writing, Sarah lays the blame for her
frustrating childhood squarely with her mother for not
appreciating and encouraging her. There was no praise
because it might make her vain and she had no recollection
of 'a caress given or received, or of any expression of
tenderness'. She attributes her slowness in learning her
ABC to this, and says that her mother 'checked her mental
growth again and again, instead of helping her to develop
it'.

   Towards the end of his life, Beth/Frances insinuates
herself into her father's affection by brushing his hair to

relieve his headaches and chattering to him while they weed the garden together. Finally, and too late, he comes to appreciate her, reads to her the *Ingoldsby Legends* and dies with her captive, bound in a fixation for him which affects her future choice of husband and her treatment of the heroes in her novels, all of whom are father figures set apart sexually by death, the Church, homosexuality, age or by all of these together.

Her father died in 1861 when Frances was seven. Her mother brought the children back to the East Riding of Yorkshire to settle near Scarborough, within reach of the Sherwoods. It seems that the Sherwoods did not want to be concerned too closely with the impoverished widow and her five children. In 1861 her brother William was farming the 543 acres of Rysome Garth and employing six men and a boy, and by 1871 he was married to Charlotte Boynton (Aunt Grace Mary Benyon in *The Beth Book*), whose brother owned Burton Agnes Hall, proudly possessed of 365 windows. Childless, William obviously did not want the servants bothered and the Manor disturbed by his ill-kempt, uneducated nephews and nieces.

In Yorkshire, Frances and Nellie ran wild for a few years – 'the aimless out-of-doors life of a girl in the later sixties and early seventies', Sarah later recalled (with historical inaccuracy because by 1868 she was at Twickenham). Their poverty by this time was only comparative. I suspect William Sherwood felt it necessary to subsidise his sister because the children had access to his library and they owned a piano which her mother taught young Frances to play. At the age of eleven she composed some songs and sent them surreptitiously to a publisher. They were returned – her first rejection – and fell into her mother's hands. The ensuing scene, when she was lectured that 'ladies only work for charity' and should never expect payment, became a lasting, galling memory. Her mother's reaction, so illogical to a sensitive child, was an important influence on her earliest feminist feelings. (Even in 1923, campaigning for fair pay at a Ladies of Limited Means sale in Bath, she mentions the 'memory of a relation's childhood' when the mother would not allow her to keep payment from a publisher.) This, and the unfairness of giving her brothers a better education than hers and Nellie's always irritated her. But she continued to play the piano, compose songs and to write and submit stories – which were all rejected.

Apart from the lack of education and the poverty of their diet in order that the boys 'might have the wherewithal to swing a cane, smoke, drink beer, play billards', Sarah's strongest memory of that period was of her dress. All her life she cared inordinately about clothes, her first involvement with the suffrage movement stemming from her interest in the Rational Dress Society. One can understand her feelings and sympathise when, amongst her other privations, she describes her appearance in 'uncouth clothes' and her repugnance for a particular frock and her brother's cast-off jacket. Mrs Bellenden Clarke thought grey a ladylike colour, and so Frances was given a dress of dove-grey for the summer. This soon became stained 'and every spot upon it was a source of misery', but the torture of a soiled frock was soon surpassed by having to wear a boy's jacket for warmth in the autumn. The 'common people' jeered, and rather than go out 'dirty and ashamed' she preferred beatings and other punishment. And it wasn't just the over-garment that was a source of ridicule. In the 1860s the crinoline or the crinolette adorned every lady of fashion; little girls' dresses, equally flounced, grew longer with their age. Poor women made do with extra material in petticoats or underskirts, and anyone could see if a girl possessed only one old flannel petticoat beneath her skirt: the local children made fun of that, too. Later, when her Great-Aunt Sarah died, Frances remade and gloried in the old lady's light lavender silks.

And so Frances' early adolescence passed in resentment,

embarrassment and a practice of self-denial brought on by religious fervour and her brothers' demands. In between, she poached rabbits from her uncle's estate, scribbled notes, ideas, stories and verses, daydreamed and flirted with the local lads.

She was 'just at an age when the half-educated girl has nothing to distract her but her own emotions' when her great-aunt, Sarah Bell, who had lived with them and who had been good to Frances, died, leaving a small annuity for her education. Like any other adolescent, she 'became subject to hysterical outbursts of garrulity, to fits of moody silence, to apparently causeless paroxysms of laughter or tears; and she was always anxious'. She also pined for the kindness of her great-aunt and finally, when Frances was fourteen, Mrs Bellenden Clarke, seeing no other way of coping with her, reluctantly decided to use the annuity to send her to school. Despite the excitement of anticipation and new clothes, her mother managed to dampen Frances' pride and pleasure in this departure, as in all others, by making her feel she was robbing her brothers. The relationship between Frances and her mother, by the time they had taken trains from the north to the south of England, was so bad that all the natural pain of parting and homesickness were swallowed in sullen dislike. And so, from her arrival at school, Frances was labelled an unnatural child.

The Royal Naval School at Twickenham occupied a great house by the river with beautiful grounds and a view of the bridge with its many arches. At first sight it seemed a promising exchange for Yorkshire, but her 'free roving outdoor habits', which had led to a healthy if not a happy life, were curbed, and she could not settle to the discipline of school. She hated the narrow classroom with its long, bare tables and hard, wooden benches, the constant noise, the method of teaching by a series of jeers and insults, the whole educational 'system of exemplary dulness', and above all the confinement and constraint.

. . . and everything else was taught in the same superficial way . . . The dull routine of the place pressed heavily upon her, and everything she had to do was irksome . . . the confinement, want of relaxation, and of proper physical training, very soon told upon their health and spirits.

They were 'not taught one thing thoroughly, not even their own language and remained handicapped to the end of their lives for want of a grounding in grammar', she also remarked – possibly as an answer to Mark Twain who had deplored her lack of it in her early novel, *The Heavenly Twins*.

'Who was William the Conqueror? When did he arrive? What did he do on landing?' were the questions set out in her history primer, each with its answer to be learned by heart and recited parrot-fashion, so that any significance was lost in the effort to be word perfect. Questions such as 'But what did the battle of Hastings *do*?' went unanswered.

When she arrived at Twickenham she had 'only a slight acquaintance with the multiplication table, and the first four rules of arithmetic', despite her mother's intensive last-minute effort to coach her through the entrance exam. Her spelling, she also recalls, was 'original' and her hand-writing 'like an old gardener but worse . . . because it has been cruelly cramped in view of the scarcity of paper, and the pressure of ideas'.[10] Again, in 'Some Recollections of My School Days' she describes the 'deadly dulness' of the routine and the frustration from lack of exercise or any outlet for the energies of a high-spirited girl: no games, an hour's 'deportment' once a fortnight and 'monotonous walks up and down the gravelled paths . . . in classes, each like a sorry caterpillar, moving reluctantly'. Her description of that first school must have been accurate because she received 'a shoal of letters' from other former pupils after the publication of *The Beth Book*. Despite her unhappiness and the close puritanical régime, she somehow and surprisingly (when we consider how sheltered her life was) learned about Josephine Butler and enthused to the other girls about her campaign to repeal the Contagious Diseases Acts – to such an extent that it led to her departure from that school.

It was in 1864, when Frances was ten, that the first of three Contagious Diseases Acts was passed. These Acts, designed to check the epidemic spread of syphilis in the armed forces, penalised women only, and became a base from which sprang feminist demands to end all inequality. In eleven listed garrison towns and seaports, the first Act provided for the forcible surgical examination of any woman suspected of being a prostitute, and her detention in a government-certified (Lock) hospital if she were found to be infected with venereal disease. The third Act, passed four years later, increased the number of towns to include two in Ireland as well as Malta and the British cantonments in India, and a plain clothes 'morals' police force was set up to arrest the possible offenders. The Acts did not provide for the control or isolation of infected men, and a Royal Commission reporting in 1871 made it clear that to inspect soldiers and sailors for symptoms would be 'degrading'. Certainly some control was necessary. Over a quarter of the British Army was infected and their death rate from syphilis, after the Crimean War, was double that of the civilian population. Certainly, too, the implementation of the Acts reduced these statistics. (Sir Henry Storks, High Commissioner of Malta, claimed, inaccurately, with their help to have wiped venereal disease from that island.) But the anger of many women – and of Josephine Butler in particular – was roused because the Acts were directed only against the women, leaving infected men to spread the disease to their wives and any other women they encountered. This argument was taken up by both men and women writing in the nineties and Sarah's most successful and controversial novel, *The Heavenly Twins*, deals with the effect of a syphilitic husband.

By rescuing the prostitute – the symbol of woman's inferior status – the campaigners could undermine male

supremacy generally. Those concerned were particularly
incensed that these Acts officially condoned prostitution by
turning such a woman into 'a vessel periodically cleansed
for public use'.[11] Mrs Butler had spent years working with
prostitutes before she began her campaign to repeal the
Acts. She knew that it was poverty, not vice, that drove so
many women on to the streets and that there could be no
real solution without drastic inprovement in their education and conditions of employment. So the two campaigns – for morality and education – marched together,
and although it took more than twenty years to abolish the
Acts, the campaign broadened during that time to fight
other inequalities, social and marital, and gained more and
more advocates of both sexes, leading slowly to female
emancipation and the vote.

Frances' enthusiasm for and involvement in this cause
began at the age of fifteen when she

formed a club to perpetuate the principles of Josephine Butler,
the social reformer. School authorities objected to her action,
and 'representations' were made by the headmistress to
the effect that another school would be more suitable for so
bright a child.[12]

She is adamant that she was not expelled and that 'her
career . . . ended honourably, if somewhat abruptly'.[13]
(Her last Half Report read 'unsatisfactory'.)

Whether it was her support for Josephine Butler that led
to her removal or whether, as she put it in *The Beth Book*, it
was her dangerous tendency to religious scepticism and her
habit of escaping to perform midnight exercises in the
moonlight, her career at Twickenham ended and she was
sent immediately to a small finishing school in Holland
Road, Kensington. Although she says that at both schools
marriage was the great ambition of most girls, the finishing
school considered that marriage was 'the only career open
to a gentlewoman and the object of her education was to
make her attractive'. To this end she entered a new world
of ease and refinement, liberty and showy 'accomplish-

ments'. Languages, music, drawing and dancing were all thoroughly taught and the handful of pupils were not only shown the cultural delights of London, but were also encouraged to read.

We do not know why she left this school as suddenly as she did, and after an even shorter period than the first, but as soon as she had settled to enjoy a sensible and disciplined education she was brought home to Yorkshire. The death of her elder sister, Margaret, and her mother's grief and need for companionship (as mentioned in *The Beth Book*) may have been the reason, though this seems improbable when we remember the lack of sympathy between them. It seems more probable that her mother considered her sufficiently well educated for marriage, and wanted the annuity back in the household for the benefit of her sons.

So Frances' formal education was over two years after it had begun, and she returned home at sixteen with marriage as her only escape from the poverty, both real and spiritual, of family life.

CHAPTER III

Marriage and the Far East: 1871–81

❧

In 1871 when he married Frances, David Chambers McFall was thirty-nine, a widower and Assistant Surgeon attached to the 34th Foot, the Indian Border Regiment. He had two sons from his first marriage who were only a little younger than his new wife, and his age and authority presented him to Frances as a good catch and an ideal substitute for her long-regretted father. Further attractions he offered the sixteen-year-old girl were escape from the drudgery of an unappreciative home and school into the only career she could anticipate; escape with a man of romantic proportions, considerable experience of the world, a man full of stories of battle and personal prowess, death and healing. David Chambers McFall was a hero and, now his active service life was complete, he could gain promotion and settle as Medical Officer of Depots – out East, it was rumoured – where he could take a wife to share his exciting life. Frances needed little prompting to accept this splendid offer. McFall, in urgent need of a mother for his two boys, flattered her effortlessly and the marriage was arranged in a matter of weeks. How and where they met I cannot discover. I can only assume that McFall was staying with friends in Yorkshire while on leave after his prolonged duties in India. Certainly the marriage had to take place before she could join him in his next appointment, many miles south in Kent.

David McFall was born in December 1832 at Magherafelt, County Londonderry, Ireland. His father, Thomas McFall, owned a livery and hostlery business in the town and his mother gave birth to nine sons and two daughters in Magherafelt where their hotel was described as 'respectable, comfortable and well-conducted'.[1] Three of his brothers were christened Archibald (two of those died), one brother studied law and later took over his father's hostlery – by then the Grand Hotel, Bangor, County Down – one became a saddle and harness maker and another emigrated to Canada. David was the youngest son. He probably learned his basic medicine with a local doctor or apothecary, for there are no details of his having qualified formally at any hospital. He is first recorded as practising as Acting Assistant Surgeon with the Royal Navy. At the age of twenty-two he was on board HMS *James Watt* during the Baltic Expedition, and was present at the bombardment of Kiel during the Crimean War. Here he tasted the first horrors of bloodshed and distinguished himself too, receiving a medal and clasp for his services. However, he resigned his commission with the Navy and enlisted in the Army. He was immediately posted to India, with the 87th Royal Irish Fusiliers and the 34th Foot, known as the Border Regiment, with the rank of Assistant Surgeon. In India, he served throughout the Mutiny and had to cope with at least three serious outbreaks of cholera. Several times he was recognised and mentioned in the War Office despatches, and received a second medal and clasp for his work in this campaign. In India, cholera presented a hazard quite as decimating as that of war, and the standard of hygiene during the native army revolt was even worse than in peacetime. In 1873 Dr James Thornton wrote:

It has long been understood by the authorities in India that removal from the affected locality is the most serviceable measure that can be adopted when cholera attacks a body of

troops . . . standing orders directing this step be taken in all
serious outbreaks of cholera [have been issued].[2]

But he added that sanitary measures for the prevention of
the disease were better, and a pure, uncontaminated water
supply best. Stamping out cholera epidemics amounted
more to clearing, cleansing and fumigating the buildings
with sulphur than to medical expertise in treating the
afflicted.

Whilst in India David McFall married Abigail, his
Colonel's daughter, and they produced three sons:
Chambers Haldane Cooke, Albert Crawford and the
youngest, whom they called Eric. Soon after Eric's birth
the family set out on the long voyage home in a troop ship
where Eric fell ill and died; he was buried at sea off the
island of St Helena. Poor Abigail did not survive the shock
of losing her baby and was also buried at sea, off Ascension
Island, leaving McFall to make his way with Haldane and
Albert, to join his brother at Bangor. The two little boys
arrived in Ireland more proficient in Hindustani than
English, appearing like Indians to their startled relations.

We can assume that McFall left the boys with their uncle
when military duties and the pursuit of a wife took him to
England, and that his courtship of Frances was hastened by
his need to provide a home for them. The poignancy of his
story and the excitement of his accounts of life in India
must have fascinated young Frances whose thirst for
knowledge of the world was as great as her need for a hero
to whom she could give her love and upon whom she could
build her future.

Early in 1871 a speedy marriage was arranged in
England. Although Sarah Grand found it difficult to recall
him with kindness, and her descriptions of him in her
novels are barbed and bitter, McFall must have appeared
splendid to the inexperienced Frances. Always well
dressed, a bit of a dandy, with very white hands and curly
dark hair, he had 'a red and white clear complexion, grey

green eyes . . . and wide-spaced teeth'. In the photographs we are struck most by the cold little eyes and a moustache that quite obscures any teeth; but the expression of disdain, and the uniform, could well have impressed the young girl. More than that, he praised her intelligence which made her 'more pleased than if he had called her beautiful'. This flattery and the urgency of his courting coincided with 'the inevitable friction' between Frances and her mother, 'the shocks and jars and difficulties and disagreements'. She says she saw no other escape from 'long dull dreary days and loneliness'. McFall offered her self-improvement as well as independence. She wrote: 'The great inducement being that I should be able to study thoroughly any subject I liked, learn languages so that I could speak them, and music so that I could play it, have command of good books, and escape from routine.'[3] Such attractions to a girl like Frances were more than enough: she never mentions any love between them, and never says that she admired anything other than his knowledge. Later, she was to describe his courtship as insensitive and mercenary, but what she subsequently wrote of husbands, suitors, and men in general, as well as of McFall in particular, was always disillusioned, disgusted. Perhaps her later reaction to him muddied the waters, distorting her memory of earlier feelings.

With no other experience of male company except that of her brothers for comparison, and isolated in a Yorkshire fishing village, McFall must have seemed a reasonable gamble. There was no reason why he should be any less suitable than the next man. She herself was the problem, for even at sixteen she felt that she had potential, that she, Frances Bellenden Clarke, had individuality, personality, a future. And her marriage to McFall was the first step towards an unspecified goal. Possibly, probably, she married in cold blood to escape an unhappy present. And despite the fact that she had been taught – and knew – nothing about men or marriage, it was the right choice for her because experience and knowledge could now flood into her confined world. Her marriage allowed her to travel and learn far more than if she had chosen to settle for some Yorkshire squire. Frances Bellenden Clarke had to be buried, but, effectively, Frances McFall was to take her place. In *The Beth Book* Sarah Grand makes up for the pain of that death of individuality by allowing her heroine to keep her surname 'for her father's sake, and also because she could not see why she should lose her identity because she had married'. To lose herself so totally in another individual, without any lasting passion to fuse that union and spark a pride in that new name, must have added to her sense of loss. Madame Sarah Grand, her third incarnation, I am sure grew out of this void.

So the wedding picture shows not just a simple pose of gallant army officer, hand on sword, and bright-eyed maiden, buttoned and bowed, skirts flounced and trimmed. The husband's bewhiskered smile reflects relief that all that wooing is over and Frances' eyes express anxiety as much as excitement. She has done the right thing, behaved as she should; she has pleased her mother, fulfilling her role as daughter and woman. Lightly she has crossed the threshold from dependence on her family to become the responsibility of her husband.

On 7 October in the same year a son was born. They christened him David Archibald Edward after his father, his McFall uncles and his maternal grandfather. McFall's two other sons, Haldane and Albert, by then eleven and nine, were probably also living with them at that time but would soon be sent away to boarding school, for they are not mentioned again until, as young army officers, they became friends with their stepmother. In December, McFall was appointed full Surgeon and Major in the 80th Royal Irish Fusiliers and for a while the family lived happily at Sandgate, Kent, where McFall settled to routine medical work at the local army depot, and Frances concentrated on the host of new experiences in her life.

Married life at first seemed a great improvement on the strange and disturbing emotions of her adolescence, when her awakening sexuality had produced discontent, black moods and fantasies. With marriage 'a sort of content' settled on her and 'that strange vague yearning ache, the presence of all things incomplete, was laid'. Although she disliked a vulgarity in McFall's behaviour and speech, for the first time in her life she felt herself admired and wanted and her personality could expand in this warmth. After years of criticism or disregard she seemed to be loved. McFall made much of her and she liked that, but it wasn't long before she became satiated with this sensuous life, the 'incessant billing and cooing, and of a coarser kind'. She began to realise that his approaches 'were for his own gratification, irrespective of hers' and, whether from frustration or disgust, she became bored by the repeated sexual act and lost 'any zest for his caresses'. Any sensual feelings she had herself were discouraged by her husband's insensitivity and by an even crueller invasion of her privacy when he started opening her letters. An introspective young woman at the best of times, she soon found no corner of her life, home, body or time that could be called her own and she began to see his behaviour as 'a breach of good taste and good feeling'. Gradually the 'habits of dutiful submission' destroyed her desire to respond, and led to cold pretence. The honeymoon was over.

But for the young wife there was considerably more to her new life than sex and she used McFall (perhaps as mercilessly as he used her) to increase her knowledge of the world. Like a leech she sucked from him any and every medical detail and fact, 'collecting material for which she had no use at the moment, and storing it without design'. At the same time, as wife of the depot surgeon she now met other officers' wives and observed their fashion in manners and dress, little of which pleased her. Fashion over-ruled common sense to an absurd extent: tight-lacing to produce a tiny waist; elegant booting to cripple the feet to the necessary admirable proportions; unhealthy tastes in clothing, feeding and rearing babies. Sarah watched and listened, noted and wrote 'The Baby's Tragedy'[4] (a short story not published until the 1890s) about the virtual murder of a baby by its mother's refusal to listen to her stalwart nurse while her head was full of fashionable misinformation.

The facts she learned from McFall about physiology and prophylactics are peppered throughout all her novels and made her work remarkable to reviewers, although initially these facts were presented as little more than mere regurgitation of almost undigested details. In 1873 she wrote and published *Two Dear Little Feet*,[5] a morality tale about tight boots which ran to 125 pages of serious lecturing. In this, her first published work, under the name of Frances E. McFall, she sets down, page after page, the names and functions of bones and ligaments, how man and giraffe both have seven neckbones, case histories of inflammation, pain, fever, death under chloroform, and finally an analysis of racial differences which typify the eugenicist attitudes of the time:

African negroes, Bushmen of Australia and, indeed, all low savage races, have broad, flat feet, thick ankles near the ground, low heels, and badly formed calves to their legs; while in the higher races the feet and legs are well formed.

Despite this advantage her heroine, Laura, cripples herself with tight boots. Her corns, inflammation and bunions lead young Frances to admonish the reader thus:

The scales of the cuticle fall off, or are rubbed off, continually, and it is the 'Rete Mucosum' which makes new scales . . . so that it is very important that it should be well-protected, and kept in good working order, else we should soon have no outside skin, and the consequence would be that we should bleed whenever we were touched.

Each page is filled with sincerity and such eagerness to

improve our understanding of our feet – an exhausting theme in no way subliminally approached in a tract which hammers home its slogan: 'a healthy mind can only exist in a healthy body'. This sentiment recurs again and again in her writing. Sixteen is a most impressionable age and poor Frances was forced to experience marriage, motherhood and medicine all at the same time. She needed time to assimilate such complex matters, to understand them and to fit them into some proportion with the rest of her knowledge. With her blow at boots, her life as a crusader began. By the age of nineteen she was in print – and on her way with husband, baby and English nursemaid to Singapore and further, hopefully enriching, experiences.

Five hectic years followed, years of experience not normally offered a Victorian girl. She travelled extensively in the Far East through Ceylon, the Straits Settlements, China and Japan. In Singapore she attended her first dance and 'got many partners being the only young girl present'.[6] She obviously delighted in pulling rank: 'As wife of a senior officer, a surgeon-Colonel [sic], she took precedence over women much older than herself.'[7] Of course it all thrilled and excited her. The baby, Archie, proved no problem with Chinese amahs and an English nurse to care for him, and she whirled from one country to another setting up house, supervising servants and still finding plenty of time to observe local customs and behaviour and to toss off little stories. Roman Catholic missionaries in Hong Kong, where McFall was attached to the Wellington Barracks and the military hospital ship *Meeanee*, were a source of information as much as inspiration, and here she began an interest in denominations other than her own and a questioning of doctrine in general. In China she had the opportunity of observing for herself the practice of foot-binding and could begin anew about feet and health:

When a girl is seven or eight years old, her mother binds them for her, and everybody approves. If the mother did otherwise, the girl herself would be the first to reproach her when she grew up. It is wonderful how they endure the torture; but public opinion has sanctioned the custom for centuries, and made it as much a duty for a Chinese woman to have small feet as it is for us to wear clothes! And yet . . . when they are taught how wrong the practice is, how it cripples them, and weakens them, and renders them unfit for their work in the world, they take off their bandages! . . . When I learnt that, and when I remember that my countrywomen bind every organ in their bodies, though they know the harm of it, and public opinion is against it, I did not feel that I had time to stay and teach the heathen.

And although she was initially struck by 'the strange appearance of the people, and the quaint humour of their art' she quickly saw through to 'the like in unlikeness', the 'familiar old tune, as it were, with a new set of variations'. So much to do, so much to learn and so many new opinions to sort out. Arranged marriages she could defend from the heart: 'The girl has no illusions to be shattered, she expects no new happiness in her married life, so that any that comes to her is clear gain.'[8] Frances was always comparing and contrasting, collecting facts and views and storing them for future use.

She wrote two pieces about her experiences in Hong Kong, 'Ah Man'[9] and 'The Great Typhoon'[10], in both of which she describes the leisured life, the servants and the atmosphere surrounding their comfortable house, the verandah 'overlooking a grove of mango trees, the heavy foliage of which formed a screen between me and inquisitive amahs and coolies who might be loitering in the road below. The fruit shone ochre against the green in the cloudless sunshine.' During her brief time in Hong Kong she experienced both an earthquake and a typhoon and she started German lessons, a part of McFall's marriage bargain that she might improve herself. In Hankow she was paid what she later called 'the greatest compliment' when her Chinese hostess requested her to arrange the flowers, which she did 'English fashion',[11] and then settled to learn the Chinese symbolism of line.

The earthquake cracked their part of the town 'from top to bottom' and, from her description, appears to have shattered part of their house. She tells of the months of heat 'from a sky bare as a lidless eye of all solace of cloud', and her compensating dreams of snow and ice; the crashing, throbbing uproar of the earth movement, the greater stillness after the shock, and the howling Chinese out in the street where she ran with her English maid to escape. In the morning she saw:

some of the buildings had slipped from the perpendicular, one here and there had collapsed altogether, great cracks appeared on others, and roofs had fallen in; but the damage looked old and accustomed already in the first glow of the sunrise.[12]

She notes that 'not less than 20,000 people lost their lives' in the typhoon which struck Hong Kong on 22 September 1874. Despite omens and portents, plagues of flies, terrified animals and birds, flotillas of junks scurrying into harbour and seeking refuge up creeks and inlets ('long before daylight they were all swept out to sea, and nothing more was heard of them'), Frances went to bed at 10.30. She awoke with a crash to find that

It was pitch dark, the wind and rain were beating in on me, the sea roaring in my ears, and I could hardly breathe. My husband heard the crash, and came running in with the servants and lights. He discovered that one of the doors had given way, and the vibration of the house had loosened a large portion of the ceiling, which had fallen upon my bed, suffocating me with dust. The strong white calico at the top of the mosquito-netting was bulged down by the weight of the plaster to within a yard of my head, but did not tear, and so saved me.[13]

In the confusion and darkness McFall and his household ran about bravely barricading doors and windows until 'it became evident that no effort of theirs could save the house'. Then Frances lost husband, child and nurse in the shrieking, crowded streets and had to make her way with the house boy through 'the furious wind and the showers of missiles, the streams of water and the broken branches of trees' to the safety of the barracks where she found the nurse and her son, and spent the rest of the night on a mattress between a mad woman and a corpse. 'The loss of life on land,' she wrote, 'was bad enough, but on the sea it was so great that for days after the storm we did not dare to go to the windows or to look at the water for fear of seeing the bodies floating about the harbour. There were not men enough left to bury them, and many drifted far out to sea, where ships reported having seen them.'

These terrifying experiences she gathered into short stories which she sent regularly to the editor of *Temple Bar* and other magazines. Although she had succeeded with the publication of *Two Dear Little Feet*, none of these editors showed any interest in her stories, and, miserably, she accumulated rejection slips. In a letter to her publisher, Richard Bentley, in 1889 she wrote:

I have been in the habit of sending the Editor of *Temple Bar* a paper ever since I was 17. I sent the first from Singapore, the next from Hong Kong, and some from Japan, and suffered agonies once they had gone. It was a whip to get them back again. But all the same I believe the Editor of *TB* is an ogre who lives above a dark cavern, eats motherless babes, and growls when anybody approaches. Probably he makes those 'returned with thanks' comments out of baby clothes.[14]

During her five years in the East, apart from writing these rejected short stories, she began to form the views on men and marriage that later became the core of her creed. She had the perfect opportunity – given to few women at the time – to see 'the agony of woman's lot in the East . . . with her own eyes', and 'to experience "the moralless monotony" [sic] and "romantic misdemeanour" which

makes up life in Anglo-Eastern communities'. An article
about her, published many years later tells us that this
oriental experience

burnt into her soul and . . . has always coloured – it may be
involuntarily and unconsciously – her views on the women's
movement in the Occident [and] warped her outlook upon
men and their ways. East of Suez, as Kipling tells us, 'There
ain't no ten commandments', but the repeal of the Decalogue
·applies mainly to the masculine gender. There is among
Europeans in the East one law for men and another for
women. This unequal dispensation had, no doubt, its effect on
the acute, alert mind of the Brigade Surgeon's young wife,
and home she came with a distinct, but not unnatural, bias
against 'mere man'.[15]

However, in her writing of this time it is the island of
Malta that figures as a hot-bed of social intrigue for
regiments abroad, and although some of her characters
have reached Malta from the East, and have names and
characteristics already described in the more naturalist
Hong Kong stories, her years in the Orient seem not to
have shocked her moral sensibilities. Either the McFalls
were posted in Malta for a short period on their way home
to England or returned there soon after: whichever, her
feeling for that island is coloured entirely by the social life
she experienced there. That the English inhabitants of
Malta seem, in the main, such cruel caricatures in her
novels could well reflect a growing dissatisfaction with
McFall. I believe that it was in Malta that she first became
disillusioned with him. The easy, artificial society she
describes was evidently attractive to him and distasteful to
her. And after the Malta period, her son Archie no longer
seems to have been important to her: thus far there had
always been a baby or a toddler in her plots. The slide to
disenchantment had begun and although she worked hard
at collecting facts, observing manners and mannerisms,
and forming theories on morality, education and employment for women, she began to feel wasted, unfulfilled.

Describing the need for work for women, she wrote shortly after, 'And all this seems to me a grievous waste of Me!'[16]

In 1879 McFall was appointed to the barracks at Norwich where he had charge of the welfare of the 5th Royal Irish Lancers, the 21st Hussars and the 1st Royal Dragoons. Frances, with little other distraction, absorbed the essence of the place to use it as Morningquest, the cathedral town where her three principal novels are set. Norwich and its surrounding countryside is the most minutely examined and most favoured background for the embryo feminists she created in her books. It was here that Frances started visiting the poor and found sympathetic friendship with people outside the Regiment. During the next two years she wrote the first part of *Ideala: A Study from Life* and planned 'The Tenor and the Boy', a strange story of transvestism, 'highly sentimental and extravagant',[17] which was finally published, almost inconsequentially, as an 'Interlude' in *The Heavenly Twins* (and much later, on its own, in 1899).

The Tenor is the leading chorister at Morningquest Cathedral, a beautiful, aesthetic young man with a 'history': he is uncertain of his origins (his father was certainly titled) and he has shot his best friend in a hunting accident. The Tenor has a spell-binding voice as well as 'dark dreamy gray eyes' and a passion for flowers. The Boy is a married woman – one of the 'heavenly twins' – who, at midnight, masquerades as her brother and ensnares the Tenor. Angelica – this dual personality – is simply trying to escape convention and the artificial relationship between the sexes. Dressed as a boy she seeks and finds comradeship with a man – a relationship which, at that time, could only exist 'man to man'. They meet at night, converse, stroll arm in arm, and develop a 'masculine' cameraderie during several months of nocturnal meet-ings – cooking bacon and eggs in the Tenor's house, arguing, joking, singing and playing the violin. Their relationship is easy, relaxed and close, with joking asides from the Boy about his 'sister' whom the Tenor idolises – appropriately, from afar – while singing in the Cathedral. (Mark Twain in his annotated copy of *The Heavenly Twins* commented: 'all this about the boy in this Book IV is very good fun indeed.')[18] But all is lost when, happily rowing together, the Boy falls overboard. Rescued by the Tenor, 'he' is carried back to the Tenor's house, wrapped in blankets and clasped in the Tenor's arms and then a lamp is lit. 'But – "God in heaven!" he cried . . . for this was not the Boy, but the Tenor's own lady, his ideal of purity.' With 'high-minded, self-contained dignity' the Tenor restores the girl (with half the brandy he would have administered to the Boy). 'His idol was shattered, the dream and hope of his life was over . . . she was . . . the dishonoured fragment of some once loved and holy thing.' Thereafter, the Tenor can only die of pneumonia – 'seized by attacks of haemoptysis' – brought on by his activities in the river and heart-sickness at the outcome. Frances' argument behind this poignant story shows her own endless chafing at the constrictions placed upon her sex and her desire for

the delight of associating with a man intimately who did not know I was a woman . . . free intercourse with your masculine mind undiluted by your masculine prejudices and proclivities with regard to my sex. . . . I wanted to *do* as well as to *be*.

'I'll have no sex in my paradise,' the Boy remarks. It was 'brotherly love undisturbed by a single violent emotion' that Frances wanted. Her married heroine escapes into this idyll, but fails; her 'lover' is all that McFall was not, but he dies. Although, as always, Frances was attacking the conventional role of married women, she could not allow the woman to win, nor the man to survive.

In February 1881, McFall, approaching fifty and retirement age, moved to Warrington, Lancashire, where, on half-pay, he became Honorary Brigade Surgeon and Medical Officer at the Orford Barracks, in charge of the health of the 8th and 40th depots. Here deeper dissatisfaction and disillusionment were to set in.

CHAPTER IV

Disillusion in Warrington: 1881–90

❀

Those years in Warrington were the bleakest and most cruel of Frances' life. She was now twenty-seven, and ten years married – old and wise enough, we can assume, to know what she wanted, and to feel the frustration of not achieving it. Many things she had not understood when she was younger now became horribly clear. The life she had chosen began to seem intolerable and she saw no means of escape.

Her writing was spurned. Since the early publication of *Two Dear Little Feet*, only four short stories had been accepted, three of them by *Aunt Judy's Magazine for Young People*[1] – not a major literary triumph. All were returned by more serious journals, and many accumulated in manuscript in her bottom drawer. The same fate also fell to her novel *Ideala: A Study from Life*[2] which she completed soon after her move to Warrington: 'no publisher would look at it'. *Ideala* was 'put away in a drawer for seven years'[3] and nothing at all was published until she paid for the novel's publication herself in 1888. Those seven years of rejection caused her as much agony as the deterioration in her domestic life, but she did not give up or change the purpose of what she wrote. Her views on marriage and the plight of married women hardened with experience, and she used those years to complete her most famous and controversial novel, *The Heavenly Twins*, as well as two others, *A Domestic Experiment*[4] and *Singularly Deluded*.[5] These two lighter-weight stories were finally published by Black-wood's in 1891 and in 1893, after she had left Warrington.

But in the meantime, stuck in that dreary town in 'a rough manufacturing district', her frustration grew and McFall's behaviour deteriorated. She hated the factory chimneys belching smoke and smuts and chemical fumes, and 'the people themselves . . . unlovely in thought, word, and deed', but far worse than that, she was now isolated with her husband without much social life or congenial companionship. To his already reprehensible habits of opening her letters, drinking, smoking in her bedroom, piling up debts ('Debts are a symptom of weakness of the moral nature'[6]), and telling her lewd stories, his sexual demands on her – usually late at night and reeking of alcohol and tobacco – continued and she also suspected he had a mistress. When she locked her bedroom door he demanded she open it saying: 'I've a legal right to come here whenever I choose': she felt contaminated by him.

'The tragedy of such a marriage,' she tells us in *The Beth Book*, 'consists in the effect of the man's mind upon the woman's, shut up with him in the closest intimacy day and night, and all the time imbibing his poisoned thoughts'. In her view he was utterly depraved and therefore depraving, and she agonised over the effect he was having on her. Against this she argued, 'We are what we allow ourselves to be'[7] and 'we always may be what we might have been',[8] but she realised that 'by tacitly acquiescing she was lending herself to inevitable corruption'. She was faced with a moral dilemma and she tried to write it out of herself in poetry and prose.

The Orford Barracks, which occupied twenty acres in the parish of St Elphins, had only been completed in 1878; the buildings were of 'red pressed bricks with string courses and ornament of Staffordshire blue brick, except the Armoury which was asphalt'.[9] It existed for regional recruitment and training for the 8th and 40th Regiments of Foot which, in the year of the McFalls' arrival, changed

their titles to the King's Regiment and the South
Lancashire Regiment. The barracks were constructed to
hold fourteen officers and about 400 troops, with stabling
for three horses, and contained a hospital with five beds.
These beds McFall could use only for brief emergencies;
any cases requiring lengthy or complicated treatment
necessarily had to be removed to the local hospitals.
Obviously McFall had to deal with soldiers infected with
venereal diseases and could not limit them to his five beds,
so the Warrington Borough Council resolved:

that all cases of infectious disease occuring within the military
depot at Orford be admitted to the Infectious Diseases
Hospital on payment by the military authorities of one guinea
per head per week.[10]

This hospital, it would be reasonable to assume, was the
local Lock hospital where suspected prostitutes could be
forcibly detained, and examined under the provisions of
the Contagious Diseases Acts. Although the Acts were suspended in 1883 and repealed in 1886, it can also be
assumed that McFall had several years of involvement with
the hospital and, being the insensitive man he undoubtedly
was, that he made no effort to keep this connection from his
wife. Frances' reaction can well be appreciated. At fifteen
her knowledge of what syphilis involved must, at most,
have been sketchy. In her late twenties, with a decade of
army medical observation behind her, she was in no doubt.
In this she was well ahead of her time, though her interest
in the disease was to be typical of many of the progressive
men and women of her class in the next decade. By the
1890s her knowledge of and interest in venereal disease
brought her notoriety and acclaim. But in 1870 a Dr
Preston wrote:

I don't like to see women discuss the matter at all. No men,
whomever they may be, admire women who openly show that
they know as much on disgusting subjects as they do

themselves, much less so those who are so indelicate as to discuss them in public.[11]

And public opinion had not changed much in the meantime.

Frances' feelings, once she had learned the facts, were definite. That McFall had connections with 'the whole horrible apparatus for the special degradation of women' was a source of humiliation as much as outrage. When she asked him 'What do you do to the men who spread it? What becomes of diseased men?' her husband in *The Beth Book* replied, 'Oh, they marry, I suppose. Anyhow that is not my business.' In *The Heavenly Twins* she makes Edith, the Bishop's carefully protected daughter, marry the debauched Sir Mosley Menteith despite the heroine's warning that 'marrying a man like that, allowing him an assured position in society, is countenancing vice, and helping to spread it', and Edith dies insane. 'The children of the depraved will be depraved,' Sarah affirms. 'The consequences become hereditary and continue from generation to generation.'[12]

Germinating at roughly the same time, and published the year after *The Heavenly Twins*, Emma Frances Brooke follows the same theme in *A Superfluous Woman*: her villain Lord Heriot is 'saturated with mental disease and feebleness', and the heroine's imbecile children exhibit 'the crimes and debauchery of generations'.[13]

I have myself known 8 of those dreadful Edith cases [Sarah wrote in 1894]. Don't you think it a disgrace to our civilisation that such a thing shd be possible? It ought to be made a criminal offence, and will, I expect, when men themselves wake up to the fact that the numbers said to be diseased by dissolute living in Europe are one in three and in America one in five, and also that the disease is incurable and has been known to recur twenty years after it has apparently disappeared. What can a father do to protect his daughter from the possibility of infection? Only ask questions. Doctors advise these men to marry, and only the most consc'tious

acknowledge that the disease is incurable. The marriage
certificate should be a certificate of health. Do you not think
we might [have] the law altered to make it so?[14]

And in an interview in 1896:

Nothing has yet been done to protect the married woman from
contagion. I hope that we shall soon see the marriage of
certain men made a criminal offence. This is one of the things
which, as women, we must press forward.[15]

These quotations underline her personal outrage and
fear. Again and again she returns to the fear of contagion
and its effect on future generations. This was, presumably,
a very real fear for her, burdened as she was with a
philandering husband and the weight of observation from
his medical practices. Although her son Archie was
growing into adolescence apparently unscathed, it would
appear that her feelings for McFall extended to him, for she
never referred to him, and in *Ideala* she kills off her
heroine's child with diphtheria at six weeks. With great
restraint, she wrote later about that period: 'I suffered
terribly from want of encouragement; it was a black time. I
was thrown back for years.'[16] A less confident woman than
Frances would have collapsed or given up. At that 'black
time' nothing seemed to be going her way and no one
understood her.

While Frances' marriage was deteriorating and her
stories were rejected, her personality clashed unhappily
with local society. 'Mrs M'Fall' (sic), we are told,

was quite a misunderstood personage in Warrington. She was
an idealist – an exotic in a strictly mercantile atmosphere – a
pioneer of the feminist movement, when it was thought
unwomanly to make any claims on behalf of women. But Mrs
M'Fall went her own way. She was brimful of ideas; and
ideas, like murder, will out. She was unconventional in dress
and in habits, and the narrow-minded little coteries around
her covered their faces with their hands – metaphorically

speaking – and . . . kept a strict look out through their fingers.[17]

Frances was evidently well known for showing off her knowledge: in 1885 'a naughty curate incensed against his rector wrote a savage satire upon the society of which the rectory was a pivot . . . and Mrs M'Fall appeared in the squib as "Mrs Tumbledown".' This squib was called *Battleton Rectory*,[18] and every character lampooned had a similar synonym. Mrs Tumbledown, friend of the rector's wife who had an 'appetite for devouring curates',

was a woman of about five-and-thirty. Her face wore a most unhappy and disappointed expression, her manner was singularly lacking in that gentleness which is a woman's great charm; and while her features, though not delicate, possessed sufficient regularity to entitle her to some amount of good looks, there was something about her which seemed to repel you, though she tried hard to make herself agreeable to some people.

On top of that vicious description, Mrs Tumbledown is referred to as a 'blue-stocking' and makes statements like:

It is my only objection to Comte's philosophy that it finds no place for the aesthetic and the beautiful.

The Buddhists seem to offer as a solution of the infinite a series of co-ordinated interchangeable expansions.

Does not Huxley say that the cosmogony of the ignorant Hebrew has done more to hinder progress?

Woman can regain her true place as being more divine than man. . . . By divine, I mean exalted over man – superior to him in every way; more brain, more force of character, just as in time she will have more animal strength.

Oh, naturally . . . husbands should always be obedient to their wives.

The doctor [her husband] likes him . . . but, then, I don't give much for his opinion; he is utterly weak.

All of this paints an awesome, overbearing portrait, but

one which can only have been based on observation
because none of Sarah's views, other than those expressed
in *Two Dear Little Feet*, had yet been published. So, however
restrained and forebearing she describes herself in her
novels, the Brigade Surgeon's wife was considered
opinionated and by no means retiring – and unconventional in dress, too. In Warrington, despite being 'quite
misunderstood' by local society, despising her husband
and receiving no encouragement for her writing, at least
she developed her character along the lines of 'we are what
we allow ourselves to be'. However unconventional, what
she allowed had strength and determination, and the
exercise of these qualities preserved her from succumbing
to frustration and dwindling into neuroticism. Opinions
and dress – and later a bicycle and a cigarette – were the
props of the New Woman. If Frances couldn't use her
energies in being likeable or loved, she could channel them
into constructing a personality that could stand alone. And
her clothes were the outward show of this inner
development.

In the eighties the idea of Rational Dress was born. The
crinoline had been a sumptuous and imposing mid-
century style suitable only for sitting on sofas, and it was
condemned for its inconvenience while Frances was still a
child. Apart from its physical size and the space it occupied
in carriage, omnibus and pew, if the hoop swept up it was
further criticised for indecency, and there was also the risk
of accident and even death to its wearer, by burning.
Modified to a crinolette, with the bulk of the dress gathered
behind, it survived with frills and flutings and false buttons
and bows, growing ever narrower until it became a simple
bustle. But still the waists were pinched and the toes
crushed into high-heeled boots, as the skirts became
tighter. At this point, reflecting the atmosphere of the
times, women began to rebel against these sartorial restrictions, and Lady Harburton founded the Rational Dress

Society in 1881, daringly introducing the divided skirt for
cycling. The bicycle and the bustle had both become
fashionable in the eighties (the bicycle has been called 'the
greatest emancipator of women in the nineteenth century')
but practical women understood the nonsense of limiting
the exhilaration of independent speed with cumbersome
clothing. They tried bloomers – an America fashion which
never conquered England – and varieties of more
voluminous skirts. They also began to realise the difficulty
of breathing deeply into whalebone-constricted lungs.
Clothes have always been symbolic of an age: cautiously,
women loosened their stays and their skirts; at least, some
did. But for people like Frances, in provincial Warrington,
this met with ridicule and scorn. 'If your dress is loose,
your morals are also' ran the general opinion. We can
assume that Sarah's dress was loose, but it matched only
the morals of her husband.

Battleton Rectory, with its cruel descriptions of Frances,
was published in 1885 and she immediately began work on
her own summary of Warrington society, *A Domestic
Experiment*,[19] in which she describes her heroine – in riposte
to the naughty curate – as having 'that ivory-smooth
delicacy of skin, lineless and transparent, which is only
preserved after extreme youth by women of well-regulated
mind and equable temperament, who do not drink wine
habitually', and she finds fun with her dissection of the two
vicars' wives: Mrs Managem 'a stout, short, gushing little
woman' and Mrs Stubstile 'tall, thin, hard, dry and
matter-of-fact'. Frances' thwarted desire to work – at
anything – comes through when her heroine wails, 'The
mere pleasure of living doesn't satisfy me as it once did. I
want an object in life.' And her hatred of her husband can
be easily seen:

What does the dirt say to the flowers? It is contact that does
it – the mere association. You have lowered me in every possible way . . . Don't I understand all the impurity of your life

without a word, and despise you for it? . . . There is no form
of vice with which you have not managed to make me familiar
. . . it is you – husbands like you – who take us from our
homes innocent, and corrupt us . . . and marvel if you find
one day that we are no better than yourselves. That is the
history of *my* married life. You have made me worthy of you,
now take the consequences!

And again:

Like most 'jolly good fellows' he had his pleasures abroad,
which were selfish, and his moods at home when he was
neither 'jolly' nor 'good', and of which his wife had the full
benefit.

In this novel she first explores love – unrequited of course
– describing the only kind of man who for her could be a
hero: titled, inhibited, spiritual, and pretty soon dead.
Lord Vaincrecourt loves her heroine, Agatha, and she
loves him and, while her horrid husband is out, they pace
the drawing room in anguish:

His countenance, beautiful always in its spiritual serenity, had
grown grey, and lost something of its ineffable youth in the
struggle . . . had she moved, had she sobbed, had she looked
up, had he seen but one sign of the suffering he knew was
there, it would have been too much for his strength. . . . She
never knew how much she had tempted him, how nearly he
had spoken and stayed.

But instead he rushes off and 'the life is crushed out of him
under a dray'. Carried back to Agatha and the scene of his
temptation, there remains only time for him to look at her
'with devouring love in his eyes, love purified and perfect',
and for her to remark, 'He was so beautiful, and he died for
me.' A perfect hero, a perfect gentleman, a perfect lover.
   Frances could not, it seems, come to terms with men in
real life and so she desexed them in print, making them too
good and spiritual, or too old and ill to approach any of her
heroines. If any man should succeed, and fall in love with
the heroine, she usually crushed him with a nasty death. A

writer can reject rejection and salve sexual longing by pinning it on the page. Frances hit back at her husband, father and brothers by emasculating the few good men in her novels, and vilifying the rest. This method proved safe and successful for her, but reduced her heroes to cardboard cut-outs, always too good or too bad to be true. Frances' male characters in these early novels can be classified as the Good, the Bad and the Sexless who happen to be referred to as 'he' but, wifeless, could equally well pass as 'she'. Most of her male creations – including all those marrying for the first time – personify varying degrees of vice and most prove to be, or to have been, 'impure'. This 'lack of proper self control' and its possible outcome makes any really masculine character suspect, and leads her heroines to avoid sex when they can. Frances can write:

In olden times a woman would have rid herself of such an incubus, and would have considered herself repaid with an hour of love. Love! She had never known love – pure, passionate, ecstatic![20]

But there must have been few men around with whom she could trust that passionate ecstasy be pure and I doubt if those would have indulged in an hour of it.

During her 'captivity' in Warrington she may have longed for a new experience with a different kind of man, but, one suspects, only in order to observe her own reactions and to attempt to balance her disillusion with her married life. Instead she took to 'poor peopling' as an antidote to Society, and as Lady Bountiful she felt happier visiting the poor and the sick than trying to impress the Warrington establishment. She applied to the Vicar of St Elphin's for work 'to vary the stultifying monotony of my elegant leisure'[21] and finally found some solace in this. Unemployment in Lancashire was chronic at that time, due not only to mechanisation in the mills but also to commercial depression. As Frances wrote: 'Soup kitchens and clothing clubs were established to prevent starvation and relieve distress, but numbers of people died nevertheless, and quite a third of the population tramped away.'[22] Conditions in the workhouse were grim and she described with compassion the plight of an elderly couple who, having sold every stick in their Church-owned cottage to pay the rent, were dragged out by the bailiffs and separated to die in squalor.[23] She did her best to help; she taught penniless young women to crochet and make woollen comforters, listened to their stories, brought flowers and plants and pictures to their rooms, and read to them from the poems of Tennyson and Longfellow. She saw for herself the horrors of charity hospitals and charity dentistry – 'where the young gentlemen learned their business' – and used all these facts and experiences in short stories which were all rejected at the time, but which were published later, after she had left her husband and Warrington.

Two events led to Frances' departure from the matrimonial home. The Married Woman's Property Act of 1882 gave women the right to keep their own property after marriage, and the publication of *Ideala* in 1888 gave her an income and the ability to survive on her own. (As recently as 1848 Caroline Norton, although coming to a financial settlement with her ex-husband, still had her earnings as a writer claimed by him.)

Frances had written most of *Ideala: A Study from Life*[24] at Norwich, and finished it on her arrival in Warrington in 1881. After many attempts to find a publisher and repeated rejections, she put the manuscript to one side for some years and finally arranged for it to be published anonymously at her own expense. Although it was more common to pay for the publishing of one's work in those days than today, this was a brave – though probably desperate – step. Anonymity was necessary because, 'My husband had a gt. dislike to having his name associated with my ideas'.[25] *Ideala* went on sale in Warrington for

3s.6d. and was marketed by E.W. Allen of Ave Maria Lane, 'an obscure London publisher'. It. was almost immediately taken up by Richard Bentley, a notably advanced publisher who had recently done well with Mrs Lynn Linton's collected articles, *The Girl of the Period*. *Ideala* was reprinted three times during the following year and was later published by Heinemann.

Ideala establishes the theme for Frances' next two important novels and introduces the feminist stalwarts (a group of women gathered together by Ideala to campaign for the New Order) that support the heroines of *The Heavenly Twins* and *The Beth Book*. Lord Dawne (the emasculated narrator) and his sister Lady Claudia see Ideala through her problems with her obnoxious husband and unrequited lover, help her to avoid a dishonourable decision to marry the latter, and draw her into their campaign for the New Order gathering 'the useless units of society about her' and turning them into 'worthy women'. Nothing much changes in Frances' philosophy from *Ideala* onwards. She agrees with Ruskin that by securing the 'order, comfort and loveliness' of the home[26] women will equally affect the outside world, that 'they have only to go home and use their influence to that end . . . and the thing will be done'. She quotes Ruskin on the title page – and he replied by sending her his amended copy, saying 'that one of his objections to the book was that he "couldn't bear funny people, however nice" '.[27] She was so 'tickled' by this that she presented the copy to Archie, but later found it in the wastepaper basket – all we have to illustrate the relationship between son and mother at that time.

In *Ideala* Frances expresses her views about the position of women, a central issue for debate in the 1880s and 1890s; and she expresses them well in advance of most other writers, as the book was completed in 1881:

The women of my time are in an unsettled state; it may be a

state of transition. . . . Principles accepted since the beginning
of time have been called in question. . . . Women want
something; they are determined to have it too; and doubtless
they would get it if they only knew what it is they want.

With its endless moralising, and somewhat naïve discussion about ideals and religion, *Ideala* is 'much more of a
treatise than *The Heavenly Twins*, for which it was evidently
a study',[28] but it also expresses more anguish than the other
novels. Her hero, Lorrimer of the 'carnal impulses', is an
appreciably good-and-bad individual, attractive enough to
give Ideala sufficient reason to leave her husband – not
that it would seem necessary to have more incentive than
the latter's flirtation with barmaids, and other
unappealing habits such as opening her letters, striking
her, locking her out of the house and abandoning his
mistress to die of scarlet fever while Ideala holds her hand.
She ends with a rousing call to arms, likening the English to
the Romans, but claiming for them superior experience
and morality:

We have the grandest and purest ideal of morality that was
ever preached on earth. . . . The future of the race has come
to be a question of morality and a question of health . . . We
want grander minds, and we must have grander bodies to
contain them. And it all rests with us women. . . . Do you
think women are less brave: No. When they realise the truth
they will fight for it. . . . They will use the weapons with
which Nature has provided them; love, constancy, self-
sacrifice, their intellectual strength, and will. And so they will
save the nation.

Ideala impressed the public, and also found a sympathetic
admirer in another writer, Mona Caird, who quotes from
it in one of her essays in *The Morality of Marriage*[29] though
without mentioning the author. (This oversight could have
occurred because *Ideala* was first published anonymously,
though by the time Caird's essays were brought out in book
form *Ideala* was published under the Heinemann imprint as
'by Sarah Grand, author of *The Heavenly Twins*'.) Mona

Caird commented on a passage in the book about the marriage contract, in which Ideala creates a sensation by arguing the immorality of using it 'to ratify a business transaction, or sanction the indulgence of a passing fancy'. Caird's views of marriage were very similar to Frances', but were better reasoned, both in her novels and in her essays. She argued for revolt, but also analysed the problems of such action.

Her views on men, however, were identical:

When we consider how vast is the number of men in any great country who are little higher than brutes, and that this never prevents them from being able through the law of marriage to obtain a victim, the breadth and depth of human misery caused in this shape alone by the abuse of the institution swells to something appalling.[30]

And on the guilt of wives who write she also summarised Frances' experience:

The woman's confidence in herself is starved or shaken. Instead of working on without question at the instigation of her talent, she stops to wonder morbidly if indeed she has the gift or the justification. Her training tends always to make her readily accept moral censure. Repeatedly assured that she is selfish and wrongheaded, the struggler loses heart, and in most cases can be finally talked into the belief that it is her true duty to make antimacassars. . . . If after keeping the house, with its minute and multitudinous demands and interruptions, bearing and training children, and performing all her duties to her relations and friends to their entire satisfaction, a woman finds that she has strength and courage for any work of her own, then she may, without serious offence, so employ the odds and ends of her energy and time. But even then, she runs the risk – nay incurs the certainty – of being dubbed selfish.[31]

Encouraged by the reception of *Ideala*, Frances began working seriously on what became *The Heavenly Twins*, working outwards from the short story, 'The Tenor and the Boy' (on which 'the publishers were obdurate' about not publishing)[32] and arranging her escape from her husband. As George Meredith complained to her much later, *The Heavenly Twins* was 'such a very long book'. It took two years to write and three to find a publisher, but was even longer in gestation. Her first theme for the new novel was the creation of a heroine who could see 'the bewildering clash of human precept with human practice', and who wanted to know the truth behind the prejudice. Her heroine's name, Evadne, was suggested by Arthur Clementi Smith, the schoolboy son of a friend.[33] And some other children, clamouring for stories about an African zodiac ring she wore, discovered the twins in a fairy story woven about the ram, the bull, the heavenly twins:

I pictured two delightful imps to whom the epithet 'heavenly' applied with amusing irony. I felt it an inspiration and pounced upon the title. . . . They would necessitate re-writing the book, but that was nothing.[34]

The twins were created, and the framework for her lecture reconstructed. Evadne took over from Ideala, stronger, resolute against her husband's 'impurity' from the start, and Frances determined to instruct women on the pitfalls of sex and marriage so that none could claim, like her, that they did not know beforehand. This theme was fundamental to her belief and was one she elaborated on in later articles and symposia.

In the meantime she tried unsuccessfully to publish the two shorter novels that had been written solely to fill out her days. Both *A Domestic Experiment* and *Singularly Deluded* draw on personal experience, but where the former concentrates on characters and emotional intrigue in Warrington, the heroine of *Singularly Deluded* rushes breathlessly back and forth across the Channel and northern France, missing death by inches in every chapter. Frances recalled the story much later as 'a poor thing written when I was trying my pen'[35] but it has a wild romp of a plot – quite unlike her normal work – and its male

characters are all more or less men of honour. From the
detailed descriptions of cross-Channel steamers and
Brittany, we can deduce that McFall must have taken
Frances on holiday there. Since the heroine shows nothing
but love for her husband, and faith in him – despite his
remarkable behaviour – and as no fear of immorality blots
the pages of the book, we can also assume that this holiday
occurred before Frances had become so bitterly dis-
enchanted with her marriage. But it wasn't until much
later, in 1892, that it was serialised in *Blackwood's Magazine*.
('But think of what it meant to a young writer in those days
to be in *Blackwood*!' she wrote to her friend.)

The heroine of *Singularly Deluded*, Gertrude Somers, is
holidaying with her husband ('one of the ablest and most
polished ornaments of the Bar') and their toddler son
beside the sea so that the overworked barrister can
recuperate from 'brain fever'. All is love, beauty, white
dresses, little waves and brilliant sunsets until he
inexplicably binds her to a telegraph pole and wanders
away. To her physical pain and chagrin is added fear for
their son who settles on a nearby railway line to sleep. A
train immediately runs over him, but without ill effect, and
when our heroine recovers from her swoon she is rescued
by the private physician to Lord Wortlebury, who feels
'sincere admiration . . . for this young creature, so cruelly
placed, and yet so strong and wise . . . in the midst of her
calamity'. So does Lord Wortlebury himself and they set
about helping her to find her husband, last seen leaving by
train for London. Throughout the long night journey to
London Gertrude is resolute: 'Her wounded arms might
burn, and her wretched body might stiffen, but be with her
husband before morning she would, if she kept her consciousness at all.' But she cannot. Instead she discovers
that he has taken a cab to Waterloo, a train to Southampton, a steamer to Jersey, and that his destination is San
Francisco via St Malo.

At each point she just misses him and while she is sipping a small bottle of Champagne to steady her stomach on the eleven-hour steam-and-sail Channel crossing, fire breaks out. Panic. But Gertrude is calm, jumps overboard, is rescued and dried out, and takes the next ferry to St Malo. Here she waits all day, and then pursues him to Dinard, to Dinan, back to St Malo and on up the river Rance. She pursues him by train to Dol, and by carriage to Mont St Michel which rises up 'gaunt and alone out of a wilderness of sand, like a cottage loaf on a bare board'. Coming back from the island, inevitably, the incoming tide towers over her, the carriage is crushed, the horse drowned and she and the driver swim ashore unscathed. (' "It's a good thing it's a warm day," Gertrude said, trying to make the best of it.')

Typically, Gertrude is not, as she says, 'subject to phases, nor as a rule to periods of exaltation and subsequent periods of reaction and depression. Reason was the pilot that had steered her so far through all her tranquil happy life.' So she gives the driver a diamond ring to cover the loss of his horse and carriage, wrings out her skirts, and walks, shoeless, for *miles* to the nearest village – where she just misses her husband again. Back at St Malo her money runs out and she has to accept her ticket to Southampton from a diffident young gentleman who turns out to be her brother's best friend at Sandhurst. Having taken the precaution of cabling Lord Wortlebury and her sister-in-law so that they could intercept her husband's earlier boat, she is released by them from prison whence she has been thrown on arrival with her young benefactor as a suspected eloper and robber. Lord Wortlebury has cunningly lured her husband on board his steam yacht and all embark on a storm-tossed passage through the Bay of Biscay at fourteen knots per hour. She hears coarse laughter and coarse words in the next cabin but is not allowed to meet the deluded man until they are in the Mediterranean and, although thoroughly occupied in

drinking and gambling, he is intrigued by hearing her play
'Ave Maria' on the piano. They meet. She screams.
' "That man," she gasped, " – is not – my –
husband!" ' So they put him ashore at Malta and sail
home again.

All is revealed in the last chapter when she discovers her
true husband, back with their son in their rented holiday
home beside the sea. He explains that he fell thirty feet into
a gully when he left her on that fateful day, was rescued by
a possessive deaf-mute shepherd, survived ten days of fever
and delirium with a dislocated ankle and finally crawled on
hands and knees all the way home to await the return of his
singularly deluded wife.

In the summer of 1890 Frances finally left the barracks,
McFall and Archie, to begin her wanderings. How often
had she thought of it, how long did she plan her departure?
How does a woman throw off the obligations and duties of
marriage and maternity? In 1890 for a woman to desert her
family proved she was a monster. However little she might
care for that family, her behaviour was automatically considered abnormal, callous, inexplicable, indefensible. And
Frances was proud and cared about public opinion. If she
had to be labelled, she certainly wanted the right label. To
desert one's home requires good reason and enormous self-
confidence – or a very thick skin. Despite her experiences
and education during nearly twenty years of marriage,
Frances was still sensitive and introspective. But she was
also driven by a belief in herself and a strong desire to
survive as an individual. She had tried to reconcile that
sense of individuality and spiritual freedom with marriage
and it was her failure which finally forced the choice: either
she had to lose herself in the wretched constrictions of her
marriage, or leave and face the world alone. Of course she
believed in Duty (a word she used often) but her concept of
it was that it applied first to herself. Personal integrity was
of the highest importance for from it sprang all good traits

of character and the power to influence others. ('Jealousy,' as she remarks in *The Beth Book*, 'is a want of faith in oneself.') And she was determined not to repeat her mother's martyrdom, whatever she had been taught about the world's expectations of a girl of gentle birth and breeding. In *Ideala*, written nine years before her decision to leave McFall, Lady Claudia, her sensible, older character, had said firmly, 'It is immoral for a woman to live with such a husband.' Frances had ample justification. She first moved to Bewsey Mount, Warrington, from where she wrote to Blackwood's who were showing interest in her work, 'Will you kindly note my change of address. I shall be here for some time now.'[36] She had left her husband with a kind of honour – for no worse reason than that she despised him – and she was able, unlike most unhappy wives, to support herself by writing. Her son, then nearly twenty, was about to embark on a theatrical career: there was little or no attachment between them, and her stepsons, both with the Army in Egypt and Abyssinia, were already showing far more concern for her. Later they became favoured guests and, indeed, Archie visited her only with reluctance. Haldane McFall, Frances' elder stepson, was already planning a literary or artistic career of his own.[37] Frances' efforts interested him and he spent 'long, long weary hours'[38] helping her edit and revise *The Heavenly Twins*. Both he and his brother stayed with her in London, where she settled soon after her move to Bewsey Mount, whenever they were home on leave.

And so Frances ended twenty painful but formative years with her husband, yielding to her desire for freedom now that she could see a possibility of supporting such independence. The 'woman of genius' was beginning to be noticed and nothing should stand in her way.

CHAPTER V

Success in London: 1890–93

The portrait of Sarah Grand, as she will now be known, is one of smart clothes, large hats and an occasional, wan smile. She was thirty-six, very much a woman of her time, and the burdens of achievement were taking the place of the frustrations of marriage. The confinement of Warrington was now exchanged for the excitement of London and a joyful sense of freedom, but her pleasure was diluted by fear and worry about the details of accommodation and livelihood. However strong she had become, Sarah must have worried about where and how she would live. But her ambition and her belief in what she had to say carried her through these early years alone until indecision and insecurity were buried in the past. With *Ideala* in print and with Blackwood's showing an interest in *A Domestic Experiment* she moved to Kensington and embarked on the selling of *The Heavenly Twins*.

She was no longer a young girl, no longer inhibited by a captious, uncaring husband; she could now believe in herself and her writing: she was indeed a New Woman – but *who* was she? McFall had made it plain that he did not appreciate being connected with her views and 'in order to save him the annoyance, I changed my name'.[1] Bellenden Clarke seemed to belong to another life and was also an unwieldy mouthful. And with her modern spirit and desire to prove that a woman could accomplish at least as much as a man, she wasn't going to become a 'George'.

Her pseudonym, Sarah Grand, she said at different times, was suggested by her stepsons;[2] came to her in a dream;[3] was taken from an old woman; or was chosen because it was brief and memorable.[4] Whatever the reason, she adopted it for *The Heavenly Twins* and never gave it up. It suited her. She swore she had never heard of the other Sarah Grand before she adopted it and it is probable she did not know the implications of the name.

The original Sarah Grand was born Catherine Noël Werlée in Madras, 1762, and at the age of fourteen married a Swiss gentleman who worked for Warren Hastings of the East India Company in Bengal. Extremely beautiful – as can be seen in her portrait by Zoffany at the Metropolitan Museum of Art, New York, and a later one by Gérard, at Versailles, – her name was soon associated with Sir Philip Francis who was 'surprised in her bedroom, and secured by the head-servant'.[5] As a result Sarah Grand was ejected from her home, and Sir Philip forced to pay her husband compensation.

Twenty years later she met Talleyrand in England, became his mistress, and married him after Napoleon had secured a dispensation for him from the Pope. Napoleon rechristened her Princess Talleyrand (though on St Helena he called her 'a disreputable character', '*sotte* and grossly ignorant'). Her ignorance, which completed her title of 'bad, beautiful and foolish', aroused as much excitement as her beauty. Napoleon mentioned that she mistook Denon for Robinson Crusoe, and chattered on to him at dinner about his Man Friday. The French enjoyed her reported malapropism 'Je suis dinde' (I am a turkey) for 'je suis des Indes' (I am from India); and Talleyrand himself said, 'Mais que voulez-vous que je fasse? Ma femme est si bête.' (What can I do? My wife is so stupid.) This proverbial stupidity led to an animated correspondence in *The Times*, but was balanced by her gracious hospitality at the Foreign Office and by her acknowledged role as the reigning beauty at Napoleon's Court. She died in 1835, nearly sixty years before our Sarah chose her name, and now lies in a neglected grave. Unwittingly, she offered a good foil or antilogy to the serious-minded, progressive, and anti-sexual woman who made her name famous again before being consigned to equal obscurity.

As an old woman in Bath our Sarah pestered the library to find the details of her namesake's history probably because public interest in the story was renewed when she became Mayoress; and she enjoyed the publicity. It is reported that

At a dinner party sitting beside Sir Frederick Pollock[6] he had asked her why she had taken the name of so disreputable a woman – she had not known about her then – she was very beautiful and very stupid said Pollock. Well [she answered] I am not beautiful and I am certainly not stupid. She told me she had taken her *nom de plume* from 'a poor old body in an almshouse'. She was dead and it couldn't hurt her. [She] wanted a simple name, without flourishes, something easy to pronounce and remember.[7]

The year after she left her husband, Sarah published *A Domestic Experiment* in Blackwood's. And *Temple Bar Magazine*, which had been returning her manuscripts for twenty years, accepted two of her short stories.[8] With the money she received she retired to a convalescent home at Kirkleatham Hall, Redcar, in Yorkshire and later to a hotel, also beside the sea, at Ramsgate, probably debilitated by the insecurity of life on her own and the first rejections of her new and to her important novel. But in between, and intermittently for the next few years, she made Kensington her base. At first a flat in Sidney House, Sinclair Road, seemed ideal and filled her with pleasure:

a sheltered harbour after long buffeting on the open sea. My first night in it, when I went to bed, I fairly hugged myself, I was so thankful to be there – alone – with no one to interfere with me. . . . I had nothing to fear. I was free! You can't think what that means to a woman who had known what it was to be always at somebody's beck and call – the kind of beck and call exercised by power without love![9]

Her move to London 'brought [her] into close contact with the leaders, in different departments, of the movement for the Emancipation of Women – such women as Eva McClaren, Emily Conebeare, Mrs Massingberd, Lady Henry Somerset, Mrs Wynford Phillips, Mrs Oscar Wilde, and many more; all women of high character and ability'.[10] While she was still in Warrington, Lady Harburton, founder and president of the Rational Dress Society, had asked Sarah to serve on her Committee, and with that privilege her circle of friends had expanded handsomely. Until then she 'had not come into touch with people of advanced views' and her own had made her 'feel like an alien, and an outsider'. But now

With these new friends I was in a new world. To hear them talk was like having doors opened and light shed on all that was obscure to me. Working with them, I came up against what Frances Power Cobbe called 'the dead stone wall' – which, she prophesied, would stay the advance of women until it was razed to the ground. A deaf ear was turned to pleas for reform made by women. The right of free speech was denied them. The newspapers boycotted reports of their meetings. The efforts men ventured to make on their behalf might be mentioned, but only to be ridiculed. It did not pay to bother about women's grievances; they had no votes. Thousands of capable women at that time were living in a state of semi-starvation, crowded out of such ill-paid occupations as were open to them. Trades and professions were divided into 'masculine' and 'feminine', but the division was only arbitrary when a woman was for doing 'masculine' work. A man might keep a baby-linen shop if it paid – anything that paid was 'masculine' – but a woman could not drive a pair of horses for profit, however good a whip she was, without incurring the odium of being 'unsexed'.[11]

So began Sarah's further education with like-minded women. She learned quickly, and soon was writing articles and even speaking in public in support of the Movement. During the nineteenth century middle-class women had increasingly involved themselves in philanthropic work. From 1834, they could be appointed Poor Law Guardians; in 1869 they were allowed to vote in Municipal elections; and in 1870 to serve on School Boards. To extend the franchise to women therefore appeared to be the next logical step, as well as being necessary to improve their educational and social position. Women's involvement in the welfare of the community had given them confidence in their ability to right social wrongs; to extend their powers to vote in Parliamentary elections was only reasonable. However, when John Stuart Mill added women's suffrage to the Reform Bill of 1867, the amendment was firmly defeated. In 1870 the Suffrage Bill was blocked by Gladstone who also quashed the Third Reform Bill in 1884. By the time Sarah became involved in the Women's Movement, there were various suffrage committees throughout the country supporting different causes, both political and social, and more and more women were becoming aware that the vote was a necessary starting point in any attempt to remedy established injustices. It wasn't until later[12] that national societies – both militant and non-militant – were formed to press specifically for the vote.

In the meantime, the modern campaigning woman was viewed either with suspicion or amusement by the public and Sarah took action to help to alter this image. Although she had more important and heartfelt points to make, in addition to her campaign for the moral health of the country, she also wrote and talked about 'the Duty that is incumbent upon all advanced women of being as pretty as they know how'. In 1893, a summary of one of her articles explained her view that 'advanced women do not pay enough attention to their appearance', and continued:

that women might have had the suffrage a long time ago if

some of the first fighters for it, some of the strong ones, had not been unprepossessing women. These two or three were held up everywhere as an awful warning of what the whole sex would become if they got the suffrage, and instead of argument, people used to say, 'if you only saw the old harridans, their dress, and their manners, who are agitating for the suffrage, it would be enough. If women are to look like that when they get the suffrage, then defend me from it.'[13]

But Sarah concentrated mainly on morality and marriage, arguing the importance of the former and the need for women to be properly enlightened about the latter:

It was time someone spoke up, and I felt that I could and determined that I would. I would expose the injustice with which women were treated, in all its cruelty, and those who were responsible for its continuance. . . . It was torture to think of it and shame to mention it. But it had to be brought in somehow. It was the cornerstone of the whole foundation. . . . The general reader required a dose for his moral health. . . . .One and all thought it impossible to do more or better than Josephine Butler was doing. The brutal way in which she had been treated was quoted as an example of the result on public opinion of any effort a woman might make to change it.[14]

Sarah now started on a three-year search for a publisher for her 'unpalatable' novel with its mischievous twins sugaring the pill 'so that it would be mistaken for a bonbon and swallowed without suspicion of its medicinal properties'. Poor Evadne, with her rational decision to exclude her new husband from her bed when she learns of his premarital incontinence, dominates the story and, as George Meredith wrote when, as a reader for Chapman & Hall, he rejected the book, 'Evadne would kill a better work with her heaviness . . . the objection is the tedium in the presentation of her'.[15] Mark Twain loathed her 'putrid' twins: 'Blank paper in the place of these twins would be a large advantage to the book.' And 'Are these tiresome creatures supposed to be funny?'[16]

But it was the 'allopathic pill' of the Bishop's daughter, and her marriage to the syphilitic Sir Mosely Menteith that created the most trouble and caused the book to be denounced as 'a product of hysteria and wilful eccentricity with something more than a savour of indelicacy; defects of balance and proportion, lack of reticence, over insistence on its moral'.[17] Many people, when the book was published, looked on her as a follower of Ibsen, but Sarah wrote in 1894, 'I had not read a line of Ibsen that I know of when I wrote *The Heavenly Twins*, and I have not even yet read *Ghosts*. Ibsen, in fact, was a name of no significance to me until I saw myself mentioned as a follower of his.'[18] One publisher wrote:

We do not say that the ideals you employ are coarse, though we have no doubt critics will be less scrupulous, but we venture to assert that they are antagonistic to all culture and refinement. . . . All delicately-minded women must feel themselves aggrieved, if not insulted, by the prominence which is given to the physical idea of marriage. . . . Even had I not the traditions of my House to go by in the case of *The Heavenly Twins*, I could not, and would not dare to place your work in the way of ladies, who compose so large a proportion of the novel-reading public.[19]

Poor Sarah; back it came, again and again, criticised and lambasted not only for its content, but also for its grammar and syntax. If any publisher applauded the manuscript for its sentiments, he slammed it as not fit to be seen by his wife or daughter. It was condemned as 'ill-constructed, crammed with ideas and opinions and prejudices and often over-written', and 'If Mrs McFall had made three novels out of her material, at least one of them would doubtless have been more satisfying to the critic'.[20] An anonymous article, purporting to be written by Mrs Humphry Ward, in *The Quarterly Review* in the year after the book was published, compares Sarah's 'scientific realism' unfavourably with that lady's equally decadent

Marcella. Mrs Ward's book is described as 'a genuine work of art, rising in one scene at least to the height and the beauty of a poem', whereas *The Heavenly Twins* is 'self-conscious, or even pedantic . . . interminably prosing . . . in art there is a degree of mental as of physical agony which must not be shown, or the audience will turn away their eyes'.[21] Plain talk about syphilis was taboo and the terrible twins weren't considered sufficiently entertaining to sugar the 'pill'. Meredith suggested, 'The writer should be advised to put this manuscript aside until she has got the art of driving a story.'[22] Most publishers' readers preferred that she bury it deep in the back garden. But Sarah had not given up with *Ideala*, and she was not to be beaten now. Even though her best friends pleaded with her not to publish 'that dreadful thing', she set about having it printed at her own expense. When it was already in sheet form, she said:

I was persuaded to show it to Mr Heinemann as a last chance, and consented reluctantly, for he was the youngest of the publishers and I expected him to be cautious for lack of experience . . . [but] Mr Heinemann was in touch with the spirit of his day, if ever a man were.[23]

William Heinemann had started his own publishing company in 1890, and had rapidly become an important figure of the decade with his introduction of foreign fiction in a cheap uniform edition in his first list, and with the publication of William Archer's translations of Ibsen. His personality and flair for what would sell made him champion many *avant garde* writers and his fairness in business made most of his authors life-long friends. As his biographer Frederic Whyte wrote about the acceptance of *The Heavenly Twins* manuscript:

she offered it to Heinemann, saying he could have the copyright for £100; it looks a small sum in the retrospect, in view of the history of the work, but we must reflect that not one novelist in a thousand earns so much money by a first effort. Heinemann admired the book and agreed, although very doubtful about his investment. The novel came out and, as everyone knows, was a quite unlooked-for success. In a few weeks' time Heinemann sent for the young authoress, told her that he proposed to tear up their agreement, substituting for it a new one by which she was to be paid 'the most favoured authors' royalties', and concluded by handing her a cheque for £1200, the amount he owed her already upon this new basis.[24]

And so, on 7 February 1893 *The Heavenly Twins* was published in three volumes at a guinea and a half, and William Heinemann's gamble paid handsomely.

It created one of the greatest sensations of literature; it certainly caused tremendous excitement in the ranks of the Feminists and anti-Feminists, and the upholders of the new and the old morality. The general public read it with interest and pleasure mainly because of the pranks of the irrepressible twins. . . . But for the Feminists the importance of the book lay in its account of the marriages made by two of the girl characters, Edith and Evadne.[25]

The launch of the book was supported by effective publicity, attributed variously to Sarah and to Heinemann, in the Strand in London. In one account Sarah herself arranged for two dolls to be dressed alike and paraded up and down.[26] In another, Heinemann met a man unsuccessfully selling a tray of balloons painted to resemble babies. 'Hold up two of your beautiful babies together and offer them for twopence as *The Heavenly Twins*,' he suggested, and the man did so with triumphant results.[27] Both Sarah and the twins became famous overnight. Better than that, the book sold. In the first year Heinemann reprinted it six times, and by the time it came out in one volume the following year nearly 20,000 copies had been sold in this country.[28] In America, Cassell's had no hesitation in accepting the book, although they expected the disapproval of the parent house in London. Published by

Cassell at one dollar, it sold at least five times as many copies in the United States as in England in its first year.[29]

'Just now everybody is reading *The Heavenly Twins*,' wrote a commentator in *Munsey's Magazine* in October 1893. It was hailed as the chief women's rights novel of the period, and made the 'Overall Best Sellers in the United States' category for the nineties. In England, despite some criticism of her 'shamelessness', the novel was generally praised. The *Athenaeum*, a most conservative journal (lampooned in *The Beth Book* as *The Patriarch*), remarked on her 'delicacy and good taste . . . which shows something more than cleverness'.[30] The *Manchester Examiner* linked her with Thomas Hardy in popularity:

As surely as *Tess of the D'Urbevilles* swept all before it last year, so surely has Sarah Grand's *Heavenly Twins* provoked the greatest sensation and comment this season. It is a most daringly original work. . . . Sarah Grand is a notable Women's Righter, but her book is the one asked for at Mudies suburban and seaside libraries, and discussed at every hotel table in the kingdom.

And so Sarah's faith in herself, and Heinemann's courage 'to break a lance with public opinion', proved more than justified. She had overcome the taboo, broken through masculine prejudice and could amend her earlier remark in *Ideala*, 'You will find that all the most objectionable books are written by women – and condemned by men who lift up their voices now, as they have done from time immemorial, to insist that we should do as they say, and not as they do'. Critical voices were certainly raised, but the 'dead stone wall' had been breached. John Lane followed Heinemann's lead with George Egerton's *Keynotes*, and the following year Emma Frances Brooke caused her heroine in *The Superfluous Woman* to follow Sarah's Edith Beale into dementia and death, after marriage to a syphilitic Lord. 'That terror' was out in the open and on the shelves, and heroines were permitted sexual feelings and relationships as never before. It may have been sheer luck that made Sarah the leader of this literary vanguard, but she must be given the credit for her years of perseverence to publish. Better novels about the oppression of women had been written before and have been since, but *The Heavenly Twins* was the first to attack male sexuality both within and outside marriage, and to expose the double standard of morality which governed this masculine stronghold.

Sarah was now living in Kensington and, when on leave from the Army, both her stepsons stayed with her, Haldane taking great interest in her literary success. Amongst the literary celebrities of the time, she became acquainted with Thomas Hardy, whose *Jude the Obscure* was yet to be written, but who had published his attack on the inequalities in divorce (adultery was allowable for men but impermissable for women) in *The Woodlanders* in 1887, and in *Tess of the D'Urbevilles* in 1891. Sarah sent him a copy of *The Heavenly Twins* as 'a very inadequate acknowledgement of all she owes to his genius', and in June that year she was found sitting in his drawing room when he came home one day.[31] He wrote to Florence Henniker that her own novel *Foiled* 'ranks far above some novels that have received much more praise: e.g. *The Heavenly Twins*' and 'Sarah Grand, who has not, to my mind, such a sympathetic and intuitive knowledge of human nature as you, has yet an immense advantage over you in this respect – in fact of having decided to offend her friends (as she told me) – and now that they are all alienated she can write boldly, and get listened to'.[32] George Bernard Shaw went further by associating her with genius:

There is always a vulgar cry both for and against every man and woman of any distinction; and from such cries you cannot keep your mind too clear if you wish to attain distinction yourself. You know the sort of thing I mean: you have heard it about Whistler, Sarah Grand, Ibsen, Wagner – everybody who has a touch of genius.[33]

Sarah had reached the top. But what could she do now?

CHAPTER VI

Fame and Freedom in France and England: 1894–98

◥◆◤

Sarah enjoyed her fame. She was interviewed, criticised, photographed, lionised. She moved to a bigger flat, bought larger and more magnificent hats, travelled on the Continent and, not prepared to rest on her laurels, used every opportunity to inform and educate her public. From the beginning this had been her aim and the notoriety of *The Heavenly Twins* gave her a position at centre stage from which she could reach a wide audience and say whatever she wished. She could publish anything – and did.

In 1893, the serialised version of *Singularly Deluded* was published as a novel by Blackwood's, and the following year Heinemann published most of her rejected stories in *Our Manifold Nature*. *The Humanitarian* took her article on 'The Moral and Manners of Appearance', and in America *The Review of Reviews* enlarged on it. And it was in *The North American Review* in 1894 that she coined the phrase, 'The New Woman'. As she said:

With the success of *The Heavenly Twins* the storm and stress of my literary career was practically over. The book caused so much clamour that I had no longer to work against the dead-weight of being unknown; and an essay, the first of several, with which I followed it, on the development of the woman of the day – whom I called 'The New Woman', still further spread my work.[1]

The New Woman became many things to many people,

but for all she stood bold, free and capable of thinking and acting for herself. The retiring, dimpled virgin, decorative and obedient, was brushed aside by the modern girl who read, knew and understood, and refused to sit quietly in a corner. Walt Whitman wrote: 'She can swim, row, ride, wrestle, shoot, run, strike, retreat, defend herself,' and described the ' "female chrysalis", putting off her absurd silken web and by rational diet and exercise . . . on the wing in search of an emancipated mate'.[2] The modern, middle-class girl, with her more sensible clothes, her bicycle and her increased opportunities for education, had taken many years to evolve but now she had a name, a banner, and could fight for qualifications and the right to work instead of languishing at home, packaged for her future husband. Once married . . . well, that was another story. Here opinions amongst the pioneers varied. Some defined equality as freedom from any vow and the abolition of the marriage contract. Others, like Sarah, advocated raising the moral standards of men and arranging for themselves a reasonably balanced place alongside their mates. Sarah repeatedly proclaimed that 'woman was never meant to be developed man'. To her the New Woman was

one who, while retaining all the grace of manner and feminine charm, had thrown off all the silliness and hysterical feebleness of her sex, and improved herself so as to be in every way the best companion for man, and without him the best fitted for a place of usefulness in the world.[3]

But even this proclamation caused trouble with the anti-feminists. There were those who believed that women, because of their biology, must be inferior to and less evolved than men. Considerable pseudo-scientific evidence was presented to 'prove' that women's brains weighed less, that they were pathologically deceptive, and that the menstrual cycle made them incapable of competing in any way with men. Then there were the women who themselves reacted against emancipation. Eliza Lynn Linton opened the debate on 'The Woman Question' in 1868[4] by arguing for reasonable education for women, for their claim to personal property, and for the rights of motherhood to be legally equal to those of paternity. Once these demands were fulfilled, Mrs Lynn Linton retreated into writing about the *duties* of women: 'The cradle lies across the door of the polling booth and bars the way to the Senate.'[5] Because 'emancipation had not proved such a success in her case as to warrant its general adoption',[6] she became a champion of domesticity, modesty and 'good-ness'; she vehemently criticised the 'Wild Women' and 'Shrieking Sisterhood', and condemned the Women's Movement as 'a gigantic mistake . . . which makes women hard and men hysterical'. In the same year that *The Heavenly Twins* was published she dedicated her latest novel to 'the sweet girls still left among us, who have no part in the new revolt, but are content to be dutiful, innocent, and sheltered'.[7]

A strong, familiar voice, but worsted in *The New Review* debate[8] the next year when most of the illustrious authors who took part sided for telling all young people the facts of life: in 'The Tree of Knowledge' Walter Besant, Bjornstjerne Bjornson, Hall Caine, Mrs Edmund Gosse, Thomas Hardy, Mrs Lynn Linton and Sarah, amongst others, all gave their opinions. A review summarises them:

Walter Besant is very outspoken as to the necessity of boys and girls being taught such leading facts of physiology as may help in the future conduct of human life. The Norwegian writer follows in the same track, and declares that knowledge must lead the van in the struggle against temptation, too ready acquiescence, and excess. Hall Caine thinks that the present generation of daughters will reap the benefit, as they will have the bloom of modesty with the safety of knowledge, a declara-tion with which the author of *The Heavenly Twins* has a certain amount of sympathy. She thinks that immoralities of all kinds are as often the result of ignorance as of a vicious nature. The author of *Tess* considers that the sons require instruction as much as the daughters, as he does not believe that the spider is invariably male and the fly invariably female. Poor Mrs Linton, as might be expected, indulges in a wail over female degeneracy, and she denounces the public discussion of such a subject as indecent and unnecessary.

Marie Corelli, too, another prolific authoress, harped on women's influence in the home and deplored any activity to alter the system. 'Why . . . unsex themselves by appearing on public platforms and prating of their Rights? Surely their rights are manifold. With them rest the strength, goodness and greatness of the next generation, in the influence they exercise over their children.'[9] And Havelock Ellis wrote: 'The New Woman ought to be aware that her condition is morbid, or, at least, hysterical . . . The liberty which she invokes will be fatal to her . . . her peculiar grace . . . is neither rugged strength nor stores of erudition, but a human nature predestined to Motherhood.'[10] Although Sarah agreed wholeheartedly with the idea of marriage and that the female role of motherhood was essential for the good of society, she was not content to murmur about duty and innocence and mounted the public platforms to explain why. Marriage was a corrupt institution because ill-educated daughters coupled with constitutionally impure and unreliable husbands made bad wives. The system must change for the institution to have any true value.

Yet Mrs Lynn Linton, with her myopia, her hatchet jaw and hairy chin – a hefty, aggressive-looking woman – resembles all the newspaper caricatures of feminists, whereas Sarah, whose first photographs were taken at this time, gazes sad and tranquil, striking poetic poses or peeping from under the most frivolous hats and bonnets, looking delicate and dumb. In her favourite photographs of herself her 'soft brown curly hair' is looped back behind her ears into an unruly chignon, accentuating a Roman profile and enhancing her desired impression of femininity

and prettiness. But when she wears a hat – generally huge
and topped with ostrich feathers or cunningly angled with
stiff pleats of material and a large rose – though she may
look smart, it adds weight to the oval face and lessens the
softening effect of the hair. Everyone who interviewed her
remarked on her charm and elegance, 'culture' and 'high-
bred manners'. She practised what she preached about
manners – slightly chilly and reserved – and about
appearance, dressing gorgeously in bead-encrusted silks
and ruched velvet. A contemporary journalist described
her as:

Something over the medium height [actually 5′ 4½″ and with
a size four shoe], and slight in figure, the face, of pure oval
shape, is crowned with soft brown curly hair; a brow that
indicates intellect and spirituality; eyes deep grey in hue; and
a complexion of delicate colouring; a serious, somewhat sad,
expression when in repose.[11]

She cared as much for her complexion as for her dress
and she was quick to advise female cyclists to beware of
'scorching in the sun without a thought for their complexions, and lose half of their attractiveness if hopelessly
sunburnt'.[12] She suggested that they copy American girls
who 'before they ride out in the heat . . . rub a little
"crême Limen" over their faces, and dust lightly over with
powder before starting, taking a little powder box with
them to supply some more if necessary on a long trip . . .
and pretty rose-leaf complexions are thereby saved
irretrievable damage'.[13] She also advocated Jeyes' Fluid in
warm water as good for the hair.[14]

Being 'not only extremely good looking, but remarkably
well dressed' certainly helped her public appearances. 'By
being inelegant, an earnest woman frustrates her own
ends.'[15] Sarah was never inelegant. But she was torn
between her desire to teach and reform – which necessitated all the parties, meetings and frivolity of living in
London – and her equal desire for solitude and the peace

of the countryside where she could get on with her writing. Both ways of life attracted her. Having worked so hard to leave the social backwaters of Warrington, she now found herself a person of influence; this made retirement seem a waste of new opportunities. She saw herself, like her heroine Beth, as 'one of the first swallows of the woman's summer' and certainly savoured the role. The difficulty lay in finding the time and the place to write her next novel and at the same time to give interviews and lectures, and satisfy the demands of London society in general. She hated London, despised the way Society lived, yearned to escape and yet felt bound by what she saw as her vocation.

This conflict led to acute depression and, while living in a vast new block of flats 'in one of the oldest roads in historic Kensington', surrounded by bowls of roses and pale china-blue walls hung with quaint daggers from her 'soldier stepsons',[16] she became aware of an unnatural force (transmuted into a supernatural experience in a story in which her heroine falls in love with a footstep on the floor above her top-floor flat).[17] Repeatedly, she felt herself drawn towards the open bedroom window and impelled to throw herself out, until her doctor, 'an advanced psychologist', advised her to leave London immediately. Sarah then sub-let the flat and moved to Paris. While she was away her tenant had the same experience, and when Sarah heard this she checked with the porter who told her that a man and a woman had both thrown themselves to their deaths from that same window. It made an effective story – with embellishments – and one which chilled the citizens of Bath when she recounted it as Mayoress.[18]

She might also have been bound to London – and disturbed – by an 'ardent impulse'. In the Preface to the collection of her stories, *Emotional Moments*, she wrote, 'In the days when these stories were written I was living in London for the first time', and while deploring the lack of true friendship and conversation, a life in which 'all individuality was obliterated', she deals, rather sadly, in several of the stories, with love and the rejection or betrayal of her heroine. And she asserts 'dry knowledge . . . is no use for creative purposes. All through Nature strong emotion is the motive of creation, and in art, also, the power to create is invariably the outcome of an ardent impulse.'[19] On discovering that her handsome lover was simply using her, one heroine announces,

The roses on my right that smelt so sweet an hour before suddenly sickened me. I sent them away. I shut the piano. I drew down the blinds that the moonlight might not stream in, and lit the gas; and in the act I tore that page of poetry out of my life.[20]

That sounds heartfelt, but with another heroine demanding, 'I want a man without unpleasant associations of any kind about him – a whole man, and not the besmirched remnants left by scores of ignoble passions',[21] we return to Sarah's earlier preoccupation, and it seems most unlikely that any man in London, as in Warrington, could live up to her ideals or standards.

When on leave, Haldane and Albert acted as escorts to the theatre where she shivered with refined disapproval at human nature in the foyer and the surrounding streets: 'powder, paint and paste-diamonds more evident than in Belgravia', she complained, and 'tight-lacing . . . carried to a more painful extent . . . the difficulty of breathing with only the upper part of the lungs free caused the bare chests to heave hideously'; giving her further opportunity to expatiate on 'how inevitably those who haunt the sewers of society deteriorate'.[22]

Her lectures and speeches were never complicated or militant, but were much enjoyed by her audience. ('She talks brilliantly, lectures with easy grace and polish . . . searching sense of humor, which is like salt to her speech.')[23] To the Pioneer Club, of which she was an early member, she spoke on 'The Want of Consideration of Others Shown in the Manners of the Day', in which she cåstigated women for elbowing men out of the way whilst window shopping in Kensington High Street. To the Sunday Lecture Society at St George's Hall, London, she lectured on 'The Art of Happiness', her most repeated theme, set out in 1900 in a forty-one-page pamphlet, and also used in her tour of America. It is easy to understand her popularity with predominantly female audiences. She spoke with authority and sense, and her argument was simple:

The ineffectual lives of so many women is one of the saddest features of the civilisation of this century. . . . One of the things that women know least about is how to make life worth living. The habit of endurance has become so inveterate in women that they will sit and suffer from evils they might quite easily remove. . . . The kindnesses of men are oftener the expression of their own satisfaction than the outcome of a desire to please.[24]

But all this activity wore her out. At the same time that *The Beth Book* was germinating and she was recalling minute details of her earlier pain and self-development, she was writing articles and stories on 'The Modern Girl' and 'The New Aspect of the Woman Question' for women's magazines in England and America. Equal grounds for divorce, the sanctity of marriage, the establishment of a 'House of Ladies' which 'would be doing more useful work on behalf of the general community than the present House of Lords is doing', and the defence of Rational Dress also took up her time. And on top of all this an anonymous article in *The Quarterly Review*[25] attacked her for 'aiming at sexual laxity' in her work, linking her with Frau Irma von Troll, an advocate for unlimited divorce, and with the infamous Oneida Creek Community in America whose members practised free love and polygamy. Arguments against her artistry and grammar she could accept, and even comments that 'her language is as new as hard study and George Eliot can make it' she could swallow. But when the author stated, 'None of these marriages [in *The Heavenly Twins*] were made in heaven; why should they not be dissolved? It must be, after all, *la pruderie anglaise* which has cut short Mrs Grand's argument in the middle, and ruined her story', she was exasperated more by the moral slur than by the misreading of her intention. The editors of *Literary World* and *Christian World* rushed to her defence, and she wrote plaintively, 'I am not even for change in the divorce laws except to equalise them. I think marriage should be made a more not a less sacred institution, and say this in so many places that no one can misunderstand me.'[26] Friends at the Athenaeum and Savile Clubs reported to her that the writer was none other than Mrs Humphry Ward who had also 'used her influence to have *The Heavenly Twins* boycotted in *The Times*'.[27] At first, Sarah refused to believe this of a fellow authoress, but a similar attack on Iota's *A Yellow Aster* in *The Times* – following Mrs Ward's glib excuse that an editorial committee of that paper had 'come to the conclusion that it would be better [for Sarah] if it [*The Heavenly Twins*] were not noticed' – prompted her to write again to her friend Mr Fisher, editor of the *Literary World*:

It seems to me such a monstrous charge, I could not believe it without the clearest evidence and I told you all I know about it. You might fairly point out however that the argument supports Mrs Ward as bitterly determined to show no favour to any other authoress. This attack on 'Iota' is worthy of the days when Messrs Lockert and Crolen[28] reviewed Harriet Martineau in the *Quarterly Magazine*, and, taking advantage of her sex, made 'gross appeals to the prudery, timidity, and ignorance of the middle classes of England, and so inflicted much suffering upon her – for views which high minded people now accept not only as containing the economics but the ethics of the question. I do not know Mrs Caffyn [Iota] at all, and I have not read any of her work, but I think she is to be congratulated upon this attack. It will help her book tremendously. And I expect she has to thank your para on the

boycotting of *The Heavenly Twins* for it. It resembles the style of
my friend in *The Quarterly* and I should fancy was done by the
same person. Mr Schültz [?] Wilson told me he had heard
from the Editor that the writer was very bitter indeed against
me, but meant to be moderate.[29]

And yet again Sarah used her friend at the *Literary World*
to vent her indignation when Emma Frances Brooke's new
book was credited to her:

I find the author of 'A Superfluous Woman' is allowing her
new book 'Transition', to be announced as by me. The
announcement I saw was in the *Daily Telegraph* and I wrote at
once to beg them to contradict it . . . I wonder if you could do
anything for me in this matter. It is a mean and unworthy
trick, I think, for an author to remain anonymous in order to
touch upon my name, and one which there will be no end to if
it is found to succeed. Any inferior and impecunious writer
would secure a certain sale by having a book announced as by
some popular author.[30]

This was a little unkind as Brooke's first novel, *A Superfluous Woman*, reflected much in Sarah's own novels –
including an enlightened, emasculated doctor as observer,
a bright young heroine who tries to escape the constrictions
of Society, disapproval of corset makers, an unhappy
marriage to a syphilitic Lord, congenitally syphilitic
children, dementia and death. It was also published within
months of *The Heavenly Twins* and by the same publisher,
Heinemann, and had carried an advertisement within its
covers for the new one-volume edition of *The Heavenly
Twins* at a price of six shillings. Brooke was by no means
'an inferior and impecunious writer' after this publication,
but Sarah was as bent on defending her own position as
Mrs Humphry Ward was concerned to protect the decency
and modesty of women.

In 1894 Sarah made convalescent escapes from London
to Kirkleatham Hall ('we are just off to the Yellow
Sands – to which I owe oceans of inspiration'[31]), and, with

a nurse, to Ramsgate, on her doctor's orders. These
convalescent holidays were taken periodically for her
'nerves', a popular therapy at a time when doctors had no
tranquillisers and anti-depressants to prescribe. Sea air,
like treatment at the Spas, was fashionable and had much
the same effect as a visit to a health farm nowadays: a
change of scene, physical and mental rest and a feeling of
being pampered to restore jaded spirits. Sarah worked
hard and conscientiously and all that she undertook was
against the current of public opinion. The stress of her
independent and unconventional life frequently brought
her to the verge of breakdown, and rest-cures beside the sea
became more and more necessary. This year, however,
each time she returned to London she soon collapsed again
and, after another unsatisfactory visit to her flat and
attempts to rent a furnished house near Burnham Beeches
as a more permanent escape, in the New Year she moved to
France, first to the Villa Mignonne at Cannes:

It is I who have been out of favour with the gods, I imagine as
they have seen fit to afflict me with a long illness from wh. I
am only just beginning to recover slowly. All work has been
stopped for six months and my corresp. has to be carried on
for the most part on postcards.[32]

She then moved to Paris where she settled at the Hôtel
des deux Mondes on the Avenue de l'Opéra. From here
she explored the city for three or four months, either with
Haldane or with a stream of other visitors. She invited
Ellen Terry to dine with her and her American friend, the
poet Agnes Tobin, and with 'my eldest stepson who has
long worshipped you from afar off'.[33] Here, too, William
Heinemann visited her. He had a flat in the Palais Royal
and came frequently to Paris. A gourmet and fluent
linguist, he treated his authors as friends and entertained
them on both sides of the Channel. Sarah had certainly met
the Edmund Gosses with him in England; in Paris he

helped her research by introducing her to cabaret and can-can:

We did the *Moulin Rouge* and the *Chat-Noir* last night – 'we'
being a respectable party. The *Moulin Rouge* is deadly dull but
the *Chat-Noir*, Meissonnier's old studio, which has had pictures
presented to it by almost every artist of any name in France,
was extremely interesting. . . . I hope, by the way, your
forecast future sales of *The Heavenly Twins* will prove true. I
have not parted with the copyright either in England or
America. I get a good royalty from each. In fact Mr
Heinemann raised my royalty five percent the other day
because *The Twins* has been so successful.[34]

Certainly the royalties were keeping her in reasonable
style and independence. Grant Allen's *The Woman Who
Did*[35] was published in 1895, and caused almost as much
stir as *The Heavenly Twins*. He received £1000 a year from
his royalties until he died four years later – and, as his
book was outsold by hers, we can assume that Sarah was
making at least that amount in each country. It is
mentioned in family papers that she made £18,000 from
The Heavenly Twins.[36] The heroine of Allen's novel, true to
New Woman fiction, is a Girton-educated girl of advanced
views which she carries to the length of refusing to marry
her lover, on principle: 'marriage itself is still an assertion
of man's supremacy over woman. . . . it ignores her
individuality.' This stand leads to a miserably impoverished life after her lover dies intestate, and the hatred of
her surprisingly conventional daughter, leaving the
heroine to take a dose of prussic acid as the only possible
solution to their problems. When asked her opinion of *The
Woman Who Did* Sarah declared, 'It seems to me that Mr
Grant Allen wants us to return to the customs of the poultry
yard. . . . The story shows . . . very clearly that women
have nothing to gain and everything to lose by renouncing
the protection which legal marriage gives.'[37] It was in
Paris, while Sarah was having tea with the Grant Allens,
that 'one of our party overhead a lady ask who I was: "Oh,

don't you know?'' was the answer – ''that's the woman who didn't.'' '38

In Paris, Sarah took to bicycling, a craze she continued avidly on her return to England, becoming a member of the Mowbray House Cycling Association and being photographed and interviewed at the handlebars. Three hours in the Bois de Boulogne with Agnes Tobin and instructors 'threading our way between carriages, cycles, and traffic of all sorts' gave her confidence and, although she had considered the sport 'only as a pursuit for very young ladies', she delighted in it. In an interview she said:

Cycling has done wonders for my health. I had been spending the winter on the Riviera, very ill from nervous prostration, and directly I took up riding I began to feel better. I think cycling is a perfect refreshment for brain workers.[39]

In Paris, she always wore bloomers for cycling – 'very much more comfortable, one feels so light and free in them'[40] – but even the mention of such dress scandalised Londoners and when she returned to England she resumed conventional skirts. In spite of her interest in Rational Dress, she considered bloomers and culottes 'exceedingly ugly', and wished someone would invent something more graceful but at the same time practical for cycling:

It is necessary for a New Woman to be very careful about her appearance. For comfort and utility there is no comparison; it takes ten years off your age to wear Rational Dress. There is nothing to catch the wind and impede your progress. I found a most astonishing difference when riding *en culotte* in Paris, indeed I never could have believed the difference it made to the ease and pleasure of riding. But the dress is so unsightly. The French women do not mind, because they are more inclined to study utility in their dress than we are; they consider it the best taste to be suitably attired for what you are doing.[41]

She suggested a long tunic over trousers as 'comfortable and yet feminine' but that was not acceptable. From a

London tailor 'at a price that inspired confidence' she purchased a cycling skirt, but:

Shortly afterwards while riding her bike, this skirt caught in the spokes of the wheel and was torn from her waist. To use her own words, she was 'a most indecent spectacle'. However, her distress was not to last long for some . . . old gentlemen with pins, rushed to her rescue, and fastened her together to the best of their poor masculine ability.[42]

So she took to wearing discreetly divided skirts and although she kept her bicycle propped in the passage outside her Kensington flat, she preferred to ride in the country.

In 1896, now well into writing *The Beth Book*, she escaped London frequently, to write and cycle amongst the Surrey hills, staying at the Burford Bridge Hotel 'a charming old world Inn still in those days. The coaches stopped there on the way to Portsmouth to bait the horses. Nelson baited his, it was said, on his way to join his ship when he was bound for Trafalgar (wasn't it?) his last voyage.'[43] Here she met George Meredith who, as a reader for Chapman & Hall, had turned down *The Heavenly Twins*. (This, for him, was not exceptional for during his thirty-five years with Chapman & Hall he had also repeatedly rejected *East Lynne*, early work by Mrs Lynn Linton, Ouida, Hardy and Shaw, *Erewhon* by Samuel Butler and Olive Schreiner's *The Story of an African Farm*, which Chapman & Hall finally published under the pseudonym Ralph Irons in 1883.) Now an old man of nearly seventy, rather deaf and with a high, loud voice, he lived alone at Flint Cottage 'on the same side of the road as the Hotel, at the foot of Box Hill',[44] with a chalet on the highest slope of his garden where he could retreat to write. Following Tennyson's death he had been appointed President of the Society of Authors and was now working on a series of odes 'in contribution to the song of French history'.[45] His anti-marriage novel, *Lord Ormont and His Arminta*, had been published in the same year as

The Heavenly Twins. He held the theory of 'leasehold marriages'[46] – that they should not have to last more than ten years – and was a fervent advocate of education as the key to female emancipation, but not at the expense of natural refinement and delicacy.

While Sarah rested and wrote at the hotel, a fellow guest was Alice Meynell, the essayist and poet, whose children were staying with Meredith.

He heard of my arrival from Mrs Meynell and immediately sent her to ask me to tea, and to excuse his not calling on account of his lameness. We immediately became fast friends. I dined, or walked, or had tea with him every day. Nothing could exceed his kindness. He took great interest in my work and helped me much both with advice and encouragement. His conversation was a feast of ideas, witticisms, anecdotes, and verses improvised at a moment's notice on any theme that occurred to him. I never saw him serious; his great mind was always at play with me. He was like a grown-up person who himself enjoys the game as much as the child he is trying to amuse.[47]

His view from Box Hill, south-east over a vast tract of champaign country to the Sussex downs ('greyhounds in flight' he described them) and almost to the sea, impressed her too, but when she remarked what an inspiration it must be he replied that the best inspiration for a writer was to look out at a brick wall.[48] However, they shared an appreciation of the countryside and his comparison of the autumn foliage to 'a dozen differently coloured torches held up in the woods'[49] appealed to her. She certainly enjoyed his company. In Gladys Singers-Bigger's diaries, cosy meetings are recorded:

She used to sit on the floor and talk to him and he would get her little bottles of Champagne which he could not share, and would say, 'Ah! Sarah! If only we had met 10 years ago!' meaning that then he would have been able to join her in the refreshment.[50]

Although Sarah had scrawled the words 'delete' and 'inaccurate' over this diary entry, seven years later she wrote: 'He always had a tiny bottle of Champagne opened for me, which he insisted on my drinking',[51] and so we can assume that it was the *gauche* wording, and perhaps the reference to her sitting on the floor, that annoyed her.

Meanwhile, *The Heavenly Twins* brought letters of praise and approval from women (and doctors) all over the world: 'Many letters from medical men, known and unknown, complimenting her on her accurate knowledge of physiology and pathology . . . [and] women in distant lands, telling her that she has done more in the cause of women and children than she will ever know.'[52] It was translated into Russian and Finnish, and serialised. Finnish women 'to whom its point of view was entirely new' besieged the publishing house in crowds for each new chapter.[53] Many stories circulated about the book:

The other day a young lady, [a] passenger to a sleepy little village on the Sussex coast, in changing trains at a junction, left the book she had been reading on the rack of the carriage she had just quitted. On arriving at her destination she discovered her loss, and, instantly making it known to the officials, they wired to the terminus: 'Heavenly Twins left in first class carriage, 3.40 down,' to which they received the following startling reply: 'No trace of twins, wire description.'[54]

But in the end *The Heavenly Twins* was blamed for ruining her literary career. 'A Mrs Forbes who used to tell fortunes told her she would never get to the top of the tree unless she kept exclusively to writing,' her friend Gladys reported.[55] Cards, palms, presentiments and vibrations were all very fashionable and influential; they recur in Sarah's novels and she evidently believed that 'that book . . . spoilt her literary career . . . as it diverted her activities into other channels'.

The Beth Book – Being a Study from the Life of Elizabeth

Caldwell Maclure, her most autobiographical novel, was written over an eighteen-month period in 1895–6, in Paris, London, at Burford Bridge, at l'Ermitage de Jean-Jacques Rousseau in the forest of Montmorency, and was finished at Cambo-les-Bains in the Basses Pyrénées. Sarah was at Cambo when it was published in the summer of 1897. This was the third and last of her serious feminist novels. Although an interviewer with *The Woman at Home* announced earlier, 'the forthcoming volume will certainly contain some of her early reminiscences of Irish life, [but] is not, I believe, a "problem" novel',[56] Beth follows Ideala, Evadne and Angelica (the female twin) as a thoroughly modern woman, moulded by experience to revolt against convention and a miserable marriage. Like Sarah, she suffers from a deprived childhood, minimal schooling and early marriage to the profligate doctor, Dan Maclure, who practises vivisection and runs a Lock hospital. Thus far, smoothed by time and distance, and with no requirement to make a story more poignant than her own experience, Sarah's characterisation and recollection are vivid, and we receive a clear picture of a countryside 'padded with pine needles', of poverty coupled with gentility, of her severe mother and instructive Great-Aunt Victoria, and of subsidiary characters like the vicar who 'would not call on anybody with less than five hundred a year . . . He had had three wives himself, and was getting through a fourth as fast as one baby a year would do it.' Beth's husband and marriage are also clearly, and venomously, observed. But once Beth escapes to London, starves in an attic, finds success through writing and lecturing, and crowns her fortune with a good and loving husband, the story becomes very much 'a study from the life of [Elizabeth Clarke McFall] a woman of genius', and thus a vehicle for Sarah's own views, and the conventions of fiction are observed only where the plot dictates another thrust towards its end. The plot becomes thick with coincidences: Beth glances into the garden from the otherwise windowless side of the house just in time to see an 'immoral' act; the right person happens to drive past the right door of the right London house at the split-second right moment. Characters are superficial and firmly manipulated to allow Beth to make statements about marriage, extra-marital relations, vivisection, VD checks for men, education, music, literary criticism, and monsters of the male sex in general. The book is very much a portrait of the artist, with her views and fears and observations, the essence of Sarah; a summary of what she knew, felt and believed. Beth, too, suffers from nervous exhaustion but, as Sarah must have bravely decided during the exhuming of her past, 'everything is but an incident with all of us, a heartbreak today, a recollection tomorrow, a source of encouragement and of inspiration eventually perhaps'.

After *The Beth Book*, Sarah left feminist argument to her articles and lectures and tried to improve the quality of her writing, striving to bury the matter in the manner of her prose. As she had written in the Preface to *Our Manifold Nature*, 'Fiction is found fault with because it is not fact, and fact, because it is not fiction. . . . Personally, I think the only art worth cultivating is the art of being interesting.'[57] Perhaps she was influenced by her reviewers, whose attention to *The Beth Book* came more because of *The Heavenly Twins* and Sarah's now famous name and public standing than for the quality of the book itself. Her 'sense of a doctrine to preach' brought as much criticism as the 'essentially coarse'[58] subject matter. The *Athenaeum* comments that 'Sarah Grand is getting very heavy handed . . . [and] . . . she cares nothing about novel-writing as an art, except in so far that it can be used as a vehicle for her doctrines'.[59] And 'Claudius Clear' in the *British Weekly*, while praising her sincerity and 'eminent talent', complains that 'no-one ever dwells long on such themes without deterioration'.[60]

Sarah was still at Cambo when the reviews came in. A criticism by Frank Danby in the *Saturday Review*[61] is typical of most, congratulating her 'immense talent, almost amounting to genius (unlike the majority of women who write on unsavoury subjects)', and makes the point that 'the first three or four hundred pages . . . contain . . . fine humour, crisp phrasing and delicate scene-painting as would suffice to make a smaller writer great and a greater writer famous'. But again, like other reviewers, he condemns her 'farcical sex maniacs' at Morningquest, and her 'strange and hideous obsession' and 'iconoclastic fervour' about the controversies 'that raged twenty years ago around the dead C.D. Acts'. Although he applauds her masterly portrayal of young Beth and the minor characters in the first part of the book, he writes: 'The remainder of the novel is merely absurd, and might have been written by any fanatic.' His comments on 'bad taste and ignorance in the later chapters' of the book were, however, surpassed by Frank Harris, editor of the *Saturday Review* at that time. Harris attacked Sarah's 'egotistic outpourings' and self-indulgence. 'We do not remember,' he complained, 'to have come across in the course of our reading such irrelevant and foolish drivel. . . . her head . . . seems to have been completely turned by the popular success of the "Heavenly Twins".' And 'from the beginning to the end not a character lives'. Harris ended his diatribe by suggesting:

If she would take a course of Balzac or Flaubert or Maupassant, she might be prevented writing any more books like the 'Beth Book', and that would be an advantage, not only to herself, but to her unwary readers.[62]

Writing immediately to her friend Mr Fisher, Sarah commented:

Mr Frank Harris overdid it in his scurrilous attack in the *Saturday Review*. He outraged the British sense of justice, and the result is a reaction which is doing good. The critics are beginning to read the book. But Mr Frank Harris himself can

have no sense of humour otherwise he, in the same paragraph
in which he proposes that I have outraged his sense of
delicacy, [would not] have recommended me to study,
amongst others, Guy de Maupassant, author of *Bel Ami*, *Une
Vie*, *La Maison Tellier* and other volumes innumerable, with the
most indecent passages in them, and all distinguished by
immorality unrelieved by a single aspiration towards something more elevating.[63]

And while staying at Cambo she replied to a request for
her views on the vote:

The real position of woman's vote now and in the future is
such a big subject to dispose of shortly. I should say that now
we are in a state of transition which leaves us still doubtful
about the future; we can only be sure of the past. Our
attitude – the attitude of thoughtful and conscientious
women – is one of watchfulness at the present time. Unscru-
pulous people are misrepresenting us and our teachings in
order to find excuses for the licence of their own conduct, and
unwise ones credit us with their own follies. I do not say that
even among ourselves there are no mistakes made; if I did I
should be claiming to be super-human. But I do say that such
mistakes have their excuse. They are the outcome of a
generous effort to relieve those who suffered hopelessly in the
old days when women allowed themselves to be persuaded that
it was a virtue to suffer in silence, and a disgrace to make
themselves conspicuous even for the purpose of removing the
causes of their suffering. The great fear among people who
know nothing of what we are working for but have their own
opinions on the subject, an obstructive set who have hampered
the progress of the world in all ages, is that the accomplish-
ment of our designs will be the death blow to all true
womanliness. In answer to these, I would ask rational people
to consider if it be likely that women (I speak of high-minded
women, not the filth and scum who come to the top in society
because of their lightness) I ask is it likely that they will let go
any grace which adds to the beauty and pleasure of life, or any
charm which has from of old strengthened their influence for
good in the world: Our object is to make life better worth
living for everyone, and in order to accomplish this we

endeavour to strengthen ourselves in all womanly attributes by developing our intelligence, by enlarging our sympathies, by expanding our hearts so that we may be better wives, better mothers, truer friends, and more useful citizens. I say our object, but at the same time I am not sure that we have any choice in the matter, for the woman's movement seems to be evolutionary – an effort of the human race to advance a step higher in its development, a result which can only be attained by making the mothers finer creatures than they have been heretofore.[64]

Sarah had no reason to love her critics but she could now reproach them from a position of strength and, unlike Hardy who ceased novel-writing after the vicious reception of *Jude the Obscure*, she obviously enjoyed writing her stinging reply to an unkind review in the *Daily Telegraph*:

My distance from home makes the receipt of papers a somewhat fitful event, and this must be my excuse for the delay in answering your delicate apostrophe to me. That you should insult Scott and Thackeray and Dickens with your approval pains me but little, since they will never hear of it; that you are so much cleverer than I am I must modestly accept your word for; that you strain yourself to be facetious and but prove yourself a dunce, I must attribute to your academic degree, and a course of the blighting wit of the common room; that you should attack me with base misrepresentation I set down to some rag of chivalry that still clings to you; that you are of ancient lineage I am willing to admit, since your putting into my mouth words and sentiments which are not mine shows you infected with the blood of Ananias; that you should take yourself as a serious judge of art is a crime for which it is painful to think you must one day settle between you and your God; but that you should write yourself down as an admirer of mine is the ugliest blow that my art has dealt me, and I take this opportunity to publicly apologise for it. Believe me, yours in sorrow for your insincerity.[65]

The mass popularity of the New Woman novel lasted no more than a decade. By the end of the nineties conventional reticence had been broken: female sexuality and the need for education and employment for women were, in differing degrees, openly debated. Women were now better informed about their rights, and the suffrage committees, united in 1897 under Millicent Fawcett as the National Union of Women's Suffrage Societies, gathered together to campaign constitutionally for the vote. The need for didactic novels waned and the work of most of these novelists became less aggressive, more subtle.

On 8 February 1898 Sarah's husband died in Warrington at his house in Folly Lane where he had spent his retirement with Archie, who was now twenty-six. Haldane and Archie were the only members of the family to attend his funeral, and his coffin, with the crown of his military cocked hat, belt and sword, was carried by sergeants from the barracks, followed by thirty colour sergeants and a detachment of the medical service. The wreaths were mostly regimental. His final estate amounted to £195 16s. 5d. to be shared between his three sons. To his wife, he left such china, drawing-room furniture, pictures and books as she might like, and a silver teapot given him by her aunt. Haldane inherited his watch and chain, gold pencil case, diamond ring and writing case; Albert, his uniform, medals, swords, pins, bedroom clock and bound volumes of *Punch*. Archie had other clocks, walking sticks, silver and curios including 'my Chinese Lantern in the hall, my spirit case and Chinese cigar box and my Japanese writing and other cabinets'. His 'good old servant' received all electro-plate cutlery, glass, linen and cooking utensils, £100 in cash and an annuity of £50. He was buried in Warrington cemetery and Sarah was now honourably free to do as she liked.

After another brief attempt at living in London ('my health would not stand the continual rush there, and work was at a standstill'),[66] Sarah bought 5 Mount Ephraim, a house 'in the country, two miles from Tunbridge Wells station, a peaceful little place with a dear old garden'[67], and began a new life near Haldane, who had now embarked on his new career as art critic and author. Her other stepson, Albert, is no longer mentioned and I can find no further trace of him.

CHAPTER VII

Suffrage and America: 1898–1920

❦❦

The 'Naughty Nineties' ended with the trial of Oscar Wilde; reaction to this stemmed the flood of progressive 'sexual' novels. The Boer War brought with it tremendous controversy in the press, and public fear of defeat. These events pushed all talk of suffrage into the background. Tunbridge Wells, a genteel spa in Kent, offered an appropriate setting for a cultured English lady. Polite manners and pedigrees abounded, as did the courtesy and high-breeding that always pleased Madame Sarah Grand. Tunbridge Wells offered her a more tranquil life than Paris and the Moulin Rouge, the anglicised Riviera or the bustle and inevitable daily involvement of London: its pace and and interests suited her in every way. She could be a big fish in this small pond; if she wished she could commune with Nature, observe the common man, involve herself in parochial matters and still be free to think and write and develop her theories and commitment to the Cause. And Haldane had just bought The Grey House at Langton, a village nearby.

Haldane had served with the West India Regiment in Africa and Abyssinia, Jamaica and Sierra Leone, 'finally succumbing to the malarial climate and being invalided out of the Army'.[1] During a lengthy convalescence he began his artistic career with an article on the illustrator Sidney Sign in *St Paul's Magazine* (by 'Hal Dane', a *nom de plume* which he subsequently dropped). He had married

Mabel Annie Plumridge, daughter of Admiral Sir James Hanway Plumridge, RN, KCB, and had a daughter, Elizabeth Genevieve Bernadine Crawford Haldane McFall. She was known as Beth but was evidently proud of her string of names: an acquaintance who clearly remembered the household when Beth was nineteen could only recall the (exaggerated) number.[2] No more is known of her mother, Mabel Annie, other than that she was mentioned in Haldane's will. Within a couple of years Sarah had left her own house at Mount Ephraim and moved into The Grey House with a Miss Harling, to run the household for the next twenty years. The apparent 'disappearance' of Haldane's wife during this time is inexplicable. Yet when Haldane died in 1928 he left, in a will drawn up in 1927, his entire estate to his wife, Mabel Annie McFall, of the same London address as his own. Visitors who wrote of the Tunbridge Wells household never mentioned her, and Sarah never referred to her. That Beth, Miss Harling, Haldane and Sarah lived in the house, all agree; Beth would have been only five when the *ménage* began. An invalid or an errant wife would have been material too good for Sarah or visiting journalists to overlook, and she could not have spent twenty years 'visiting her parents'.

Haldane, while pursuing his literary and artistic career, and researching the pedigrees of his more illustrious friends, 'became his stepmother's assistant, advisor, and alleged business-manager'.[3] As Major Haldane McFall he also wrote articles and essays on art and the theatre for many magazines, including the *Illustrated London News*. He is best known for volumes on the *History of Painting* (1911), publications on Beardsley, Whistler and eighteenth-century French artists; studies of Henry Irving (1906), of Ibsen (1907); and a novel, *The Wooings of Jezebel Pettyfer* (1898), the first edition of which, with a bare-breasted Jezebel designed by Haldane himself on the cover, had to be withdrawn because it outraged the Watch Committees.[4]

Sarah now settled to a life of dignity and respect, with

plenty of time to improve her literary style and examine her political attitudes. But the message in her articles remained the same, with a series on modern girls and young men, the choice of wife and husband, the new women and the old, and the how, when and why of marriage:

The New Woman can be hard on man, but it is because she believes in him and loves him. She recognises his infinite possibilities. She sees the God in him, and means to banish the brute.[5]

In a 'Warning', printed in place of an introduction in a pamphlet expounding her views, which sold 10,000 copies in England and America during its first year,[6] she notes that her public assumes 'I think all men objectionable, all marriages failures, all English girls ill-mannered', and goes on to cement this impression. The Modern Girl has been rescued from being 'a dependant and a parasite from the cradle to the grave', but now tends to selfishness and conceit and 'sufficient attention has not been paid to her manners'. But 'women are farther advanced morally than men, less sunk in sensuality'; 'young university men' are beyond the pale. In a review of *Marriage Questions in Fiction*[7] she restates her opinion that 'the woman movement [is] an effort to raise the race a step higher in the scale of being [and] makes for law and order . . . [which is] bitterly opposed by the base and the sensual'. Although proposing fair and equal grounds for legal separation, she stands firm against 'absolute' divorce. 'Divorce permitting remarriage has proved worse than a failure' both in England and America and 'greater facility for divorce means more self-indulgence for those who are that way inclined, and more misery for the rest – especially the women and children'. She also advocates 'individuals *should* suffer – they should glory in suffering and self-sacrifice for the good of the community'. Her creed distilled much of the popular philosophy of the time, combining Darwinian eugenics with a moral feminism that asked for women no more than a fair marriage free of vice. However, like many feminists of today, she rebelled against male-orientated terminology:

Why woman-question rather than human-question or humanity-question, or any other expression which would suggest the combined interests of men and women, since they cannot be separated?[8]

In politics Sarah's concerns reflected the preoccupations of the nation. The Boer War – particularly the fear that it would be lost – affected the country profoundly. Many intellectuals spoke against it, each after his own fashion – Hardy and Sarah's friend, Meredith, avidly following the strategic tactics, perceiving faults on both sides. The *Morning Leader*, fervently Liberal, castigated the government for its imperialism and 'worship of force', and particularly for sending out and maintaining a force 'not far short of 200,000 men, and driving all the sources of national energy into a single channel' when defeat was imminent. Sarah, joining fellow authors, MPs and the clergy, drew upon her early army experience as much as her idealism when she wrote:

War betokens a want of wit on the part of the rulers and governors; it is an ugly old anachronism. Strength and wisdom are required to keep the peace, but anyone can pick a quarrel. A strong government sends army enough to the dis-affected region to inspire respect – this by way of precaution, of object-lesson; then it enters into those endless negotiations, those endless disputes which are so useful as an outlet for ill-feeling, and also as a means of exciting and interesting the more turbulent spirits, so as to keep them out of mischief. Meanwhile, able agents are set to work beneath the surface to spread friendly feeling; to encourage commerce, which is the best bond of union between nations; and to promote inter-marriage, which is the natural means of amalgamation; and to do all else that makes for peace and goodwill. Had this policy been pursued at the Cape there would have been no Boer War.[9]

She also attempted a story set in South Africa during the war; the hero of this story, a prisoner, expiates his thoroughly bad life by breaking parole to free his cell-mate, with inevitable and disastrous consequences.[10] (This story is less affecting to read than her advice to governments in the *Morning Leader*.)

Sarah had moved into The Grey House at the height of the war, and was holding court as 'a cultured English Lady' and 'our distinguished hostess'.[11] Haldane had just published *The Wooings of Jezebel Pettyfer* which now labelled him as 'her clever step-son',[12] and her own *Babs the Impossible* was being serialised in *The Lady's Realm* and was published by Hutchinson. Later she described *Babs the Impossible* to her friend Gladys as 'palpably a pot-boiler', written 'as a serial very quickly, before *Ideala*' (in the 1870s) when she 'thought she could write without revising'.[13] But it serves as a link between her feminist trilogy and the later novels, and is more accomplished and detailed than her earlier work, which leads one to assume that thirty years later in talking to Gladys she had forgotten the revision. (Later still she wrote, 'I dug it out of a book I wrote when I was a girl, and must have been unwittingly infected with the mood and manner of that time of life – the teaching-preaching-know-better-than-everybody time of life, when some of us are for improving everybody except ourselves.'[14] It is a far less 'improving' book than any of the feminist trilogy; and Babs, an endearing young heroine, has a freshness and bounce denied Sarah's feminists. Like Beth – though from parental incompetence rather than from poverty – Babs was 'deprived of the means of intellectual development' and arranges her own education in the world. Where Beth chooses books and improves her mind, Babs follows instinct and innocence, seeks caresses and lives for sensual satisfaction. Her irrepressible spirit is more spontaneous than the Twins', and carries her through flirtations, puppy love for the noble, most restrained, Lord Cadenhouse, the adolescent pain of rejection, and on to the hopefully happy ending in which Cadenhouse, pledged to Another (her aunt), is presumed to be waiting when Babs returns from an impetuous voyage to the East. Splendidly eccentric characters, like Babs' mother and Mr Capel Augustus Jellybond Tinney, smack of Dickens; sensuality is emphasised by descriptive passages on cooking and eating (plans for seduction surround elaborate menus in forests and tents); prognostications, Tarot cards and intimations of the occult link the earthy behaviour of the secondary characters with the symbolism of Cadenhouse, busy in his tower cultivating his sixth sense, and practising being 'angelic' ('knowledge comes from the spirit, it dwells not in matter'.). Babs, however, knows otherwise and having aroused him with kisses during illicit midnight visits to his tower, copes with his engagement to her aunt by the characteristically impulsive declaration to the poor spinster that he loves only Babs, leaving her aunt with no alternative but to release him. Her mother, always placated by the thought of food, wears 'hides and heads and tails of dead creatures [sables] all over her, displayed regardless of art as of expense'. Her mother's lover – who ultimately stands as Conservative candidate for the area in spite of his humble origins – dabbles in mesmerism and illusions, and seduces most of the female neighbourhood, mixing opalescent drinks of uncanny effect.

Young Babs certainly shines with her unprincipled and indecorous behaviour but, as leaven, her tutor, a university graduate, is a woman in all things admirable. She can quote Florence Nightingale and Josephine Butler, and cites Aesop as 'the only slave I can think of who distinguished himself in literature. A subjugated race produces no great work of art' (this in defence of women who could or would make their mark). She triumphs, despite Babs, by marrying Babs' guardian (object of Babs' earlier passion). Thus marriage remains the aim and reward for all.

Babs is Sarah's simplest, most compact story. She told Gladys that it was adapted as a stage play by some Americans who 'had submitted it to her, but they had so vulgarised it that she could not consent to its production. Later she heard that they had produced it under another name and had made a million dollars with it.'[15] Allowances must be made for exaggeration, as with all Gladys' reports, particularly as Sarah also apparently told her that she 'collaborated on a play of *The Heavenly Twins* with Robert Buchanan, but the English and American copyrights clashed'.[16] The adaptation of *Babs* is just credible – with enormous encapsulation – but to have brought *The Heavenly Twins* to the stage would have required an amazing feat of reconstruction.

In June of that year Athol Forbes, a clergyman, visited 'this gifted authoress' to write his impressions for *The Lady's World*.[17] Having often quoted her in his sermons, he expected 'a keen, hard debater with a touch of cynicism . . . pessimism, and . . . pride', but like all her interviewers he was captivated by her 'charming smile, and a sweet low voice' and admitted 'she was, in fact, all that the New Woman ought to be and nothing she is popularly supposed to be'. The 'merry party' for luncheon included Haldane and conversation ranged over Berkeley's *Philosophical Speculations,* old brandy, ghosts, publishers, religion, her interest in parochial work, reincarnation, and the New Woman ('You invented her,' Forbes remarked). He watched her closely and 'was struck by the remarkable change of expression' when she laughed: 'She might suddenly have had ten years taken off her age.' When Haldane showed him photographs of her 'not generally given to visitors, each picture might have represented a different person. In some she looked fifty years of age [she was then forty-six], in others she did not appear to be more than

twenty, yet all had been taken within the last two years.'
Watching her face while she held forth about the New
Woman, 'I fancied I saw there the history of patience,
tenacity, and courage, and I ventured to think, somewhere
in her life there is to be found some great act of self-
sacrifice'. But he didn't venture to enquire.

Sarah was now lecturing more, her most popular
subjects being 'The Art of Happiness' and 'Mere Man'.
Her humorous approach to serious subjects in a serious
world, and her ease and presence on the platform
guaranteed her audiences: she was in much demand. She
lectured to groups and clubs across the country and Major
Pond, who made a living organising lecture tours in
America, visited her in 1901. He 'so interested her in his
tales of fortunes won on the lecture field through his
auspices, that although she had decided some time ago not
to come to America, she could not resist this practical
appeal'.[18] *Babs the Impossible* was now published in
America, and *The Heavenly Twins* still had a readership:
'Street & Smith, having bought the plates [of *The Heavenly
Twins*] from Cassell, brought out a new edition at twenty
cents, giving the book a new lease of life.'[19] Although the
women's clubs of America were not 'particularly anxious
to engage the services of Madame Grand . . . there [were]
enough other organisations that [did] want her to assure
the success of her American tour'.

On the voyage to New York with Major Pond in
October 1901 she enjoyed the company of Sir Henry
Irving and Ellen Terry. This was to be the seventh and last
American tour of Irving's company and neither star felt
well. Irving suffered from sciatica and died in 1905. As
Ellen Terry wrote: 'In 1901 I was ill and hated the parts I
was playing in America. The Lyceum company was not
what it had been. Everything was changed.'[20] But, as
usual, they travelled sumptuously with the entire company and staff from the Lyceum and all their scenery and
properties. We do not know if the actress had accepted
Sarah's invitation to tea with Haldane in Paris,

but certainly they had met before. Sarah recalled her on board 'sitting on the floor cracking walnuts in her hands like a monkey and picking them out and eating them', and Irving 'kindly allowed her trunks to go through with theirs to save her trouble with the Customs officers'.[21] This sounds like a doubtful advantage when we learn that, confronted by Customs and unable to think of anything to declare, Sarah was prompted by the official: ' "Tobacco?" he ventured [and] Ellen Terry cut in with "She smokes like a chimney!" '

Sarah reported that she lectured for four months to students at Barnard College, New York, Bryn Mawr, Pennsylvania, San Francisco and Chicago, shaking hands endlessly at receptions in her honour, though told by some that 'they liked her but they did not like her lectures'.[22] At Bryn Mawr she said, 'Afterwards one of [the students] stood up and came forward to the platform carrying a bunch of chrysanthemums whose stalks were almost as tall as herself, and presented them saying, "We want to give you these because we like you very much". '[23] In Chicago Sarah refused to enter a slaughterhouse and told Gladys that after that stand 'the Americans liked her better and said nicer things about her'.[24] (Ellen Terry had also avoided the slaughterhouse in 1883 – evidently the prime excursion for any visitor to the city – writing: 'I never visited the stock-yards. I had no curiosity to see a live pig turned in fifteen minutes into ham, sausages, hair-oil, and the binding for a Bible!')[25]

Sarah also stayed with Agnes Tobin in San Francisco, and with Mark Twain in Connecticut. Twain, who had 'beguiled his time during one of his sea voyages' criticising and annotating *The Heavenly Twins*, came to admire Sarah. For all his arguments against her 'putrid twins' and her often dreadful grammar, he wrote, 'but never mind that, it is a strong, good book!'[26] An interest in twins united them, although they used them for different reasons: Sarah to show sex discrimination, both educational and social,

Twain to contrast good and evil in his book *Pudd'nhead
Wilson and Those Extraordinary Twins*[27] which he began in
1892, the year before publication of Sarah's novel. They
also discussed Shaw, whose works Twain had 'at his
fingers ends: he seemed to know every character and every
play . . . He said in his slow, almost sad way: "Yes, GBS
gets there, where he wants to go, every time" '.[28] Although
American feminists were disappointed by Sarah's frivolity, the trip proved a success and she was described in
Harper's Weekly as:

Clever, accomplished, and charming, she talks brilliantly, and
lectures with easy grace and polish. People who rush to hear
her in the hope that her lectures will savor of the problems in
The Heavenly Twins and *Babs The Impossible* will be disappointed, but they will be agreeably surprised in other ways by
her searching sense of humor, which is like salt to her speech,
as it is to her writing. Upon one occasion she sent a London
audience into screams of laughter when, after repeating the
cry from Australia, 'Send us two thousand wives,' she
retorted, 'In behalf of two thousand English Benedicks I reply,
Take ours! Take ours!' I just missed hearing her lecture on
'Mere Man', at one time in London, but a friend of mine who
heard her says that she entered upon the subject 'with a gasp'.
'It is so hard,' she went on, 'to know how to treat the agitating
thing, but man that is born of woman must be more than a
mere joke.' Man, she thought, it was scarcely necessary to
take seriously, because he takes himself quite seriously enough
for all purposes of humanity. She admitted meekly that she
had known some nice men in her time, and that as fetchers
and carriers they had actually been of real use sometimes. It
will be seen that Madame Grand's lectures are as impregnated
with the spirit of fun and sly humor, not to speak of sarcasm,
as was her latest book, *Babs The Impossible*. Like *Mere Man*, it is
scarcely necessary to take *Babs* seriously, because Madame
Grand herself takes her quite seriously enough. But, as a
source of entertainment, both as author and lecturer, she does
not fail her patrons.[29]

Home again in Tunbridge Wells the problem of finance

suddenly had to be faced. Sales of Sarah's books had dropped during the Boer War 'and [are] not likely to recover until I write another';[30] writing and lecturing provided an unreliable income. Haldane was no better placed to support the household. Presumably his expenses were high, for he had now become a member of Frank Harris' coterie in London,[31] was working on his three-volume history of painting, and hoping one day to publish a series of pedigrees 'in an artistic form, and with portraits, [when] I can afford it'.[32] Sarah now began to search for a further series of lectures, promising her literary agent one entitled 'Her Infinite Variety'. These financial worries, and a winter's attack of influenza, brought her to the verge of breakdown again and forced her into a two-month Weir Mitchell rest cure.[33] After that, a diagnosis of neuresthenia led her to threaten cancellation of all activities for six months. But the lectures were resumed – 'Mere Man' and 'Things We Forget to Remember' taking her through November – and she even enjoyed lecturing without payment in Birmingham to the Ruskin Society, following the example of Mrs Humphry Ward and Mrs Pearl Craigie.

By 1907 her fortunes had changed again, she was lecturing about seventy times a year; she was hardly ever at home. 'I find it fascinating work and also think I am profiting by it in many ways. I see so many phases of life, so many specimens of humanity.'[34] The limelight, as much as the opportunities for observation and the financial reward, appealed to her. Her later memories of that time dwell on applause:

Harrogate used to be very kind to me when I lectured there. It was the first place to call me back at the end after I had left the platform, and give me a rousing cheer. It never occurred to me that such a thing could happen. I had not noticed that the applause continued and was saying good night to the attendant in the Cloak Room when the Secretary, looking somewhat irate, asked me if I would not be *good* enough to *show* myself to the audience again just for a moment.[35]

The reason for her success remained, I believe, the light and humorous approach to her subject matter and the *panache* of her delivery. No doubt her audiences took her seriously: she meant every word she spoke. Although Sarah's topics may seem superficial and even frivolous, they provided a contrast to the new militancy of the feminists under the charismatic leadership of the Pankhursts, and the growing fervour and anxiety of the feminist debate. To many, Sarah's approach supported the argument that women were rational, able and intellectually equal to men.

In 1903 Emmeline Pankhurst had started her own franchise group in Manchester: the Women's Social and Political Union. This group, which shortly based itself in London, was formed to demand the vote 'on the same grounds as it is or may be held by men'[36] and, ruled autocratically by Emmeline with the help of her daughter, Christabel, became the revolutionary branch of the movement. The NUWSS, under Millicent Fawcett, remained democratic and constitutional, its members disapproving when Emmeline and Christabel later roused the suffragettes to militant action. The Pankhursts were guided by an urge to purify the male population almost as strong as their desire for the vote ('Votes for women, Chastity for men'), and these emotions would seem to coincide with Sarah's, but Sarah aligned herself with the non-militant suffragists under Mrs Fawcett. Despite their similarity of age, their marriages to older men, their husbands' coincidental deaths in the same year, and the passionate devotion that each inspired in another woman (Ethel Smyth for Emmeline, Gladys Singers-Bigger for Sarah), their tactics were different: Mrs Pankhurst was prepared to use any weapon to achieve her goal whereas Sarah believed in the spoken and written word. She joined the Women Writers' Suffrage League, an auxiliary of the NUWSS, whose methods 'are the methods proper to writers – the use of the pen . . . Women writers [were] urged to join the League.

A body of writers working for a common cause cannot fail to influence public opinion.'[37]

In 1908 the Pankhursts instigated the first attacks on property and the NUWSS broke links with their party. The WSPU itself split later with Sylvia, the youngest Pankhurst daughter, forming the breakaway East London Federation. At that time Sarah wrote to Bertha Newcombe, and while agreeing for her name to be included as a contributor to the *Coming Citizen*, deplored 'the differences that prevent all parties combining to produce one really good paper. Personally, I do not understand these differences in a common cause; they are usually so petty. I am ready to appear on any platform and write for any paper that is for Women's Suffrage.'[38] In the same year Sarah made a speech before the International Women's Suffrage Alliance in London in which she said that 'the vote was as much the need of the nature of modern, progressive woman as was the need of birds to fly or fish to swim'. The suffrage movement, she added, was 'altogether evolutionary'.[39] Sarah's involvement with the Cause led her to inaugurate a Tunbridge Wells branch of the Women's Citizens' Association and to become Vice-President of the Women's Suffrage Society, President of the local branch of the National Council of Women and President, and Chairman and principal speaker of the Tunbridge Wells branch of the NUWSS.

From 1911 'the argument of the broken window pane' took over from debate and the rift widened between suffragettes and suffragists. Apart from breaking windows, the suffragettes used arson, acid bombs, pepper and snuff in letters and wrote in acid on golf courses and bowling greens. Sarah's position as President of the local NUWSS required all her tact and diplomacy to smooth anti-suffrage feeling in the town, which grew as militant action increased. These years until the outbreak of the First World War were hectic for her with meetings, lectures, marches and rallies. In 1913, just before the NUWSS

Pilgrimage to London, local antagonism soared when the
town's cricket pavilion was destroyed by militants.[40]
However, the propaganda value of the Pilgrimage
managed to overcome the fury of the townspeople and
shortly afterwards the Tunbridge Wells branch comprised
165 Members and 278 Friends.[41] The Pilgrimage,
organised by the NUWSS, drew men and women throughout the country to converge on London for a mass meeting
in Hyde Park. With banners and bands the ranks swelled
as the Pilgrimage progressed down the roads of England,
and processions grew daily with lectures and meetings in
every town and village along the way. The Kentish
'Pilgrims' Way' held fifty-five meetings in twenty-five
days, mainly in the open air – on Ramsgate Sands, for
instance – selling the *Common Cause*, 'the organ of the
Women's Movement for Reform', and collecting money
and members. In the first Annual Report of the NUWSS
Kentish Federation, that year, credit was given to
Tunbridge Wells for 'the large contingent of pilgrims
under the leadership of its President, Madame Sarah
Grand'.

In 1914, with the outbreak of war, feminist activity was
suspended. When war was declared Sarah wrote to Mrs
Fawcett:

Madame, as there has been no time to consult the committee
of this branch, I am authorised by our Vice-Presidents, Lady
Matthews and Miss Galt, to reply to your letter of the 5th
August myself . . . We hereby agree with you as to the desir-
ability of ceasing propaganda work at the present crisis and
are prepared to co-operate in whatever scheme the Borough or
other existing agency may make.[42]

At about this time Katharine Tynan, a prolific novelist
and journalist from Dublin, moved to live nearby at South-
borough. She notes: 'There was a strong Suffrage party in
Tunbridge Wells. I was caught into the law-abiding one
– the National Union of Women's Suffrage Societies.

They were on the whole quite reasonable people.'[43] However, she was not impressed by Tunbridge Wells' society
with its majority of widows and spinsters, and her
memories of Sarah from years earlier at literary London
dinners did not lead her to anticipate friendship with the
local President. 'We differed so much on so many things,'
she wrote vaguely in one of her volumes of reminiscence.
But when they did meet, Sarah 'was a green oasis in the
arid waste of Tunbridge Wells'.[44]

She came in one November afternoon between the lights a tall
dark figure. She was wearing something soft and black –
coming swiftly, with the softest voice, the softest hands, the
sweetest heart. It was like the process known as conversion
. . . As lightning leaps from a cloud, love came . . . We were
less poor that day . . . Sarah is one of the women who, having
won you, keeps you. There are no coldnesses, no wearinesses
possible in loving her.[45]

Katharine Tynan wrote this newspaper article in 1922,
following the announcement that Sarah was to become
Mayoress of Bath, and it was based on her already
published reminiscences. There is no particular significance in her emotional wording, Tynan wrote effusively
about many women whom she had met.

   During these years of political and social activity, and
despite the demands such work made upon her time, Sarah
embarked on her second trilogy, of which only two parts
were ever written: *Adnam's Orchard*, published by
Heinemann in 1912, and *The Winged Victory* in 1916. In
these she is more benevolent towards her male characters,
all of whom are more mature, though less interesting than
her earlier 'heroes'. Perhaps she was influenced by criticism, perhaps, too, she had matured, for she wrote to her
friend Mr Fisher, Editor of *Literary World*, who had submitted to her a personal sketch in 1907:

But why, I wonder, do you all accuse me of bitterness against
the male sex? It is quite a convention, and I, personally,

cannot make out what gave rise to it. There are thirteen men
in *The Heavenly Twins*, and only one of them is an out and out
bad lot. I can think of no mere male man's novel with so low a
percentage. Then nobody gets on better with men than I
do – as well with men as with women. No, there never has
been any bitterness in my novels, so please get it out from
here.[46]

These two novels explore ambition in elaborate detail
and at great length, the first of a man, the second of a
woman. Adnam's ambition is to bring his derelict orchard
to bloom by using modern methods of intensive culture;
Ella (the 'Winged Victory') works to revive lace-making in
the same highly organised fashion. Both Adnam and Ella
are defeated in the end, one materially, the other spiri-
tually. Each novel can be read as complete in itself, but
they are linked together by their principal characters, and
particularly by 'the Nemesis which pursues and ultimately
overtakes the Duke of Castlefield Saye and those involved,
as victims or otherwise, with him, in the sin of his youth
[adultery]'.[47] Parallels between the two novels abound,
and the writing becomes increasingly 'clever' and
pedantic. Sarah's pleasure in the turning of a phrase or the
insertion of abstruse learning becomes more and more
apparent.

In the first book, Adnam's mother, Ursula, a German
aristocrat, represents culture, sensitivity, mysticism,
expressing Sarah's persona and views. Ursula makes most
of the enlightened remarks about women's rights, morality
and politics, plays the piano and practises psychic tumbler
moving. 'The modern woman,' she says, 'is not yet free
from the restrictions imposed upon her by institutions
which have survived their time and become a hindrance to
progress, she has only too often either to fight or to
abandon for ever the right to be herself and use her faculties
to the full extent of her capacity'.[48] At the end of the
nineteenth century, when Adnam is cultivating his
orchard, agriculture in England was in decline: much

wheat, butter and cheese were imported, and new technology was threatening old-fashioned farming methods and ideas. Sarah was well informed of the details of intensive culture 'as in France', and is as descriptive about the setting up of crop rotation as she is about the collapse of the upper classes. 'The brains have been bred out of us or fooled away,' says the squire, and Sarah, as narrator, purrs, 'the last worth lingering in decadent families is usually found in women'. Adnam, with his honesty, dedication and heroic stature, should reap the success of his orchard, win the fair lady, Ella, and live happily ever after. Instead, his father and mother die, the land reverts to his wretched half-brother and poor Adnam strides off into the sunset to seek a new fortune.

In *The Winged Victory*, the heroine, Ella, expresses Sarah's sensitivity, refinement, presentiments of spirits and second sight, but the mystical role is shared with Gregor Strangworth, a moralising old bore who remarks, 'to have the senses of a lower nature dominated and their function held in suspense by the consummate response of the spirit, is to experience the undiluted pleasure that is divine'. He objects to a brooch as 'one of those gross phallic symbols'. 'If you knew its meaning,' he tells Ella, 'you would cast it into the fire.' But I doubt if Sarah knew the meaning herself for, referring later to a mourning tiepin she says: 'The seemingly simple design was the phallic symbol of maternity.' In this book she finds space for self-congratulation when, discussing the modern hero, she defines him as:

Clean! The women began it, and were plentifully bespattered with mud for daring, but they stuck to it. They exposed the inside of the cup and the platter, the dirt and the disease . . . 'There is no reforming a rotten constitution,' they said, 'Let the mentally and physically tainted be set apart, and give us clean men.'

She also observes that 'women are not so easily beaten by

misfortune as men are; they resist to the last gasp . . . and
the curling pins in their hair were proof that they had not
abandoned hope'. And she suggests: 'A woman who does
not live with a man is apt to be lop-sided; neither men nor
women develop fully apart.' But Sarah does not permit
Ella to 'develop fully'. Although Ella loves the Duke's son,
Lord Melton, and secretly marries him, before their love
can be consummated they discover that the Duke is also
her father. Melton has no alternative but to gallop over a
cliff-top to his death.

With the object of her infatuation in the first two
volumes thus despatched, the final volume would probably
have united Ella with Adnam. But by 1916, and wearied by
war work, Sarah possibly felt bored to death by them both.
The tying and tidying up of all the loose ends and con-
verging parallels from the first two volumes may well have
broken the reader's spirit, for Sarah leaves precious little to
the reader's imagination. She presents Adnam and Ella as
destined for each other by birth (each has one aristocratic
and one peasant parent), each is a heroic figure in the eyes
of the villagers, each fights for independence (the odds
against Adnam being lack of funds, against Ella being the
burden of too much 'patronage'); both are honourable
people. The secondary characters in these two novels have
odd quirks and characteristics that help pad out the
primary narrative: Lord Terry de Beach and Julius
Harkles are derivative of Shakespeare's Sir Toby Belch
and Sir Andrew Aguecheek; Col Drinden, one of Ella's
admirers in London, is a heterosexual Oscar Wilde; Pecky
Tim, her pageboy, reads like the Artful Dodger; the Duke
and Duchess dither and bring calamity on themselves by
avoiding facts and evading issues in the style of most
fictional dukes and duchesses. More credibly than in the
earlier novels, the characters show a mixture of bad and
good, but the protagonists haven't the strength, conviction
or purpose of Beth or Evadne. It doesn't really matter what
happens to them. The canvas is broader, the grass greener,

the country town of Closeminster echoes Hardy, London is a bustle of carriages, with poverty in the streets and idleness in the Clubs, but so much eccentric behaviour is portrayed by so many outrageous characters that one loses sight of the central theme and cares more for the detail than for the novels as a whole.

Yet Sarah had progressed. It would have been surprising if she had produced another *Heavenly Twins* at the age of sixty and she was reacting now to different pressures in a quite different social atmosphere. By 1916 her desire to improve society was well enough exercised in making speeches and running the Tunbridge Wells branch of the NUWSS; fervent suffrage novels had been out of fashion for some time and, with the exception of *Babs the Impossible* which she admits was mostly written long before, she had not attempted a work of fiction since *The Beth Book*, twenty years earlier. With age she had become more objective, relishing her role as a pillar of society.

With the war, women's energies were transferred from the battle for the vote into nursing, driving ambulances, caring for refugees; they also filled the jobs left vacant by men. This unexpected opportunity came at a time when proof of ability was all that remained necessary for emancipation. The arguments had been debated again and again, the dead stone wall of male hostility repeatedly attacked, but all this activity had not won women the vote. Now they united to help the country in any way they could: the conventional, passive wartime role of knitting and weeping was past. Despite their lack of training, they entered factories and workshops and 'in a few weeks they learnt to perform most unexpectedly difficult mechanical operations, and they turned from being daughters at home, or parlourmaids, or whatever they had been before, into charge hands, tool setters, or factory supervisors, with the utmost readiness and success'.[49] At first this aroused the hostility of male workers but soon the employment of women became essential in munition centres, in the forces

and on the land, and their success at this work 'startled
men of all kinds into forming a new and more favourable
judgement of the female sex'.[50] These achievements made
a new Franchise Bill inevitable and, despite a dwindling
collection of 'antis' (like Mrs Humphry Ward who had
been President of the Anti-Suffrage League as long ago as
1908), the Bill was passed and the vote finally granted to
women over thirty in February 1918.

Sarah's war work was unsatisfying to a woman of her
calibre. The Mayor of Tunbridge Wells was apparently
'opposed to Women's Suffrage and he distrusted her in
consequence'. At last, however, he agreed to allow her to
set up a depot to collect clothes for refugees 'but they got
little recognition, though one woman died of over-exer-
tion',[51] and she seems to have spent as much time turning
old uniforms into pen wipers – not very demanding for a
woman capable of fine lace and crochet work, and not
much of a contribution to the war effort. No wonder her
enthusiasm for Tunbridge Wells waned and she became
more interested in Haldane's daughter, Beth, who had
now left her boarding school, Downe House, and brought
life and laughter to The Grey House. During the war
Sarah had experienced with Beth bombing raids and
alarms over Tunbridge Wells, which lay in the flight path
from Germany to London. She also had time for social life
and lunched with Hardy and his wife at Margate and with
Siegfried Sassoon and his mother.[52] With Beth's company
and with regiments stationed nearby, young army officers
visited and 'had entrée to the house [which] was a very
welcome change from the life of billets and barracks and
formal dinners in the Officers' Mess'.[53] One officer
remembers Beth's automatic writing in a state of trance.
Sarah proudly showed him something Beth had written the
previous evening 'in a strong masculine hand [which]
seemed to be the kind of message that an artillery officer in
a forward position might telephone to his battery . . . and
finished with the words ''through the head, out'' and a

name . . . of a great friend of Betty's [sic], a gunner officer
in France. The name appeared in the casualty lists a few
days later.'[54] Beth was, and remained, Sarah's closest
relative – more like a daughter than step-granddaughter.
She married just before Sarah left Tunbridge Wells and
later her own daughter, Felicitas, was sent to boarding
school at Weston-super-Mare, near Sarah's home in Bath.

Towards the end of the war, through their enthusiasm
for her lectures and personality, Sarah had met the
Tindalls, Rachel Mary and her brother William, strong
Quakers of about her own age. Their friendship flourished
through a shared interest in reading and the countryside.
At this time the family at The Grey House began to break
up: Beth was to marry, and Haldane, demobilised from the
army, probably preferred to return to London to be
amongst his friends. Sarah saw no enjoyable future or
prestige in staying in Tunbridge Wells; the Tindalls were
also planning to leave. Together they discussed suitable
areas for retirement and Bath, another spa, a much
favoured city with all amenities for the elderly, and a
leisured style similar to Tunbridge Wells, presented itself
as a choice of romantic proportions. They could imagine:

a crowd of celebrated persons, all jumbled together regardless
of chronology, in the atmosphere of the Eighteenth Century,
and a vaguely visualized Pump Room. Jane Austen, of
course, and Fanny Burney, Dickens, Mr Pickwick, Mr
Dombey, Pope – a whole host of characters, real and
fictitious, all well known to us, whether they had lived in the
flesh or not . . . And, at any rate, it was not far away, and
would do for a change.[55]

All three warmed to the idea and William Tindall bought
the beautiful mansion, Crowe Hall, on Widcombe Hill for
£15,000. Could there be a more suitable shrine for a
famous novelist in retirement too? Sarah could not have
afforded such luxury by herself, such an elegant address.
The beauty of Bath's Georgian crescents, circles and

squares would soothe her, Bath's history and literary
associations would suit her and possibly even inspire her.
Bath seemed, above all, 'a place where one could end one's
days tranquilly, simply looking back on one's life work'.[56]
A pleasing idea and an appropriate setting for a new life.

PART II

Her Devoted Friend

The end of Sarah's life as seen through
the Diaries of Gladys Singers-Bigger,
introduced and edited by Gillian Kersley

NOTE

The Diaries of Gladys Singers-Bigger which comprise most of Part II of this book have been cut by about one-third. In some places punctuation has been altered or added for clarity; I have also broken some of her longer passages into paragraphs for ease of reading. For the same reason, dates have been standardised and the ending of a volume is not shown. Three dots (. . .) precede a cut in the text and any material within square brackets is mine: [– – –?] represents an indecipherable word or words in the original text.

Gladys frequently wrote up her diary later than the day indicated (for example, she describes how she spent St Patrick's day under March 16) and she sometimes annotated her own text, shown in '( )' brackets here.

CHAPTER VIII

Bath – Enter Gladys: 1922–27

❦

Crowe Hall stands half way up Widcombe Hill, one of the seven hills of Bath, surrounded by thirty-eight acres of wooded grounds. On the terrace, which fronts the south-facing façade of the mansion, we can imagine Sarah strolling with William and Rachel Mary Tindall, three elderly people enjoying tranquillity against an elegant background. Behind them, arched French windows lead into the library-study with its lined bookshelves, old prints and Sarah's own favourite pictures. Beyond the terrace with its wide flagstones, lawns and stone balustrades descend into the valley through lime trees, oaks, beeches, ornamental shrubs, fern-clad banks and unexpected vistas. Rising on the opposite slope are the grounds of Prior Park, the mansion built for Ralph Allen, the entrepreneur who set up the postal system, and whose quarries provided the stone for the buildings of Bath. He had employed John Wood the elder to create a Palladian-style country house near his quarries which, incidentally, enhanced the later view from Crowe Hall. John Wood had been responsible for designing and developing the most important architectural features of Bath – Queen Square, the Circus, and the Royal Crescent, the latter modified by his son. Prior Park was considered by him an example of how Allen's stonework could be employed 'to much greater Advantage, and in much greater Variety of Uses than it had ever appeared in any other Structure'.[1] Allen had been elected Mayor while living at Prior Park in 1742.

Tranquillity at Crowe Hall, however, was not to last. Within two years of their arrival in Bath, in the autumn of 1922, it was announced that Madame Sarah Grand, at the age of sixty-eight, had been offered the position of first lady of the city. This offer, and her acceptance, brought journalists again to her door and revived her name across the country. 'Madame *who*?' they had choroused in the newspaper offices. 'Sarah *who*? Wrote *what*?' The name of Sarah Grand, separated by thirty hectic years from her notoriety as author of *The Heavenly Twins*, had faded to the extent that if anyone could remember her they assumed she must be dead. *Who's Who* and old news cutting files disgorged details to those who were interested. One newspaper announced that 'Mrs Sarah Bernhardt is to be Mayoress next year'.[2] (That famous Sarah died the following year.) The *Glasgow Herald*, with more accuracy, wondered: 'Who knows but a new work of fiction may result, and a new Jane Austen rise in Jane Austen's city, one hundred years after the first.'[3] The local paper noted that: 'Madame Sarah Grand, the Distinguished Novelist, has acceded to an invitation by the Mayor-Designate, Alderman Cedric Chivers, and has consented to act as Mayoress during the ensuing municipal year.'[4]

Alderman Chivers was a well-known local philanthropist and a widower, in his seventieth year. A brilliant businessman, he was founder of book-binding companies in Bath, London and New York and originated the card index system. He had crossed the Atlantic 120 times and had served the city as an alderman for many years. A Mayor requires a Mayoress to share civic duties, to balance his splendour and attend functions when he is otherwise occupied. The Mayoress is normally the Mayor's wife and usually passes her year in his shadow at official dinners, opening bazaars and flower shows, and presenting prizes to school girls. Sarah was an appropriate choice for this role and Cedric Chivers knew what he was doing when he invited her to join him. In a close-knit society like Bath, Mr Chivers would have met Sarah at social gatherings, and her grace, charm and past experience on any platform would have marked her as an invaluable consort. This, coupled with his generosity to the city and the splendour of his entertainment, ensured them the longest consecutive run in office since the mayoralty was established in 1189. At the outset, to enhance the dignity of the Mayoress, Mr Chivers presented the city with a new chain of office for Sarah to wear. This chain comprises an early eighteenth-century German belt of silver-gilt links, from which hangs the Mayoress' gold badge of office.

During the last two years of their six-year mayoralty, Cedric Chivers was frequently ill and Sarah carried out most of his civic duties, throwing all her energies into civic functions, opening flower shows, bazaars and buildings, presenting cups and certificates, making speeches and impressing the citizens of Bath by her dedication and personality. On Chivers' death she was asked informally if she would stand as Mayor in her own right, but she refused.

But in 1922 hardly anyone in Bath had heard of her. Although Heinemann had just published her last collection of short stories, *Variety*, and were to reissue *The Heavenly Twins* the following year, her novels were out of print and all that anyone could have read of hers, locally, was what she called an 'apostrophe' on the city 'Exquisite Bath, Impressions of a Newcomer', printed in the local paper a few months earlier. In this she had written:

Our appreciation of the beautiful is apt to be discounted by us. Does the born Bathonian, when he looks from his window at night see through a veil of lilac mist a fairy city, jewelled with yellow topaz, and feel its charms? Or is it only to his accustomed eyes a familiar expanse of streets and crescents, thickly sprinkled with fog-bedimmed lights; which interests him not at all, because his object in looking out was just to see what sort of weather it was? In many cases it must be so, yet it is good to think that in many more the lovely scene never fails of its effect.[5]

Sarah was vague about her duties and had no idea of how arduous they were to become. She told a local reporter: 'Of course I feel that, as Mayoress, I am just taking the responsibility for the little things that are not suitable for the Mayor to do, and that a woman ought really to do. The Mayoress is a sort of *aide-de-camp* to the Mayor.'[6] But she was embarking on six years of hard and selfless labour which would establish her in the hearts and minds of Bath's citizens. To the strength of her personality she now added the charm and gentleness of age and she became a popular Mayoress.

Amongst those citizens who were dazzled by her perfor-mance was Gladys Singers-Bigger, a spinster in her thirties. Instantly captivated by the Mayoress, Gladys was drawn into a tortuous, intense relationship which con-tinued until Sarah's death. Although Sarah by no means returned the passion with which she was courted for the next eighteen years, she enjoyed the matriarchal role Gladys thrust upon her, the power and the flattery. She had no real need of Gladys' friendship and never treated her as an equal, yet she never actively discouraged Gladys and would fuel her ardour when it showed signs of flag-ging. Passively, with dignity, she accepted the supreme position of archetypal mother-figure.

Gladys, the born under-dog, lived in Bath with her suffocating, scarlet-wigged mother and her bright and beautiful sister, Ina, an actress who, as Louise Regnis ('Singer' backwards), understudied Phyllis Nielsen Terry[7] on her South African tour. Despite the fact that their mother was an inn-keeper's daughter from Denver, Colorado, theirs was a typically 'Victorian' English middle-class family with a life-style of tea parties and good works. Gladys had been born in Denver in 1889, where her father, Hew Singers-Bigger, a rich and handsome engineer from Decham Hall, Gateshead, had been working, probably on a hydro-electric scheme. When he returned to England with the hotel keeper's daughter and their first child he had funds enough for a good establishment in London. But following his death, his fortune was lost in the Wall Street crash. His wife and daughters had no business sense and, to cope with their problems, they all became fervent Christian Scientists, and prayed for guidance. Funds dwindled and, although the daughters worried, little altered in their life-style. Of course one must have at least one maid – there were three in their first home in Bath – one must pay visits and be visited and spend one's seasonal holidays in hotels. (Mother, remembered for her red wig and somewhat startling make-up, complained immediately if the hotels were not good enough and they often moved on to another.) But, typically, the only fitting occupation for the Singers-Bigger girls remained good works. ('Ladies only work for charity,' as Sarah had been taught sixty years earlier.) Ina's elocution lessons were seen simply as a lady-like encouragement for her dramatic talent, and the short-hand classes that Gladys found so muddling were allowed in order to help her as Honorary Secretary to the Dickens Fellowship. There was no thought of earning a living, and later, when Gladys spent months typing 'A Sarah Grand Miscellany', collecting quotations from Sarah's works for publication, she refused any reimbursement but rushed out to buy Sarah another present. This way of life – narrow, claustrophobic and, to a considerable degree, anachronistic – was one of the absurdities Sarah had exposed in her novels nearly thirty years earlier. Ina was able to escape through her theatrical work, but Gladys lived the life of a Victorian spinster daughter, always at home, buried in the routine of family life.

Gladys ('Gem' to her friends) is remembered as 'a clever

girl but so unutterably dull', overshadowed by her sister,
'quiet, retiring and very plain', 'shy, awkward, always in
someone else's shadow'.[8] She had been well enough educated, but was reared to become an accomplished
'Victorian' wife, not to survive alone in the twentieth
century. Her chances of meeting an appropriate husband
were dramatically lessened by the toll of the war, and an
appropriate husband for Gladys could only mean one rich
enough to support her. She had fallen for 'a dear old Dutch
artist' who taught at Downside and had a little studio in the
city, but, although 'terribly keen on her', he had no means
to support her and finally left the district and married a
widow.[9] Gladys' romantic nature craved an emotional
outlet, a release from the frustrations of her narrow life,
someone to care for her, someone of her own to love, something to involve her 'spirit' as much as her time. Her dogs,
on whom she lavished affection, were no substitute. So she
immersed herself in work for the Poetry Circle and the
Dickens Fellowship, and organised teas for 'poor weakly
children in the city'. And she kept a diary. Gladys had
literary pretensions, unrealised apart from one slim
volume of poetry, *The Animals' Gospel*,[10] and the papers she
read to the Poetry Circle. So it is not surprising that she
kept a journal in which she noted everything that happened
to her, her family and her pets, what she read, and whom
she met. She recorded the tea parties with lesser celebrities
attracted by her mother's imposing presence and Ina's
talent, and almost daily she noted what they ate and wore,
and what they discussed; all the trivialities of a trivial life.

The Singers-Biggers lived at 12 Marlborough Buildings, at the far end of the Royal Crescent overlooking
the great curve of the Crescent field where Gladys kept
three sheep – one of which she named Sarah. They also
owned two dogs, Bozzy and Barny, and much of Gladys'
time was occupied in walking the dogs, feeding the sheep
on toast crumbs and tending the grave of her old
dachshund, Karl, in the Parade Gardens. Otherwise,

apart from her charity work, she arranged the flowers for her mother and attended her tea parties.

And then in 1925 she met Madame Sarah Grand, saw her at a civic reception or two, heard her speak, read her books, shook her hand. Sarah was by now well established in her role as Mayoress; having had a year's break, she was in her second term in office. She was seventy-one, refined, dignified, concerned and eminently feminine. She also represented authority and demanded respect and admiration. Her age, experience and fame were added qualifications for the role of mother-goddess and Gladys tumbled eagerly into the part of vestal virgin and slave. Gladys already had a larger-than-life mother of her own, but Gladys had to share her regard with her bright and beautiful younger sister, and besides, Gladys did not want an ordinary mother. An emotionally immature woman, she sought romance, sexual sublimation perhaps, a satisfying religion – fulfilment for her soul if not her body. She needed someone better, kinder, more loving, more impressive than any 'normal' mother. She wanted an ideal, a symbol, a goddess. Their early meetings were formal, but already from afar Gladys had fallen under the Mayoress' spell – in spite of finding her cold, aloof and certainly not encouraging. Nonetheless, Gladys pressed on, invited Sarah to the Dickens Birthday Commemoration Dinner and from her diary of that year we can see that the seeds of hero worship were sown.

At the Dinner the Mayoress looked 'unutterably bored . . . but wholly aristocratic and polite' in 'a black *charmeuse* with black lace and a pearl collar and chain of office and large brooch of diamonds encircling a diamond monogram; thick grey hair piled on the crown of her head in rolls, most distinguished'.[11] Ina and Gladys had laid a small spray of violets and primroses at her place with a card bearing a quotation from *The Beth Book*. Gladys stumbled on Madame Grand's train at the head of the stairs while ushering her from the cloakroom ('I begged her pardon and fortunately had not torn it but it was like me to do a stupid thing like that') and dreamed of her all night 'until by some strange yet appropriate metamorphosis she turned into Mother'. Later the Mayoress wrote 'thanking us with much delicacy and sweetness for the flowers' not having seen the name on the card until her arrival home. And Gladys wrote (after a great deal of consultation with Ina and Mother) 'to tell her how delighted we should be if it were ever possible for her to come and see us here and spend a quiet hour or two'.[12] There was no reply.

Throughout that year Gladys' passion grew, fed only by the public encounters she engineered; it wasn't until 1927 that Sarah finally weakened and invited her to tea. This invitation was the encouragement Gladys sought and now, as well as bombarding Sarah with letters, Gladys began a series of diaries devoted exclusively to Sarah. The Mayoress's role as mother figure was established with Gladys calling her Darling Madame, Motherkins, Mother of my Spirit, Mother Angel, but treating her also with a petulance and jealousy that hints at a repressed and sexual emotion. Gladys' concern that each should wear the other's ring might simply illustrate her pleasure in exchanging gifts – particularly as Sarah gave reluctantly, and nearly always forgot Gladys' birthday – but Gladys' holy awe of this exchange, the symbolism of the third finger on which she wore hers, her jealousy of Sarah's wedding ring, and her references to Sarah as Bride of my Spirit, leads one to suspect otherwise. Her passion for Sarah takes its place in a long line of female friendships, its lesbian nature unconsummated, even unacknowledged.

Sarah's feelings for Gladys were usually cordial, sometimes chilly, occasionally frigid – for Gladys' exuberance must have been trying to someone whose emotions were by then so disciplined. Her friend Miss Tindall suited her better; yet she could not help being flattered by the younger woman's attention and by her single-minded adoration. She encouraged Gladys with letters as much as conversation; but the 'schoolgirlieness' and emotion always irritated her, and she could not accept Gladys as an equal.

The year passed. A brilliant year for Bath due mainly to the generosity of the Mayor. Apart from entertaining the Sanitary Engineers from seventeen countries, organised by the League of Nations, opening Bath's first Lending Library (57,123 books issued during the first six months) and donating pictures to brighten the classrooms of local schools, the Mayor and Mayoress welcomed 250 doctors to a BMA Conference when the city became, in gaiety and colour, like a scene from the Arabian Nights. Balls and banquets, fairy lights and roses all over the Abbey church-yard and the Roman baths; concerts, plays, processions: all this was enjoyed as much by the citizens as by the visitors. Ina and Gladys, with visiting cousins, joined the festivities, dancing and dining and returning home late, drinking Champagne of which 'the supply was also very generous, but I was fearful of its strength – a man near us was purposely called to the telephone and did not reappear!'[13]

Then Gladys resumed her humdrum life of shorthand lessons, walking the dogs, writing scenes from the life of Pope ('rather sterile – I can see pictures but they do not develop into any plot'), preparing, too, a paper for the Poetry Circle on Austin Dobson. Ina meanwhile taught elocution, produced amateurs in *Much Ado* (commented upon favourably in *The Times*) and was offered an Australian tour playing the lead in Eden Philpotts' *The Farmer's Wife*.

For a third and fourth term Cedric Chivers and Madame Sarah Grand were elected to office. Their partnership was now an undoubted success. Month after month she opened fairs, bazaars and shows of flowers or cattle or paintings, presented certificates and prizes to

schoolgirls, singers or swimmers; buns and crackers to
poor children. She unveiled tablets to the famous dead and
entertained the famous living. With the Mayor she
welcomed Public Health officials, Printers, the Federation
of Commercial Travellers, Canadian undergraduates,
Master Builders, Chartered Accountants, the Waterworks
Association, Municipal and County Engineers, German
railway officials, British and Irish Millers, the Farmers of
South Africa, the Tramways and Light Railways
Association, as well as Shaw, Chesterton, Earl Haig,
Catherine Booth, Lord Allenby and the Prince of Wales.
Taking the chair at the annual meeting of the Church of
England Temperance Society she remarked on 'the
increased sobriety in rural areas' and was commended for
her 'unflagging interest'. Addressing the British Israel
World Federation she told them 'what the Jew has
done – a wonderful record'. She exhorted the country:
'England must grow more food', and in 'a vigorous
speech' as President of the National Women Citizens'
Association could say with authority 'in 1850 women were
so "cabin'd, cribb'd, confined" that they could not have
helped win the War'. For all this she was applauded in the
Evening Standard as 'one of the rare examples of a literary
light to whom social sovereignty in civic life appeals, and it
is more remarkable since her hobbies are sociology, music
and country life'.[14]

In the midst of all this activity, in January 1926, local headlines exclaimed: *Fire Disaster at Crowe Hall – Mayoress of
Bath's Home Burnt Out – Early Morning Blaze Lights Up The
City*[15] After a reception at the Chamber of Commerce – the
Mayoress, unaccompanied by the Mayor, in low-cut black
dress and a wealth of carnations – tragedy struck, and
more than half the building was gutted, throwing the
Tindalls, the Mayoress and their four servants out in their
night clothes and killing the cook. A good breeze and a
feeble water supply helped the flames through the house

until all that remained intact was the billiard room and the library and 'masses of charred, smoking or steaming timber and a floor ankle-deep in water' elsewhere. (Later, from a study of the house plan, it became apparent that smouldering soot, in a flue from the kitchen fire in the oldest part of the house, had set light to a sitting room adjoining Miss Tindall's bedroom.)

Sarah was now forced to find other lodgings and her younger sister Nellie's retirement from nursing pointed to their sharing expenses. (The Tindalls had the house rebuilt, but they had become somewhat irritated by the common assumption – encouraged by Sarah – that she owned their home; nevertheless, they all remained close friends thereafter.) Sarah and Nellie rented 7 Sion Hill Place, in a small terrace high above Bath on the other side of the city from Widcombe Hill. The sisters shared this house until Nellie's death in 1939. Edna, their maid from 1928–33, arrived at Sion Hill Place when she was sixteen. She remembers all the details of their life there: she took Sarah her early tea at 7.00, then later her breakfast of coffee and toast (Miss Clarke preferred kidney and bacon). For lunch Sarah's favourite meal was steamed batter pudding with a lump of brown sugar and butter; for supper, chestnuts and cheese sauce on toast, the chestnuts boiled for ten minutes and dipped in salt. 'Madame Grand couldn't do a thing for herself, couldn't even make a cup of coffee, never came to the kitchen. I used to eat her fruit for her or Mrs Taylor (the cook) would get annoyed.'[16] Sarah smoked Three Castles tobacco – Edna would buy her two ounces at a time – 'When she had finished her lunch I'd run upstairs, put her eiderdown on her couch and make up two cigarettes with her little machine.' When Sarah returned at night from a mayoral function, Edna would watch from her upstairs window, the chauffeur peeped the horn at the corner and Edna would have the door open by the time the car arrived. She would take the bouquet – 'real carnations' – and put it in a bucket of water and then follow Madame Grand upstairs to put away her clothes.

During 1926 Gladys continued to organise teas for the poor
children of the city and sold flags to help the Mayoress. She
read Chorus to Ina's Juliet, wearing a white dress trimmed
with silver beads, and won the Sonnet Class in the
elocution competitions: 'Ina had told me not to rely on
myself but on a Higher Power and I tried to think rightly
and to remember what I had read in Christian Science and
Lord Haldane.'[17] She continued her pursuit of the
Mayoress by letters, a poem and a pot of cream sent from
Dorset, and described each casual meeting. 'One has the
impulse to go out and kill dragons for her, and then
something she does or says or looks denies the wistful
appeal for understanding, and one feels more strongly than
ever that impulse is unnecessary and undesired.'[18]

Gladys' everyday diary stopped abruptly in June 1926.
In 1927, she began afresh, giving the new volume the title
Ideala's Gift: The Record of a Dear Friendship. During the
sixteen years covered by this Record, the Singers-Bigger
family plunged further into poverty but these serious
problems receive little mention. Once Sarah had weakened
under the shoal of letters and contrived meetings, and
invited Gladys to tea, she placed herself on an altar, more
as tabernacle than sacrifice, and remained the focus of
Gladys' life until long after her own death.

To understand Sarah's effect in this her final role we
must turn to Gladys' Record – seven volumes in which
each daily or weekly meeting is minutely recorded and the
storms and calms of their relationship described. Today a
woman would be aware that an open record of such a
friendship with another woman would be interpreted,
misinterpreted, analysed and discussed. But Gladys wrote
straight from the heart with the intention of glorifying her
'Darling Madame' and in order to have the diary 'as a
record of days so dear to me, so that in the years to come I
may perhaps be able to live them over through its

medium'. The Record began, and blossomed, as a hymn to Sarah. It fulfilled Gladys' twin needs to concentrate on Sarah and be with her even when apart, and to pour her feelings on to paper. For all its minute detail and claustrophobic content, the Record is in many places more poetic than anything Sarah herself had written. Gladys knew she could write and it becomes apparent that an ulterior motive for keeping the Record was to offer it to Sarah as much as proof of ability as for approval. The Record not only bound Sarah to her; it was also a form of catharsis and compensated Gladys for her feelings of inadequacy on other fronts.

From the Record we learn a great deal about Sarah's personality and see her, too, in her final role as a dominant mother-figure long after she had abandoned this very position with her own child. Although one could say that Sarah was born to the role, or had achieved it through experience and her need to dominate and be appreciated, this final persona was literally thrust upon her: she had little hope of escape. That Gladys represented all the narrow, dependent, Victorian attitudes that Sarah had earlier fought so hard to alter makes their friendship all the more ironic. But, despite Sarah's often brutal disregard, Gladys proved unshakeable in her devotion and in the end Sarah gave in and accepted the 'maternity' Gladys forced upon her.

Extract from pages attached to Volume I of Gladys' Record of a Dear Friendship: 'Account of Our First Meetings as Friends'

March/April 1927

I do not know quite how to record the wonderful blessing that has come to me since last I wrote in this book. It is so dear to me that I do not wish to lose its details but also it is so sacred that I hesitate to write of it in full. I will give it therefore in language which only reverence holds restrained and without, I hope, revealing any confidence she would rather that I left unwritten.

I have always, it seems to me, longed for Madame Grand's friendship even when, discouraged by her apparent aloofness I have sought to crush the wish for it out of my heart. That it is at last, at long last, mine and mine as surely as her spirit is steadfast, is still something of a miracle to me but a miracle that is becoming with our every meeting more and more natural.

On Christmas Eve I plucked up courage to send her a verse of mine entitled 'Nearing Christmas' which I had had printed as Cards. A day or two after she wrote to me in answer a letter full of such sweet and generous praise that I felt as if a light had been shed over me. I wrote as much to her and looked forward to meeting her with twofold happiness at the Walcot Tea to Poor Children which as usual I had organised for the Dickens Fellowship and to which she had promised to come being again Mayoress of Bath this year.

When she arrived with her sister, Miss Bellenden Clarke, I was busy with the children and Ina dressed as a clown received her, calling later to me. I looked for her in vain in my agitation, noting Miss Clarke's likeness to her and fearing for a moment she had not come. 'The Mayoress!' said Ina to me, 'You blind bat!' and I turned to find her quietly waiting my recognition with her dear blue eyes misty but clear as one sees the sky on a sunny morning above the sea. I apologised and she spoke of having been driven by mistake to Twerton, but above the talk our thoughts were communing more seriously. I led her to the top of the room to the rather untidy platform where the children greeted her.

Later when the entertainment began I helped her down, very nearly kicking a huge man who at first refused to move out of the way! Finally she helped us give out the crackers looking so sweet and gracious, tossing the last ones into eager outstretched hands. We had presented her with a Dresden China Columbine and Ina had put it in her car. When she left she picked up the parcel and sat with it on her lap looking as excited and pleased as any of the children. Before that though, we had a photo taken and to avoid keeping her standing I stopped the entertainment and got the photographer to do it at once. She allowed me to place her in the centre of the Hall and I stood beside her as perforce I could not get out of the row in which I found myself, and then she shook hands with me, catching mine with unconventional cordiality and so left.

The next evening we were at Milk Street. I had hoped against hope she might come but felt it was too much to expect and busied myself as usual marshalling the children and giving out the bags of buns. I had just finished one lot when I turned and saw her standing like an answer to a prayer, very still with her hands folded. How she got in with no one to receive her I can't think.

I brought her a can of tea warning her it was wet and she went off with it to pour into the children's mugs. I had chosen a light one but that finished she took a heavier one and worked as hard as any of us. When the entertainment began she took the chair I offered her, and I noticed once that she furtively wiped her eyes with her handkerchief. We had no flowers for her, not having expected her, so Mrs Goossens and I ran out to get her some. We had to go as far as Ralph Allen's shop before we found anything presentable and we ran most of the way there and back, I anxious not to miss a moment of her presence. We chose some pink and white carnations. When I got my breath again I knelt beside her chair and whispered a request that she stay to help us with.the crackers. She inclined her head gently in acquiescence and I reseated myself. True to her promise she distributed most of the crackers, first stopping at Mrs Cotterell's suggestion to address a little speech to the children from the head of the room. She predicted that we should all be together again next December and asked them in the meantime to be true to school and country. As I listened to the hesitant heartfelt sentences, I was near tears and when she concluded she turned as if drawn to me with a little wistful appeal in her eyes and I nodded reassuringly. I followed her down the room to take the boxes and to save her from overcrowding as the kiddies surged round her. At the door she paused to thank me for the little figure we had given her. I got out some stumbling phrases in response, hoping it wasn't broken and added that it had wanted to belong to her for a long time. 'I don't know whether I shall be able to live up to it,' she said and Ina doffed her cap and holding out the carnations replied the only thing she could: that that would not be difficult.

'You must come and see where I have put it some day,' Madame said and Ina and I both murmured, 'We should love to,' and then she was gone.

As Secretary for the Teas it was my happy duty to write to thank her for coming twice like that, and for once I discarded conventionality and wrote as I felt. I told her how seldom I felt I dared speak to her but how I went on caring none the less and admiring her gentle graciousness. When it was gone I went through agonies of apprehension in case she might consider it an impertinence, but one evening at tea when I was least expecting it, a letter from her was at my place. A letter that met me halfway with gentle understanding and tender but restrained feeling. It sent me into the twilit garden in a maze of thankfulness and reverence, for I felt at last the friendship might be mine, despite my unworthiness to receive it.

I met her the following Tuesday afternoon at the Bath Avon Branch BESS Social[19] held at the Orange Tea Rooms in Pultney Street. She was dressed in brown and came into the room with her characteristic quietness. Assured of her understanding I went forward as quietly to greet her, and she lifted her eyes blue with unsuspected radiance to my face and asked me to come and sit beside her. I went but, with the little table between us, after one spasmodic effort to be conversational I became tongue-tied. Rita[20] crossed to where we were sitting and I perforce rose to give her my place.

Madame made no effort to detain me and I was undecided what to do. Finally I went to collect other eatables and returned with a plate of scones. I caught a searching glance from her, quickly veiled, as I put the scones on the table beside her, and my heart throbbed a response. 'Embarras de chois,' she said (using the old French instead of 'richesses') but I could not reply. Again I hesitated what to do and at last brought a chair and sat between them facing the wall, saying I hoped I should not be in the way and immediately felt a touch of impatience in the atmosphere; tho' I believe I am doing her an injustice to say so, it would have been justified none the less! The conversation in which Miss Tyler joined turned on crossword puzzles. Madame said her sister was interested in them and that she often supplied her with words she had forgotten but which came back suddenly and that she didn't use a dictionary. 'But, Madame,' I ventured, remembering Ina's opinion that such was necessary to find the least well-known word, 'You ought to use a dictionary.' And again without warning she lifted her girlish challenging blue eyes directly upon me, large and limpid like blue lamps full of that happy comprehending radiance, and I felt in its light that every barrier went down between us and that I entered the shrine of her spirit. I felt my whole being dissolve and soften in sudden adoration and knew not what I said, the one word 'dictionary' reiterated itself on my lips with some foolish qualification as to her being too clever really to need one. And then seeing my danger she let fall her lids again and seemed, in consideration for me, to shrink into herself and to make her little frail body as inconspicuous as possible.

So the time went on and other conversations. She listened attentively to Rita's monologue on the book the latter is writing, putting in an occasional sympathetic remark. I left them talking when I felt *de trop* but I hovered near, drawn by that dear magnet, so that when Mother came over to show Ina's new photos I sat down again and took my share in the exhibition. Madame smoked one cigarette and then drew her gloves over her little white hands with her wedding ring shining heavily on her delicate finger. She rose to go and I rose too. Ina was busily engaged giving out the result of a competition and Madame said not to disturb her. 'I will see Madame Grand down,' I offered with unwonted boldness and together we went to the door, where I made one more effort to attract Ina's attention but she didn't see. So turning to Madame I said, 'You don't mind, do you, you understand,' and she acquiesced. I shut the door behind us and on the instant we were alone and the little gentle gracious figure in my keeping. Never can I forget the strength of the feeling that then gripped me, as we began slowly step by step and in silence unbreakable to descend the narrow staircase. It was like a bridge building and yet dividing us, a bridge of such spiritual strong substance that I felt it would have borne even a material body. It was physically impossible for me to address her, but at last she overcame the spell and spoke, saying quietly that she hoped we would come to see her some day but that she would have to ask us separately as the table was so small, and I replied naturally enough and then after another pause, I thanked her for her letter.

We were at the foot of the stairs and she gave me her hand. I held it as if it were something which might break and moved as I was muttered, 'It was so sweet of you to write to me like that,' but she met my awkward humble gratitude with her own better controlled and thanked me for mine, yet with a like humility. And then she left me, going out into the dark street on foot to pay another call nearby. I stood awhile in a dream and then climbed the stairs again now empty of that gentle presence and re-entered the room where they clapped me, but I was too happy, too reverent to reply. Before we left I managed to secure the end of the one cigarette she had smoked and to bring it away in my bag. That night I wrote to her an amplification of my thanks and more fully in answer to her letter.

The following days because she did not at once reply were again filled with apprehension. I feared I had lost her and cried and tortured myself to a frenzy . . ..

Unable long to bear Madame's silence I wrote again and greatly daring once more in obedience to a sudden impulse I asked her if she and her sister would come to the Poetry Society Meeting on March 16th which we had arranged to hold here at home and at which I was due to read a paper on Songs of the Spinning Wheel which I intended to illustrate with music, etc. She did not keep me waiting any longer for a reply but wrote in the most gracious manner possible accepting the invitation and adding a little postscript which made me deeply happy.

On February 7th we met again at the Dickens Fellowship Dinner at the Red House. But again I was in a foolish mood. She looked different without her hat and though she smiled and waved to me genially and I bowed, I could make no further advance and was positively rude in my efforts to avoid speaking to her. Once she stood quite near me while Mr Green Armytage was talking to me. I saw she was alone for the moment but I could not move and it was left for Mr G.A. to go to her, while I having hovered a second turned and fled to the other side of the room to speak to Miss Masters. All through dinner I was in an agony of nervousness and anger with myself for having behaved so, and as the long entertainment neared its close my agitation grew.

Madame ate scarcely anything and neither did I, the menu being vile in every respect. When speeches began she gave her own graceful tribute saying that some people held that Dickens had never drawn the character of a gentleman, but she thought there was no truer gentleman in literature than Lester Dedlock and Mr Jarndyce and she spoke delicately and feelingly of the first's consideration for his caring wife. She held the black ribbon on which she carries her glasses with one little hand nearest me, with her white glove tucked up round her wrist.

During Mr Weatherby's long tirade I was able to observe her closely as he was sitting on her other side, and I could see her across the Lord Mayor of Bristol and the President, both of whom were leaning back. I felt she was conscious of my scrutiny for without turning her head her grey-green eyes were watching and observant of all that passed around her. Finally we rose. I dug my nails in my hand and forced myself to stand in her path as she came down the table, and then my hand was in hers still ungloved and the contact quieted me by magic.

'I never seem to have a chance of speaking to you,' I said and she finished the sentence as it were for me in gentle rejoinder while her dear kind eyes promised better things in the future. 'We shall have a chance on the 16th,' she said, remembering wonderfully the date.

'There was something I wanted to ask you,' I ventured and then stopped. She waited in quiet patience for me to recover myself and I pushed a chair or two out of the way. Touching her wrist to gain confidence by renewed contact I asked if I might include a quotation from one of her books in my paper. She gave me permission without hesitation, trusting me and I thanked her. But I could not now leave her. I hung about her as she took her leave of the President and Mr G.A. 'I loved what you said, Madame,' I announced with diffidence, but she did not reply though G.A. enthusiastically agreed. I followed her out then into the front of the shop and she at the door turned to shake hands again and not realising my proximity gave a little shy start of surprise. Not displeased however she held out her little gloveless hand and I put mine into it. And through them our natures seemed to melt into one another in that gentle lingering clasp, without pressure yet clinging, warm and yet sure. Her hand was like a rose with the sun on it and for long I felt the fragrance of its touch . . .

CHAPTER IX

The Lesser Boswell: 1927–28

⊙⊙

Framed at the door the Mayoress stands
Looking her regal best,
White gloves upon her slender hands
And diamonds at her breast.
   Cloaked in a mantle hyacinth blue
   Veiling yet richer guise,
   She stands as still as statues do –
   Sadness in her eyes.

Thronged by the Poor the Mayoress moves,
Granting to each small guest
The bag of cakes her smile improves –
Paper bags at her breast.
   Clad in the simplest gown is she,
   Seeming 'mid childish cries
   A radiance set from marble free –
   Gladness in her eyes.[1]

Volume I of Gladys' Record covers eighteen months, showing the growth of her passion for 'Darling Madame' and Sarah's often irritated acceptance of it. Their letters,[2] treasured by Gladys, complement the diary, revealing amidst much trivia several snappish remarks from Sarah about returned presents and female friendship: 'I should like you to understand friendship as I do. More as men do – with each other. Theirs are the more lasting friendships. Women are such self-tormentors.'[3] Gladys tormented herself with minute worries about their relationship, stressed her own social gaffes and solecisms, clumsiness and gaucheries, but managed to record slights and rebuffs from Sarah as well intended. Although sometimes understandably puzzled and annoyed by Gladys' forceful devotion, Sarah appears to have tolerated if not encouraged these effusions and by the end of this volume their friendship was established. This period was their honeymoon, with a loving Gladys lingering on their frequent meetings and tea parties, a woman who, despite her anxiety, was happy and fulfilled. On New Year's Eve Gladys summarised their first year in a letter:

You have taught me so much in a mental way, too. I have kept a record of some of your conversations; Ina calls it the 'lesser Boswell'!! Perhaps you would like to censor them some day . . . If I were asked I think I should say that one of your greatest gifts to me has been a truer sense of values; you know so well what matters and what is negligible; and you never seem either in conduct or writing to confuse issues.

During this period, Sarah continued to act as Mayoress. On 24 July 1928, after an operation at Millbank Hospital, Haldane died, and was buried at Highgate Cemetery.[4] In his will he left his entire estate to his wife 'of the same address'. Sarah, as seen through Gladys' eyes, said and did nothing about Haldane's death. After living with him for twenty years and helping to bring up his daughter, she registered no emotion for the watchful Gladys to report. Her Bellenden-Clarke nephew (Commander Francis Drake Clarke, son of Sarah's older brother, Edward) and his wife are mentioned in Gladys' diary, and Haldane's daughter, Beth visited her in October of that year and more frequently thereafter, but we do not know if Sarah attended Haldane's funeral. We can only assume that she never mentioned him and that she was not noticeably grief-stricken.

Ideala's Gift: The Record of a Dear Friendship

Bath, April 18, 1927

[Sarah is seventy-two and Gladys thirty-eight]

Yesterday I went for the first time to tea with Madame Sarah Grand. I had been reciting at the Baptist Church for the Oldfield Park Brotherhood and arrived still rather agitated from that somewhat alarming ordeal. The taxi turned in through the gates to Sion Hill Place and up the avenue along the Pomander Walk Terrace at the top with its green space with trees in front, and stopped at No. 7 in glorious sunshine. I paid the man and rang the electric bell. An elderly woman opened the door and I stepped into the little hall passage with its low toned blue and caramel carpet. She asked my name and I divested myself of my coat and left my umbrella and a magazine on the table. She then led me up two short flights of stairs, white and blue predominating, into the drawing room.

There Madame greeted me with her dear quietness to which my restlessness is so great a contrast. She was dressed in brown, cloth I think, with a high collar and an old fashioned chain. I was horribly nervous and took some time to calm myself sufficiently even to answer her gentle questions as to how I had got on, coherently. At last I said I hadn't got over it quite yet and looked at her appealingly. She answered my glance with her beautiful understanding and patience and gave me time to collect my thoughts. She leaning her grey-white head against a brown velvet cushion. Blue and cream coloured cretonnes made a perfect setting for her pale face and grey-blue eyes, and the wallpaper of cream, with a faint pattern of flowers, shed back the light from the two windows upon her serenely. A green earthenware jug held a bunch of pale pink carnations in one corner. On the mantel were ornaments of odd kinds, green and cream but no clock, neither did I remark any photos. There were old prints in the room and an oil painting or two. Behind me two large china cabinets were filled with curios and between them a white azalea was reflected in 'an old fashioned circular mirror in an old gilt frame. A sofa was placed between the windows. This was all I could take in at a first glance round.

Soon the door opened and her sister, Miss Clarke, entered. I rose and hastened to thank her for the pot of dainty pink spirea she had sent me yesterday. She was almost as nervous as myself and we were pretty feeble to start with. I said it was such an uncommon flower to choose and she said she hoped it was the one she wanted and hoped I liked the pink better than white. I said it went perfectly in my room with its green tapestry wallpaper and she replied that at Easter it was difficult to get flowers, the fallacy of which struck me so that I stopped completely and did not even reply when she took refuge in the weather . . . whereat Madame came to our rescue and thence the conversation took a turn for the better and I, having calmed down at last, was able to answer with something like intelligence.

We spoke of American papers, mother's nationality and my own birthplace, Denver, of the vulgarity of American journalism and Madame wondered how it was when there were so many refined and educated Americans that they could tolerate such vulgar exploitation of their Press. She told how when she had visited America she had been interviewed 24 times in 24 hours and how angered she had been by a particular reporter for whose paper she had promised to write, when he called her 'Sarah' all the way through his article and ended up by implying that 'Sarah' was a 'real good fellow'. She sent for the Editor and put it to him that he would not care for his own family to be treated in that way and he agreed. She did not however write for that paper after!

We spoke also of California and Arizona. I mentioned too having read Harold Spender's *The Fire of Life*[5] and his high ideals of journalism. Madame had read it of course and said she had liked him better through it. I wondered how he could remember the details of so many transactions and this led us to talk of diaries and journals generally.

The tea-bell went about now and Madame got up with that decision of movement which she shows on occasion and which reveals the latent energy of her spirit. Her quiet repose of manner being anything but lethargic, there is always the possibility and capability of immediate action behind it. She went downstairs, I pausing to admire a view of the little oblong garden from the landing and of a bright coral patch over the wall which I recognised as Japonica. There was newly sown grass in the garden centre as Madame said she liked to see the green and there were white and yellow little flowers bordering it, primulas or violas. Several old prints were on the walls near us, especially a fine mezzotint of Charlotte Brontë's, her Wellington, which was the first picture I had noted as I entered. This was curious I felt as I have often thought there is a certain affinity between Madame's writings and those of Charlotte Brontë. It is a matter of courageous spirit, a striking out for herself and an abiding by the consequences, the prejudices of others. Madame is too a Yorkshire woman by birth . . .

We entered the dining room on the ground floor front. Here the walls are a sunny sparrows' (or thrushes'?) egg blue, cool and clear as the sea and against that background her dear eyes took on an added blueness and an added graciousness. She was happy in my company as I in hers and several times she laughed with more naturalness than I have ever yet seen her display, her white rose face going pink with enjoyment of some joke. The table was oblong oval of polished mahogany or rosewood and there was a yellowy vase of daffodils in the centre. The silver was bright and with raised flower patterns. A crochet-edged cloth covered the tea tray and crochet doilys were on the cake plates. I learnt after that Madame liked crocheting, but like me, her sister prefers knitting. I can see her small hands raised at that dainty work, so suited to her and to them. In the window was a large, tall green pitcher filled with pussy-willows, on the desk table in a corner by the window beneath a bookcase, a vase of lilies-of-the-valley. Over the mantel an oil painting in warm sunny browns and greens of a wind-mill and a larger oil painting above the sideboard. A beautiful inlaid chair also caught my fancy. On the table between the cakes was an elaborate silver cigarette box, inscribed. Madame poured out the tea, I sitting on the left of the table and Miss Clarke at the other end. Madame passed the milk and cream and sugar down to us. The milk looked so like the cream that this began the conversation which turned on farms and eatables generally . . . Madame who doesn't eat meat spoke of its effect on health and gradually our discourse turned to Christian Science. Never shall I forget the considerate broadmindedness with which she listened to my views on this subject, allowing me to ride my hobby (if that is not too flippant an expression for a sacred subject) with undiminished interest and encouragement, and telling me anecdotes which went to prove my points rather than her own at every pause . . . But, said I at last, I didn't come here to talk Christian Science. At once she reassured me and said it interested her to hear about it. My eyes delighted in the loveliness of her kind expression, in the blueness of her direct gaze, and I loved her with all the best that was in me. Turning to her sister, I found her eyes fixed on me too, darker in shade, more prominent and strangely wistful. I felt I would like to help, all unworthy as I was . . .

I had a generous supply of plum cake, home-made, cut for me by Miss Clarke and we sat some time over tea. Madame asked me to pass her the cigarettes but, finding there were only a few in the box, she got up and went to a drawer in the side-board whence she replenished it, and lit one for herself as I had said I didn't smoke . . .

'Shall we go upstairs now?' she said and I rejoined that I ought to go but she kept me and I, only too happy to stay, asked her to turn me out when she got tired of me. She smiled and together we re-ascended the stairs to the drawing room, whereupon she pulled forward a card table which I helped her to adjust and Miss Clarke seated herself on the sofa to play Patience. In the meantime, Madame drew me to one of the cabinets to point out where she had placed the little china dancer we had given her at Christmas. She had kept the card I had painted to go with it and placed it under her so that the painting showed. Bless her dear heart. Fancy keeping a little thing like that! I explained why we had chosen it, as a Columbine from a clown (my sister having dressed as a clown for the children's party at which we presented it) . . . We sat down then to the Patience, Madame helping her sister so kindly. She smoked another cigarette, remarking that she shouldn't have a second but she would today because I was there. Once she leaned back in her chair and whether it was the light from the window on her or the smoke from her cigarette I don't know, but she seemed to go all silvery in a pearly radiance, her thick silver hair swathed carelessly on the crown of her head with the little curls arrayed as a fringe, her blue eyes soft but clear against the moonlight blue of the cretonnes, her face pale and sweet veiled in the grey-blue smoke, she made a memorable picture drawn as it were in pastelle too ethereal even for ivory. I felt it was her angel spirit shining forth suddenly and illuminating her like an Easter Lily. 'My little Mother', 'My little Holy Mother'.

We spoke of fortune telling and she told me how the night before or a few days before the fire at Crowe Hall she had just been playing with some cards and picked out one or two at random, not intending to tell her fortune. They were what she called 'the speedy card' something to happen quickly. Danger by fire: and the death card with a woman. The cook lost her life in the fire and Madame said it made her feel rather frightened when it all turned out exactly in accord with the cards. I asked her to tell mine, at the suggestion of Miss Clarke, and she told me to cut and wish. I wished that I might come again to this peaceful and holy refuge beside her many times and the wish card came up. I had chosen the blue pack, and there was a new admirer – a lover she said – in my fortune and she pointed to a dark knave on whom she insisted my thoughts were resting. No, they're not, I answered rudely! but when she said a friend might be coming from the country I agreed that might be likely.

I spoke of a house to let next door and said we'd come and take it; Madame smiled and said it was only half a house. I was sure she wouldn't want us because of the dogs!

I made another move to go and said if I didn't she would do what she had in my dream. She wanted to know what I had dreamed and I told her that I had stayed so late that she had retired upstairs in despair and Miss Clarke had stayed with me politely, but fatigued! She turned on me with her indulgent kindly smile, her eyes encouraging, seeming to enfold me happily. Well, wait till you're turned out! she said gently. I reminded her that I was coming to the Waifs and Strays Address on the Wednesday and also of her promise to send an auto-graphed book to Ina's stall and I asked to choose one that I hadn't read as I wanted to buy it. Which have you read? she asked and I numerated them while she listened with quiet dignity and acquiescence to the list of her published works, all but three of which I mentioned.

I asked for *The Tenor and the Boy* misled by the fact of its having been published separately and felt rather foolish when she said it was an interlude in *The Heavenly Twins*. Have you read *Babs the Impossible*? asked Miss Clarke. No, I replied. But that is out of print, Madame told us, so she insisted she would get us *The Heavenly Twins* and said she only had to drop a PC to her

publishers. I said it was some years since I had read it . . . I think
this was the sum of our converse except at tea she had mentioned
the *Life of Ninon de l' Enclos*[6] asking if I had read it and recounting
how she had preserved her charm into late old age, with a certain
wistfulness and underlying courage of voice and look. I had seen
a cinema story with her as heroine, I told her. Also Madame had
invited me to go with her to the opera, *The Mikado*, on the
Thursday and I had happily accepted.

On leaving I invited Miss Clarke to come to tea one day and
she quite eagerly said she would if I would name one . . . We
fixed Tuesday. It is no good asking you, Madame, I know, said
I, as I reached the door. She shook her head. Certainly not
Tuesday, she replied. Mother feels awfully about it, I said, you
do so much for me and we can't return it. I don't do anything,
she said gently following me out of the room and downstairs. I
had her little hand in mine as we went and on the last steps I
kissed it with love and gratitude and adoration in my heart. She
yielded it to me but said nothing and I picked up my cloak with
which she helped me. The maid came up the kitchen stairs but
Madame dismissed her, saying she would see me out. But the
memory of our farewell is too dear to me to be related in detail.
Let me respect it here as I respected her in those moments. She
came out into the breezy sunshine and I thanked her and left her
and immediately longed to be with her again . . .

May 13th

On the Friday morning I was dressing leisurely, when our daily
charwoman entered, out of breath and holding her side.
'Madame Sarah Grand has rung up, Miss, I told her you were
not down yet and she said would you telephone as soon as you
were.' I flung on a few more things, bathed my face in cold water,
and hurried down and for the first time rang her up. Her dear
voice sounded near and blessed me with her presence even
though unseen. 'I am sorry, I'm afraid I got you up too early,'
she began. 'Oh, my dear,' I answered 'I'm ashamed of myself,'
and I was, heartily, for it was after 9.30 and she already at work.
She laughed and went on to ask me to tea with her that Sunday
and to come early as she was expecting friends later. Needless to
say, I accepted with the utmost alacrity and then proceeded to
live for that day.

May 15th

Taking her at her word, I went early. It was just on 4 o'clock
when I arrived and was met by a younger and smiling maid who
led me upstairs to the drawing room. Madame was not yet down
and I told the maid to ask her not to hurry as I knew I was early. I
sat down and had time to notice the carpet was a deeper blue than
I had thought, that there were birds in the pattern of the
cretonne, that there was a second sofa against the wall behind
me, that the ornaments on the mantel were more elaborate than I
had first noted, that there were two Bouchers on the walls, the
blues and greens and pinks of which toned in delicately with the
decorations, that a fern had replaced the white azalea before the
mirror, that plant having been placed on the right of the fire, and
that there was no piano in that room.

The door opened and Madame entered. I jumped up and went
quickly to greet her. She gave me both her hands, her eyes turquoise as she faced the light. She was dressed simply but richly in
black velvet with Cluny lace at her throat; her silver hair was
more softly arranged than I had seen it before, swathed with a
little wave in it on the crown of her head and the curls combed out
into a softening fringe on her forehead. One felt that here was
living history as one might have felt in the presence of a Queen,
but one was also conscious of some intangible flower-like quality
that suggested nothing more clearly than a white rose. She sat
down in her favourite chair with her little feet close together, her
hands on her knees playing with the silver plaque pendant
attached to the chain she wore last Sunday. This she turned and
re-turned as she talked . . .

We began to speak of old dances, but were interrupted by the
entrance of her guests, two elderly ladies . . . and their friend
. . . Miss Arbuthnot was younger and rugged of countenance
and very badly dressed, but pleasant, and I was glad she fell to
my lot, and we talked quite easily. Soon the tea-bell rang and we
went down-stairs to the dining room. The two older ladies sat on
either side of Madame, my place being indicated by Miss Clarke
as next Miss Denny. The conversation being more or less general
I did not hear all Madame said until the repast was well
advanced. A small bouquet of pink carnations and ferns filled the
centre of the table, there were lace edgings to the mats, not
crochet, and there were cakes made to resemble nests with tiny

eggs of different colours in them, which we discussed.

Suddenly I heard Madame refer to the unveiling of the Harrison tablet[7] by Lord Haldane[8] and to the banquet which preceded it at which Lord Haldane was the guest of honour. 'He has been a friend of mine for many years,' she said quietly, not looking at me, tho' she must have recalled the confidence of my admiration for him which I made in one of my letters to her. I felt how truly safe such confidences were with her and did not regret my expansiveness . . . Madame asked me if I would like some of the cake on the other side of the table, calling me for the first time by my Christian name, 'Gem'. Earlier Madame said wistfully that she had made many acquaintances and that she hoped she had made some friends, since coming to Bath. A chorus of protesting acquiescence greeted this remark, but she did not pursue it and I said nothing.

It was about now that, excited and nervous as I was, I made a small social break by laughing suddenly more loudly than I had intended. I saw Miss Arbuthnot exchange glances with Miss Clarke but Madame gave no indication that she had heard, and I do not know even now whether she noticed it, her consideration as hostess being grace itself. I felt awful for a while and listened in a kind of horror of stupefaction and regret to what Madame was saying. She was talking of the new Prayer Book – 'I suppose it is one's innate conservatism,' she said, 'But I don't like the . . . word love for charity' . . . Soon after we broke up and went out into the hall. Here at the foot of the stairs Madame paused in reply to Miss Arbuthnot's admiration of the mezzotint of Wellington. We stood and looked at it and Madame told us how it had greatly resembled a chauffeur she once employed and whom she had called Wellington in consequence. Once they brought him in to show it to him, but he took exception to the nose saying it was not like his. 'Wait till you get to that age and it will be!' Madame told him. I was standing leaning against the bannister and could not refrain from uttering my thought in the silence that followed the laugh with which this reminiscence was greeted. 'Charlotte Brontë's hero!' I said. No one answered and I wondered if Madame had heard. Miss Arbuthnot passed me and went on upstairs.

We were side by side on the stairs and I felt Madame's little hand grasp my coat at the waist. I thought she meant to urge me on and I quickened my steps, but she held me back and, without speaking, we went up slowly together. On the landing she detained me, pointing out another print and for a sacred moment or two her delicate figure was close against mine, and I was conscious again of the fragrant bodily reserve which is hers and which makes her proximity purifying as a breath of the Spirit. We moved into the drawing room to be met with the bathos of crossword puzzles and a ballot. Discussion of both ensued and of what we considered the most necessary adjunct to a house. Miss Arbuthnot and I agreed in thinking mains drainage indispensible and were voted most unromantic . . .

Madame sat on the sofa, persistently upright, looking whiter and whiter and more and more like a white rose, till I feared she might in reality change into one if we did not relieve her of our presence. I therefore put on my gloves during a short conversation with Miss Clarke in which she thanked me again for our kindness to her in her illness. 'I should have liked to have done much more,' I replied, handing her a poem I had copied for her by Geoffrey Fyson[9] . . . I said farewell and departed, walking home elated by their kindness, tortured by my remembered break, and wondering why Madame had at first looked so frequently at my shoes!!

May 17th

To the Theatre with Madame. I made a careful toilette, washing my hair, and Ina helping me with ironing silk stockings and white petticoat. I wore my new mauve evening gown and black coat, with violets and grey shoes and stockings and a new Champagne-coloured bag . . . I had no difficulty in talking to Mrs Devenish, a fair woman of the Victorian type with ample presence and a pink brocade cloak with pearls and lace, that suggested by the way she held it the well-known picture of the young Queen receiving the news of her accession! She is even more nervous of dear Madame Grand than I am on occasion, so I felt rather superior . . . Madame used her lorgnettes which she wears loosely strung on a gold chain so that one hears the ring running up and down the links as she moves them. It is a characteristic of her and does not irritate as it might in someone else. Another little sensitive habit of hers is to bite her lips . . . Madame looked at me with her kindly comprehending eyes, darkly grey in this light and indulgent of any mistake I might commit and so knowledgeable of my every weakness I felt safe, but a veritable child beside her. Mrs D. spoke of Madame's work as Mayoress and how active she had shown herself. 'But you are mistaken,' Madame answered, 'I am not active naturally, I am contemplative. All this is not natural to me,' she repeated, 'I prefer a contemplative life.'

Once she spread out her little hand, remarking how soiled her gloves were, 'I think it must be the black cloak,' she said and rubbed her hand against it. I lifted my eyes to her dear face and met her gaze bent on me. She knows I love her hands and her pretty white gloves are a special attraction for me. It was a Masonic moment between us – and thereafter, fearing she was wearied, I longed, sitting just behind her with the outline of her grey head and slim upright form before me, to put my arms round her so she might rest, or to take her right away from all she had owned was unnatural to her studious nature.

When the Mayor returned she looked at him critically and, noticing his Mayoral jewel was crooked, she told him to put it straight as it 'offended her eyes!' He offered us each a lemon-drop from an old gold snuff box . . . on leaving I hesitated, watching Madame's retreating figure till she was swallowed up in the motor and then we entered ours. But in heart and spirit I was with her.

June 11th

> There were wings in your eyes tonight
> Little blue wings that fluttered
> As if your thoughts took flight
> Beyond the words you uttered.
>
> There were wings tonight in your eyes
> Petal sweet wings of azure
> As if like dainty butterflies
> They shyly danced a measure.
>
> There were wings in my eyes as well
> Moth-like brown wings that brushed them
> As if so fragile were the spell
> A deeper glance had crushed them.

Yet those wings in our eyes tonight
Thought-laden wings unbroken
Were strong to bear in words despite
The love we left unspoken.

October 13th

I have been in two minds about continuing the story of
Madame's friendship for me, first because it has seemed at times
too near and dear and sacred to me to write about, secondly
because I have not always had the time or the inclination to do it
justice and feared to give false impressions. I would rather recollect in dreams her kindness and sweetness; or I would pour out
my thoughts of her to her directly by letter and this left me
undesirous of further writing. But now I feel that to leave no
record of so lovely an influence is equally impossible and that
since I have been privileged to spend so many happy and profit-
able hours in her presence it is only right, she being the celebrated woman she is, to chronicle if not every word and detail, at
least enough to bring her however faintly before those who may
hereafter discover this book.

My recollections of the past half year are a series of pictures of
her, each different, yet each informed with gentle dignity and
unruffled calm, sometimes maintained by effort but always
achieved. She gives her little hands to one instinctively, they are
as appealing, unconsciously so, as a child's, like petals which the
sun expands, and they are soft to touch but firm. It is her first
expression of friendship and contradicts her reserve of bearing.
Her eyes, which are so often shadowed by a deep sorrowfulness,
soften at times into an exquisite tenderness; dilate with thought,
horizon blue themselves absorbing the horizon distance in their
depths; or grow intent as if she brought a weight to bear behind
them to help their concentration. With the progress of the year
they seem to grow a paler turquoise and the first frost seems to
touch them to a glacial tint in her pale face. Not cold wholly, for
there is always the glow of her heart to warm them when she will.
At times her features are almost rugged in their tragedy, set rock-
like, and then at a word they melt into indulgent understanding,
her whole face lightens and gentles as if touched by an angel's
wing, and her little pointed smile, asking for understanding
in its turn, makes one her willing slave. Her voice has a

strange quality of thickness about it which at first is discon-
certing, but which becomes so dearly characteristic on better
acquaintance that one loves to hear it and craves for it when
absent. She speaks slowly but without the suspicion of a drawl; at
times she will answer some question with a simple monosyllable
unqualified, as when I asked her one day after tea if I might come
and sit on the floor beside her. She stopped to reach for a cigarette
then answered quietly the one word 'Yes' without further
comment. Another time I offered to hold her sun-shade over her.
She moved slightly away from me and replied, as briefly, 'No'.
One has to grow accustomed to these small curbs, and to me who
am restless and eager for argument and assurances, they are
good, calming, controlling, fascinating and galling all in one.
Once when we were motoring home together from the Guildhall
I inadvertently touched the blind of the car and it fell with a
clatter. I naturally apologised for breaking it, but she gave no
sign of having noticed the *contretemps*, neither by word nor gesture
nor look. It simply might not have happened. She has a larger
sense of values and sees events in better proportion than most
of us.

Quite recently I was at the Reception given to the Federation
of Musical Competitions at the Pump Room. Madame was
wearing a dress of art blue velvet trimmed with silver lace with
which she carried a bouquet of deep pink flowers. There were
close silver leaves bound round her silver hair and the lights
made her eyes look darker than usual, and her train taller. There
was a touch of an older fashion in her toilette but she did not look
old-fashioned, only beautiful and imposing with some added
quality of magic about her quite indefinable. Fairy Godmother
she appeared to me who worship her – magic and sacred and
motherly. She wears her dresses lower than is the custom nowadays, but not in caprice. Her soft neck revealed suggests
only the phrase 'breasts of her compassion' and seems to offer a
resting-place for the aching heads of all the world. Mother,
Mother and again Mother, are the words that recur to one as one
sits beside her. Yet once when I told her she meant Motherhood
to me, she gazed sadly and quietly out before her down the hill
on the crest of which we were resting and said she never thought
she was motherly, she thought she was more of a comrade.
Tonight she said laughingly that she didn't know what she

looked like in this dress. 'You look adorable,' I replied and meant
it. 'This dress is the Queen in Hamlet after the wedding,' she
added a minute or two later. 'Ah, Madame,' I said. 'How can
you say such things?' But I was happy she had worn it, because
she had earlier asked my advice about it . . .

After my arrival I was carried away from her and was forced to
spend the evening listening to music and conversation which
bored me and increased my restlessness and longing for her to
such a pitch that I felt I would go to any lengths to find her. I
looked everywhere for her and, such were the crowds, had just
given up in despair when turning down a corridor to seek the
cloak room, intending to go home, I came directly upon the
Mayoral party on their way to the Terrace. I feared she would
pass me by but, true friend that she is, she looked up and held out
her hand, drawing me to her side, warming my chilled hand in
hers. I had been down in the ruins of the Roman Baths, I
explained and as we passed through the swing doors to the open
terrace overlooking the large bath with its dark gulf and fairy
lights below us, she threw her velvet train round her bare
shoulders. I was standing near her and slipped my hand beneath
its folds timidly till I found her arm and held her close. Oh, the
peace of having found her at last, the utter completed joy of our
at-oneness. My love for her beat almost painfully in my heart out
towards her, and she, after one observant glance at me, respected
our moment and we fell upon silence, sinking into it as into the
soft darkness around us. Then she drew my attention quietly as
one would speak hushed words in church to the Abbey wraith-
like above, and gently moved away towards the doors. As I held
them for her she spoke quickly. 'Let us cling together,' she said,
'or we shall be separated again.' There were others about us but
they were ignorant of what that moment had meant to me, and
Madame covered up my vagueness with information about a
concert Miss Harford was organising for her Fresh Air Fund.[10]
So we reached the dance room and Madame, after seating herself
in a corner, perforce had to move again to pilot a new acquaintance to the Baths once more. She leaned towards me and gave
me instructions to keep her chair, instructions which I fully
intended to carry out . . . [in the bustle of meeting friends,
Gladys loses the chair to another] I feared her anger horribly and
as I took my place once more beside her I said imploringly, 'You

are not cross with me, are you?' She bent her dear eyes, tender, comprehending on mine and reassured me, 'No, why should I be?' – and then I shot her a glance of such passionate adoration and gratitude that she must have thought me about to kneel at her feet, as indeed I was fain to do. But I never regained any sense of proportion that night and when I got home I penned her a fervent apology. I referred to it again later, and this is how she checked me: '. . . for the rest what on earth is the matter with you? I don't want you to tell me, only to consider whether you may not be worrying your poor self about nothing at all.'

October 19th

The day I received that fresh air answer to my emotionalism was Ina's birthday. She had brought her sister Miss Clarke to tea with us and the latter handed me the note. Later Rita[11] came in to bid Ina farewell prior to her South African tour, and when the bell rang a third time I turned questioningly to Ina. 'That will be Madame calling for Miss Clarke,' she hinted. It needed no more. I was flinging open the front door and was down the steps almost before the words were uttered . . . I pulled myself together to announce her. While she entered I slipped away to search for her particular brand of cigarette, but when I had found it she still preferred her own and I seated myself with my back to the fire on the floor at her feet. Ever and anon she turned her sweet face to look with softened eyes down into mine, as she smoked, listening quietly to our criticism of Edna's wedding and accepting Rita's congratulations on her re-election as Mayoress with reserve and modesty. 'It takes all my strength,' she told us and we could well believe the statement . . .

October 21st

We talked of clothes as women will. She is all woman on this subject, unexpectedly enough it seems to interest her however often the topic is raised. It is doubtless a relaxation, and by little remarks of approval and suggestion I think I have given her an added interest in her appearance. For long she wore nothing but black, or black and white, occasionally brown or tan. But since I said she could wear colours and that they suited her she has adopted less sombre toilettes. I remember an emerald lining to a black cloak which she wore thrown back at the opening of the

Bath & West Show and which looked like a University gown.

. . . 'My best speeches come to me of a morning when I am making my bed,' she informed me.[12] '*Making* your bed, Madame?' I questioned in surprise. 'Yes,' she answered gently, 'I always make my own bed, I like it made in a special way and it gives me exercise.' I looked at her with the adoration I felt, and then away in front of me while the tears came to my eyes and threatened to fall. She observed my emotion and remained silent herself, till I regained composure. Somehow the thought of her, delicate and frail as a flower, disciplining herself in this daily fashion, at her age, touched me as I have rarely been touched before. 'I think,' I said when I could speak, 'that I have only made my own bed about three times in my life.' Soon after this conversation our housemaid's holiday gave me an opportunity to follow Madame's example and since then I have kept it up steadily, a daily service of loyalty to my admiration for her, a daily communion of occupation. 'I think you are so wise to keep up your bed making,' she wrote later in a letter to me. 'What we women need is regular exercise.'

. . . Rita was her guest at the Concert as well as myself . . . I told Madame I had been reading *Adnam's Orchard* and liked it so much . . . She told me she had intended to write a trilogy of which that was the first volume and *The Winged Victory* the second, but that the War had then intervened and altered everything.

1928

March 4th

Let me recall one or two mental portraits I have of her, remembered and framed by my love for her, but alas not as vividly as I could wish. If only one could instantaneously record forever the gracious form, the appropriate background, as they present themselves at the moment in every detail, how dear the gallery. One morning I was selling flowers for the YMCA at her depot outside the Guildhall. It was a fresh, grey rather windy morning and I had rung her up to tell her to put on something warm. Her car stopped a little way up towards the corner and as she came towards me for a second I could not believe it was her. She looked ten years younger in a neat dark blue tailor-made with a dark red

velour hat, a striped shirt blouse of fawn and dark red with a dark
red tie to match. 'My clove carnation,' I called her afterwards,
deep and rich and fragrant as that flower, and her friendship is
like that too. We walked shoulder to shoulder selling the flowers,
she with a tin for the money, I with the tray of flowers. Never
have I felt such peace or such utter contentment in anyone's
company before or since.

She laid herself out to be *sweet* to me that day, giving me her full
attention as she will at times, making up a thousandfold for being
distrait and distant a day or two before . . .

March 5th

Let me now recall another portrait of her standing on the Guildhall platform at an evening gathering of the Bath Secondary
Schools' Prize Giving. She was in black, an ornament in the
shape of a small diamante ostrich feather sparkling in her hat
brim. Behind her shone the great glass to Ralph Allen's portrait
and reflected in its surface the glittering crystal chandelier – it
was as if my Snow Queen stood surrounded by her grotto of
icicles, pure and clear and cold as herself in some moods . . .

March 6th

It is curious how I hunger for her presence at times. A week is
usually the extent of my being able to do without her, in a purer
sense she is an appetite to me, a spiritual appetite. Things assume
a different appearance when I am with her. She sweetens the
atmosphere like a flower and my heart melts into charity for all
the world in her company; my outlook is clarified, my energies
stimulated and encouraged to effort while my thoughts are
quietened. Yet she never dictates, she leaves one absolutely
free and, while influencing, never seems to try to do so . . .
Sometimes I have felt her hold herself in suspense as it were,
when I have referred to her writing. She seldom mentions it
herself and yet is ready to respond with modest and subdued
pleasure if you do so. When I have quoted from her books as I
have on occasion she seems to catch her breath in expectation,
her habitual quiet demeanour caught into deeper stillness until
the words have been uttered. I think she holds her gift in
reverance, in trust, and in triumph and in sorrow, so far
removed from self advertisement or conceit that one is apt to

overlook at times the fact that Authorship is natural and dear to her and to forget in her self effacement the fame that has been hers.

April 16th

Madame is independent. Despite the submissiveness with which she accedes to arrangements made for her at public meetings, in her private life she is rigourously independent. 'I wish you would let me do things for you,' I have said but she will never permit me in any way to 'fag' for her unless I do it without her knowledge . . . I reminded her she had not replied to my offer of doing secretarial work for her. 'I couldn't let you do that – I haven't enough' – yet I knew she had. 'I can do nothing for you,' I lamented discouraged and laid my cheek on her hands which were then in my clasp. Suddenly I looked up and found her eyes bent on me with all the depth and tragedy of the ocean in their gaze but she withdrew them and reached for a cigarette . . .

One knows she knows all there is to be known of life and mankind and yet instinctively if there is something said that is not quite nice one seeks to shield her from hearing it and criticises one's own speech lest some chance word should sully her confidence. People have told me that she can appreciate a risky story, if so she may do so from bravado, sheer mischief or with the design of character drawing, but her true self is as free from taint as the white rose I have chosen as her flower. Often things one thinks one will say to her have a way of becoming vapid and foolish in her presence and remain unsaid. I have told her everything about myself but she keeps her own counsel and I know little of her actual history. I have come very close to her in confession and mental communion . . .

April 22nd

Last Thursday evening Madame called for me in her car to go with me to the Dickens Fellowship Dramatic Entertainment in aid of the Children's Teas at Holy Trinity Church Hall . . . After a separation of some weeks we were together again. I had brought her three white roses and as we swept along Marlborough Lane I held them out to her and asked if she would wear them. 'I should like to,' she replied and in the paling sunset I laid them against her breast. Her white face and silver hair, her white gloved hands hovering about the flowers like butterflies or petals fallen free accentuated her likeness to them and a sudden wave of tenderness overcame me. Her indefinable charm reached me like music. 'Oh, my dear,' I said 'it's so lovely to be with you again – I haven't seen you for such ages.' She concurred gently. 'There was a white rose in the sky this evening,' I went on inconsequently. 'Was there?' she asked, humouring me as if I were in truth her child . . . The car was jolting too much to permit of my pinning the flowers in her coat and she said she thought I should have to wait till we were still. Then we drew up and I pinned the roses on her cloak with two brooches I had brought. 'How many pins have you got?' she enquired amusedly, but she made no effort to do it herself and let me arrange her as I would – which was badly as we could scarcely see in the dark and I was nervous. But she wore them proudly and I was happy as ever with her . . . How I savoured to the full the distinction of walking up the crowded hall with her and how privileged I felt as I took my seat beside the special chair reserved for her in the middle of the second row.

Her eyes, as she looked at me with indulgent fondness, were like bluebells seen at evening when the mists turn them grey, and they kept their dear expression unaltered for me all the evening and when I returned to her after making my own speech half-way through the programme, it was like coming home to an unchanged tenderness which no success or failure could alter, augment or diminish . . . She told me the Mayor was going away soon and then she would be less tied. For during his long illness she has had more – infinitely more – than her share of work and during his convalescence she has visited him constantly, sitting with him as she told me from 4 to 9 sometimes to let the nurse off. 'He is used to having me about,' she said when I said I thought that was too much to expect of her. We spoke of poetry and she told me that all hers was burnt in the fire at Crowe Hall. 'I was not meant to be a poet!' she remarked but I begged to differ remembering the prose poetry of her novels . . . She said nothing in praise or blame of my effort at a speech and I did not ask her for an opinion. Her being beside me made everything else fade into insignificance. She liked the Readings better than the acted scenes, she said, and we spoke of her sister and Beth (her step-grand-daughter) who is staying with her – and again of poetry – and were just in complete accord.

May 17th

Holy Footsteps

Oh! never say thy feet are clay
When hour by hour and day by day
They walk along a heavenly way
And where they pass disperse the gray
While gentle steps, like words they pray.

All hushed and modest is their tread,
But one would miss thee overhead
Dear feet by light and loving sped
So small and yet so royally led
And shod with faith where most had bled.

. . . Madame performed her Chairman duties with her usual quiet sweetness and efficiency, putting on her 'owly' glasses to read the notes. She told us *à propos* of Barnard College in New York, whence Miss Caroline Spurgeon[13] had written, that she herself, during a visit to America, had been given a reception there. The guest of the evening was of course required to stand and shake hands with countless people while first one lady then another, to relieve her, did the introducing. After an hour or so of this Madame felt very much exhausted and a lady saw that she was looking tired and asked if she would like a glass of iced water! 'I was feeling as if I could have drunk a bottle of Champagne,' said Madame laughing. The next day the paper remarked that she had more colour than American women which was evidently not considered to her advantage, and that she did not smile as much as Americans who smiled all the time. 'But if you had been standing all that time you would not have felt like smiling either! But they were all very kind and meant it in good part and sent me beautiful flowers to the boat next day. And that's all I have to tell you of my association with Barnard College.' Ripples of laughter attended this recital but for some reason of constraint there was no applause and when Madame sat down she seemed to retire into herself a little shyly, reviewing what she had said a trifle anxiously and looking at her notes without seeing them . . .

Whit Sunday May 27th

This is a digression. There is much left out that will be inserted later, only today she has seemed so near me I want to record how happy I have been in that consciousness, even though to all seeming we have been absent from each other. Last night I wrote to her after a longer interval than usual. I have not felt worthy or able to address her for a while but this morning she came back to me and I took the letter up to Sion Hill Place and dropped it in her letter box. The precincts, as I call the avenue of trees leading to her retired terrace, looked more than usually inviting. I lingered in it, picking a branch here and there of cow parsley, remembering how she had recently told me the name of that plant, and tucking a sprig of it in the flap of the envelope foolishly and sentimentally enough with the aid of a hairpin! My dogs trotted happily on in front or came back to enquire into my tardiness in following them. I went on and passed her door, admiring the majestic beech in full leaf and the semi-circular lawn under the trees of which some children were playing across the road in front of her house.

I stood dreaming and murmuring to her as I have stood so many times after days spent in her company, recalling her words to me by the tree trunk near the railings on the right-hand side, gazing out on St Stephen's Church framed in an opening of foliage. Then I continued my walk and sat down on the High Common choosing a seat just below the one on which we sat on the wonderful Sunday so recently enjoyed. The breeze was stirring the delicate mist of cow parsley above the buttercups till it looked like her silver hair and I watched it lovingly – she has shown me beauty everywhere, even beauty in a weed. Glancing back, the sun on the paint of our seat turned it too to silver. I felt surrounded by whiteness, the holiness of the day and her nearness – a sense of light and wings, my Paraclete. And in the evening on my way to service passing down the hill where we drove the night I gave her the white roses, I saw a thrush perched on a stone pillar to one of the gateways singing his hymn of thanksgiving for the day and his gift of the Spirit, regardless of those who stayed their steps to listen. He delivered himself of his message then fluttered down into the garden and disappeared. A woman sang in the church her fuller song of praise and at sunset the clouds were like the tiny breast feathers of a bird. 'And

I will take away your stony heart and give you a heart of flesh.'
Ah! my beloved, I am resting on yours tonight, close to you in
purity and peace.

May 28th

Madame has rarely reproved me, and then so gently that one
might have mistaken her words for a caress. Once, twice she has
remonstrated with me for giving her presents. The first time she
told me how she had once yielded to the same impulse of giving
and had had her gift returned. The pain the incident caused her
had made her determined never to cause the like to another – the
desire to 'pay back', to avenge herself by inflicting similar
suffering has no part in her . . .

She had invited me to tea one Sunday. On the day I had developed a sore throat and, fearful in case I should give her a cold, I
rang up to say I could not come. A few days later she was driving
me to Mrs Devenish's house and enquired how I was and I
described how the cold had not materialised after all. She had
asked some friends to meet me. 'And,' I said contritely, 'I spoilt
your party.' Madame then put me for the first time unmistakably
in my place. 'You did not spoil my party,' she said with gentle
dignity. 'No of course not,' I rejoined hastily. But she did not
pursue the point and when later, tempting fate, I showed her I
was foolishly hurt by something she had written to me, she was
patience itself with my mood. 'Such a cruel little mother,' I
reproached her. 'Don't say that,' she replied, hurt in turn and
laying her hand a moment on mine. 'You quite misunderstood
me.' When – suddenly melting, as I intended all along – I
clasped her arm beside me, 'It's Christmas time, don't let us
quarrel,' she met me with a cordial 'No.'

At the party there were crackers. Madame was beside me and
we attempted to pull one between us but it refused to break. I
chose another but the same thing happened and I took it for a
good omen – our friendship could not be broken either, pull as
we would! We are bound in spirit and in a deeper love. When we
reached home I said to her lowly, 'I can't do without you.'
'There is no need,' she answered me, 'J'y suis, j'y reste.' . . .

June 5th

. . . It had rained heavily as I made my way up to her house and when I reached her I was disgruntled not only by the weather but by finding that she was not alone as I had hoped, having come full of many things I wished to talk to her about. Her sister was in the room and, much as I liked her, I was irritated by her unexpected presence. The conversation turned upon Chesterton[14] and I said, with a good deal of quite ignorant arrogance as I have read very little of his works, that I thought him a *poseur*, that his prose was affected, since people had begun to expect that style from him it had become forced. Madame disagreed with her usual deference for another's opinion, saying that she was sure I should not think that if I met him, that he was so bland and child-like. 'We are not agreeing today,' I said half in jest, half in regret. She smiled good naturedly. 'If you knew Chesterton I'm sure you would like him,' she repeated. 'I'm sure I should,' I replied, humbled and anxious to make amends and an end to our small sparring bout.

I had, while Madame had been on holiday, sent her at her request a dissertation I had written on *The Heavenly Twins* and the impression the book had made on me at a second reading – there was much in my composition which had worried me when I thought of how it might strike her and now I flung my hand towards her appealingly. 'You didn't mind all I said about *The Heavenly Twins*, did you?' I asked her. 'I loved it,' she said simply. It was then that I sought permission to sit on the floor at her feet and she gave it in the one word 'Yes'. I sat facing the fireplace and she rested her hand like a feather an instant on my shoulder, but I reached up and brought it round till I could lay my cheek against it and my lips – preoccupied with a confession I had made to her in that composition, longing yet unable to speak of it again with her here beside me, conscious of her sympathy and understanding but utterly incapable of breaking the barrier of reserve . . . I spoke of Marie Corelli,[15] asking Madame if she had ever met her and whether she was as bad as people made out, sure that Madame's humanity would have found some saving grace in her, but to my regret Madame said she had once refused an introduction to her and that she could not read her novels, they were not English and they were so 'improving'. 'But you are improving too,' I caught her up. 'Oh not in that way I hope!' she rejoined in horrified disclaimer . . .

We talked of quotation Calendars and I offered to do one of

Madame's works, but she said Miss Tindall had already completed one. I said I should do it for my own use then and instanced those I had kept of Pope, Shelley and Lord Haldane. 'He is a great man,' Madame remarked seriously, but though she had known him many years she confessed to never having read a word of his writings. I warmed to the subject and we discussed his philosophy. Once or twice I made a move to go but she detained me owing to the rain, very kindly. At last I took out my powder puff, apologising for using it. Madame said she always preferred powder leaves just rubbed over the face as they cleaned the skin as well . . .

June 8th

Having come so far in this book, I look back and, remembering my promise to show it to her, I am dissatisfied. There are some people who are, or who seem to be, wholly of this earth and there is less difficulty in portraying them objectively. But there are others who, like Madame, live apparently on the borderland of Spirit. These are they whom it is almost impossible to characterise. One moment they are here, ordinary mortals to all intents and purposes, the next they have eluded one, or else become so vividly and so thrillingly significant that human language is rendered abortive by a revelation beyond it. I have sought to fix the indescribable, but its nature being spiritual I recognise that I have failed for this very reason, not merely from lack of the highest talent in writing. My greatest sorrow and my greatest glory is at once that the realisation of our most perfect moments evaporates all too quickly. I seek to recapture the experience and it is gone, and yet to comfort me, sometimes unannounced from the heaven which is its home, it will return suddenly in all its beauty and poignant tenderness and I kneel to remember a loveliness not of this world. Spirit dawns in her and summers all her being, visibly, like something outside her taking possession of her gracious body. I have never been so conscious of the coming and going of spirit in anyone, yet there is no suggestion of duality about her . . .

Annunciation

If like a flower I might slip into thy hand,
Silently, secretly, a silver like wand,

Only my fragrance to bid thee understand,
What caused my petals there so purely to expand.

If like a bird I might speed one to thy feet,
Fearlessly, modestly, a humble sparrow sweet,
Only my grace-notes to echo the heart's beat,
Unnoticed in my coming; in my going fleet.

If like a poem I might live within thy mind,
Latently, beauteously a thought with thine entwined,
Only a rhythm to tell thee I was kind,
And ready of recall when thou wouldst comfort find.

Never then I'd hesitate love to come to thee,
Flower unto a flower and wings where wings should be,
Only one more song to the soul of harmony,
To mingle thus ignored were all enough for me.

June 10th

Today had been Madame's [seventy-fourth] Birthday and I have
been to tea with her. She had something in the nature of a party
and as I look back on it, it seems to me that she could not have collected types more strongly contrasted. There was Mrs Glynn
Stewart, old in years, exaggerated in dress, of a refined vulgarity
in conversation which to me is particularly objectionable, an
avowed *bonne-viveuse* if one can use that term, with a gloss of
superficial cleverness culled from her association with well-
known people, travelled, insincere and coquettish when she
ought to know better, doubtless good-hearted and possibly
amusing in some moods if not taken seriously. There was Miss
Katherine Kimball, a famous etcher, a South American (this is
rather bitter; I did not know her well and may have been unjust)
with intent blue eyes and naïveté of manner aided by her almost
foreign accent and trick of holding her head on one side, inno-
cently ingratiating, slow of speech, unerring of judgement, not
one to whom one could talk flippancies; she was dressed in a
severe home spun tailor-made with white turned down collar and
a round black felt hat which made her dumpy figure look almost
deformed and her rather broad face rounder. And there was Miss
Harford, bouncing, but not quite so bouncing as usual, wearing just the shade of pink sleeveless jumper she should avoid,
very rubicund, rather self-important but pleasant withal

and entirely English; she, too, ingratiating but in a totally different way. There was Miss Clarke – and there was one – and
there was my Birthday Lady in her character of White Rose
today looking pale and a little thin, possibly in contradistinction
to the grosser figures surrounding her, and doubly refined. One
would not have guessed however that the past week has been one
of successive social efforts. She was as ever grace itself in her role
of hostess, concentrating on each in turn and bringing the
peculiar gifts of all to the notice of all, regulating the conversation
with quiet question, quiet comment and little laughs that flattered and encouraged. As the talk was so general, I cannot record
it in detail but gradually her words will come back to me, as they
do, like music or verse.

But I want to picture her at tea with her Birthday cake before
her. Mrs Taylor, her housekeeper, had chosen it, she told us, and
as I murmured to her it could not have been better found for it
was a white-iced plum cake decorated with a white sugar rose in
the centre and little white and yellow roses round the edge, in
some other substance more lasting. There were pink forget-me-
nots also in the middle and a silver motto 'Birthday Wishes' to
complete the top. A ruffle of paper round it she ignored when
called upon to cut the cake and I saved the situation by peeling it
off a little way. I had asked for one of the side roses and now I
warned her not to cut into it. She disentangled it from its crumbs
and tossed it playfully on my plate and I later pinned it on my
dress with her brooch which I was wearing. But she soon gave up
the effort of cutting and I asked permission to help her . . .

I had sent her the cushion I had been embroidering for her and
she had it well in evidence in the drawing room, showing it to
everyone so kindly, and thanked me in her own dear way which
makes my work for her light and eagerly performed. I was able to
do her another little service by running downstairs for the
matches she had forgotten, and in helping myself to a cigarette I
noted the inscription on the silver box I had often admired. It was
from Haldane McFall. Mrs Glynn Stewart and I had a discussion
as to whether Herbert Schmalz[16] painted flowers or not, but,
as I was in a position to know that he had recently taken to this
branch of art, I came off more or less victoriously. All remained
silent during this passage of arms and I didn't know whether I
had been brave or singularly rude in holding my own!

I was the first to leave and my rising was a signal for Mrs Glynn Stewart also to go, for which I was glad for Madame's sake but exasperated for my own, for Madame's dear intention of coming down with me alone and of giving me a few words to myself at the door was thus frustrated. I said to her, 'Don't come down, Madame,' but she stood with her darling obstinacy in kind deeds, and answered unwaveringly 'I always do,' and she did. Her sweet eyes fluttered up to my face, provocative and shy. I clasped her hand tightly and blessed her again and so left her . . .

June 13th

Alexandra Day[17] once more and my dear wild rose and I were together again. It was Sir Harry[18] and Lady Hatt's Garden Party to the Electrical Association Conference in Victoria Park. Miss Clarke called for me and we joined the Mayor and Mayoress at their table on the lawn. Later Miss Clarke and I found deck chairs nearer the band-stand and there Madame came to us and I sat between them. Miss Clarke mentioned that Miss Hatt was to visit Castle Bally in Ireland. 'But that wouldn't be our Castle Bally,' argued Madame in reply. 'Our's was in County Mayo.' She told me they were born in Ireland though her people were originally from Yorkshire. She said too that the Belfast people claim her as Irish and always on St Patrick's Day the Council sends her some shamrock and she went on to relate how one of her stepdaughters[19] when visiting Ireland had been received here and there with much ceremony, she could not understand why, until someone asked, 'You are Sarah Grand, aren't you?' A case of reflected glory.

She looked indescribably charming and as I turned, noting her starry eyes, her softly arranged white curls beneath the arch of her black crinoline hat, and her face like a pale pink cloud, it was as if I gazed at a miniature dawn and I could not help exclaiming, 'You look so sweet today.' She gave her little embarrassed laugh and her eyes flickered in girlish shyness, renouncing the compliment and yet appreciative of it. She told me that three engagements all at the same time had been made for her at the Guildhall for tomorrow! And that this morning she had spent in the Institution Gardens being photographed in the group of the Electrical delegates, 600 strong . . . Her dress was made for her without a fitting and sent from London – of black georgette

and silk lace, a wide band across the front of the bodice in pink
which was really flushed rose like her face and veiled again with
the lace. I said I thought her hat could stand a little more trimming and she confessed to having taken some of the flowers off it.
Not that kind of flower, I thought, which was of black felt, but a
scarcely tinted pink chiffon rose to accentuate the touch of pink
on the dress. But I doubt if she troubles to make the alteration.
She was wearing the favours demanded of the day and her gold
chain of office, which gave the necessary tinge of yellow to complete the illusion she creates of a rose herself; a white rose, a pink
rose, a wild fair rose with delicate petals spread to the stillness of
the reverent air.

June 14th

If Madame ever reads this she will think it sentimental. 'You
see,' she impressed upon me once, 'I'm not sentimental.' 'Am I
very sentimental?' I questioned. 'You are rather,' she returned
with her usual frankness that doesn't hurt because it is a part of
her sincerity and the reliability of her friendship. She defines that
fault as 'indulgence in emotion for its own sake'.

But to live over today is my aim tonight. If I fall into that error,
forgive it, my little Mother, as you forgive me all things. She had
invited me to the tea party she was holding in the Assembly
Rooms to the Women's Section of the Electrical Association.
When I arrived I found the Club Room packed to suffocation
and she at the entrance to the hot room still valiantly receiving
her guests. She clasped my hand cordially and whispered, 'It's
an awful rabble! Go and find Nellie' (her sister). I acted on her
advice and discovered Miss Clarke, with two cups of tea in
imminent danger of being upset, doing her work of distribution.
I took the hint and thereafter, only stopping to take my cloak off,
I too helped to hand cups and cake. Later there were a few
speeches, Madame welcoming the delegates in well chosen words
and they responding with a vote of thanks and admiration for her
work now and in the days gone by . . . Madame now joined us
saying as she had not ordered the car until a quarter to 5 we
should have time to go round the Electrical Exhibition in the
main rooms. What a contrast were these exhibits to the 18th
Century Rooms – modernity in all its latest guises . . .
We saw the sunray lamps (the violet ray one being my one

point of interest!) and any amount of refrigerators, geysers, stoves and cookers. At last the tour of inspection came to an end and I made to bid her farewell, but she offered to drive me home and though it meant waiting some added minutes till I went to fetch my things, she persisted in her kind intention. I bundled myself in, after scattering the crowd right and left to permit of a hasty excursion to and from the cloakroom. Miss Clarke most kindly sat on a little seat and I beside Madame.

What was my joy unspeakable (literally for I could not reply) when she said, 'Come home with me and rest a bit.' Of course I went and we talked happily on the way – such unexpected good fortune going to my head blissfully. 'I hate machinery,' she informed me. At the door she was met by Mrs Taylor with the message from the Mayor that he would call for her at a quarter past seven. I had no idea she had to go out again that evening and offered to take myself off there and then, but she made way for me and urged me to go upstairs and I, nothing loath, complied. 'Sit down and have a cigarette,' which I proceeded to do on the floor beside her, having first lighted hers for her on my knees. This morning I had bought her a small pale pink shell flower to go on her hat of yesterday with some black satin leaves to soften it. I now laid the box on her lap and opened it, explaining my intention. She seemed to take a liking for them and said we would try them on the hat later . . . I asked her if she had felt the recent earth tremors but she had not and I related how one night I had become rather frightened, deciding to keep awake until the prophesied time was over, and so read her book, *Our Manifold Nature*. Turning to 'Ah Man', what was my agitation to find it was all about an earthquake.[20] Was it true? I asked after we had laughed together, and was sobered on the instant by her assurance that it was, and that thousands of people had been engulfed by a tidal wave. She pictured for me how a huge battleship had had to keep full steam ahead in order to remain at anchor and how two enormous blocks of granite the size of her two sofas had been swept 30 ft up the road. 'And you were asleep?' I prompted. 'Yes, it happened just as it is described! The day was airless and the barometer kept falling. We felt something was coming.' 'And you were taken to the hills?' 'Yes,' she repeated, 'it all happened as described.' But out of deference for the memory of the faithful Ah Man I did not refer to him, fearing to pain her.

And now she said she would go up and get her hat and we would try the flower on it. 'Get a cushion,' she urged me, 'if you must sit on the floor.' But I hugged her arm and swore I was perfectly comfortable and, when she had gone, I kissed the oblong velvet cushion against which she had been leaning . . . She returned with her little crinoline straw and handed it to me with scissors and pins and I sat on the sofa contrarily reluctant now to unpick the flower already on it, in black felt and silver. But she said it looked like a French funeral so, having tried the pink flower and it having met with her approval, I snipped off the other and pinned in my spray in its place. 'You will have to try it on,' I said gently, for she was reluctant to remove her other hat, thinking her hair would not be tidy. She did as I suggested, however, and sitting there in the semi-twilight of the darkening afternoon, her soft white hair loosened and crushed after her long and tiring day, her wistful eyes so anxious to look her best, she was enough to wring the heart out of one's body with tenderness for her. I poised it lightly, scarce daring to touch her and yet longing to press the dear white head to my heart. I loved her then as never before, with a poignancy that will haunt me to my dying day and a reverence that held me then and will hold me in her thrall forever. She rose and walked to the glass . . . As the time was getting on we decided that I should come to finish it another day . . . And so I kissed my liege lady's hand again and she even came to the door with me, and my trio of wonderful happy days, the happiest and most wonderful, closed. As I looked up at her windows from the Avenue I exclaimed through my tears in Ferdinand's words, 'Oh! you Wonder!'[21]

June 15th

Today is the birthday of the man I loved, but if I could have him back, even if he gave me all the love I mistakenly imagined he was ready to offer me once, and it meant losing Madame's friendship I would say no – a thousand times no! Thus it is that God makes up to us with fairer, holier gifts for all we suffer if we do but trust in him. Madame said her white dress if she chose it must not be too bridal and yet she has often suggested a Bride to me in her approach, timid and yet sure of her attraction – a Bride of the Spirit, for the thought of her wedded is peculiarly

Sarah's favourite publicity photograph, taken when she was in her late thirties.

Right: D.C. McFall, probably on his return to Ireland after service in India and following the death of his first wife in the late 1860s.

Signed oil portrait of Sarah (dated 1896) by Alfred Praga (1867–1949) presented to the City of Bath by Archibald Carlaw Grand in 1943. She is described in the programme to a recent exhibition of the portrait as 'wearing a dark brown cloth coat trimmed with black (either jet beads or bobble fringe) and with large leg-of-mutton shaped sleeves. Her wide black hat is tied under the chin with black ribbon and she carries a fur muff.'

Sarah in one of her many hats, *The Lady's World*, June 1900.

A caricature of Sarah and 'Mere Man' from *Harper's Weekly*, 2 November 1901.

Below: The Dickens Commemoration Dinner, 7 February 1925, at Fortts Restaurant, Bath. L. to R. standing: Miss S. Ruskin, Louise Regnis (Ina Singers-Bigger), Miss D. Gandy, Mrs Revell, Dr Richards, Miss F. Tylee, Miss Masters. L. to R. seated: Mrs Preston King, Gladys Singers-Bigger, Madame Sarah Grand, Alderman T. Sturge Cotterell, Mrs Ingham.

A portrait of Gladys at the age of thirty, on the back of which she has
noted 'pale blue and crystals'.

Facing page: Mrs Singers-Bigger 'taken in the Morning Room, 12
Marlborough Buildings, Bath, by Muriel Blackburne', 1923.

Above left: Sarah as Mayoress of Bath in 1925. *Above right*: Alderman Cedric Chivers, J.P., Mayor of Bath, c. 1925.

Crowe Hall, Widcombe Hill, Bath, where Sarah lived with Mr and Miss Tindall from 1920–26. The picture shows the south façade with Sarah's library-study on the ground floor, right, and her bedroom above.

Gladys' photograph of Sarah's eighty-third birthday party at The Royal Hotel, Weston-super-Mare, Somerset, 10 June 1937. Left to right standing: Miss Kimball, Miss Bellenden-Clarke (Sarah's sister Nellie), Felicitas Robbins (Sarah's step-great grand daughter, 'Winkie'), Miss Tindall, Miss Oliver. Left to right seated: Mrs Sonnenschein, Madame Sarah Grand, Miss Harford. *Below left*: Sarah presenting certificates at the Adult Schools Home Arts and Crafts Exhibition, 27 April 1933.
Below right: One of Gladys' poems for Sarah.

On the Loan of an umbrella
To S.G.

It rained! and with the rain my spirits
    fell,
Until, like fairy-guardians of old,
Into my hand you put your talisman
Which made the drops in lovelier variety
Prospective flowers that strewed my onward
    way.
For on your side umbrella perched unseen
The woodland elves and green-clad meadow-
    fays
Intent on showering blossoms to the earth
Where mortals waved their coronation flags
And thought of emblems in the shape of flower.
The daisy and the daffodil were there,
Rough thistle and the stately fleur-de-luce;
Ubiquitous, the tiny shamrock ran
To vie with oak-leaves for the rose's kiss

Sarah aged eighty-six with Bobby, her cat.

painful to me. Nevertheless no one could have been more fitted for wifehood than she, so loyal, so tactful, so willing to give and take in understanding comradeship, so slow to anger and loath to condemn and to argue.

One night, however, I must have gone to sleep in a pronounced 'jealousy complex' (according to the modern psychological jargon) for I dreamt she was to be married and woke in an agony of apprehension which clouded my whole day, anathematising the man she intended to honour with a violence that was a revelation to me! I have watched men's demeanour towards her. It is invariably one of respect, of salutary awe for her reputation, judgement, attainment; of curiosity before the sense of mystery and dignity that surrounds her, or of true fellowship arising from a feeling of knowing where they are with an experienced woman of the world. She blossoms in the society of the distinguished in rank or achievement, as in an air native to her, and I have seen her smile on an official guest of the opposite sex with a pronounced sweetness which had nothing of caprice in it but a natural feminine exertion of a charm she knows herself to possess. It had in it too a touch of indulgence as coming from a superior who while not yielding her supremacy could afford to disguise it for the moment . . . Madame rarely, if ever, uses any term of endearment in speech. She has her rare and doubly precious one for me in her letters, but it lies, as it were, beneath the surface and unacknowledged between us when face to face. I cast a net of 'darlings' over her and knot it with frequent 'angels' but, while permitting the exuberance, she does not respond except by that permission which is much from her and valued by me accordingly.

We are neither of us in our first youth and sometimes the terror of losing her overcomes me, it may be on a walk or at prayer beside her picture. The tears rise to mourn her too early and then a voice prompts me, 'Oh make haste to love her, withhold no tender word, shower all that thy love bids thee shower at her feet, for it may not be for long.' And then another will come in consolation, saying, 'You have eternity in which to love her, she does not comprehend haste, peace, be still, for her spirit is calm and so you will the better commune with her.' And then sometimes she will come to me suddenly as in a dream and I am caught up to her mother heart in an ecstasy of divine enfoldment as never yet in reality.

Like daisy petals from your heart
Your little hands are rayed
And from that golden centre start
Behests at once obeyed.

But as obedient to the sun
The whole sweet flower expands
So answer to the love of one
Both heart and little hands.

June 20th

On Saturday the 16th, after lunch I had just settled myself to paste cuttings and photos in my sister's scrap book – a record of her South African tour – when the bell rang. Mother and I wondered idly what or who it could be. I was in a black and white jumper and my old green skirt, my hair more or less anyhow, when the door was flung open and our little parlourmaid Burcombe announced 'Madame Grand!' The surprise was electric. She came in imperturbable as ever, dressed in a neat black cloth coat and skirt with a white muslin front and her black hat with the gold buckle, looking fresh and untired. I welcomed her eagerly and Mother thought of a cigarette and we soon had her comfortable in my chair by the window. She had been lunching at Crowe with Miss Tindall and said, as she was passing our door and had the afternoon to herself, she thought she would call for me and take me home to do the hat. I was full of joy at the prospect and, in a state of excitement, dashed upstairs to change, descending, just as she had finished her smoke, in my grey with a coral blouse.

And so I was whisked off in the fairy coach to the fairy house, goldenly set like the heart of one of the moon daisies she remarked in the field adjoining the Avenue, saying she thought that was a pretty name for them.

We talked of girls keeping shops for something to occupy their time and I cited one or two I had known of. She related the story of one Society woman who had taken up millinery but who as a result was much put upon by her friends who never paid their accounts. I referred to *The Wingèd Victory, à propos*. She said she knew all that set depicted in the book, that she had moved in both sets. 'You know it was said of Queen Victoria that she was not in Society,' she added smiling. I mentioned Lord Terry de Beach[22] and Madame informed me that a certain Sir Tollemache Sinclair was his prototype. He had been a 'very bad old man', as she expressed it, but was in a state of repentance and would sometimes eat nothing but peaches and milk. He used to come and talk to her for 7 hours at a stretch and would ask her for her influence with Editors . . . I said again that she ought to write her memoirs, but again she said she couldn't 'because she could not tell the truth', but she had felt she had to do him and had! Did you write before you published? I questioned. Oh yes, she answered, I was always writing. Of verses she said those in *Ideala* and *The Beth Book* are her own and she had had to make up a legend for the story of 'Eugenia' in *Our Manifold Nature*.

She spoke too of her war work, relating how the Mayor of Tunbridge Wells was opposed to Women's Suffrage and that he distrusted her in consequence. At last, however, he had said they might collect clothes for refugees and she organised the depot which proved most successful. But they got little recognition and though one woman died of over exertion all they received at the end was a 'type written letter of thanks'. This with a wry little smile . . .

I finished the trimming of the hat and handed it to her. 'My little mother,' I said kissing her hand, 'I would do so much more for you if you would let me.' But she seemed to feel a qualm of conscience at my calling her that and rose restlessly, for once referring to my own mother and what she must think of her. 'She says you have been the making of me,' I returned, quoting. Madame has never once usurped my mother's place actively. I have in my great love for her thrust the relationship upon her, apologising for needing two, each filling a need of my nature. 'Mother of my Spirit,' I called her, and once, yes once, she wrote she would have been glad to have me as a daughter. Now I went to her and took my accustomed place at her feet and something prompted me to ask her a question. Madame wears almost constantly a necklet of silver, like silver beads, to which is attached three round crystal globes in silver and graduated in size. They lie close against her throat, are uncommon and much identified with her. I have wondered occasionally as to their history and I said now, 'May I ask you a question? Don't tell me if you would rather not.' And then it was out in a rush before I realised my error in speaking, 'Why do you wear those crystals?' I felt her spirit withdraw like a sensitive plant rudely touched, and she spoke without an instant's hesitation, with a quiet decision that admitted of no argument, 'I never tell that to anyone.'

I lifted eyes wide with regret and astonishment to her sweet face bent seriously above me – 'All right, darling, I didn't mean to intrude.' 'I'm sure you didn't,' she replied, but the very certainty and considerateness of her answer implied a doubt and I suffered under it, forced to forego discussion. She went on to relate how she had once given a crystal necklace to a servant who had not appreciated it. 'I don't suppose she knew the difference,' I rejoined, and Madame said she always liked to give good things to maids to educate their taste . . . She showed me how Grant Allen had taught her to hold a pen so as to avoid writer's cramp – between her first and second fingers. But I could not get over my unhappy feeling of remorse at having hurt her by seeking her confidence so mistakenly and I grew silent, a sad uneasiness spoiling moments that should have been full of perfect companionship and peace . . .

The tea bell interrupted us and, unable to bear the strain of dissimulation longer, I turned to her impulsively reverting to my fault, 'I am so sorry I asked about those things,' I burst out, and would have put my arm about her but she eluded me and started to her feet. I felt all I cared for in life was with her slipping from me. 'I wouldn't offend you for anything on this earth,' I stammered and Madame, looking down upon me from the mantel near which she stood, answered as before, 'I'm sure you wouldn't.' Again the implied doubt, in that I had already done so, stung me like a lash. But it was impossible to continue my self reproaches before her determination to close the episode and I had, in deference to her wish, to stem my longing to come to a better understanding. I craved her pardon in words but she rather proved it mine in acts, and was kindness itself and consideration all through tea and afterwards, but the sense of my own unworthiness hung heavily upon me. It would with anyone else have meant little, but with Madame so dearly reserved, who maintains that 'friendship is hedged about with delicacy', I felt myself to have fallen in her estimation in giving way to what must have seemed an idle curiosity.

After tea we went out in the garden and stood beside the White Rose I had given her last year which is again in lovely bloom, but its fairness had no word to say to us and we were cold to its significance . . .

June 24th

Back in the drawing room I was told to sit on the sofa and sit on the sofa I did, feeling very much in disgrace, though Madame's kind manner never changed nor did the affectionate regard of her blue eyes alter. I mentioned a rather foolish letter which had appeared in the paper signed by Lady Peirse in reply to an objectionable post card she had received. Madame thought it was a mistake to have replied to it in any way and recounted how following the occasion when she herself had taken the chair at a meeting convened in aid of the starving German children on the Ruhr not long after the war,[23] she had been bombarded with abusive post cards and letters to which she had wisely vouchsafed no answer. She told me that feeling had run very high at the meeting and she had not been allowed to speak. At last she had made up her mind to bring it to a close because she had feared the opposers would wreck the room. Jordan, the Mayor's Officer,[24] had stationed himself at the side entrance to the Banqueting Hall and when Madame descended from the platform at once took charge of her, tho' she was at the time ex-Mayoress (it being the year after her first in office). He piloted her and, at her request, the rest of the platform party by a special passage-way which brought them safely out at the Police Station. 'But I would do it again,' said Madame with spirit. 'I know, I thought it so jolly courageous of you,' I rejoined. 'It was the first thing, except your books, which made me take an interest in you.' 'It wasn't courageous,' she answered. 'I just didn't care for people's opinion – if I know myself right I decide for myself. I never take advice.' . . . 'You know what General Booth[25] said?' she asked me. 'No? He used to say that if Moses had had a Committee he would never have crossed the Red Sea.' And in the laugh that followed Miss Clarke entered with the flowers she had been arranging. 'You're looking tired,' she said to Madame, and I took the hint. Madame came with me to the door. Outside the drawing room I hesitated for some reason. 'Go down,' Madame's voice was suddenly imperative behind me. It seemed to surprise herself for she immediately softened it to regrets for turning me out like this. But I obeyed her submissively and went down without more ado. In the hall a sharp shower of rain was visible above the transom. At once she became all eagerness to detain me or to make me accept a large umbrella which she called 'Mr Harkles' but I would have neither and in the little altercation that followed the tension was lightened, endearing terms uttered and with her standing on the stairs calling to her sister to come and stop me, I waved her a farewell kiss and departed naturally and happily. Under a tree in the Avenue the moon daisies showed like stars, brilliantly white just beyond the fringe of shadow and soon the rain was over. But not my remorse for the moments of pain I have given her, and when I got in I threw myself on the floor by her picture and cried and cried.

June 26th

I bore it for a day or two, then having found a little coloured moonstone brooch which I thought might go with the flower I had sewn on her hat, to hide the stalks at the side, I sent it to her with a letter of penitence, asking her pardon. I said as the ornament was only on approval I would ring up to know if it would do, and call for it if not.

In the morning I did as I had suggested . . . Madame's voice blessed me. She said that she couldn't decide for herself and in any case could not fasten it in for herself and that I had better come to do it for her. I gasped with relief and pleasure but had the grace to demur. 'If I come so often you'll get so tired of me,' I hesitated. 'No,' she said simply. 'Come after five, I have something to do till then.' And so it was settled.

Lights and shades were making will-o'-the-wisp illuminations on the hills as I climbed up to my Paradise and I rested, so as not to be too early, on the common watching them. In her Avenue I picked up the half of a thin fragile blue egg and carried it in with me asking Edna, the new maid, if she knew what bird's it was, but she could not tell me. Madame heard our voices and opened the door of the drawing room to greet me before we had reached it, and stood waiting to draw me in and back into her confidence. I felt myself forgiven and hastened towards her. So tiny she looked and yet so great, with that atmosphere of tradition of which one is ever conscious in her presence surrounding her; so homely and yet so queenly in her dark blue coat and skirt and the clove carnation blouse of which I had so happy a memory. Her eyes so blue made a light for one, and together with the all apparent stature of her mind silenced me, so that I could not utter the joy I felt to be welcomed by her like this again. She understood and filled the pause and then I asked her what the little egg was. She came and inspected it in my hand. 'If it has black spots it is a thrush's – yes, that is a thrush's,' she decided . . .

She invited me to sit down and have a cigarette and waited on me, offering me the silver box and tossing me a box of matches. I lit up but no sooner had I done so than the thing went out. 'I wonder why it is,' I said, 'that whenever I light a cigarette it goes out?' 'Because you don't light it,' she replied calmly. 'What sarc!' I exclaimed and we looked at one another laughingly with, for me, the tears of fondness very near the surface. My heart brimmed with relief and love, and kissed her with unfelt kisses . . . I was determined not to outstay my welcome and made a move to go, but she detained me offering me another cigarette and when I refused she said I could watch her smoke. Nothing loath, I sat by her side on the sofa and watched. I was a trifle behind her, placed so, and when she smiled as she did once I could only see the corner of her mouth, but crinkled in the dearest way, the little fullnesses broke into kissable indentations and its sadness and self repression dispersed in a softening ripple of amusement that fled as soon as seen, like a sun-beam. We talked of our letting our house and Madame gave herself to the consideration of our difficulties with unselfish interest, suggesting and advising . . . I would have wrapped her up in my heart but I offered her no caress today, loving her the more. She came out on to the doorstep and in parting we were yet bound in harmony and true understanding.

July 12th

Soon after this I attended the Mayoral Reception to the Society of Architects and took Priscilla Gordon with me. There was a long queue waiting to be received when we arrived at the Pump Room and we attached ourselves to it. I was wearing my blue and silver and, in hopes that I might have an opportunity of speaking to Madame, I had put the little rainbow brooch which I felt she wanted and had bought for her, in an envelope in my bag. When

I reached her, I had an impression of 'downiness', of soft pink, and a light of recognition in the dear eyes but for a second upon me. I passed on and we were immediately hailed by Dolly Gandy. I watched Madame continue her greetings from a distance. She was carrying a bouquet of pale pink and deeper old rose and mauve carnations. Soon Priscilla and I escaped into the quieter concert hall which was cleared, except for supper tables round the sides, for dancing. Here Dolly followed us and we amused ourselves, being the only group in the room, by giving 'dares' to one another in true schoolgirl fashion. There had lately been a craze for a certain jazz tune entitled 'The Room with a View' and as the members of the Orchestra were taking their places, I 'dared' Priscilla to go up on the platform and call up to them to ask if they had the new tune. She would not go so I went myself and put the question, whereupon she followed suit with 'And have you got "I Can't Help Loving That Man"? ' making our breach of convention all the worse. We laughed a good deal over our temerity in this and over recollections of historical dares when suddenly the Mayor and Mayoress, accompanied by several distinguished Architects and other guests entered the room in ceremonial procession. I turned to gaze at Madame when half way across the polished floor she spoke to me. 'Are you going to perform?' she asked, referring to our isolated position and the proximity of a piano. The whole imposing train paused for my answer. I went up to her and murmured something feeble in explanation. The Mayor looked stonily at me, the distinguished Architects were non-plussed, but Madame smiled graciously and moved on, satisfied that she had pleased me, nay, raised me to the seventh heaven of adoration as only she knows how. She seemed to me majestic as the Queen herself and oh! so much dearer, and like a tender sunset cloud on the fringe of a starlit night – for her dress was black chantilly lace over soft pink and she wore a floating scarf of pink net about her shoulders which, together with the harmonising flowers, completed a picture of such womanliness and grace mingled with dignity that I rejoiced anew in her notice as in a newly conferred title of honour.

She went through the doors of the hall and out on to the terrace, making the round with the Mayor, and I saw her pass in and out among the statues and pillars without haste, threading her way with mild patience, conforming to all the ceremonies of the occasion. And then I saw her no more that night until the hour of 11 had struck when again the Mayoral procession entered the Fountain Room, on their way to depart. There was something infinitely charming in the appearance of this strangely assorted couple, the Mayor not without his own good looks and dignity and that atmosphere of history less solid but more flamboyant than that which surrounds Madame, the atmosphere which in his case brings back all the prosperity of Beau Nash's rule and makes one feel that one will be glad hereafter that one lived in Bath under his; obviously soothed by Madame's presence; obviously considerate of it, and the Mayoress clothed in the condescending grace of her intellect, moving beside him like his better genius . . . They were gone and I had had no other chance to speak to her. My one aim and ambition when Madame is Mayoress is to make myself as inconspicuous as possible, and when my ambition is realised and she does not see me, then my heart descends to my boots and I am miserable. So it was tonight. I allowed a few minutes to elapse and then, thinking they must have disappeared from the entrance, I piloted Priscilla out of the dancing room. What was my delight to find Madame still standing at the entrance, waiting while the Mayor donned his coat. I held out my hand, thanking her and ignoring everyone else. She responded, lifting her eyes a little strained and red with the late hours and smoke. But nothing could dim their limpid beauty nor the spirit of truth in their depths. And I didn't care for appearances. I took out the folded envelope with the brooch inside and asked her to take it home in her bag. I put it there myself while she obediently held it open, not knowing what I was up to but showing no surprise. 'Put it in your bag,' I had said and she replied, 'Yes.' Oh the dear familiar sweetness of her voice on the word, intimate, humorous; my friend and not the Mayoress! And when we left her and went to gather our things in the cloakroom she followed us in and, dazzled, looked round for me till she found me and asked if we had a car ordered to fetch us. I could have thrown my arms round her, but answered conventionally with thanks in the affirmative. One more glimpse I had of her, like a Marquise at the window of her own motor which should have been a glass coach and then would not have been worthy to carry her.

It is curious how Madame seems to expand and grow tall when fulfilling any official duty. And then she will put off her height with the ceremony and condescend, in intimacy, to the stature which justifies one of my names for her 'Little Flower', a little flower whom one could press within one's heart so tiny does she seem and easily enveloped. Early this summer I had much ado not to take her flowers from our garden every day, each as it unfolded its beauty seemed to plead to go to her. The forget-me-nots said they were like her eyes, conscience blue, the wallflowers that they were steadfast as she, the primrose that she is quite as prim as they in some moods (how prim I look, she commented once on her photo and 'very much chain', referring to the Chain of Office she was wearing). The lilies-of-the-valley vowed she loves them, and the cherry blossoms were jealous of the white roses and maintained they resembled her most because they are more delicate. And so they do when she is at home, but not when she is Mayoress because then she is regal. And even the buttercups held that they had some of her simplicity of taste and a fair proportion of her heart's gold. I gathered her some on May 6th, one of the most perfect days I ever remember. Let me now recall it and entitle it after the poem I read that evening: *Day That I Have Loved*.

I look from a golden autumn back to a golden spring and the one seems the reflection of the other. I spent that morning gathering buttercups and going to service as I always like to do when I am to see her, to spend a little preparatory time in the presence of the spirit 'who owns each waiting hour'. At 4.30 I was dressed and looking for her from the doorstep. I saw her coming towards me and told myself again that she was like a bride as she moved, and I hurried to meet her. She lifted her sun shade in greeting and smiled her provocative little tucked-in smile, as much as to say, 'Here I am, such as I am. I hope you are satisfied, for I am glad to be with you.' The day was perfect. It couldn't have been nicer, we agreed. A dog chased the sheep as we got to my door and we paused to see him captured. Madame threw her sun shade down nonchalantly on our box-seat with a clatter that might have broken its handle, about the only noisy thing she has ever been guilty of! and we entered the morning room. She sat beside the bowl of buttercups, now upright and widely open like a miniature sunburst in her honour, and remarked upon them and upon the bowl which she thought just the right shade of green. Soon she and Mother and I were all talking pleasantly . . .

I showed her a book I had recently been given, *The Prophet* by Kahlil Gibran,[26] and she correctly guessed the author was an Arab. We talked of Ina and the Victoria Falls which she said were three miles long and could not be seen all at once. Tea, or rather coffee over, I went to gather her some white lilac in the garden and returned to find her looking at our Cloisonné vases which she wondered were Italian or Japanese. She said I might walk home with her . . . Half way up the first hill we stopped to admire the vivid green of a tree against the young blue sky and she remarked the clarity of the atmosphere. 'I did make a fool of myself the other night,' I burst out, seeking to put aside the little shyness and reserve which settles upon us when I have written her something in confidence and find it difficult either to ignore or speak of when face to face . . . 'I should never apply the word "intrusive" to you,' she reassured me now gently. 'I am so afraid of being like others in Bath, to whom if one gives an inch they take an ell,' I urged in self excuse. But she surprised me by the tender seriousness of her answering reproach, 'I should have thought you would have drifted towards me naturally,' she said – no more.

'When you go away,' I began. 'Yes,' she encouraged me. 'I am going to give you the Lesser Boswell to read,' I continued. 'What's that?' she questioned. 'It's all about you,' I replied, having in mind this book. 'Which one of me?' she asked mischievously. 'Yes,' I rejoined, 'there are many,' seeing the justice of her claim, countering my arrogance. But she opined that if I had written with the design of showing it to her that 'that rather spoils it'. I assured her that it was only recently I had taken that decision, in case anything happened to me and the book were found, and in case I had said anything in it of which she disapproved. We agreed that we liked the path into which we now turned, and I told her how I had day-dreamed meetings with her there, when I had heard she was coming to live near and before she had become my friend, and how they had been realised.

We walked on slowly in perfect harmony and to my joy she suggested our sitting to rest on one of the seats on the hilly pathway, whence the view of the city in the mellow evening light was fair as a dream indeed. She opened her dark green sunshade and

I sat beside her plucking at the lilac leaves in my hand, rolling one into a little green cigarette and at peace with all the world. No sense of making conversation disturbed me. I left it to her lazily, happy in the sound of her dear voice, the details of her sorrow-worn face clear to me like the dropping petals of a rose, especially the soft fullness beneath her eyes, which would have been assuaged like the mark of tears by a soothing touch. She was in her dark blue *charmeuse* and grey and was wearing the blue straw hat with the grey flowers of velvet. It had slipped a little back with the exertion of the walk and beneath the brim the tight grey curls peeped with the air of slight exhaustion . . . We spoke of the houses on the hill opposite wondering which part of Bath they were and I told her of the street which at night looked like an illuminated S – her initial emblazoned on the City. . . . A dog stayed his steps at the end of our seat looking at me sympathetic-ally with friendly brown eyes, and I called him darling indis-criminately having just used the term to her but, such was my happy and expansive mood, all and sundry were darlings to me at that moment . . . She said she had never been a suffragette, that she had not agreed with their methods after their opening of the campaign, that they had done 'cruel things'. It was not so much the vote she cared for – 'I hate party politics,' she said – but she thought for working girls it was right, and that there should be equality of opportunity in professions. I lamented my inability to give myself wholeheartedly to any cause. 'If you were fully convinced you would fight.' . . . Later continuing our discussion she counselled me, 'Never seek to con-vert the individual, speak to the masses . . .'

But it was not only what she said to me. Her conversation had been full of interest, grave and humorous, rallying and kind, but it was rather the lingering blessing of her manner towards me that made this walk so memorable and dear. She was like the Sabbath prolonging the tenderness of its benediction and when we reached her step she asked me in to see her sister, so that our wonderful day might not come even here to its close . . . If ever I have lamented, 'Never the time and the place and the loved one altogether', I retract the words now, for that day all loveliness in earth and sky and in the heart of my friend combined to bless me. I watched the evening darken slowly and felt a great peace and a great joy and a great sadness as night approached. I had

been fed with a heavenly manna and was satisfied, but yet there
was pain in the declining hour and so I read the poem:

> 'Close in the nest is folded every weary wing,
> Hushed all the joyful voices and we who held you dear,
> Eastward we turn and homeward alone, remembering
> Day that I loved, day that I loved, the night is here.'

September 13th

One Sunday last winter I had invited Madame to tea with the
understanding that she would pay a visit to my bedroom in order
to see where I had placed her photo and also that I might show her
some of my other treasures. But alas, tho' we arranged the new
gold and green tea-set in the drawing room, the afternoon turned
out hopelessly wet and as Madame never uses the car on a
Sunday and as she always keeps to a decision once formed, I
remembered her warning that she would not come if it rained
and so ceased to expect her. Later in the week however as if she
divined the extent of my disappointment she rang up and asked
herself to tea and to the postponed inspection. This time she
came and duly christened the new tea service with coffee! . . .

[Gladys here reports previously mentioned anecdotes about
Sir Henry Irving and Ellen Terry.] Now Ellen Terry having lost
her memory often goes up to a policeman when out to ask where
she is going and the police who all know who she is tell her they
think she must be going home.[27] When she came here to unveil
the Siddons tablet[28] in 1922, Madame spoke to her at the
luncheon and asked her if she remembered her, mentioning her
name. 'Sarah Grand, Sarah Grand,' said Terry as if she were the
one friend she had longed to meet again, but Madame knew she
had no recollection of her whatever. . .

I now urged her to accompany me upstairs. She complied, telling me to show her the way, but I said we would go together and I
linked my arm in hers and we climbed the steps slowly, she
remarking on the wall paper and enquiring if it were a Morris
paper and stopping on the landing to look out of the window and
down at the row of gardens, each planted with individual taste
and indicative of the characters of their owners. We entered my
room, I closed the window and turned on the electric stove,
inviting her to my armchair beside it. I had placed a vase of lilies-
of-the-valley by her portrait and she paused, looking down at

them. 'Oh lilies!' she exclaimed in a tone that made me feel, as
once before when she uttered a like exclamation, that they are
favourites with her. Only that – she made no further comment
on the picture.

On a small table near the fire I had arranged a bowl of blue
hyacinths, some sweets and cigarettes. And I now took my usual
position at her feet offering her the sweets. But she refused, so I
took them instead saying we must have our midnight feast and
she helped herself to a cigarette which I lighted for her, and
joined her, smoking one myself . . . I questioned her if she were
happy when she was writing. 'Oh yes,' she answered, 'it is my
recreation.' And she gave one to understand that she had accomplished her literary works in intervals of more exacting employment. She told me she had written an essay once on happiness,
herself – that the *Winged Victory* (which she pronounced without
stressing the ed) was out of print and that the new publisher
would have none of her![29] *The Heavenly Twins* she said was stereo-
typed and could always therefore be reissued . . . Madame spoke
of voice production in contradistinction to elocution, saying she
never had any difficulty in filling a hall. 'My funny voice as you
call it,' she added, referring to a letter of mine in which I had
said, 'Do you know what a funny dear voice you have?' Now the
tears of tenderness sprang into my eyes and I leaned forward to
kiss her knees. Her little black clothed knees so close that I could
almost touch both with my lips in one kiss. 'Your funny voice,' I
repeated brokenly. 'I think it is like a corncrake!' she rejoined
jokingly to restore my composure. She related how she spoke of
'the happiness of talk' to Mr Cross (George Eliot's husband)[30]
and how he had said she meant 'conversation'. 'No,' she had
maintained, 'just talk like we are talking now.'

She said she thought I wouldn't like her novel *Babs the Impossible*. I amused her by telling her I had kept the cigarette that she
had smoked at the Orange Tea Rooms on the occasion of our first
meeting as friends and then I substantiated my statement by
showing it to her in its little silver snuff box. She laughed, and
entered girlishly with young understanding and sympathy into
my nonsense, when I took the one she had just finished and put it
beside the other. Humouring me she half teased me into
believing it was the one I had smoked which I was on the point of

saving, but I had the vulgar proof of having sucked mine, she having used a holder to smoke hers! The evening darkened without; within the glow became brighter and warmer and, shining upward, threw into strong relief the almost rugged lines of her features . . .

At last she rose, taking a look round, and stood before the window. A calendar, *The Light of the World*, illustrating great thoughts, hung on the shutter and above it some cardboard blue birds saved from one of last year's. 'Blue Birds,' she ejaculated. 'Yes,' I apologised. 'I'm afraid my room is an awful mix up.' 'I like mix ups,' she reassured me. Hers, she said, was in white and gold and her desk was always littered. My room she thought neat . . . I asked if I might give her the lilies and she said, 'I should like them.' I tied the lilies in a bunch with some ribbon and we descended the stairs again, the car having been announced. In the hall, after taking leave of Mother and saying she 'had enjoyed every minute', I gave them into her hand and was rewarded by the sweet upward glance of shy gratitude and she was gone.

September 15th

Sometimes there is a strange blankness, almost a blindness in her eyes – then it is that she is not seeing with them but with her mind. But if you claim her attention, her spirit wakes in their depths, timidly at first they meet your own, then with a directness that both withholds and reveals, and it is as if a blue flower spoke to you with the intelligence of another sphere, thrillingly, etherically sweet. Always, no matter with what confidence or sympathy we have parted, when we meet the next time I have to begin all over again to woo her from her reserve. Always I know that behind the still almost cold exterior there is a paradise of tenderness, beyond the wall a garden of fairest thoughts and sometimes she herself will set the door to her heart ajar. But frequently I have to push it with delicate hands, refusing to be discouraged. And yet when occasion warrants, she will be bold in her devotion to me; then no witnesses count and we are alone in our loyalty even in a crowd. She never shows surprise at any foolishness I may be guilty of, nor does she ever seek for ulterior motives . . . She is patient and long suffering with my sensitiveness, but has often given salutary clichés to my sentimentalism.

Often I have known her to put her little foot in it, as when she told me, without any thought of hurting, that she rarely wore grey after I had given her a grey bag. And again, that she had not been able to rouse herself to the effort of writing to me. It is because she has habituated herself to telling the truth . . . I have never been able to talk with anyone in the spirit before, but suddenly in absence her thoughts reach me and I answer, like Samuel, 'I am here.' Above the turmoil of other interests, above despondency, above fits of temper or laziness, the call will come, silver sweet and clear, and I am with her. This is my only hope and comfort when I contemplate the loss of one who is beyond all reckoning dear, that she may so come even unto the end.

September 17th

On June 6th I had been invited to two functions. One was a lecture at the Guildhall in aid of a Bird Sanctuary to be formed in Bath and the other was a Bazaar organised by the Salvation Army. I questioned only where I was most likely to find the Mayoress and decided on the Guildhall. When it was over Madame, having seen me in the audience, waved to me and I started towards her, as it were also on wings. We met at the foot of the platform, I indescribably joyful at our reunion, and she asked me to drive home with her . . . She was wearing the little white rose ring I had given her at Easter, on her finger next her wedding ring and the sight of it there woke my heart into a greater consciousness of love for her and a deeper need of her trust. I called to her, and for but the fourth time in all our hours of friendship she gave me the sacrament of her sweet face to kiss. Outside, her little lawn was thick with daisies and the remembrance of her was as of a white dove against my breast.

October 3rd

On July 8th Madame accepted an invitation to tea prior to our respective holidays. She had been suffering from sciatica so that her coming on foot was a brave tribute to our friendship . . . How happy we were! That wonderful unseen cord of sympathy and love binding us in willing, mystic union; on the instant in accord too, like notes attuned in all their tones and overtones. We entered the morning room in conscious harmony than which I ask no sweeter heaven, and Mother drew Madame's attention to the little white calf which had recently been born in the field . . . And I followed her over to the window putting my arm round her while together – together we gazed at the milky patch on the further green, so soon, alas! to disappear. Then she sat down and our usual pleasant talk ensued . . . I had arranged some strawberries in a Beleek basket in the centre with Beleek vases of white roses on either side. I helped her lovingly to the largest strawberries and we had coffee and thoroughly enjoyed it.

. . . Back in the morning room Mother offered cigarettes. 'I smoke too much,' Madame accused herself. 'Oh no, I don't think you do,' Mother was beginning politely. 'Don't tell her that,' I cut in. 'She does smoke too much though it is very disrespectful to say so,' I continued looking at her with apology and adoration. 'I like to be told my faults,' Madame encouraged me. 'It is the only fault she has,' I said, turning to Mother. 'How do you know?' asked the latter. But I was arrogant with my two years' experience of so perfect a character and persisted in my assertion. To Madame, smoking is I think more than it appears. A cigarette is the symbol of her feminine emancipation and the smoke the flag of her freedom . . .

Soon after this she rose to leave and asked me to accompany her home. I gathered up the white roses and together we started, despite the threat of rain, on foot, tho' I had offered to ring for a taxi . . . We walked on slowly until we came to the top where we sat down on the seat beside the telephone box. The wood was damp and I warned her not to stay there, but she said she didn't fear it if I didn't and so we stayed awhile. 'It is only a Scotch mist,' she remarked of the fine rain which now began to fall faintly, the mists sweeping from the opposite hills and darkening the dull afternoon.

Madame drew from her wedding finger the little ring I had given her at Easter, asking me to take it back as she felt Ina would not like her to have it as it had been a gift from my sister to me. I assured her otherwise and besought her to keep it, saying I should cry if she didn't. And in truth the tears had sprung to my eyes. 'See I am crying already,' I said and looked at her with eyes brimming. Madame, my darling, returned my gaze with a kind of wondering incredulity which changed to conviction, and slowly she replaced the ring, making room for it by taking off another. This she also half replaced and then quietly again withdrew it, offering it to me almost timidly, saying she would like me to have it if I cared for it. I took it from her reverently, overwhelmed at the gift and then asked her to put it on for me. 'Which finger will you have it on?' she enquired. I hesitated but a second. 'I shall never use this one now,' I replied, and without demur or surprise she put it on the third finger of my left hand, saying only she hoped it would not be too big. 'Oh Mother,' I murmured as I gazed at it, and then 'I am not worthy to wear your ring!' 'Hmm?' she questioned. But I could say no more and we got up to continue our walk up St Winifred's Lane . . .

Now she related me the history of the ring. How it had belonged to a Miss Walford who had given it to a Miss Heath and how it had figured in a case of law. How when the Miss Heath had died Madame had been asked to choose a remembrance and how she had chosen this little ring for its history and because it was not very valuable, only about £5 she said! 'And I have worn it ever since,' she ended. 'And now I have given it to you and some day you can give it to someone else.' 'Never, never,' I promised, my voice low and my heart full. The ring has three diamonds, the centre one in a star shaped setting. And so we came to the little straight terrace road leading into her domain. And today as once before I offered to hold her umbrella and today she gave it into my hand, tucking her own dear hand beneath my arm and so we walked up to her door. I could not help contrasting this occasion with that on which she had answered me, moving slightly away, with a single 'no' when I made to take her sun-shade. I thanked her for all she had done for me saying I should never have got through this winter without her. 'I don't know what I do,' she returned, 'I never can understand!'

[In December Sarah read this first volume of *The Record* and wrote to Gladys]

7 Sion Hill Place
Bath

16th Dec. 1928

Everybody's Gem but my Gladys
I was just going to answer your letter of the 10th when the

Diary arrived. Let me reassure you at once. There was no need to be in a panic about it. I really think I have been able to read it from your point of view as well as my own, and it has interested me greatly. Rather, in some respects, as fairy tales and fiction interest me. It has the faults of your qualities, and I allow for the licence to which the poetical bent in your attitude entitles you. We do not quarrel with the [artist?] for enhancing the [ordinary?] in nature, nor with the poet for doing the same for a friend. We know that the beauty that charms us is created by the magic of moonlight in the one case and of the poet's [mind?] in another, and are [captured?] by it all the [same?]. Only a prosaic [cavelling?] would break the charm by questioning its reality. We only wish it were so, with regard to the lady you describe. It is true that I never met her, but I do know a good deal about her, and there is little or nothing in what I know that shows her to me from your point of view. I only wish there were. As it is she is only to me an ordinary mortal transfigured at [- - -] by the magic of your love. What perhaps you sensed in her were latent possibilities, such as so many of us have in reserve for great occasions without knowing it; the springs of action; those actions to which we rise, as much to our own surprise sometimes as to other people's.

All the same I make bold to say that her friendship has done you good, by [letting?] you out of yourself at a difficult time, and you have only [not?] been the happier for it because you have yet to be [aware?] of tormenting yourself. All the bad moments you have had were about trifles which, at the worst, should hardly have cost you a passing qualm.

I have no time to go into details this morning. We must talk it over. There are things to be corrected if you are to keep the diary, noticeably lapses of memory. In several places you have misquoted me or misunderstood what I said. It is difficult to report conversation accurately and requires great practice.

I am so glad to hear that you have secured the house you wanted. I do hope you will soon all be happily settled in it, and that all will go well with you from now on. You will be all amongst friends there and much nearer to me, which will be one advantage. I don't see any of the [ladies?] you mention as - - but [constant?] they are and dear.

I hope to see you soon. It will be as soon as I can. But I am all in arrears with my shoppings for Christmas and . . .

I wish you good hunting, dear heart, as the animals say in *The Jungle Book*.

Ever yours lovingly
Sarah Grand

CHAPTER X

Sunday Afternoon Land: 1928–34

There were wings in your eyes tonight
Little blue wings that fluttered
As if your thoughts took flight
Beyond the words you uttered.

There were wings tonight in your eyes
Petal-sweet wings of azure,
As if like dainty butterflies
They shyly danced a measure.

There were wings in my eyes as well
Moth-like brown wings that brushed them,
As if so fragile were the spell
A deeper glance had crushed them.

Yet those wings in our eyes tonight
Thought-laden wings unbroken,
Were strong to bear in words despite
The love we left unspoken. [1]

Gladys' record continues, filling three more volumes – more than 100,000 words – describing six idyllic years full of Sunday tea parties, conversations and encounters, salted with occasional misunderstandings; the 'Sunday Afternoon Land' later fondly remembered by Sarah. As each of these three volumes of her journal was completed Gladys offered it up to Sarah for approval or destruction:

You see my Dearest I feel I must not keep it without your sanction because anything might happen to me and it might be found – though I have written it with no other intention than as a record of days so dear to me, so that in the years to come I may perhaps be able to live them over through its medium . . . But my Mother angel, if you want me to I will destroy it. We will burn it together.[2]

That was followed by 'Wise and Beautiful Writer of a wise and beautiful letter'[3] but Sarah's wise and beautiful words are not to be found. However, Sarah's reaction to another such offering is characteristic and gentle:

It was all very interesting to me, more especially in the revelation of yourself which it conveys. For your interpretation of me you deserve a place among those who are [joyful?] because they loved much. You make the common mistake of trying to express the inexpressible, and lose spiritual perception in the effort. Great [diarists?] have wrestled with the difficulty and kept examples of these failures which should serve as a warning not to make that attempt. There is a language of the heart, but there is no mental or material form which gives expression to what is immeasurably beyond and above what our hearts know of love; we must be exalted above all that in order to come into touch with the plane where love is, the spiritual plane. We must escape from our physical prison and rise to the higher plane to love truly, and leave it at that. To do otherwise makes confusion worse [– – –]. For the present I have locked the Diary up safely. We must have some big talks about it as soon as we can.[4]

During this period Sarah considered adapting *Babs the Impossible* for the stage, with Ina's assistance, and Gladys laboured over an anthology of quotations from Sarah's work. This anthology began with a suggestion of a Sarah Grand 'Book of Days' in calendar form (a letter from Miss Tindall praising the idea insists it would sell well in America) and grew into *A Sarah Grand Miscellany of Counsels and Conclusions* on subjects ranging through Sympathy, Friendship, Forgiveness, Courage, Dress, Marriage, Happiness, Punishment, etc. Most quotations were taken from *The Heavenly Twins* and *The Beth Book*, which Gladys by now knew inside out, and were annotated and amended by Sarah with such additions as:

The Position of Women – It is hard to determine whether man was created to make women weep or to keep them laughing (in their sleeves). Probably he was intended to answer both purposes.

Reflections – 'The tender grace of a day that is dead' is not to be revived by a fifty guinea auburn wig.

This last addition was possibly suggested when Sarah wrote to tell Gladys that an old hat Gladys had restored for her

is being worn every day. Nelly [sic] says I look nice in it. What she means is that it looks nice. I caught a glimpse, haphazard, in a mirror yesterday I was passing in the city of a dowdy figure which I did not recognise at the first glance. (Was *that* the face that launched a thousand ships!) There is no more looking nice for this sort of wreck.[5]

Dr Charles Whitby, a local clergyman, philosopher and admirer, who had made the original suggestion, wrote a useful introduction[6] to the proposed book and encouraged the project which they hoped to publish with a foreword by the Dowager Duchess of Beaufort.[7] Sarah and Haldane's daughter, Beth, discussed it with the publishers Grant Richards but offered it first to Heinemann:

Now we must get the thing off. Beth described it in one of her letters to Grant Richards, and he assured her he was greatly interested and would like to see it. So that is one string to our bow. But I feel that it is only fair to try Heinemann's first.[8]

But no interest was shown and Sarah wrote to Gladys consoling her over the failure of their first attempt to place it.

I was prepared for it and took it as a matter of course. It was sure to receive immediate attention and the reason for not letting me know their decision no doubt was the one I gave Dr Whitby. They did not want to publish it. Heinemann's does not publish that sort of thing as a rule, and at the same time they disliked having to refuse it. The excuse they finally hit upon was a good one. Such a publication at the present time is bound to be a failure financially. You must take it as only a check. Check No 1. It will be a case of *reculer pour mieux sauter*, you will see.[9]

Gladys did not give up. She abbreviated the book and it was finally printed locally under a new title: '*The Breath of Life*: *A Short Anthology of Quotations for Days and Months, from the Works of Sarah Grand*, to be sold for the benefit of the Mayoress Fresh Air Fund, Bath, price one shilling' (2s. 6d. autographed). The cover was decorated with drawings of a ragged child, fairies, imps and rabbits in a pastoral setting. Gladys worked unflaggingly for months on this, not only compiling the quotations, but typing all the drafts and redrafts, negotiating with printers and designers, checking proofs, painting the posters by hand, arranging publicity and delivering handbills, selling the pamphlet for weeks in cafés and departmental stores in the city and paying for the printing costs out of her own pocket. In all, it made £58 for the fund for poor city children, each day's selling never bringing in more than a couple of pounds.

While Gladys refused to accept any reimbursement for her work and continued to shower Sarah with flowers and presents, the Singers-Bigger finances were draining away at increasing speed. They sold their house in Marlborough Place overlooking the Royal Crescent lawns and moved up the hill to a less fashionable area, to 12 St James's Square. They sold the grand piano (replacing it with a Steinway upright), sold some china and talked of moving right away to Sidmouth. But there were compensations. Sarah wrote with increasing warmth: 'Ever yours, dearest, S.G.' (1929), and 'It is such a lovely

morning I should so like to be with you in the flesh as well as
the spirit' (1930), encouraging Gladys to a state bordering
on hysteria, but also giving her relief from the sordid
financial worries at home. Gladys in her turn wrote:

I could have sat in the mud in Milsom Street and howled for
you like a lost child, but I had just enough sense to go on
quietly home, and then I think your car passed me in George
Street and Oh! I wanted you.[10]

I went in the garden and called and called to you the other
night; I wanted you so – so badly Mother. You give me everything that makes life worth living and I can return you so little
except love and prayers and so I echo your lament with more
truth – my Dear, my only Dear, Your Gladys.[11]

Such letters were exchanged sometimes three times a day.
Sarah would write:

I wonder if you noticed the sunrise at 8 o'clock this morning.
It was so lovely as I saw it from my window through the bare
brown branches of the trees. I thought of you as I watched the
colours change and sent you my love and every good wish. I
thought of you too last night as the old year waned.[12]

Sarah did not always choose her words carefully enough
and it took her many years to realise how much more
Gladys could read into them. Poor Gladys grasped at every
encouragement and very little was required to bring on an
emotional outburst. Throughout November 1934 Gladys
was miserable and Sarah, in her favourite role as school
marm, wrote her letters about friendship:

I cannot stand schoolgirlieness and how schoolgirly, alas!
women are apt to be in their friendships. Why can't they be
friends as men are? Men rarely make any display of feeling
. . . Can you imagine a man exchanging notes on the subject
of their feelings and inspecting each other . . . Men are so
much more sympathetic deep down than women, so much
more observant, so much less self centred . . . It was a man to
whom I was grumpy of late, who laughed at me and said

'You're all out of sorts and ought to be in bed.' Not one of the women about me had observed that . . . You mustn't come near me again till I am not all out of sorts, dear one.[13]

All of this Gladys humbly accepted and, when the lectures were over, bounced back to her normal exuberance.

One conversation – about Virginia Woolf's *A Room of One's Own*, mentioned in the Record and amplified in letters – illustrates the different personalities of the two women. Gladys' turn of mind and her attitudes were often conservative and ill-informed and Sarah made painstaking and kindly attempts to educate her to some understanding of the freedom a woman could and should expect. This particular exchange demonstrates, too, the immense intellectual inequality between them and explains why Sarah felt more sense of kinship with Miss Tindall. It also shows why she treated Gladys as though she were little more than a child. This of course suited Gladys who wanted to be mothered by Sarah, and to some degree the charm of the diary depends on the infantile quality of their relationship. This letter from Sarah, dated 26 January 1930, summarises the problem:

I shall be so interested to hear your revised opinion of parts at least of *A Room of One's Own*. Your first impression was unexpected enough to be a shock. It had never struck me that you were an ultra Victorian. The grown up girls used to [attack?] me when I was in the schoolroom, and just beginning to rebel vociferously, with the same arguments. You make me feel young again, an experience one always delights in. But why should you apologise for differing from me just because I gave you the book? It is dull to have a friend who sees only from my point of view, dull to be always in agreement. Differences of opinion are interesting not irritating, to discuss; they keep up the conversation and give point to it. There is value, too, in an opposite point of view, and [enlightenment?]when it is discussed with the breadth and breeding that saves one from bitterness. There are [wide?] differences of opinion on the subject of this book, some of them curiously

unexpected. I lent my copy to Miss Tindall, half expecting her
to dislike it, but she wrote yesterday: 'I am so much *enjoying*
your book (*Room*) – but I can't read it all at once – much of it
is too too poignant – it brings back much that I would rather
forget.' You might think that she had had everything in life,
wealth, position, and friends, that heart could desire. Will you
be able to imagine, I wonder, what the one thing necessary
was, which was denied her. You have been singularly
fortunate if you cannot – or, to me, singularly content with
the lot that was mapped out for you – I mean too content ever
to be aware of how some were being cramped and suffering by
being forcibly kept in places in which they had no room to
expand*. I am all with you in regard to the Woman's Sphere,
only I don't see it as contained in the walls of a house. The
whole world is the Woman's Sphere. And, in my experience,
the best home-makers are the women who know well the world
outside of the customary and conventional limits.

But I am lecturing, and it isn't fair when you are not here to
defend your position. Besides I really ought not to be gossip-
ing with you. I have a piece of work on hand that I must finish
for Beth to type before she goes back to Weston-s-M on
Tuesday. It is that which has prevented my writing to you
every day since Thursday. A case of duty first. But always by
the time I had finished work for the day, I was [– – –] myself.
Don't please, feel that I do not neglect you in the most
important particular. I think of you often, with love.

Ever yours, Sarah Grand.

(* You do not even realise that the liberty of action you
[are] enjoying was won for you by women who had to fight for
it till they dropped dead, [– – –] in very truth.)

In 1929 Cedric Chivers died, ending Sarah's public life
abruptly. In 1932 she relinquished the Presidency of the
local National Council of Women, and in 1933 she made
her last public speech. In 1934 Gladys first met Sarah's
son.

After his mother left Warrington, and probably after his
father's death, David Archibald Edward McFall had

studied drama as a pupil of Sarah Thorne's, at Margate. Sarah Thorne also coached 'the Vanbrughs, Arthur Bourchier and others as well known',[14] and through her Archie must have been introduced to other actor-managers such as the Boucicaults. He later joined Mrs Bandman-Palmer's company playing small Shakespearian roles before turning to light comedy with some success. He continued this unspectacular career all his life, more often than not 'resting' or working as stage manager for repertory companies, and, when all that failed, as it did increasingly, he became dependent upon his mother – a role that aggravated them both. 'As he put it himself, he did not retire from the stage, the stage retired from him.'[15] He assumed the name of Archie Carlaw Grand presumably hoping that some of Sarah's fame would rub off on him and, like her, was never afterwards called McFall, though he was proud of his family heritage and told Gladys about the Clan Chattan 'of which the McFalls have the honour to be a minor sept'.[16] Although Sarah's stepsons had often stayed with her, Archie appears not to have visited his mother for any length of time until she was in Bath. It is understandable that he should have felt embittered by her desertion of himself and his father, and his letters to Gladys show a robust and healthy disregard for his mother whom he referred to as S.G.:

To my mind, searching for excuses or extenuations for strange or unusual parental behaviour is mere waste of time – like raking for moss-agates in a bay of pebbles. There is never any useful purpose in reviving 'has-beens.'[17] When you say that you got some good coffee at Sion Hill you simply amaze me – it will take years to obliterate the memory of the filthy coffee they gave me at Christmas to say nothing of some of the food efforts.[18]

In 1931 Archie first visited Bath Theatre Royal in a production of Charles III, and in 1934 when he met Gladys, he was again in Bath, as stage manager of Ina's play, *Arising Out of the Minutes*. On these occasions he stayed with his mother at Sion Hill Place. Their relationship had by now become calm and cordial; more than sixty years old, and periodically dependent on Sarah, Archie had little alternative, and Sarah began to take an interest in her son. She had already discussed him with Gladys in 1931:

Archie has two small parts in the Nigel Playfair play neither of which give him a chance to show what he can do but he is glad to be doing something again. It was Phyllis N. Terry's husband who got him the engagement.[19]

And when he was next in Bath she became more expansive about him:

I do hope Archie will prove to have really been of some use. I have heard that he is a good stage manager. But I don't think he has ever dealt with amateurs before. I am amused by what you say about his appearance. He has been mistaken for Lord Rosebury[20] (I haven't a notion how to spell his name) but you will know who I mean. I think Archie looks like a bishop in mufti. Daisy Ross describes the effect of what she calls his 'dukecal voice' when he asked for a pound of beefsteak one day in a butcher's shop. Heredity plays queer tricks. He was made to play the part of a sometime gentleman of property of the non-sporting type, a bit *dilettante*, loving flowers and animals and kind to them. He is essentially kind, punctilious, scrupulous, honourable, *au-déla de la lettre*. The kind of thing known as 'a gentleman' for short. And of course he has his faults and peculiarities . . . Please wish Ina a brilliant success on Thursday with my love. She deserves it. Archie . . . thinks her a great actress.[21]

Archie expresses himself as 'proud and pleased' with Ina's presentation, and her complimentary note. He says he has not had many compliments of that kind during the 30 years he has been stage manager . . . The little change did him good. He has been sadly depressed of late, and no wonder.[22]

I am glad to hear that Ina's play is attracting attention. It seems to have brought Archie a [streak?] of luck. A mention of him in a notice of it which appeared in a London paper

probably acted as a reminder that he was still alive. At any rate
he was offered a small part in the try out of Ridley's new play
'Glory Be'[23] at the Arts Club last Sunday and was com-
plimented by the producer after the performance. It is to be
repeated next Sunday, with a view to [placing?] it in a West
End Theatre. It has had a 'good press', it seems, so 'Here's
hope!' as Archie says.[24]

During much of this period Beth stayed at Sion Hill
Place. Beth was a sensible, amusing woman, refreshingly
irreverent; she typed Sarah's official correspondence and
any articles she may have begun, tried writing herself and
became friendly with Edna, the maid. It was a convenient
arrangement for her to stay with Sarah because her
daughter, Felicitas (nicknamed Winkie), was at school
nearby, and she was separating from her husband, a
King's Messenger stationed in Germany. Presumably,
when she had found somewhere else to live, Beth departed
leaving Sarah *in loco parentis* for Winkie. At the time of
Sarah's death she was living near Aberdeen. Winkie, 'a
dreamy, poetic child',[25] was born in 1921; according to
Gladys she went on to Bedford College when she had
finished at the convent, and married two years before
Sarah died. Beth also had two sons, one of whom, Patrick
Michael Robbins, died in 1939. A schoolboy, he was
accidentally poisoned and, as Sarah reported to Gladys,
'Beth herself was prostrated with grief. It is a cruel
misfortune which has robbed the other boy of his brother.
They had never been separated.'[26](However, Gladys only
refers to 'Dick' or 'Donald' as a young boy visiting Sion
Hill Place with Beth.)

Bath 1928

September 14th

The front door open, a vase of single dahlias on the table, the
dear perfume of the house. Madame was sitting facing the door,
on the sofa, engaged in a game of Patience. She rose as I entered,

looking white and pulled down by her recent illness. I asked
about her eye which was giving her trouble with inflammation,
but she avoided my glance sensitively and sat down in another
chair, putting on gold-rimmed spectacles and saying she could
see me at any rate. I replied I had grown fat, to which she
answered that I was before too thin and enquired how tall I was.
She told me she was 5ft 4½ and weighed just on 10st. 'One's
muscles get set as one grows older and one weighs more,' she
said. She thought she had strained her eye reading at night
because she can't sleep. Talking of my sister Ina not getting a
theatrical engagement, she spoke for the first time to me of her
son Archie saying he had been with the Boucicaults and after had
been out two years before he had got anything to do.

I went and sat beside her chair having divested myself of my
coat; she liked the green buttonhole which went with my hat. I
drew her attention to the ring she had given me and then she
thanked me for the little scent bottle I had brought her from
London, reproaching herself for not having mentioned it earlier:
'I really am a pig!' I asked her if she had found the note I had put
inside and to discourage sentiment on my part she told me she
had got it out with a hairpin! We discussed my plan for buying a
house in St James's Square. She strongly disapproved of my
investing my capital in such a scheme and made various other
suggestions. We also spoke of Beth and of her little daughter
Winkie who is being educated at the Sacré Coeur, Weston S.
Mare[27] and is quite at home there with the Mother Superior,
swinging her rosary back and forth and being called Sister
Felicitas . . .

And then Madame turned to me with an effort and asked,
'Does it look very badly?' The appeal broke something in my
heart and I hastened to reassure her. 'No of course not, my
Sweet, but you must take care of them, they are such lovely eyes.'
It was such pain to me to see them like this, dimmed as if her
spirit had receded from them, taking with it all their colour and
much of their expression. They are so much a part of her that she
seemed but half herself without their speaking aid. But that
appeal proved she was still with me and in my response we were
at one again, her little soft hand close against my cheek . . . Then
we spoke of the Mayoralty and she told me as a great secret, 'at
least I'm not going to be Mayor of Bath'. And how she

had been approached to take the Mayor's place and that he should be her deputy. She said one is not formally invited until one offers in a sense, so that the Mayor had asked her and she had refused. She couldn't let him be her deputy! But she had said she was game to continue Mayoress for as long as she could with the understanding that she might resign if she found it too much for her. I tried to dissuade her and she acknowledged she wanted to live her own life, especially at this end of it but she felt as he was so ill she could not refuse him. She was, she said, accustomed to entertaining, had had it all her life so it didn't tire her. In some ways she liked the work . . .

October 6th

It was like waking from a bad dream to be with her again. My little Mother was wearing a plaid skirt in shades of pink and fawn. She looked stronger and her eyes, though weak still and pale behind her 'owly' glasses, appeared brighter and more expressive. Her whole bearing was more energetic and she moved more quickly and with greater ease. Her colour too was healthier and had a tinge of pink. She was using the bag I had sent her and told Miss Clarke that she had discovered the donor. I had put a card inside but she had not guessed it was I, as I had not signed it. 'For my Treasure's treasures', I had written. 'If you have many people who write to you like that I shall be jealous,' I teased her and she laughed with some of her old appreciation of fun, enjoying with simplicity the flattering chaff. She said that everyone she had shown the card to had thought it was printed. 'Well I wish you wouldn't show these things,' I cried and again she laughed with me, neither confessing to or denying my earlier implication. I gave her some red roses and a sprig of honeysuckle, saying I had seen on a film that one only gave red roses to people one loves, so she must have red now as well as white, and the honeysuckle was because she was so sweet. She replied, fingering them gently and laying them against her breast, that she had a vase upstairs for the flowers that were specially hers . . .

I had much I wanted to say to her but as usual my problems faded into insignificance in her presence. I have never felt more clearly the difference of her plane and mine. Her state of consciousness is above mine at every point – that we meet at all is remarkable – it is only love that has taught me her language and a perception of what is fair, for it is not natural to me. Neither is the lower, I feel myself betwixt and between. Ah, lean down and lift me to them, Mother, Mother! And so she did, for in bidding farewell – after promising to come to see us as she 'must not forget how to walk' – she kissed my cheek of her own dear accord, and I left her ennobled by that accolade.

November 9th

We decided to witness the Mayor Making and arrived with Miss Lloyd at the Guildhall. After some demurring on Jordan's (the Mayor's Officer) part and courageous persuasion on Miss Lloyd's, we were taken upstairs past the Mayor's parlour to the Council Chamber. I had never before visited this imposing and beautiful room and as we slid into our places in the polished wood gallery I felt the elation that always comes to one when a building satisfies my taste. Highly polished walnut furniture, curved desks and table, chairs and carving above and around the Mayoral chair, a pale wine-coloured carpet, pink marble pillars and dark oil-paintings of former Mayors dusky in gilt frames. The Arms of Bath in evidence and outside the brilliant sunshine of a glorious November morning.

The Councillors entered in twos and threes, their robes showing a dull sapphire and here and there came the more sombre violet of an Alderman. Reporters sat at the centre table and wives of Councillors just beneath us. The three women Councillors looked rather peculiar with their stiff three cornered hats in black felt, a little top heavy. Mrs Devenish was still wearing her moonstone necklace and ear-rings, with a pale green jersey beneath the dark blue robe. Mrs Latter Parsons looked like a dried up chicken in glasses with a funny crest entirely out of keeping with the general effect. Jordan carefully arranged the scarlet robe destined for the Mayor over the back of his chair and later the Mace bearers entered, placing the City maces cross-wise on their stands in front of the Mayor's desk on the dais, where they gleamed golden and impressive.

Very quietly, Madame came into the room by a side door and made her way to the top of the chambers, where she was greeted by Sir Harry Hatt. She was carrying a bouquet of multi-coloured carnations, scarlet, red, mauve, yellow and pale pink. She was in a black cloak with an oppossum collar and wore her black velvet hat with the diamante ostrich feather ornament I loved so much. She was pale but not as tired looking as I had expected, though she stumbled slightly as she climbed towards the rostrum and turned smiling with her darling irresistible charm to Sir Harry Hatt who started forward to assist her. As ever, one's heart went out to her with a great wave of tenderness and concern and one involuntarily exclaimed, 'She is a darling!' as if the discovery were new. Once seated on the chair immediately at the left of the throne, she surveyed the room with composure and I think found us in the gallery for she looked towards us several times.

Soon the Mayor entered and took his place of honour . . . The Mayor and she having been unanimously re-instated he was helped once more into his scarlet robe by Jordan who also placed the chain of office round his neck. Sir Harry Hatt performed the like service for Madame. It rested a moment outside her fur collar and she smilingly adjusted it for herself, lifting the corners of the fur so that it set more gracefully on her shoulders, and clasping the hook in front, patting it almost with affection. It was a touching moment for me and the tears sprang to my eyes as I saw her re-assume the badge of her captivity to a fine ideal for the sake of duty and friendship. The Mayor then took the oath standing and signed the Roll of Mayors and then turned at once and shook hands with Madame. Thereupon he addressed the Council . . . ending with a personal tribute to the Mayoress for so gallantly – 'I think I may say gallantly' – coming to his aid earlier in the year. We could hear the Abbey bells ringing their announcing joyous chime to the City.

. . . Once or twice Madame looked out at the slanting brightness of a sunbeam striking athwart the roofs, and at the patch of blue sky above. And once she held my eyes with her own remotely yet intently as if she would transfer a message to my heart. It was not a similar smiling gaze as once before, slowly dawning into spiritual beauty, but a serious look as of a plea for understanding, a laying on of a trust, a 'remember me' infinitely sad, infinitely deeply calm and loving, like resignation or leave taking. Once a fleeting shadow accentuated her age and look of ill health and a fear gripped me, spreading its shock upon my shoulders as of something foreboding, but it was but fleeting. As ever, her motherhood called me and, as ever, I seemed to melt into a child, to dwindle into babyhood in her presence, desiring only to be held close against the breast to which I seem to belong, to feel the softness and purity of its all enveloping, all comprehending sympathy . . .

December 6th

Madame invited me to go with her to the concert at the Guildhall in aid of the Red Cross. She called for me accompanied by Miss Bellenden Clarke and Miss Harford. . . At the foot of the stairs we met Jordan who approached Madame with the news that the Mayor had had a fainting fit. Madame took it calmly and together we went out of the building and crossed the muddy road to walk to Fortts for tea. As we passed the brightly lighted shops my Darling who was in front arm-in-arm with Miss Harford, turned gaily saying, 'Choose anything and I'll buy it for you!' She was in a holiday mood which the news she had received had heightened rather than depressed with an unacknowledged prospect of coming freedom . . .

All at once we became conscious that the orchestra was playing the *Barcarolle* from *The Tales of Hoffmann*. Miss Clarke looked at Madame with a kind of understanding apprehension. For a moment Madame resisted the appeal of the music then, with an intensity of expression I have seldom heard her use, she said, 'I hope to God that someone will play that when I am dying.' [It was played on a gramophone at The Grange, Calne, a few days before her death – see P358] 'Oh Madame,' I cried, half in pain, half in incredulity. 'Do you love it so?' She nodded, then suddenly she was rapt from us into a trance of memory. Her dear eyes so beautifully old, so tenderly young were suffused, her mouth folded in a line of such poignant sweetness that I could not look again. Her little hands on the table before her moved occasionally to the beat of the music and of her heart. No one else could have given themselves up to emotion of the kind at such a moment without seeming to pose, but in her it was different, it was so strong, so holy, that we respected it as a confidence first, and then we began to partake of it as a communion. And I felt in those moments that my love for her, and Miss Harford's, joined with that other remembered love of hers and went up between us as a flame purified and never to be forgotten.

December 14th

I had tea with Mrs Sonnenschein who lives in Madame's terrace, at No. 4. I had taken the diary I had kept . . . that which I call 'The Lesser Boswell' for fun, determining to leave it for Madame to read, as I went home. It was dark when I left Mrs Sonnenschein's and I walked up and down the terrace in the cold irresolutely for some minutes before I rang Madame's bell and handed in the book. It was, I felt, a real test of her friendship but one which it was due to her I should make.

December 17th

She did not keep me long in suspense. This day she sent me the wise and beautiful letter which I have enclosed at the end of the first volume of *Ideala's Gift* [the diary].

December 21st

I saw her at the Venture Club. We were a little shy of each other. Avoiding and seeking her eyes, at last I met them and knew she understood. My test had not failed, she asked me as we parted when I wanted her to come to the Teas. I replied fervently, 'I always want you,' touching her hand in farewell as she held the back of a chair. And she laughed – we were happy.

Bath 1929

. . . On the 30th of January 1929, the Mayor of Bath, Alderman Cedric Chivers, passed away. Rain had fallen for two days, a continuous misty rain that seemed as if the City was weeping its coming loss. The shops displayed mourning. At night I wrote to dear Madame in sympathy. On February 1st I was desperately depressed that I could not help my dear through the morrow.

February 2nd

The day of the funeral and again the rain poured. As soon as my sister arrived home from a visit, she joined me and together we drove to the Abbey. We had to stand some time but got in at last. When the coffin was carried in through the centre doors, it was draped with a violet pall bordered with red and gold lettered text. A wreath of beautiful red and creamy roses from Madame and one of carnations rested upon it. Madame walked close after. So tiny and sad she looked with the dark rim of her glasses making even her sweet eyes mourn. She was in black with white tulle round her throat. I felt too awfully for her. I did not know I could suffer vicariously with such pain. Yet I mourned personally too, the end of a golden era for Bath. It was like the closing of an illuminated missal. We had another glimpse of my Darling, looking straight before her at the funeral motor just in front of her car, as they moved slowly up Union Street. I wrote to her – she was so brave.

February 7th

I took some mauve tulips to dear Madame and asked about her, glad to have good news. Madame telephoned on my return and invited me to see her after tea. I went at 4.30 and was with my Darling till 6 and was happy and at peace at last. She was in her quietest black. I have kept no detailed record of our conversation. That day was too holy; but sitting at her feet I asked her if she ever came to me in spirit as I had at times imagined. She sat silent for a few moments pulling gently at my wristlet watch as if she would annihilate time between us and then replied gently, evasively, 'I think of you often' . . . She showed me a little box Winkie had painted. Then, I put my arms about her in farewell, and for an instant she bowed her head upon my shoulder. 'My dear, my dear, I know what you've been through – I know, I know,' my heart spoke to her. At once she rallied herself and me, looking up. 'Nonsense!' she said, 'I haven't been through anything,' and moved from me across the room. She had given her youth and her health to us all, and that was her pronouncement upon her sacrifice and devotion. As I walked down the Avenue my face was bathed in tears, and the glimmering lights in the valley were blurred and shattered by them . . .

April 12th

A letter from my Angel Madame who never fails me when I appeal to her, asking me to tea and to read her my paper on *Dickens and Detail* this afternoon . . .

May 29th

. . . I spent the morning buying things and preparing for this afternoon when my darling Madame came to tea. She was looking so much better despite a tooth which had been giving her pain, and was in a particularly happy mood. One little curl of her fringe came over the brim of her hat. She said Norwich Cathedral satisfied her most of all the Cathedrals she had seen . . . Bret Harte[29] blamed American women for taking on the characteristics of other nationalities if they lived long out of America.

Miss Clarke was with her and we showed them both over our new house, 12 St James's Square. Madame stayed awhile in my room and I called her attention to some of my souvenirs. 'I do remember some things,' she said, reproaching gently my mistrust of her recollection of them and the occasions they marked . . . Before she went she left one of her cards in each of our bedrooms, turning down the corners to signify a personal visit and writing a message of goodwill on Mother's. No one, I told her, kneeling before her, would think of and do such dear things. I kissed her impulsively and then feared I had hurt her because of her tooth, but she reassured me and returned my kiss with tenderness. I wanted to go to Weston-super-Mare whence she was bound, on her birthday, but she gently told me Beth had prior right on that day and she would ask me down on another day. I felt a swift revulsion of feeling, the old pain of never being the first. But I crushed it down, unworthy, and when later I went on the Common I remembered only the deep and wistful sincerity of her kiss.

June 18th

Thanks to my Darling, who spared herself not at all to give me pleasure, I had one of the happiest days of my life alone with her at Weston-super-Mare. When I arrived rather nervous and flustered, she was standing outside the Atlantic Hotel with her back to me and her sunshade up, looking out to sea. I ran up to her and she turned with the sea still in her eyes. We went into the Moorish lounge for a cigarette and then had lunch in the big dining room whence I could see the bay and headland to the left. She let me choose every course and had the same herself, even to my plebeian choice of ginger beer to drink which she pretended gaily afterwards had gone to her head. When Madame gave a tip to the waiter it was as if she conferred a blessing with it.

Afterwards we tidied ourselves in the cloakroom and I would

have fastened her glove for her but that she had done it herself.
'Darling,' I said. 'Hm?' she asked looking up questioningly.
'Just Darling,' I answered and we went out along the front and
took a tram to Anchor Head . . . She spoke of friends who had
gone and said, 'It was rather pathetic to be a survival.' 'Long
may you continue to be one,' I rejoined and clasped her hand
with a sudden realisation of what life without her would be for
me. She had mentioned a whole list of (titled) people who she was
friends with at one time, Lady Henry Somerset[30] among them,
and said they were all dead, only Lady Jackson[31] and herself
remained. Once at a rather stiff dinner there was a lull in the conversation and she had heard her own voice 'trained to carry' say,
'I like my drinks strong!' This was *à propos* of the strong cup of tea
I had poured out for her. She related the gist of an article written
at her expense when she courageously wore the new costume in
Paris, then thought very daring. The article ended with the
words: 'Some day she will look at it and wonder how she could!'
She described, too, the Convent where she was staying. She rose,
she told me, at 6 a.m. and made tea for Beth and Miss Harford
who, I thought, should have made it for her. When we first went
into the lounge before lunch Darling told me she had been
reading a story by John Buchan and added, she liked boys' books
as they were so clean. 'I am quite a well known character here!'
she said referring to the Hotel. 'And not only here!' I caught her
up, pleased with my complimentary repartee which pleased her
too I think. I had to catch the 5.2 train back to Bath and Darling
insisted on my taking her little packet of matches in case I needed
them . . .

July 2nd

My so happy day was followed by a period of slight misunderstanding with my Darling. It came about through a letter. It had
reference to confidences and how these, if reported, may fail in
accuracy. Madame has all an Irishwoman's pride of family and
respect for ancient names, which traits are in direct contrast to
the Christian Liberalism of her Creed. In a Revolution I can
better imagine her going to the Guillotine than wearing the
bonnet-rouge, for though a rebel at heart in some ways, she is
instinctively an aristocrat in essentials. Finely wrought as a
sword; that honourable weapon is an appropriate symbol for her

who relies upon justice to point the way through conflicting ideas of conduct. In a former diary I had wrongly repeated an item of conversation which seemed to countenance an occupation of a relative out of keeping with his birth and the facts of the case. Darling reminded me of the slip, which she had corrected, in warning me of others and I was stung to retort by taking a mean advantage of her in citing an example which was true in my own family, of which up to then she had known nothing. Instead of treating me to the silence I deserved she wrote, opening her response with the cry of 'Oh I say, my dear . . . don't . . .' I recall now the capitulation of my own pride to that cry and how I sprang out of bed in happy tears to answer it, to tell her she had come back to me, so that the letter might reach her before night-fall and our little difference be healed. By July 8th she was at home again.

July 22nd

I walked up to see my Darling Madame. Miss Clarke stayed in the room during the whole time so we didn't have the quiet talk together I had so hoped for. Madame was playing Emperor Patience, the game which Napoleon played I believe on the eve of Austerlitz. We spoke of him and Madame referred to his mas-sacre of prisoners in Egypt as unpardonable. She looked at the book on lace which I had brought to show her. It was one I had bought for Mother long ago as a birthday present after we had read Madame's novel *The Winged Victory*. I told her it was a souvenir of the pleasure we had derived in reading her work . . .

July 31st

By a joyful chance I met my Darling Madame just as I took Bozzy out, at the corner of Park Street and walked with her to the Circus. Unfortunately, I let my dear black dog Bozzy off the lead for a moment and in trying to catch him quickly again I collided with Madame and nearly upset her. But she never lost her dignity and absolved me with blue eyes flickering with amusement . . .

[During the following three months they both take holidays and Sarah suffers from headaches and colds which prevent Gladys from visiting as often as usual.]

November 24th

A letter from Madame Darling to ask me not to come today as her son Archie had arrived unexpectedly and they had family confidences to talk about. Such a happy and excited little mother . . .

Bath 1930

January 14th

. . . While I was making my bed a book, *A Room of One's Own* by Virginia Woolf, came for me from Madame with a darling letter. She had written in the book, copying a eulogistic critique with characteristic generosity to a fellow author, ignoring the fact that she herself had said it all long before. I was very happy and thanked her at once.

More women have distinguished themselves than men in a state of subjection. Aessop is the only slave I can think of who distinguished himself in literature. A subjugated race produces no great work of art; why do you expect a subjugated sex to produce more than a subjugated race under similar circumstances. *Babs the Impossible*

January 19th

I went to tea with my Darling Madame . . . Beth and Miss Clarke at tea. We talked of ghosts and paper combines and inter-viewing. Upstairs we discussed *A Room of One's Own* which I criticised adversely. She disagreed with my opinion and men-tioned a grandmother who had spent most of her time brushing her hair through sheer boredom. She spoke of *Middlemarch*[32] as the best study of town and country life ever written, saying she had known both. 'And men are sometimes right,' she replied to what I said on a certain question. She lent me *The Hidden City* by Sir Philip Gibbs[33] recommending *The Six Mrs Greens*[34] as another book worth reading. I used my cigarette holder which she had given me, for the first time . . . Madame spoke of Anthony Hope's[35] advice at a public dinner 'to take a gulp of Cham-pagne before speaking'. I replied I thought this a fallacy, that drink made one think one was being brilliant but that the effect on others was to the contrary . . . Her eyes were like lavender pools but her little face was white and rather thin. She put her hand on my shoulder coming down the stairs and came out to the doorstep, advising me to go by the lightest way. . . .

The weeks following I was not wholly myself for the dog I loved so, my black ·Bozzy, was suffering from his last illness and on February 24th I had to part with him. I wrote constantly and sent foolish things to my Darling who, in her patience, accepted them. On the 8th I heard she had had a touch of flu. I heard from her on St Valentine's day and on the 18th she telephoned to ask after Bozzy and said I might come to tea on the Friday.

I think God gave me that respite to prepare and strengthen me for what followed, for I spent one of the happiest and most peaceful afternoons of my life in the paradisal company of my dear . . .

On the 1st of March I met Dr Whitby who told me of a project to compile a Day Book of quotations from the works of Madame Sarah Grand, for which he was writing a preface.

On the 3rd a letter came from my Darling asking me to contribute my favourite quotations to the contemplated book. I had already begun a calendar of my own so I had only to look out a few more. The next day I wrote to her and another letter came from her about my Bozzy . . .

March 23rd

I went to tea with my Darling through the rain and through my tears for Bozzy. She was in her amethyst velvet, and Miss Clarke was there. At tea, in the drawing room (it was served on the card table by the sofa and we drew up to it comfortably) she ate very little and rose instead to light a cigarette. Then she told me she had been feeling very sore about the oil portrait of herself by Praga[36] which the late Mayor had given her, and which she had allowed the Victoria Galleries to house for her. Apparently the Executors of Alderman Chivers have appropriated the picture . . . We talked of *Babs the Impossible* her novel, and she said it was so palpably 'a pot-boiler' that she wouldn't have written it now as she would have been afraid of hurting people's feelings. I said I liked Miss Spice but 'she's so silly' Darling replied and said she preferred Mr Jellybond-Tinney.

. . . We talked too of Mrs Meynell,[37] a life of whom Madame had been reading. She told me how Mrs Meynell would sit in her room, surrounded by noisy children and write her poetry on her knee in pencil, and added that she had wonderful powers of concentration.

Madame stayed at the Burford Bridge Hotel with her when her children were visiting George Meredith whose house was not large enough to hold Mrs Meynell too. She wished to introduce him to Madame but Madame demurred, knowing he was in ill health, and said if he wished to know her, he would call. (Sure enough he intimated his desire to be presented and came, and they were good friends.) He was suffering from locomotor attaxi then and could only walk slowly. She would go with him sometimes. 'Did he talk like his books?' I asked. 'No,' she replied, 'he was not obscure.' She used to sit on the floor and talk to him and he would get her little bottles of Champagne which he could not share, and would say, 'Ah! Sarah! if only we had met 10 years ago!' (meaning that then he would have been able to join her in the refreshment).[38]

She told me of a black brocade dress which she wore in Paris but which a Parisian dressmaker insisted on making over for her and adding just the touch that made all the difference, a *chou* of blue ribbon. 'And it was worth it,' she mused, and I could well believe how lovely she had looked. She told me that her first dance was at Singapore. She was only 18 but had been married two years. She got many partners being the only young girl present. She told me, too, that she married to get away from School which she hated . . . Beth, Madame says, is very psychic and writes verses and essays and is not at all like the woman she appears to be, it amuses her to shock people and make them think her wicked.

I asked Madame who 'Ella' would marry after *The Winged Victory* fiasco, and she replied that she had thought of marrying her to Adnam. She suggested my adopting an orphan to console myself for losing Bozzy. 'Pets don't last,' she said . . . She insisted on my wearing Beth's mackintosh home and went herself to get it down for me, helping me into it. We went into the dining room while I put on my rubber boots and then in the hall I held her close and the nightmare of these last weeks lifted from me. The pain of love was alleviated by love itself . . .

April 2nd

I had a letter from Miss Tylee offering me the secretaryship of the Poetry Circle. This threw me into uncertainty as to the wisest course of action so I telephoned to my Darling and asked if I might come and ask her advice. We met on the hill and when she heard my problem she said not to tie myself down to anything more like that. We had a happy time walking up and down the terrace, she said her one weapon of defence was 'indifference'. She believed in preserving one's liberty of action. She spoke of 'Pussy Cat Gosse' (Sir Edmund Gosse)[39] and told me he was as clever in conversation as in his writing, but could be a rather unkind critic. I was most relieved at her decision and acted on her advice, declining the post, and have never regretted the step.

April 3rd

I went up to my Darling to help her sort her quotations at 11 a.m. It was pouring with rain. I spent a happy morning, she is wonderful. Standing by the fireplace in her little jacket she was full of energy and spoke to me of her relations as to an audience, her words so beautifully chosen and graphic. She said she thought she was the reaction from a line of women who had always thought it a duty to suppress themselves. She said too that she thought she could work with me as a Secretary, that I had a critical faculty; most women judged by feeling. She also said that she thought I had served my apprenticeship to the 'Societies' and should now do other things.

She liked finding passages in her books which she agreed with, they came quite new to her, and we talked of the comfort one's own words hold for one when as an inspiration they are rediscovered. She became impatient of the monotony of the work soon and struck it for a cigarette, and we sat looking at the fire and I read her my letter to Miss Tylee which she thought could not have been better. In the afternoon Miss Tindall left the MS of *The Day Book* as Madame had consented to my working on it at home. (The following paragraph was written later:

On the 5th I began my work on it, and was very absorbed and contented. Barney, Bozzy's brother, sat with me. It was the beginning of a year's application and coming at this time of my need it is scarcely too much to say that it saved my reason and restored my interest in life. My mother joins me in feeling a lasting gratitude to Madame for thus helping me. I sorted and arranged the quotations according to days and subjects and took them as I completed the months to Beth to type, or she would come to me, and then I would correct the typed script.)

April 13th

I went up to Darling Madame in the morning and was happy reading her the extra quotations I had selected for her Book. Beth said she wanted some 'spicey bits' and quoted one she remembered from *The Winged Victory*. Madame sat beside me, saying at intervals, 'Yes, that's true isn't it? I agree with that!' 'Yes, put that in,' and of the 'Sociocrat' passage she said she was glad I had included it. Of the Dawn description in *The Beth Book*, Beth opined it must have been written on the East Coast as the country, being flat, was not referred to. Madame agreed. It was a memory of her childhood, her first sunrise . . . Of the fine grief passage of widowhood in *The Heavenly Twins* Beth said, 'No one would talk like that!' 'They do in books,' answered Madame . . . Madame lit a cigarette at last as she felt it was becoming embarrassing. Beth wanted a section devoted to animals and thought again that we needed more 'spicey bits' as all that was sob-stuff. Madame was strong in her approval of the passage against vivisection and said later that it was interesting to see the different tastes of those who had chosen selections. Miss Harford had inclined to love and marriage. Beth picked up a copy of *Adnam's Orchard* and asked if the man on the 'jacket' were Adnam. 'No,' replied Madame, 'that is his drunken brother.' Beth remarked that it was dedicated to her Great-Aunt. I felt Madame retreat into herself with girlish sensitiveness. 'Have you any objection?' she asked with forced naturalness. Beth had stumbled on a secret that was sacred and I was a witness, but one who was privileged and trusted. 'The Lady' meant much to my Darling, as much possibly as she in her purity and sweetness means to me, or so I imagine. I learnt later that Beth called Miss Tindall 'Great-Aunt'.

May 3rd

After tea I went to see my Darling, and was happy for the first time truly since Bozzy went. Madame was in her grey and blue. We spoke of her verse and I made bold to criticise. I said I felt the verse form cramped her, that she was more poetical in her prose. She accepted my strictures with such beautiful quiet humility and dignity. She replied that she had never thought much of her verses but she had loved making them. Had I noticed that there was always melody in them? Sometimes she had put them to music to sing them . . .

June 10th

My Dárling's [seventy-sixth] Birthday.
I wrote to her; then I went in the town to buy her two pairs of gloves of augment the present of scarves I had chosen for her. The morning was cool and grey with slight rain at intervals. I had difficulty in getting the flowers right and the ribbon did not satisfy me. However I arranged the parcel at last and rushed up the hill with it just before one o'clock.

I meditated how hard our pleasures are made for us; this hill is always the preliminary to the joy of seeing or being near my Darling and is, as it were, a purifying penance and preparation. The door was ajar but I rang to give the parcel to Edna. The flowers were wine shades of sweet peas, pink roses, and little old fashioned pinks. I was beginning my reason for being late when Edna cut me short by saying that Madame had asked to see me if I called. I was hot and flustered and did not expect to be asked in, nor did I feel dressed fit to see her. However, with happiness I entered, shook hands with Miss Clarke in the dining room, put my glove on again to shake hands with Madame as I felt my hands too warm and ran up the stairs.

At the top of the first flight my Darling met me. I stopped in adoration, looking up at her. Oh, she looked so sweet, so lovely standing there. My Birthday Lady! A white rose drooped against her breast, and beside it was my ivory brooch of carved lilies-of-the-valley, round her neck she wore a string of beads like amethysts, and her hair was done low on her neck as she wore it when a girl. Her face so pure and white contrasted with her black dress and her eyes like love-in-a-mist looked down at me with wistful beauty through her owly glasses. I wished her many happy returns knowing that were such not possible here on earth they were assured to her in eternity. And then my Angel Mother clasped me to her closely and kissed me with all the loving energy of her being, many times, nor found me wanting in response. There was something of triumph, something of joy and something suggesting the clinging sadness of farewell in her embrace.

Queen of her years, she descended the stairs then beside me, and gazing at her I could only reiterate, 'How sweet you look,' and kissed her again. But she was her reserved dear self once more, and let me with a little laugh into the sitting room . . .

June 15th

. . . We spoke of poetry – Roy Campbell's[40] – I said he was very strong; 'He is rank in places,' Madame rejoined. But we both liked *The Zebra* and some of his similes and metaphors . . . I mistook the poem of 'the languid sunset, Mother of roses' for his, in *Ideala*. Madame repeated it by heart but was sure it was not his, but could not recall the author. (Later I found it was by Andrew Lang[41].) We also spoke of Segrave's[42] death. She thought it was right to make such attempts as it preserved the virility and venturesome spirit of our manhood. Amy Johnson[43] too she admired for showing that a woman can do such things as well as men. She spoke of her with pride and enthusiasm, sitting forward on her chair. To have stopped her, as someone suggested to her she should have been, would, she said, have been interfering with the liberty of the subject. I talked of the rocket idea for reaching the moon, and she told me that Sir Edward Ball[44] had once informed her that an express train going for a hundred years would only just reach Mars . . .

June 25th

My Darling came with me to Fuller's in Milsom Street where we discussed my idea for a lace exhibition like the one described in *The Winged Victory*, for the Fresh Air Fund. She turned it down however as she did not think it would attract a large enough crowd and wanted me to work a conventional concert with Miss Harford. I was disappointed and jealous and refused, saying that I wouldn't work with her. Madame took my categorical no in silence and dropped the subject. I felt awful, angry with myself for hurting her but full of stubborn pride. We finished our coffee and then walked down and up Milsom Street with a sense of sad constraint over all we said . . .

July 6th

. . . I went to see my own Darling. Madame was in a white voile dress with mauvey-blue roses to pattern it and black ribbon to trim it. I corrected some of the MS . . . When I asked her if she still loved me, she replied, 'I am not conscious of any difference in my feelings towards you'. So dearly ambiguous!. . .

July 17th

. . . She told us an anecdote of her visit to Chicago of how she was trapped to go to the abattoirs and as soon as she got to the gates and realised where she was, refused to enter. The papers next morning had headlines 'Sarah baulks at blood' . . .

September 20th

I wrote to Darling for the – I daren't say how many times since last seeing her and taking back a book, and no sooner had I finished my letter than my blessed one rang up to ask me to go to tea tomorrow. I had been guilty of tampering with her poems, suggesting a line or a word here and there in some that were waiting revisal and she forgave me my officiousness, so humble and sweet.

September 21st

I was lost in contemplation of a title for her Anthology as I turned the corner of the road to her Terrace and, glancing up, I saw her standing there smiling at me, in welcome. She had come to meet me, my blue and silver lady and it was only afterwards that the symbolism of her being there when I had the word 'nets' in my mind, as it were on the shore, came to me.

We went into the dining room to await tea. And she took off her little felt hat and sat looking more white-roseate than ever, though one just touched with pink, and I gazed at her with a soft wonder, and then went on my knees beside her and holding her white cloud face in my hands kissed her. She was surprised at my admiration but indulged me with accustomed quietness . . . She spoke appreciatively of a military training for men and said that the young officers who came to visit her when her step-sons were young were all so neat and tidy, whereas academic training seemed to encourage bad manners. Albert McFall for whom a diplomatic position had been made at Malta wrote to thank her for bringing them up strictly in these respects and making them fit for any society. Madame said she insisted that Beth should make Winkie change for dinner, and said, 'If Grandma could, she could!' She told me she thought one should never repeat a private conversation as things were so easily misunderstood. (And here am I doing so!) I could not persuade her to continue the work for long as she has lost interest a little in it, so we smoked and talked happily until time to go . . . She told me too how someone had not recognised her with her glasses on. 'But,' I answered, 'it is not only that, your whole personality is unmistakable. Anyone who has known you would never forget you,' and I reached up enfolding her, and she bent towards me slowly, to meet my kiss, my own darling Mother.

. . . I had written her a letter before she telephoned the other day and read some of it to her. 'That is all worth reading,' I said, but Darling took it from me saying, 'That is my letter,' and put it in her bag. It pleased me that she should want it as I have always thought that my numerous epistles must weary her, so I wrote her another love letter, just a tiny one before I came upstairs tonight . . .

September 28th

Madame talked to me of Marie Corelli[45] and said she was so violent in the expression of her views but that she had the gift of rousing people's feelings to agree with her, right or wrong. Madame first saw her sitting on a sofa in a blouse and skirt and a sailor hat, quite a slim little figure. Someone said, 'That's Marie Corelli,' and Madame replied, 'And who may Marie Corelli be?' She had not then heard of her. Another time was in a cloakroom. Madame was talking when Marie Corelli came in and stood before the glass which occupied the whole end of the long room. She was then a dumpy figure dressed in a hot shade of pale blue and had flaming auburn hair. Madame declined an introduction and spread out her little hand in recollected avoidance but said she might not be so intolerant now.

My dear said she couldn't write her memoirs as she knew too much that she could not make public, that she knew things which would 'smash' her enemies if she cared to publish them. 'Most people,' I began, 'would not care about that' (i.e. hurting people's feelings). 'But,' she replied without a vestige of arrogance but simply stating a self-evident fact, 'I am not most people.' 'No indeed you are not,' I agreed quickly, touching her knee with loving apology. Coming downstairs she grasped my dress at the waist with her darling hand and then moved it up to my shoulder, leaning upon me. Ah, press heavily, my beloved burden – so pleaded my heart, joyous and tremulous at once beneath her weight . . .

October 12th

. . . Miss Tindall has suggested *A Sarah Grand Miscellany* for the title of the book and as the word had also gone through my mind as a possible one, I agreed eagerly and we settled on that . . .

November 1st

We read of Mr Tindall's sudden death and I wrote and took a letter of sympathy up to my dear at night. I did not go on the Sunday. She wrote me a dear brave letter on the Monday . . .

November 20th

. . . She made me sad at something she said regarding letters, accusing me of having shown hers; she said she could not write naturally to me. I had not done so and assured her I had not (later I found she had taken a jest I had made in one of mine, pretending I had sold one of hers to Mr Wright, seriously – I was able to show her the letter still in my possession and she let me have it back as proof that she trusted me) . . . She wishes she could love more; she confessed that she was utterly indifferent to most people and never hated except in flashes. I told her that I too could count the names of those I truly loved on my fingers, Mother, Ina, herself and my old nurse Susie, and we were very near in that hour, her soft hand there to hold, the mystery we talked of made less frightening and less dividing. I said the memory of that time with her would be a help in days to come . . .

December 21st

I spent the whole day embroidering a sack with a Xmas Tree in wool to take her presents and those for the household . . .

Bath 1931

January 13th

We talked of the book which Miss Clarke had given me, *The*

Ninth Vibration, by Adams Beck.[46] I said its teaching filled that
gap of the after life and Darling replied that the doctrine of Reincarnation was so comforting to her. I asked whether according to
it, our present relationship would remain the same in another life
and she said she thought they did. We spoke of men, and women
not being able to see the fascination other women held for them. I
said I thought one could but that men were so easily taken in.
'There is the physical side to be thought of,' she replied firmly.
We talked of Christina Rossetti and her meeting with Mrs
Tynan.[47] Madame said she had never heard Mrs Tynan speak of
her. Mrs Tynan was 'a dear' . . .

She recalled the luncheon parties she herself used to give to all
these people when in London and told me that Mrs Meynell
greatly admired Coventry Patmore[48] but that Francis Thompson's[49] adoration was not returned. He was at one time down and
out owing to taking opium.

She ordered a car to be rung up as we were finishing and it
gave me a thrill to hear her pronounce her name with unconscious dignity – Madame Sarah Grand – the dearest name in all
the world to me and the most powerful . . .

During the next weeks my sister had measles and I had to content myself with writing to Madame, as we were in quarantine.
Even on February 6th when she rang me up from Crowe Hall to
ask me to tea, I had to refuse. It was heaven to hear her voice
again. We discussed the idea of love being tidal, I mean divine
love itself, and she liked it and thought it would work up well. I
wrote 3 sonnets on the theme and sent them to her . . .

March 16th

I spent the whole day completing the Miscellany for my Darling
. . . On St Patrick's Day I woke with a bad cold but got up as I
had promised Darling she should have the Miscellany. I walked
up with it, my eyes streaming in the lovely sunlight and saw the
sweetest squirrel in Madame's Avenue. My Darling answered
next day . . .

March 24th

Darling rang up to ask me to tea at Crowe Hall on the morrow.

March 25th

I drove up in brilliant sunshine through the soft spring air and
beside me I had the first primroses and violets, softly illumined
by the sunbeams. I had a new hat on and was distinctly nervous.
When I got out at the gates I was scarcely ready to walk up the
drive and hesitated as on that long ago day when we left our
basket of wild flowers. I rang the bell at last under the portico
having had time to notice the pale stars of the early primroses
already out among the rockery plants on the bank above the
road. A kind of Gothic screen divided off the hall and I took my
coat off and was then led through the spacious entrance hall to the
drawing room door on the left of the sweeping staircase. There
my Darling was waiting for me, dressed in her purple velvet
making an unforgettable picture with a vase of deep wine-
coloured tulips behind her and some royal blue-purple daisies in
a pot beside her. The walls were a cool grey. I gave her my
humble offering of primroses saying that I feared they were not
'hot'. For a second she wondered what I meant, then she remembered her words in *The Beth Book*: 'Do you know which I like best,
hot primroses, when you pick them in the sun and lay them
against your cheek, they are all warm you know and then they are
good.'

After a while she took me through the adjoining room which
used to be her sitting room, on to the Terrace. The breeze lifted
her hair from her forehead and she put her hand up to keep her
curls in place. The lawns sloped down to stone balustrades and
seemingly met the grounds of Prior Park. There was a stone
elephant in an open recess and Darling took me round on the
other side of the house whence she pointed out a glimpse of
Widcombe Church and Sarah Fielding's house.[50] Above us were
the windows of her own room with shutters flung back. We had
tea in the hall at a round table beneath the staircase with still
darker tulips gracing the centre dainty repast. But I did not feel
wholly at ease though happy as always with my Darling friend
who was as natural and as dear to me as ever. The proximity of
the stairs and gallery above did not make for privacy and I wondered if Miss Tindall intended coming down. She did not appear
however and I was duly relieved. I regret that I kept no record of
our conversation. My interest was more especially concentrated
in sight and feeling. We went back to the drawing room after tea

and Darling showed me the title page she had drafted for the Miscellany, written in her own hand on pale Wedgewood blue paper, with my own name as Editor. I could not help crying a little and knelt beside her and kissed and thanked her. It was not only gratified vanity but gladness in her own dear loyalty which was willing to give me the honour and acknowledgement of my work. She came to the door with me when I left, and when I told her she was like a violet, she threw her eyes self mockingly to heaven and repeated, 'a modest violet!' but she did herself injustice, my little flower. I left her at the entrance to her palace and walked home with difficulty, keeping the piece of paper with that precious inscription from being crumpled by the wind, and surrounded by a golden haze of sun and happiness . . . Later I had the page framed in silver. I heard from Darling next day. She did not know it was my birthday but it was almost as if she had timed it to arrive there on purpose . . .

April 5th, Easter Sunday

. . . She talked of making her Will at tea, and whether it was wise to choose the Public Trustee or the Bank and of the question of Executors. She told me how she wished to leave her money in trust for three lives, and spoke of the Central Argentines[51] as having gone down to one per cent. She said she should destroy her present Will because, without consulting her wishes, the lawyer had put himself down as Executor. She turned with relief to a cigarette.

. . . Madame told me she wrote *Babs the Impossible* as a serial very quickly, before *Ideala* and thought then she could write without revising, now she wonders how she could have done it! . . .

Darling mentioned her son who was playing in a recent production, *Charles III* . . .

April 26th

. . . She told me that Mrs Massingberd[52] who founded The Pioneer Club always used to read the poem of *The Heavenly Twins* in public. Madame did not like Clemence Dane's *Will Shakespeare*[53] which I had lent her and said it was a libel on the dead. She said *The Beth Book* had been published in America and she had not been able to go through it properly, hence mistakes had crept in. She lent me Masefield's Poems and let me take back the Miscellany again to re-correct . . .

June 6th

My heart is full of tears tonight because I felt her to be sad although she denied it, and tired, so tired, like a weary child, though she made gallant pretence at gaiety. Like a drooping flower. She stood to receive me, wearing her grey and blue and the soft tan feather boa, with the black hat I once trimmed for her so long ago . . . She confessed that she did not like Dante nor Milton; disapproved strongly of the play we had seen – *The Barretts of Wimpole Street*[54] – and said only a Frenchman could have put that interpretation on it (the father's love). We talked of my paper on Masefield and Beauty . . . As I sat at her feet I asked what had become of the white rose ring I had given her. Had she lost it? No, she had it still and was going to give it back to me some day. Without meaning to hurt me she said, 'One does things for a time and then drops them'. I told her I had worn her ring without taking it off since the day she gave it me and we spoke of the other one which I wear to guard it, with a line from one of her books on it ('The test of the spiritual lies in its continuity'), and how I wrap them in a 'nightgown' at night, at which she laughed. Did I wash in it she asked, and I replied, 'Yes'. I thought the stones well set. In a pause I looked up to find so tragic a look in her dear eyes, such a depth of mystery that I was disturbed. She awoke quickly as from a trance, brief yet profound, and caught at the sleeve of my dress with sudden force as at a straw, and immediately was herself again. I reached up to her asking if she were sad, but she smiled at once and said no . . .

August 2nd

. . . Talking of critics she said that when she first published, the only paper that gave her any real helpful criticism was the *Saturday Review* which picked out faults in syntax and grammar very helpful to a young writer. Beth said that Madame altered *The Winged Victory* half way through and she had to type it over for her. Madame had got tired of Ella Banks and so changed some of it. Beth continued that Miss Tindall had had a 'purity campaign' and took exception to the incident where Lord Terry is taken home on the floor of the cab. But Beth insisted on its being kept in, happily . . . I told her that Mother had heard me talking to her over the phone and how she had counted 4 'darlings' – 'You must sicken Madame,' Mother said. Madame laughed at this sally, but gave no opinion for or against.

August 8th

Some devil of inharmony possessed me this morning when I went up to Darling to go through the Miscellany again. Instead of enjoying her interest and delighting in the amendments she suggested, I implicitly disapproved and was reluctant to alter, partly through laziness and partly through hurt that she could so disturb what I hoped was the final symmetry of the fair copy. A coffee stain on the pages I had so prized upset me likewise and when Madame suggested the interpolation of whole scenes in place of shorter quotations my heart descended to my boots. I hid my discomfiture I hope as well as I could and truly wished to please her, but it was an effort to appear acquiescent and then my Darling launched into a project for writing a play round *Babs the Impossible* and I could not enthuse as I dislike anything to do with the theatre and wished her to be untouched by that germ! She told me some Americans had adapted the story and had submitted it to her, but they had so vulgarised it that she would not consent to its production. Later she heard that they had produced it under another name and had made a million dollars with it!

She had collaborated on a play of *The Heavenly Twins* with Robert Buchanan,[55.] but the English and American copyrights clashed and it couldn't be done as they blocked each other. I asked couldn't it be arranged on a sharing basis, but she answered, flushing sensitively and looking at me appealingly, that it was all so sordid . . . She invited me to tea tomorrow. I held her little hand and replied, 'Don't you think you have seen enough of me?' 'No,' she replied, and so I consented, but went home vaguely restless and later the mood assumed foolish proportions and I cried and was utterly miserable and couldn't work.

August 9th

I almost made up my mind not to go today, but thank Heaven I did not decide to give in to my hysteria and bad temper. The sun was shining, the air cool as in Switzerland from the snows and, once I started to walk, the nightmare began to evaporate and was utterly dispersed when I found myself suddenly in my Beloved's presence . . . I had taken her a book on playwriting by William Archer[56] which Ina had sent her and this brought back the subject of her own play. She had met William Archer once as a girl and later at dinner when Mayoress here. She wanted to know Ina's opinion of the project and generously suggested they should collaborate – 'by Sarah Grand and Louise Regnis' (Ina's stage name) would look well, she thought! She thought the dialogue would be easy. She had always found dialogue easy to write; if one had been accustomed to hearing clever people talk as she had all her life, it was simple! She showed a deep interest in her characters and spoke of them almost as actual people . . . This led us to the subject of copyright and mention of Dickens in America. Darling said that Heinemann had told her and she thought it was true (tho' he did not always speak the truth), that *The HT* was the first book printed after the American Law of Copyright had been passed and the last book to be published in three volumes, just before the 7/6 novels came in . . .

We talked too of fortune telling, and of Beth's Bohemian acquaintances, one of whom, a woman, who had studied dermatology said that 'Adern's' and other creams on the market were fatal to the complexion, that only wax should be used. She would try a little on one's hand and then make it up to suit individual cases. I told Madame of my affliction of acne as a girl and she was dear and sympathetic. She said she had never done anything to her skin and had kept her clear complexion till she was 50 . . .

October 22nd

. . . We talked politics too with the election[57] uppermost in our minds. She felt still in sympathy with the Liberal point of view but said her vote would neutralise her sister's who is a Conservative; they would neutralise each other and therefore and partly because she was undecided she thought she would not register her vote this time. 'Oh but,' I exclaimed, 'people say that it's such an awful thing not to vote.' But she replied to the effect that it did not matter to her what people said. Faithful as ever to her independent spirit, in the winter of her life still strong in the courage of her own course. 'You rebel!' I cried brokenly . . . We talked of books and authors and of free trade. Her ideal was of free trade for all the world. But that will never be, I thought. Not in our time, she replied. She told me how in a train once, going I think she said to Exeter where she was going to lecture, she got into conversation with a fellow passenger on the subject of politics. As she neared her destination he asked her to tell him with whom he had been talking. At that moment the train drew up and her maid grasped her suitcase and she got out flinging back over her shoulder through sheer mischief the name 'Marie Corelli'. She heard a gasp, but never knew if he believed her or no . . . Madame said she (Marie Corelli) looked *canaille franche-ment* – just as Ouida was but Ouida was taken up by the best society[58] . . . She could not believe that Virginia Woolf had written *A Room of One's Own* as well as *The Lighthouse*. She thought *Miss Mole*[59] the greatest novel of last year . . .

November 15th

. . . Beth was home and we three sat beside the fire all cosy and as usual I chattered and chattered in perfect happiness. She told me that when she went first to Tunbridge Wells it was very Conservative and she was not popular when she arrived being a Liberal and Suffragist, but at length she won them . . .

Once she had asked Clara Codd[60] to lecture at an At Home, thinking it was rather a daring thing to do, but they loved it and for old time's sake when Clara Codd spoke on Krishnamurti[61] in Bath, Madame consented to take the Chair for her. We spoke of Suffragettes and Madame said she did not approve of their methods when they became so violent and was not too pleased to read an account making out that she had taken part in a procession on a coach, published in a book of Sylvia Pankhurst's.[62] She deplored, though, those women who had inveighed against the suffrage and opposed it but who now that it was won for them, took every advantage of it.

Of another illustration, in a Life of Edmund Gosse's,[63] she thought, Mrs Knight had laughingly said Madame looked as if she were taking part in 'a dissipated party'. It was a group of Sir Edmund and Lady Gosse, herself and Agnes Tobyn [sic] at whose feet Mr Heinemann, the publisher, was stretched at full length.

She sat allowing Beth to express the most outrageous opinions on voting and patriotism, without protest, as if she knew that time would ameliorate her judgements . . .

Bath 1932

January 7th

Today was memorable for my asking if she had suffered after writing *The Heavenly Twins*. The question arose from my telling her how it had been mentioned as a best seller in a recent letter in the *Sunday Times*[64] and the reason for its success asked for, and how I had replied with the result that my letter had not been published, and how I had gone through agonies fearing she might not like what I had said if it did appear. She looked at me with fond forgiving eyes, understanding my every qualm, and so I asked her if she had never gone through similar trepidation . . . about her book she maintained she had not, that she had such good friends at her back. 'But didn't you ever at night?' I insisted. 'Didn't you ever "grovel" over what you had written?' 'No, never,' she answered. 'Not even when such horrid things were said about you?' 'No, it put me on my mettle!' She was sure she was right.

Beth broke in that it was good advertisement and that Gemini (June) people were distinguished for cock-sureness. But I knew better, with her sensitiveness. I know she suffered, and I know her for a moral heroine. Given the genius, I said, the ability, I might have written the book but I should never have weathered the storm.

'It put me on my mettle,' she repeated. She said she had profited by her critics pointing out her faults and agreed with them. Oh faults, I said, I don't mean them, but the theme of the book. She would not give in though and Beth quoted Arthur Waugh's[65] reference to the dire result of sowing wild oats. Darling laughed heartily at the euphemism. Well, I concluded, I think you were wonderful and courageous and I don't know how you didn't. Beth said that Madame had allowed Miss Tindall to correct *The Winged Victory* and that Beth still thought the alteration in one case which she had made, a pity . . .

I felt again that I was on another strata, problems smoothed themselves out and seemed negligible. And I seemed too as if I had never left her – we go on uninterruptedly however long the parting. She comforted me saying we would meet again soon.

Outside there were white clouds like doves on the dark sky and the stars sparkled down at the lights of the city till they all looked like a shower of diamonds.

January 24th

My Darling told me over the phone yesterday that her cook-housekeeper, Mrs Taylor, had had a seizure and was going home that day. She added that the quotation for the day in her calendar was 'Keep smiling'. So this afternoon I went prepared to have a picnic tea, but not prepared for the news which met me. Beth opened the door and after I had taken off my coat I turned to see my Darling standing in the dining room, in her thrush brown dress. I threw my arms round her kissing her and feeling my own cheek cold against her warm one. 'Did I strike a chill through you?' I asked, and went on to ask how Mrs Taylor was. Madame with her quiet directness replied, 'She's dead.' I was dreadfully shocked, more especially for Madame's sake. 'Yes,' chimed in Beth, 'we have a full blown corpse upstairs,' and she purposely treated the subject in as unemotional a way as possible, protesting that she felt nothing and that there was nothing there anyhow. 'Oh, but the shock!' I murmured. 'Death is death whatever you may say,' said my Darling . . .

After this I bestirred myself to try to take her mind off this tragic happening, for I could see that although her dear face looked well, she was much shaken, her little hands and her lips were tremulous, she was biting them constantly and her eyes filled with tears now and then . . . But at tea she was actually able to repeat two or more stanzas of Swinburne's *The North Sea*[66] and responded to the beauty and passion of the lines ('and then come the flickering grasses') and I was carried away too by the loveliness of the words like the change of a key in music . . .

We moved back to the fire after tea. I could not eat the cake, feeling it might be Mrs Taylor's last. We none of us tasted it. Madame refused a second cigarette, then changed her mind and rose to reach for the box of Players. She and Beth used spills to light it, but I took a match, forgetting! We talked of a book I had been reading, *A Tenement in Soho*,[67] and while on the subject I heard a motor draw up [the undertakers] and the unmistakable sounds of wood scraping as the doors were opened. I guessed what it was but said nothing. Later Madame wrote to tell me that it was then that the men had come and gone, so that when I went all was over, thank God for her sake.

Beth left us for a few precious moments ostensibly to go to look up the title of a film we wanted to see; there was silence for a while. I felt icebound and my heart reached out to my Darling in an agony of inexpressible sympathy as she sat a little huddled in her chair.

February 7th

Beth came to meet me and there were japonicas on the hall table. My Darling was sitting looking rather sad by the fireplace in the dining room when I entered and I embraced her as she rose . . . 'Religion is a life,' she said. 'Religion is a binding down,' rejoined Beth, 'from *liguor*, to bind.' 'That does not make it so because they have given it that name,' my Darling answered gently but finally.

The talk now turned to the club spirit manifested by R. Catholics and non-Conformists. Madame was glad Winkie had gone to a R. Catholic school as she would have connections with it all her life. I recalled the time when Madame unveiled a tablet to Wesley in New King Street and said as it was in the twilight I could see only the lighted plaque and her white glove.

She told me she had come across a boxful of her white gloves the other day and wondered what she would do with them as she would not want to wear them again for a long time, as she never went out now at night and did I think any singers in Bath would like them. I replied that I had always coveted a pair and she promised to send me one. They would be ones in which she had shaken hands with hundreds of people. Some were cleaned, but I insisted I did not want those but just as she had taken them off. She could send them for St Valentine's Day! (She never did!)

We talked of sentiment and sentimentality as an old discussion and she quoted 'Leslie Stephens'[68] definition, supplementing it herself with sentimental people are not in love with the person at all, they enjoy the emotion of love . . .

Beth said to succeed one must write something shocking, but I thought that phase was passing. Madame mentioned Mary Borden's novel, *The Woman with White Eyes*,[69] as being unnecessarily horrid in detail. After such books one needed a mental bath. Passing over these delicately, she gave us a clear outline of the plot, remembering all the names and characters. 'It seems to have made an impression on you,' commented Beth as she finished. I was struck by the unfaltering power of memory she had displayed, the reserve force of her mentality, so vital and clear at her age . . .

She told me that her own son had written in a very complimentary way of Ina's acting and tact in dealing with leading ladies and promised to copy out his observations for me, a promise she fulfilled . . .

March 27th, Easter Sunday

. . . There was a chocolate cake with 'chocolate' written on it and she laughed at the obviousness of the lettering – what else could it be? The new cook was not good at cakes. I told her about the miniature I had had painted of her and said the eyes were not blue enough. She answered that I was the only one who had ever seen her eyes as blue. I was surprised because I thought it a self-evident fact tho' they change to green and grey at times. Everyone says they are grey, she told me. But they are like the sea I said, like sapphires and sometimes turquoise. They are not blue today – it depends on your mood . . .

When I asked about my new idea for the Miscellany, she replied that she thought that work was out of time with the present, out of time with the mood of today, and that any further application would be time lost. I told her it would be recreation for me and begged to be allowed to do it and she gave her 'slow leave'.

. . . She kissed me lovingly. I reminded her she had not sent me her old gloves and she said she would try to find a decent pair. I answered I did not want a *decent* pair! and said I would send notes every day to remind her! . . .

April 24th

. . . We discussed *The Fountain*[70] by Charles Morgan, she mentioning it in a voice which relegated it to a lower rank than the works we had just had in mind. She thought it was summed up by what the Baron had said, that 'the man was a cad who had stolen another man's wife'. Characteristically she stood up for the woman when I said she had egged the man on. 'Ah, no doubt she tempted him,' but it was his fault, she maintained. I argued that he had written her quite nice letters and it was she who had said she could not live up to his ideal of her. I read one or two extracts I had copied about the philosophy, but I could not persuade her to enter deeply into the discussion . . . She liked the little note-book in which I had copied the quotations. I read her one or two on other subjects; one in a review of a book on Blake. She con-fessed never to have felt attracted by that poet, in which avowal we were both in complete accord. She said she felt the same way about Milton tho' of course he was on a higher plane. I instanced the poet of *The Shropshire Lad*[71] as another of my aversions and gave 'an assumed simplicity which didn't ring true' as my reason. Madame nodded understandingly but said she had always meant to read it and had never done so yet. Robert Louis Stevenson was another of my *bêtes noires* of literature and Darling thought that his popularity depended upon the generation still living who had known and loved the man himself, that he was a most lovable personality, but that his works were not so wonderful . . .

As we sat talking I noticed a long silver hair on the table beside me, now cleared of the tea things, and asked her if she thought it was one of hers. 'It is probably one of the maid's,' she chaffed me, seeing me begin to wind it about my fingers lovingly and she rose and took it from me smiling and threw it in the fire. Some-thing in her manner of doing it brought tears to my eyes and I caught her little hand in mine as she returned to her place. And I told her, still half crying, how I had kept and lost and kept again tho' uncertain of its identity one I had found in the hat I had trimmed for her. She laughed at me tenderly, treating me like a child, mothering me in her looks, so wistful and gentle, under-standing my tears and not far from them herself. 'The soul's Rialto hath its merchandise',[72] I quoted, saying how people always exchanged locks of hair in the old days . . .

May 1st

The morning had been glorious, a real May Day, but I was suf-fering from neuralgia, having read late. At last I took some aspirin and went to lie down, but I was impatient to see my Darling and soon rose to begin dressing. My headache passed off in anticipation and I was well when I began to ascend to hill. Large drops of rain began to fall, the weather having changed, and I had difficulty in shielding the fragile plant of blue primroses I was taking her . . . I had wanted to be with her and the realisation, the gratification of that need did not in any way fall below my expectation, it excelled it and I gloried in the completeness of joy which her presence and companionship give me . . . She told me why she had wanted the quotations typed from the Foreword to the *Heavenly Twins*. It seemed that an American – a Mrs Plowsdale or Plowsday – had lately taken interest in the manuscript of the *Heavenly Twins* and, hearing Madame wished to dispose of it, had said that she knew Miss Barlow, a sister of the head of Sotheby's. When she went back to London she asked Miss Barlow to lunch and spoke to her about the MS, later writing to ask Madame how much she would put on it as reserve. Darling replied that she would not let it go cheaply. Pressed for a more definite answer she mentioned £4000 to £5000. They wrote back saying they did not think it would fetch so much as the work of a living author. But evidently they have not dropped the idea. Darling put up the price because as she said she felt it would not be fair to Archie (her son) to sell it at a small price now for her own convenience when later he might get so much more for it. They had been looking at the Foreword together and Madame thought it would amuse her to have that extract, being an American, about Mark Twain . . .

We spoke of the new hats which look as if they were blown on to the side of one's head and Dearest thought that they were not only 'vulgarising' but that they made a woman look 'impudent'. She thought one shouldn't follow the fashion sheep-like, and she had refused to wear certain hats just because everyone wore them . . .

We talked of her soft silver hair and she said her maid had spoilt the natural curls and waves by persuading her to put her fringe in curl papers. 'It hangs down straight in straws over my nose now,' she told me, 'when it is not curled.' Mrs Gerald Paget thought she ought to have it *ondulé* but Madame had refused again because she would not slavishly follow the dictates of fashion. Mrs Paget has lovely hair and one day when they were out driving, Madame and a friend with her took off her hat and fluffed her hair all about her face pretending they were two attendants out with a lunatic. Mrs Paget acted up to the joke and smiled and bowed to everyone like the Queen, and 'You should have seen their faces,' said Darling, adding rather wistfully how soon women grew out of being able to play jokes like that, that men were able to enjoy them much longer . . .

. . . This was an opportunity to ask her about [the ring], as I had worried as to whether with my washing up and other house-work I might lose the stones from it. Darling thought they were well set. Would you, I asked pressing the point, would you rather I should keep it on and risk losing the stones, or would you rather I took it off in case. I told her it was the ring itself I valued most. Of course you wouldn't like to lose the stones, she added. And in the pause of hesitation, Miss Clarke entered and my decision was made – the ring, God willing, shall never leave my finger where my Darling placed it that happy day so long ago.

(*1950* I still wear it tho' sometimes I fear the Rheumatic swell-ing of my other fingers may force me to remove it eventually.)
. . . (*1959* I had to remove the ring and did not wear it for some months until I found I could slip it on the little finger of my right hand.) . . .

May 15th

At tea we mentioned the late Sir Arthur Carlton,[73] and I referred to his abnormally small hands. Madame said she did not like small hands on men or women, that in America when she had had to shake hands with so many at the receptions held in her honour she had been struck by the tiny hands of the women, some of which had made her feel quite creepy . . .

She accepted the 2nd vol. of *Ideala's Gift*, the Diary I had been keeping of our meetings since 1928, with interest. I told her I did not wish her to read it particularly but that I felt it was my duty to show it to her. As she saw me out I said I hoped she would not be offended by it. Darling did not reply, but I knew I could trust her . . .

To S. G. June 10th 1932 (her 78th birthday)

> Oh not unguided we, life's pilgrims, wend
> Our steps, exploring this world's wilderness,
> Love blazed the trail where tangled branches bend,
> Where meadow flowers and white rose thickets press,
> Along the route we recognise his sign,
> The linked hearts that witness to the way,

> Ours but to kiss with faithful lips and twine
> More deeply still the carved device today,
> That others passing may behold and cry,
> 'Twas here they went!' and bless our memory . . .

Sept. 13th

'Love me?' I asked her as I kissed her, making up the little rift we had had. 'Mm,' she answered, 'and laugh at you too sometimes, when you are schoolgirly and won't grow up.'

December 11th

. . . A Mrs Forbes who used to tell fortunes told her she would never get to the top of the tree unless she kept exclusively to writing. That book *The Heavenly Twins* spoilt her literary career, my Darling said, as it diverted her activities into other channels and it took her a long time to get back again . . . I asked if she still had the MS of the *HT* and this led me to mention the MS of the *Trial of Warren Hastings*[74] which I read had been sold for £70 and eventually gone to America. 'Sarah Grand had some connection with Warren Hastings,' she said. I thought she was speaking of herself in the 3rd person and leant forward, laughing and interested. 'She was divorced I think because of him and then came back to Europe and married Talleyrand.' I then realised she was speaking of Madame Grand, but I said I didn't know her name was also Sarah. Yes, she had made sure it was and at a dinner party sitting beside Sir Frederick Pollock he had asked her why she had taken the name of so disreputable a woman. She had not known about her then. 'She was very beautiful and very stupid,' said Pollock. 'Well,' answered Darling, 'I am not beautiful and I am certainly not stupid.' She told me she had taken her *nom de plume* from 'a poor old body in an almshouse'. She was dead and it couldn't hurt her. Darling wanted a simple name, without flourishes, something easy to pronounce and remember. So many of her friends were taking high-sounding names or the names of men. She thought and thought, and then one night she had a dream and woke with the name of Sarah Grand on her lips and knew that that was what she wanted. 'And did you know the old woman at the almshouse?' I asked. 'Oh yes,' Darling replied, 'I was very fond of her. She used to come and see me. She was always very much intrigued by syphons and thought they were medicine.' Darling would say, I know you would like some soda-water and she would answer: I think it would do me good, and the funny thing was, added my Darling mischievously looking at me with her shy sweet eyes, it always had the desired effect!! An instance of mind over matter! She had the face of a Botticelli if you can imagine a Botticelli grown old.

Later she told me that a scurrilous newspaper article published about herself in America had made out that she was a divorced woman. She was annoyed at the time and almost decided to bring a Case. However she was advised to take no notice and after-wards she thought that in all probability the journalist had con-fused her with her historical predecessor – and that that was the way many stories had got about.

Bath 1933

March 5th

. . . She suddenly plunged into reminiscences of famous people and spoke of George Eliot. She had not known her but she had known Hale White (Mark Rutherford)[75] who was a neighbour of hers at Groombridge when Madame lived at Langton. He used to speak of George Eliot as beautiful, contrary to the usual belief in her plainness, and would describe her with her hair all about her. Madame suspected him of having been in love with G.E. There were years which were unaccounted for in her life before she met G. Lewis and some said she had a lover during that time. Accounts differed respecting her. Mrs Frederic Harrison,[76] for instance, used to say that she was altogether too solemn towards the end of her life and worried even about the meanings of words, but another friend of Madame's described her as playing like a kitten. It depended on the character of the observer, she thought, one calling forth one quality and one another. Madame spoke too of Watts Dunton.[77] The last time she saw him was at the Lyceum Theatre. Heinemann asked her if he might bring him to her and if she would 'take charge' of him as he was deaf and rather an incubus to others not so kindly disposed. She consented and he remained with her during the whole of the performance. She said that people were unjust regarding his friendship with Swinburne. The latter was going the way of Rossetti before Dunton took him in hand. It was not true to say Swinburne never wrote well after, for to her mind he wrote the finest of his poems after he went to live with Dunton – *By the North Sea* – but in any case it was only to be expected that his powers of writing would decline with the years. 'All those are dead,' she added after a pause, wistfully, but I felt they still lived in her speech.

We discussed the respective virtues of German and French literature and she spoke of the 'ponderosity' of the German as opposed to the clarity of the French. She did not like the way the French treated serious subjects, too much on the surface, words, words.

I read her a cutting regarding the symbolism of the Japanese style of arranging flowers – one for Heaven, high, one for humanity a little lower, and one for earth the lowest of all. She said when she was in Hankow she was invited to arrange the flowers at a Japanese lady's house. This was the greatest compliment they could pay you. She did not realise it at the time and merely arranged them in the English fashion and had often wondered since what they had thought of her effort . . .

In a pause before this I told her as delicately as I could the plot of *Mädchen in Uniform*,[78] the German film of school girl life which we had recently seen at the Assembly Rooms. Her ejaculations of interest and encouragement were wordless and more like cries of pain; she made no comment when I finished. She was not 'shocked', yet it came as a shock to her. Thereafter we talked of visits to the Continent . . . We spoke too of Austin Dobson's[79] poems which she liked – 'such dainty work'.

March 19th

. . . I related some difficulties we had had recently with our dogs, but added I could not live without them. 'Something alive for company.' She understood and told me that at one time her publisher Mr Heinemann had felt the need of something alive 'to go back to' and had kept a goldfish for company. Later he bought a Siamese cat![80] . . . After a silence that lasted for some minutes, she asked me, hesitantly withdrawing herself into the farthest corner of the chair and clasping her hands as if she wrung them, did I ever feel fear as if something terrible were impending? My impulse was to put my arms about her but I resisted it and instanced an occasion lately when I had thought the day was fateful and news had come of a great earthquake, and called her 'Darling' comfortingly. 'I hope you may not be right,' I went on, 'because you are very psychic, aren't you?' 'I am sometimes,' she answered. I suggested the possibility of war, keeping her fear on a general basis though I have suspected it had some personal application, and opined that things looked very like it. 'Horribly, I think,' was her reply, reluctant but convinced. Thereafter we talked of air raids and how all the windows on her hill at Tunbridge Wells had been shattered, but her house was left uninjured. How Beth had wakened at the bomb and cried out, 'Oh Nan, what is it?' and how she had replied, 'Nothing, dearie, it's only a bomb.' She got the servants downstairs and afterwards had made a little festivity of it with refreshments.

We then spoke of the Russian Film recently shown by the Adult School here in Bath which had caused, together with their contemplated Russian studies, some controversy. I asked her if she had read the letters in the paper and she told me she had. Madame thought that it was permissible to study conditions in Russia providing there was no bias on the side of Communism. She agreed with the letters which had stressed the fact that the School existed primarily for Christian study.

. . . Miss Clarke happened to say that she did not care for the sound of the German language. This was tantamount to a challenge to my Darling. She dissented gently and as an example to support her own view of its beauty, she recited the poem 'Kennst du das Land?'[81] with a sensitive shyness yet tremulous eagerness to share her perception with us. And there was another poem which I could not follow so well, that had in it the recurring word 'Schloss'. This she told us she had learnt at Hong Kong where she had taken German lessons. Her instructress desired her to learn perhaps one verse if she could for next time and Madame surprised her by reciting all twelve and by having translated the whole poem into her own original verse for the following lesson! . . .

April 9th

. . . She told me that Miss Tindall wanted her to spend her birthday with her at Clan House again this year. I, with recollections of what I had felt to be her ordeal last year, spoke my thought. 'How trying,' I said. My Darling challenged the word and my meaning. I told her that I thought celebrations of the kind were always rather trying and that I thought she had found that one so . . . I intimated that I did not feel that a family party of the kind demanded such ceremony as it was accorded, but Madame spoke in praise of ceremony and the value of etiquette. 'You gave me the impression that you were unhappy,' I urged. She sat down by the fire and looked at me. 'How little you understand me,' she said so gently that I could not be wounded by the quiet regret of her tone. 'Perhaps I understand someone I think to be you and who is not you,' I ventured . . . It had brought us nearer in spirit than we had been for weeks past and I could bear to be told that I did not understand her for that reason . . . and when she kissed me farewell the sacred depth of her nature surrounded me like the ocean and I sank in it like a shell in an element that is greater and wider than itself . . .

April 16th, Easter Sunday

I sit down on the morrow of one of the happiest Easter Days I have ever spent to live it again in retrospect. The sun was shining brightly, the air cool from the sea, the spirit of primroses abroad. I walked up to see my Darling.

When Edna showed me into the drawing room she was not there, but the room itself never looked more lovely in my eyes, so welcoming, so homely, so refined. My white roses stood by the door, a vase of tawny wallflowers were beside the Mayor's picture and below it in a taller glass my two Arum lilies . . . In the corner my Bleeding Hearts hung gracefully. I was glad her room was a bower of flowers, even to the little bowl of japonica on another side table. I stood looking at the familiar yet ever new dearness of the scene, feeling it somehow unreal and fleeting in its comfortable variety and warmth.

Then I heard her footsteps and she was with me and I in the tender depth of her loving embrace . . . She remarked my feather ruffle, not quite liking it, so I took it off but she said I looked spring-like in my green dress . . . When tea came in she nodded towards the muffin dish I had given her praising it with Edna's concordance and we drew up to the table. She said she was going to take to sending me back my gifts, and I laughed, saying I thought she had last night when the bell rang, but that as I had had her initials put on it, I hoped she wouldn't. I did not feel that she had quite liked the dish and when later she took out her silver cigarette case which was rather dull and worn remarking how badly it looked compared with 'that flashing – – –' I was sure she would have preferred something less new.

. . . When tea was finished she led me up the uncarpeted stone stairs, admitting me into her bedroom now papered in dove grey paper like distemper, having a faint flush of pink in it. The windows were still uncurtained and the room was dismantled [for redecorating]. But I could realise a little of how it would look when completed. The tiles in the fireplace were primrose yellow (she had forgotten these but thought they could be easily arranged) and a lavabo stood against the farther wall to one side. In the centre now of the room was her bed, mahogany head and foot in open railing design and a little dressing table with a cream coloured curtain back was piled against it among miscellaneous objects and a bundle of odd pieces of wallpaper on the floor. Beside us was a fine inlaid mahogany and satin wood chest of drawers, all that remained of her big wardrobe from the fire. The handles were rings with lions' heads, and the drawers were curved outwards. We walked to the window and stood together looking out on to the lovely scene, the lawn and the further field to Sion Hill and to the left, with a mauve haze over it, a glimpse of the City . . . Those were holy moments and very dear to me. Another milestone in our friendship, the first time she had shown me her own room, and even now she had the shield of its disorder, precluding any undue sense of intimacy. So she preserved her reserve even here . . . Darling was looking her dear, dear self again, gently aged, mellowly young, now animated with little smiles bringing the indentations about her sensitive mouth into being, and now relapsing into quietude which was companionable and not today distant. In short she exercised her own peculiar charm to the utmost, a charm that I defy anyone to resist when she chooses to exert it. Oh! Dear Weaver of Happy Spells, how often I have experienced it and how ever new and potent it seems . . .

As I stood up to go she referred again to the roses: 'There is nothing so lovely as a white rose,' she said, and I thought in my heart that was true when it takes human form as in her. 'Every time they catch my eye I think that,' she continued, and then, with a certain shy restraint as she put her dear arms motherly about me and kissed me again in farewell, 'Well, thank you for everything but don't do it again.' I caught her hand, but she gave a little exclamation of pain. 'Did I hurt you, lovely?' I asked in consternation and kissed her fingers. 'Yes,' she answered, 'you did – my rheumatism.' 'Your ring,' I suggested, for it was her left hand with her wedding ring upon it. 'My old bones,' she rejoined smiling ruefully and rubbing them. 'I am so sorry,' and I looked all the love and repentance and gratitude I could as she stood poised on the first step of the upward stairs . . .

April 30th

My Darling was looking rather white and pinched today – one could scarcely have taken her for the same woman who had attended that public ceremony last Thursday when she had pre-sented certificates at the Adult Schools' Exhibition. Our con-versation soon reverted to it and I asked her how she had felt afterwards. She told me she had been making speeches all night long and had not been able to sleep. She was discouraged that it had taken so much out of her and despite my compliments main-tained that she had not come up to her form. She had not said all she had wanted to say. This she had done earlier in the Autumn at the National Council of Women when she relinquished the Presidency,[82] but now she was disappointed in herself and again said she would not in future attend public functions for fear of being asked to speak. She had been invited to the Authors' Club Dinner at which Lord Crawford[83] was to take the Chair, and Mr Ramsay MacDonald[84] to be a guest, but she said all her friends in London were dead; if she should go to a Hotel she would go to the Metropole. She would be quite 'a veteran' if she did go, she smiled . . .

I outlined a scheme I had for a new Miscellany, a very short one, just a pamphlet to be sold in aid of the Mayoress' Fresh Air Fund, as she had desired the larger work to be, had we been able to publish it. Darling listened indulgently and I was delighted to see approvingly, saying that 'It is as good a way as any other of over tiring yourself!' and stipulating only that the price of printing should come out of the sale.

May 8th

Instead of resting I worked all the afternoon on the new pamphlet.

May 12th

Went to the printers, Dando & Gerrish, to leave the Pamphlet for estimate. Felt encouraged to think we might be able to afford to have it printed. Wrote to my own Darling in a sunbeam all about the Eventide Home Bazaar and tea party, the paradise garden and the Dickens-like scene of the old people presenting posies to the Mayor and Catherine Booth, and to welcome Darling to Weston.

May 13th

At lunch the estimate for printing the booklet came and to my horror was for £15.10.0. for 1000 copies. Desperately disappointed.

May 15th

Went out to talk over the pamphlet with Dando & Gerrish. Got him to say he would do 500 for £9.

May 16th

I wrote to the Mayoress, Mrs Rhodes-Cook, about the booklet and also to Mr Payne, ARCA Art Master at the Technical College, asking him to design a border for the cover. Gave order to Dando & Gerrish for 500 at £9. A dear letter from Darling.

May 18th

. . . Letter from the Mayor refusing to allow me to sell the Pamphlet on the street but suggesting I might be able to get permission from trades-people to sell it on their premises. (This later we did and it was the means of our collecting the bulk of our contribution of £58 to the Fund.)

May 19th

Wrote to Darling confessing all I had done with regard to the booklet.

May 22nd

My Darling in her faithfulness and dear indulgence of me had written absolving me from my precipitancy over the Pamphlet . . .

May 25th

.Began correcting the galley proofs of *The Breath of Life* (the title of the new Pamphlet). Very tiring and the long paper slipped about. Then I wrote to my Darling to welcome her at Clan House on the morrow and to tell her the proofs had come.

May 30th

Went to the Technical College to see Mr Payne about the cover and after some hesitation chose the pale blue rather than the purple which Madame had favoured. We thought the latter was too sombre for the subject matter.

June 1st

Wrote to Darling with additional quotations appropriate to the theme which I had discovered. Went to Dando & Gerrish with the Pamphlet. Corrected proof and talked to them about it.

June 2nd

Letter from Madame saying she did not like the quotation I had suggested for title page, so decided to eliminate it . . .

June 7th

A dear letter from Madame which inspired me anew. Interviewed several booksellers asking them to stock the Pamphlet and was on the whole successful. Bought Darling a lovely Holy Grail cup in Scotch glass like the sea for her birthday . . .

June 15th

Saw an advertisement in the *Morning Post* of a booklet on an asthma cure called *The Breath of Life*. Unlucky coincidence . . .

June 26th

Early this morning the first consignment of *The Breath of Life* booklet arrived. Wrote to Darling and sent her one after reading it nervously through. Went to various booksellers taking advance copies.

June 27th

Letter from Darling approving of the booklet but wanted my name on it, and Mr Payne's . . .

July 3rd

Rang up Darling who said she didn't want to sign any of the booklets as they were not hers! I told her tenderly not to be silly. When I asked her how much signed copies should be sold for, she said 'one and six', 6d. only for her signature! We fixed it at 2/6 . . .

July 4th

After lunch I took some leaflets announcing the booklet. The Crescent was like a furnace. Left a letter on Mr Green-Armytage in reply to a lovely one from him on Darling's writing, which I sent her. Went to interview Mr Harold Fortt to ask if we might sell the booklet there. Mr. Fortt charming and gave ready permission. Paid bill at Dandos, £13.10.0. for 1000 copies, and ordered a poster . . . After dinner wrote to 'Hoppy' to thank her for the notice she had written in the *Chronicle* and rang up Mrs T. Sturge Cotterell, an ex-Mayoress, to ask her to help me sell . . .

July 7th

Took twelve copies of the booklet to Clan for Darling to sign. I left leaflets in Sydney Place, at shops, Pump Room and at hotels. Went to *Evening World* office and ordered papers. Left hand bills round the Circus and Brock Street. Went out again to leave booklets at Jones's in Margarets Buildings.

July 8th

Darling left the signed booklets. Our little dog Roy died . . .

July 12th

Got up early and did as much housework as I could, then took taxi to Fortts where the head assistant helped me very kindly get ready the table with the booklets . . . suddenly I saw my Darling Madame looking so beautiful in brown with pearls and a new brown straw hat, and white gloves. She was her 'Mayoressy' self again and I thrilled to the old magnetism, feeling I could worship her . . . One woman refused to take a booklet because she said Madame had 'fed' the children on the Ruhr. It was this woman's 82nd birthday and one wondered how anyone could reach that age with so little charity . . .

June 10th

My Darling's birthday was a day of fleeting clouds and sunshine cooler than we had had it of late. I drove up to Clan House by taxi arriving a little before the time for tea, 4.15 and the first of the party. Miss Tindall came out of the room the right hand side to greet me, closely followed by Madame. I apologised for being early. 'But why shouldn't you be early?' Miss Tindall said kindly, and then I turned to Darling and wished her Many Happy Returns. She was looking well, her face softly pink, her eyes blue and brimming with affectionate appreciation of what I had sent her. Her dress was that *bois-de-rose* with lawn which I had so much liked last year in the Autumn when she had first worn it and at her breast a little piece of white satin ribbon escaped in a bow and softened the line of the bodice. As we entered the drawing room I saw the roses in the cup vase I had given her. They were not the colours I had ordered and there were so many that some were already dropping. I was struck with disappointment, a sensation which all the afternoon I was utterly unable to shake off. 'Did Coles send those?' I asked, and explained that I had had to telephone for them and there they were not right. 'But,' said my Darling, 'we thought them so lovely when they came.' She was using the bag, and it went surprisingly with her dress, but she liked the toy sealyhams representing *The Heavenly Twins* (so labelled on a black plinth) best of anything, just as I knew she would, and carried it about and showed it to the others who now began to arrive.

Miss Kimball to whom I talked; Miss Harford and her sister, Mrs Pelly, a thin woman with a big nose which she had dipped in a flour barrel, so that it looked blue compared with the rest of her face. She was wearing large pearls and beautiful emerald and diamond rings. She gave Madame a little cheap *Cloisonné* ash tray which Darling received as graciously as if it had been something priceless, and rose and put it on the table. Miss Harford presented her with a book, saying that she had had some ribbon to tie it up with but had lost it. I reminded her rather tactlessly of a similar *contretemps* she had had last year and she came and sat on the sofa to discuss the point and talked with me till tea was announced. As we walked from one room to the other, Madame gave me her hand saying lowly, 'Miss Tindall has arranged the table – she wants you to sit on her left!' So Miss Harford was beside Madame. This was fair as last year I had sat there, but I felt isolated, and the more so since Miss Tindall talked chiefly to Mrs Pelly. I suddenly discovered Mother's letter to Madame in my bag and asked permission to pass it to her, before I should forget it. I felt this was a break of etiquette! Somehow I always feel there that I don't know how to behave. When at Madame's own house, all is so natural. There were the loveliest pink and white carnations on the table in a silver rose bowl. They were from Miss Kimball and we all admired them, I jealously enough for they were far lovelier than my roses. I ought to have rejoiced in them . . .

There were strawberries of Miss Tindall's own growing in a Worcester china stand. As I passed it, twice I clicked it against another plate, another awkwardness of which I should not have been guilty elsewhere. I shook myself mentally telling myself to buck up and be agreeable and succeeded better.

Tea over, we adjourned, each waiting for the other to exit politely. Miss Tindall took some of the company round the garden, Darling having managed to see that we should have a few minutes together. She came and sat on the sofa and we talked . . . She told me she had heard from Beth 'somewhere on the Sussex Downs' but that she had not referred to Winkie. Darling had not heard from Winkie either though her longing for a letter was reflected in her confession that she had written a day or two ago to the child to tell her she was going to have a birthday. I had in that moment a glimpse of the heart-rending tragedy of age and loneliness . . . She referred to my card as being lovely and then added, in reply to my saying I had copied the design of the stork, 'One of my first recollections is of seeing a dead stork.' This was a cruel blow to me because I felt I had reminded her of a painful memory. She described it as lying in a shed: 'So it was funny you should have chosen a stork,' but she had no intention of hurting my feelings and it was just the kind of unconscious blunder which one would have expected her character 'Ideala' to have made! Remembering this I loved her for it, it being so essentially herself . . . Soon after this we were rejoined by the others. First by Miss Harford . . . Madame very gently and tactfully suggested that her dress would be better if lengthened, looking at her with kindly interested eyes, a true friend. She liked my black satin dress for she said, 'That will look nice till it falls off you!' Miss Harford offered to drive me back. It was kind of her but I got out of it . . .

July 16th (at Sion Hill Place.)

Dressed and went up to my Darling. The storm clouds cleared away as I arrived and I found her in the dining room wearing her dark blue dress. It was lovely to be with her alone in her own home again . . . She unlocked her desk to please me and we sat together while she showed me portraits of herself and family. It was such a beautiful happy intimate time, journeying with her into the past, tracing her present self in her younger portraits. She showed me photos of her home in London, the dining room, drawing room and hall with African spears and curios on the walls. She gave me a print of one photo and also an illustration of herself from a paper. There were some of which she had said, 'I had a figure in those days!' and one wearing the latest creation from Paris, a short waisted black satin coat and a toggle with an upright loop of a bow in front for trimming, her hand holding a simple lily, and there was one taken by Miss Ross, looking up quickly with a cigarette in her hand full of life and cleverness. There was one also of her son Archie in profile, and some of Beth very charming about the time of her marriage . . .

August 6th

. . . Darling lent me *The Temple Magazine* for 1896 with an article by herself in it on *The Modern Girl*.[85] She spoke too of Harriet Martineau[86] and said that she (Mme) had all her books and of what a statesman had said of her, 'Everything is being upset by the little deaf woman of Norwich!' . . .

August 13th

Dressed and went up to my Darling. I ate a large tea for me . . .
We talked of the Blue Shirts in Ireland. 'Blue shirts, red shirts,
bronze shirts,' she smiled, 'They were all started by Garibaldi!'
. . . She did not think that France would ever return to a
monarchy, but Germany might and she wondered what the
Kaiser thought of all the happenings there since his abdication.
She had met Sybil Ruskin's grandmother,[87] Mrs Raphael, at San
Remo where the latter had had a quarrel with a bosom friend
over 'Bridge' and the rule of silence during play, and they never
spoke again to each other! Darling was in her dark blue
dress . . .

August 27th

Another glorious day. I put on my fawn net dress to go to tea with
my Darling. She had been to the postbox and kept her hat on, her
brown straw with her *bois-de-rose* dress. We had a happy tea and
were in sympathy again . . . She said one must write continually
if one did not want to be forgotten by the public. She said that the
Americans liked her better and said nicer things about her when
she refused to enter the slaughterhouse at Chicago than they had
before. Someone had said it was such a wonderful sight but she
could not feel it was that, however expeditiously they were killed.
She related how she had heard of a child who had patted and then
kissed the side of a beast hung up in a butcher's shop. Unless we
had been brought up to see them all our lives, she said, we could
not bear the sight of a butcher's shop. I spoke of the lamb being
killed in the opening chapter of *The Beth Book* and asked if it were
true. 'Yes,' she replied. 'They used to be killed in the open
street.' She had put nothing but what was historical in that book
as she wanted to make it sound sincere . . .

September 3rd

. . . At tea I mentioned that I was reading Clough.[88] I quoted the
poem 'Say Not the Trouble Naught Availeth', and Darling
answered with the verse about 'the tired waves vainly breaking'.
We both thrilled to the particular loveliness of the words and
Darling said that he would always live by that one poem. She did
not know his works very well. She had been given a volume of his

poems by Bram Stoker[89] when she was staying at a golfing centre in Scotland . . .

I had recently lent my Darling an old journal of mine to read, in which I had kept a record of our first meetings together with other matters and conversations. Now suddenly she referred to it, with that difficult utterance to which deep feeling impels one, her sweet face suffused with the flush of generous faith, a noble indignation paramount. 'Divorce!' she cried. 'What was that about divorce? There was never any divorce between us. I loved my husband. My man would have done anything to defend me, he would not have hurt me for the world. It was a great sorrow to him when the rumour got about. I think he would turn in his grave if he thought . . . But I know why it was, I think . . .' and with a gradual but swift reversion to self-control and calm, she recalled what she had once before told me of the wife of Talley-rand who bore the same name. (This was the sense of her broken sentences conveyed to me, I do not pretend to have remembered them in their exact order.) I had felt struck with dismay at the unexpected strength of her emotion, and at the thought that I had ignorantly offended her, for I could not recall the passage to which she alluded in my diary. It was a remark I had recorded, she told me, of Mrs Humphrey's, and in that moment in the dawn light of the love and faith of other years which was flooding her still and was actual and present with her, I had to readjust all my romantic fancies about her. I had to replace my identification of her own married life with that of Beth in *The Beth Book* and to substitute a deeper and purer reality, a simpler and lovelier verity.[90]

She went on then to other passages. 'I think your associates were not very nice, they were so censorious no one could stand up against that kind of detailed criticism,' she said referring to a criticism of her smoking. 'I should never ask any young girl to smoke, I don't think it is good for them and I should never say, "Have a fag"!' 'No,' I replied. 'You would much more likely have said, "Have a cig"!' She laughed at that and went on to tell me how shocked even the Mayor had been when she began as Mayoress to smoke in public. The first time he had suggested that she should have a screen put round her, but before the end he always had cigarettes ready for her and bought her boxes of them. At the luncheon party held in honour of Viscount

Haldane, she was seated next to him, and was talking so inter-
estedly that she forgot to light up after and so give the signal for
the ladies to smoke. The Mayor sent Jordan round to remind her
that Lady Horner was waiting for her example before lighting
her own cigarette, and that was the only time, Darling added,
that the Mayor came near to rebuking me for a neglect of my
duties as Mayoress . . .

Madame rose on that and I touched her hand remorsefully.
'You didn't mind me giving you that book to read?' I asked. She
turned and looked at me sincerely. 'No, of course not,' she
replied. . . .

Upstairs I thanked her for sending me the number of *The Vote*[91]
with the article in it about and by her. She told me that the writer,
Mrs McCracken, had written to ask her her views on women of
the day and for some anecdotes, and she had complied rather
hastily. Mrs McCracken had later asked to be allowed to incor-
porate Madame's letter in the article. Darling could not then
recall all she had said but did not think it could offend anyone but
the Editor of *The Fortnightly*. This was Frank Harris and he was
dead, so she gave her permission. Madame went on to relate how
after Frank Harris' attack on her in *The Fortnightly*[92], her publisher Heinemann had insisted that she should attend a semi-
public luncheon. The party was seated when Frank Harris
entered and looking round the table asked in a voice that all could
hear, 'And where is the lady who – – –?' Madame turned to Mr
Heinemann and enquired clearly, 'Who is the little man with the
big voice?' whereupon Frank Harris subsided discomforted. At
the end of the luncheon Mr Heinemann detained both Madame
and her reviler and standing them together called upon him to
apologise. This he surprisingly did at once without demur and
kissed her hand. Mrs Hepworth Dixon,[93] my Darling said, went
round carrying the good news. 'He never tried to harm me
again,' she said.

Later Mrs Walters[94] on *The Times* asked them both to tea.
Harris asked to be permitted to call, but Darling, with her little
languid drawl, replied no, a busy man like him had no time for
making calls, and she did not think that they would agree if he
did. He took it very well, she added, with pardonable pleasure in
the recollection of this peaceful routing of an enemy . . .

Miss Clarke had come in and asked us if we had had a pleasant talk. I said that Madame had been scintillating and that I had almost asked her to stop in case I should forget all she had told me. 'Oh don't take notes,' she laughed. I was silent, loving her for a few moments when her dear voice broke in on my reverie. 'Have a cig?' she asked and then as I looked up quickly, the love light in my eyes, she altered it chaffingly to 'Have a fag?' and I reached out and touched her knee, worshipping the under-standing amusement in her eyes . . .

September 10th

I failed to develop my notes of this Sunday and can now only record one or two sentences. It was a very warm day and Darling was in her lace dress, the black one, her arms as I remember it bare – 'One gets used to being uncovered,' she said quaintly . . . I told her of someone who affected the modern fashion of tinted nails and this led to the discussion of other kinds of make up. 'All artificialty is repellent,' she said thus summing up the matter with finality. I mentioned a book of sayings by Pearsall-Smith, a review of which I had recently read. She had known his mother Mrs Pearsall-Smith[95] and spoke of her as tall, nice look-ing and elderly. 'One of my friends accused me of only caring for humanity as a whole and not for single specimens,' she volun-teered later, adding, 'She died.' Of the Church Darling said, 'It has nothing to say to me now,' and 'Catholics get more pleasure out of their religion – they are encouraged to pray about more things.' . . .

September 24th

After lunch I dressed to go to see my Darling, the first time in a fortnight. Ina and the dear dogs walked up with me. Madame opened the inner door, the outer being already ajar, to my ring and gave me her gloved hand. She had been to the post. 'How do you do,' she said and I rejoined as ceremoniously, 'How do you do,' and again, with a break in my voice, 'How do you do.' She was wearing the hat I trimmed for her and said she liked the shape better than any she had and that it was so difficult to find one suited to her age.

We talked of the Sitwells at tea and *Cavalcade*.[96] She said she thought there was one big moment when the two young people turned away from the taff-rail and one saw the word *Titanic* on

the lifebelt. She liked Diana Wynyard as being in appearance
well bred but she did not like the dresses which she did not think
were like they wore – not accurate to period. I said that I cried at
the departure of the troop ship for South Africa and Madame
replied, 'So did I, I remember it all so well.' But on the whole she
thought it just missed fire . . . I asked her if she had expected me
last Sunday, as she saw me downstairs. 'No,' she replied quietly,
'I didn't want you – not last Sunday.' She said it so seriously
that I felt it to be intentional. 'I always let you know,' she continued. I rallied from the implied rebuke and asked if we could
not come to some arrangement, saying I would always come in
future unless I heard to the contrary. Darling fell in with this. 'It
must be an awful fag for you to have to telephone always,' I
added. She came out into the Autumn sunshine, mellow as it was
and almost copper coloured. Dr Daymond next door had only
just ceased playing Bach. Madame had said that that music
always made her think of the player and not of the music as it was
so intricate. (*1964* What a good comment and how true.) We
spoke of the light and I turned, and she met my kiss lovingly, forgivingly, but I felt somehow that I had fallen from grace in some
subtle way . . .

October 22nd

. . . She told me it was ten years this year since she became
Mayoress for the first time. In that time 26 of her friends had
died, 8 of whom only were women . . . In her holy way she made
me feel today that I was beloved of her. I put my hand on her knee
and she laid hers upon it. Miss Clarke said, as I made an effort to
go, 'She does not want to outstay her welcome,' and Darling
rejoined, 'That implies that she could do so.'

   I took a tender farewell of her, blessing her and saying, 'I do
love you,' to which she answered, 'I am glad you do,' with a note
of sincerity and true rejoicing in her voice . . .

November 19th

. . . In an ill-advised moment I began reading her comments on
my Diary of our Friendship at night, and then the Diary itself,
sitting rapt and cold till after midnight, when in tears of memory
and tenderness I heard a sound on the landing which scared me.
It was only the clock but I got quickly to bed. But sleep I could

not, aching all over nearly all night. Felt tired next day but wrote to Darling . . .

December 3rd

The wind was high, she said it was a foreboding wind; it rarely has that feeling in it like the last pages of *Villette* . . . She produced a little paper-bound booklet on the value of vegetables which she presented to me as my Christmas present! and related an anecdote of Tennyson watching his wife and another woman taking an affectionate farewell of each other in the hall and commenting, 'What hypocrites you women are!' . . .

December 24th

Finished my imitation plum pudding and put the presents inside, dressed and started up the hill with it to Darling. Rested here and there as the weight was appalling. At the top of St Winifred's Lane I rested it on the low wall outside a cottage. Within, the voice of a man could be heard simply reading the Gospel Story. Children's laughter reached me from a further room and outside all was still, the twilight deepening. The moment had a concentrated significance and epitomised the Christmas meaning. I went on, and on entering I gave Edna the parcel and ran upstairs and went into the drawing room unannounced. I had asked Madame and Winkie not to watch from the window in case they should see the surprise destined for the morning and there they both were seated on the sofa hand in hand with the blinds drawn, the firelight on Winkie's red dress and on Darling's violet velvet, like two children they were . . . At last I had to go, my best bit of Christmas over. Darling one kissed and embraced me in the hall and I looked into her twilight eyes. I kissed Winkie and went from them warm hearted. Darling's Xmas letter I 'wore' all day.

Bath 1934

January 7th

I went to see my Darling. She was wearing the cardigan I gave her and looked well in it . . . Yesterday I had been to tea with Miss Gordon Gibson who was very much exercised in her mind because the late Mr Mead had 'come through' at a spiritualist seance as at his worst, and using slang! He said that Mme Blavatsky and Annie Besant are always fighting while all Paradise looks on. I repeated this story to Darling and with a flake of her old humour she replied, smiling, that it was strange that 'all Paradise' should think it worth while to watch! . . .

January 14th

I walked up to my Darling carrying an old yellow velvet dress of Mother's which I was to wear as the Marquise St. Evrémonde[97] at the Dickens Fellowship Party next day. There was a west wind and I found my Darling sitting on the sofa with her hair done on top of her head, all silvery *pouffes*, wearing her mauve cardigan over her blue dress. The twilight was soft blue behind her, the silver tea things before her shining faintly. She looked the spirit of a bluebell . . . She had been reading about Hans Anderson and we talked cosily of books; she suspected that I did not quite like *The Camberwell Miracle*[98] and I criticised it frankly. Darling said it had the essence of religion for her. She said she believed whatever belief she was reading about at the moment was true, and added in a low voice that she didn't think she had any religion or philosophy. That was because I had said that books on doctrine depressed me unless I agreed with them . . . She mentioned a book, *High Rising*,[99] by Thirkell which she had enjoyed and sent back to the library by mistake as she had not quite finished it. Edna the maid is leaving and we talked of domestics generally . . . Siegfried Sassoon[100] had lately married, she told me, and he and his bride spent Xmas at Tunbridge Wells and had Xmas Dinner with Daisy Ross[101] on boiled eggs, etc.

January 28th

I had been disappointed during the week by her not coming to tea as I had asked her, for she never comes now. I went to see her, feeling still a little sore. We talked of Stead[102] whom she had know, and of ghost stories . . . This lead us again to *The Camberwell Miracle*. 'You are as orthodox as anyone,' she said. We also talked of marriage. 'One lives on affection in marriage,' she said opining that love was not necessary. Her great-grandmother had 15 children. We spoke of a blue bag I had given her which she never used. It appeared Miss Tindall had said it was too good to use. This upset me very much. The next day I felt utterly downcast and miserable, and imagined a lot of foolish things. But after lunch I discovered a letter from my angel friend in the box and it broke me up. I cried and hugged it and then lay down and slept off my bad temper . . .

March 6th (At Clan House)

We left the dining room and its deepening shade to go to the drawing room where we meant to turn on the light but we found a golden sunset illuminating the room as with a lamp, lighting to an added glory the yellow jasmine in the window and the deeper orange azalea which repeated the tones of the rays in solid form. My Darling was in her purple velvet, purple and gold the colours of the crocuses that bordered the pathway without. I sat at her feet on the soft sheepskin rug and showed her the lace bobbins I had brought. She held them like the stems of flowers and the perfume of violets pervaded the air. Her face that had looked so faded and ill took on a faint animation and her eyes were bent upon me with their old kindness. I thought of the day she had so sat above me when she visited my room in the long ago, her face rock-like in its strength. Her influence seemed to come to me like a separate and moving entity between us, flowing quietly. I gave myself up to its charm and told her in the sunset beauty all my weaknesses and endeavours. And then I reached up and kissed her, begging her to get well soon and not to worry as she had been doing. And I held her hand with its wedding ring to my lips, saying I had not seen her for so long; such a little hand it looked. She suffered my embraces gladly but with her usual admonitory withdrawal . . . Welcomed her home on the 9th with some tulips . . .

April 4th

Sold the booklet with Miss Margaret Lloyd at the Pump Room Hotel, early during the luncheon hour. The Manager and the Head Porter most kind and helpful . . . We made £3.4.0.

April 15th

. . . I asked her to what cause she attributed her present debility and she replied that it was worry about the servants and also anxiety about Winkie and Beth.[103] The telegram summoning

Winkie home had upset her and also she had been working hard
before, writing. She had gone about perhaps too much, she
agreed, with Winkie during her stay at Christmas. But of the two
first factors, she said she went down before things like that,
adding merely as a matter of self observation, 'I am very sensitive.' 'I know you are,' I agreed. Darling said she thought that
every woman who could ought to marry, and we talked also of
expenditure and our own financial troubles. She told me
that nearly the whole of her capital was invested in the
Argentine[104] . . .

April 27th

. . . She had been reading a book on Christian Science, but
called it 'a farrago of nonsense'. She had closed her mind against
it, saying Mrs Eddy[105] talked of mind continuously when she
meant spirit, and repeated herself over and over again as if we
were idiots . . . Today she was as violently opposed as ever to the
teaching and flung back the book I had lent her as if it were
worthless. I read her Lord Haldane's definition of God as
Subject, but she refused to see that the Universe required a per-
cipient mind for its existence and seemed able to conceive of it as
self-existent. I gave up the argument, since I realised that her
intelligence is moulded on totally different lines from mine. But
the disagreement was a stimulus and I loved her all the more for
it . . .

May 6th

. . . Darling told me she used to work with Mrs Frederic Harrison though not herself a Positivist.[106] Madame helped her with
her girls' club taking the recreation evenings for years while she
was in London; they met at Newton Hall and had meetings on
Sunday. Mrs Harrison was a convinced Positivist . . .

June 3rd

. . . Of Reynolds' portrait of Mrs Siddons as the tragic muse, she
told me that Baroness Burdett Coutts[107] had had the original in
an alcove and below it she had always kept the red velvet chair on
which Mrs Siddons had sat to be painted . . .

June 6th

I went out to get a cigarette case for Darling . . . In the evening I sewed ruching in the sleeves of the black lace coat I am giving to Darling tomorrow.

June 10th [Sarah's eightieth birthday]

Everything in nature this morning seemed saying it was the 10th of June. Holiness wrapped the day compact of summer and Sabbath and associations with her. We took her presents up in the hot sunshine, white iris and roses I had picked in the garden. Afterwards I went to tea. Her field looked like a corner from the golden age, tall grasses and yellow flowers mingled with moon daisies and cow parsley and the Jersey cow in its soft luxuriance through which the sun shone as through hair and over which the trees waved, framing it in coolness and shadow. My Darling met me on the stairs, clad in her purple velvet and wearing her pearl bead necklace. She looked white and tired. Referring to the iris she said she always liked nature's finishing touches, nothing could have been more right than those touches of yellow on the petals. Miss Clarke came in to tea and Darling said nothing about my offerings all through the meal. We had hot seed cake and Bath buns.

Upstairs alone afterwards my Darling showed me the lace spread on the sofa and said she liked the texture, the pattern and colour of the lining, also the barbaric buckle. She said too that I had excelled myself in painting the card. She liked the form and design inside. She asked me what I had meant by the winged feet and I answered, 'A message,' to which she replied, 'I thought so.' She fingered the scent bottle, and we talked of that, and she showed me a basket which Miss Tindall's maids at Clan House had sent her with their cards. One referred to its being a special birthday (her 80th?). Darling said she had felt poorly yesterday, tired by looking at photos and drawings the day before, and had feared she would have to leave the tea table but she had got through . . . Darling thanked me again for all I had done and for my letter and on that her dear voice broke and I knew she was essentially herself and near to me in that second. For such revelations, fleeting as they are now, one endures the long withdrawal of her spirit and the eclipse of her old responsiveness. I recognised my own dear love in that moment and kissed her hand with tears and so left her, my heart wrung with love and pity yet blessed with an indescribable sense of spiritual beauty. Beth had not written but Darling hoped that a letter might come to-morrow . . .

June 19th

. . . As against accepting the whole of the Bible as inspired, she quoted certain bloodthirsty passages in Leviticus which she could not accept. She thought the present Oxford Movement[108] a kind of non-conformist revival among the upper classes . . . The other day, she said, she was trying to think of pleasant things, but asked herself, 'Has nothing happy befallen me?' and she could think of no unalloyed happiness. But, I suggested, surely there were days she would like to live over. She agreed that there had been days of excitement, which is a kind of happiness. I told her there were many happy ones in my life, many spent with her. 'That is a nice thing to say to me,' she rejoined. She said her happiest times had been when she had written her verses, that they had come without effort. She recalled 'Day That I Have Loved' by Rupert Brooke[109] and thought he was truly inspired by that poem. She said I was lucky to be able to 'grind it out' in writing, that she always had to wait for the moment . . . She spoke of one of her own first stories which was published in *Blackwood's Magazine*[110] and could not think how it was ever taken as it was so childishly written. 'But it was a good story,' she added . . . Talking of writing she said she could read her own works as critically and with as little feeling as if they were by someone else. She had so read *Adnam's Orchard* lately, but thought it so much over written. 'If I had had the strength I would have liked to rewrite it and make it into a story,' she commented . . .

July 4th

Sold the booklet at the Bath Rose Show in tropical heat in one of the tents. Had to keep going out for air. Ina got me some ham sandwiches . . .

On the *12th August* I was with her again and she talked of visiting Hardy every year at Max Gate. She suggested that her son Archie should take part in Ina's contemplated production of the play *Arising Out of the Minutes* . . .

August 26th

Went to see Darling; though I felt almost unable to do so I was very glad I did. As we were walking upstairs after tea my Darling amused me by taking exception to the ultra-modern sleeves of my dress which she said were 'an offence'. I apologised for them saying they were the fashion and I didn't much care for them myself . . . and so we entered the drawing room. I noted Miss Kimball's etching of Chateau Gaillard. Madame told me how once she was sitting next to Tree[111] at a dinner party when Julia Nielson[112] was seated a little way off. Tree turned to Darling and asked, 'Isn't she gorgeous?' We agreed that 'gorgeous' was perhaps the best word to describe her at her best.

I talked too of Lord Houghton's biography.[113] Darling said she had come across a book by Miss Martineau and in it a letter to her (Madame) relative Bellenden Clarke referring to Lord Houghton and saying that he had been 'an angel of goodness to her' (to Miss Martineau that is). We discussed *Kingdom Come*[114] by Hugh Redwood, I saying that books like that did me only temporary good. Darling said I had never felt the call to act, had never been converted, that things would be quite different to me if I had, that I should do things in quite a different spirit.[115] Christ would be 'an ever present reality' she said, accepting the phrase . . .

When Miss Clarke came in I referred to *Vogue* and to an article by Pamela Hinkson, a daughter, Darling said, of Katharine Tynan. I asked if Madame ever took that paper and she smilingly retorted that it was 'too low'. I said I censored the things I brought her. She liked the *Moon of Bath*[116] and said one hoped that things had been like that. Miss Clarke gave me cuttings from *The Daily Mail* of Dickens' *Life of Our Lord* . . .

Darling said there was great excitement at Clan House about the Royal engagement.[117] Miss Clarke had interesting letters from Lady Thomas the wife of the Prince of Wales' Private Secretary, so had already had an inkling of how things stood. Lady T. sent them fashion papers from time to time . . . We agreed that white roses would soon be fashionable as the Prince had given some to his fiancée. We talked of Winkie coming, she is 14.

September 2nd

. . . She told me she had witnessed the Diamond Jubilee Procession from the house of the Baroness Burdett Coutts which was opposite the St James's Park and when she, the Baroness, appeared on the balcony the people cheered her more than the Queen. The Baron said he wished he could have gone to the Abbey and Madame replied without thinking, 'Well, why didn't you?' 'I couldn't leave her,' he answered. This was Madame's first recollection, afterwards she thought it must have been one of the Coronation processions, and we then talked of the fallibility of history and how few people are born with accurate memories and how stories get altered in the telling. Talking of books carrying germs, and lending libraries, Darling said that letters could undoubtedly carry illness and that her son Archie once had diphtheria. She wrote about it to his brother [stepbrother] and he contracted it. He in his turn wrote while ill to an Uncle who caught the disease and died from it . . .

September 11th

I took Winkie to tea at Green St Fortts, Ina coming with us. Took her after to the Victoria Galleries and to see the Roman Baths and Abbey. She was flatteringly and pleasantly interested in everything. We took the bus home . . .

September 30th

My Darling told me that she had had a letter from a lady in Washington saying that ever since she was sixteen she had read *The Heavenly Twins* once a year, and that it was interesting to remember what Bjornsen Bjornsen[118] had said in his criticism 'that *The Tenor and the Boy* might have been deleted as it had no bearing on the story'. 'Of course,' my Darling commented, 'we know that that is so. It is not necessary to the story, but what interested me was that Bjornsen Bjornsen had reviewed the book, I did not know that he had done so.' She wished she knew what he had said further and could obtain a copy of his criticism. *The Heavenly Twins* she told me in addition was translated into Russian and Finnish. A Baroness Alexandra(?) translated it into the latter language. Darling could not remember her other name, but she had said that as it came out in parts, the Finnish women, to whom its point of view was entirely new, beseiged the office in crowds. There was a white rose on the drawing-room table and Winkie was wearing Madame's crystal necklace, her most characteristic ornament of which I had such a poignant memory. Madame had given it to Winkie . . .

October 25th

A letter from Mr Grand, Madame's son who had agreed to take part in my sister's play *Arising Out of the Minutes* for competition at the Arts Club at Bristol. I rang up Darling on the question of putting him up and she said of course he would stay with them. I wrote to him to that effect . . .

October 26th 1934.

I met Madame's son Archie for the first time. As he stood beneath the light in the morning room that evening blinking with a slightly puzzled expression at the illumination of our strange faces, his fingers touching, he had a decided look of his mother. But this likeness lay not so much in actual feature as in expression. Not tall and rather thick-set his figure reminded me also of Lord Haldane's. He was then a man over 60 [63]. As an actor he had grace of movement despite his weight and he possessed a sense of humour, sometimes rather coarse, which kept us in a state of hilarity that was new to me and stimulating. At rehearsal he took a masterful hand, with Ina's concurrence, in the production. Later I discovered a strain of sensitiveness in him and he would manifest a streak of poetry in what he did and said at sudden moments which was unexpected and oddly appealing. Quick to take offence, hot-tempered, stubborn, there was no moving him once entered upon. He had had a hard life made more so by his unbridled impulses which seemed to me never to have outgrown the nursery and forgivable for that reason.

November 4th

I went up to Darling wearing my new chenille dress, a kind of burnt sienna in shade. 'You are an orange lily tonight,' she commented. She talked of Archie and I sat on the sofa beside her and spoke of Mayoral days.

Fancying I had lately seen a difference in her demeanour towards me I wrote to tell her my fears on this next day. Two letters from her followed evincing a salutary impatience with my 'schoolgirliness' which she said she hated and saying that when her women friends talked of change it put her on her guard as she had lost friends that way before. I cried and was cast down until the 9th when I sent her my usual remembrance of the date and was rewarded by a kind acknowledgement.

November 18th

I made it all up with my Darling and was unspeakably happy. She had on her violet dress and I gave her a pink rose. The little cat came in, for we were in the dining room. She shaded her eyes with her hand then leaned above the fire with her hands clasped near her chin.

> And blessings on the falling out
> That all the more endears,
> When we fall out with those we love
> And kiss again with tears.

November 28th

My loved one, taking some reference I had made to my impecunious state in a letter, with touching seriousness, sent me a cheque for £15 as a loan to tide me over Christmas. I wrote and blessed her but did not cash the cheque, though she allowed me to keep it in souvenir of her kindness and generosity . . .

December 9th

I went to tea with Darling Madame. She told me how she was once asked by a certain *coterie* to give a lecture. It was rather a compliment to be asked to speak to these people and her lecture was entitled 'Mere Man', which took an hour and twenty minutes to read. Directly she began she knew it was unsuited to her audience who were not taking it in. So she read the opening and the most amusing passages and finished up quickly, to be met with a chorus of 'Charmin', charmin'!' They only wanted to see her and to say they had heard her speak . . . And furthermore [she] announced, 'I am not interested any more in the franchise of women, I think it has gone far enough.'

December 23rd

. . . She talked at tea of her sister's work as a trained nurse, how she had stood out for shorter hours and against probationers working in the scullery. She had taken on mental cases, studying the science of will power and had also been a masseuse. Once when abroad a doctor had come to her and told her he had a case of atrophy which was mental and persuaded her to accept it. The patient turned out to be Edith Wharton.[119] They took to each other and Miss Clarke went to America with her and finally completed the cure . . .

Darling was reading *The Memoirs of Gertrude Atherton*.[120] She noted that the author mentioned parties which Madame had attended and enumerated everyone but herself. *The Heavenly Twins* was published 1903 – *Patience Sparhawk* 1905. Madame recalled Thomas Hardy coming to her own At Homes. He would bring a rather large tall hat in with him and sit with it on his knees. He liked to sit with his feet inside the fender and would talk when the other guests had gone . . . Darling said she always waited for people to come to her.

People had to go to Meredith at the time Gertrude Atherton spoke of him because he was suffering then from locomotor attaxi and could not get about much. Darling mentioned that she had some relatives called Boynton[121] who live at Burton Agnes near Hull. There, in the hall, is kept a woman's skull, that of a member of the family in the time of Queen Elizabeth who was so badly treated that she died. She willed that her skull should be kept in the hall and a great misfortune should befall anyone who removed it. The present owner had it buried [but] so many were the things that went wrong as a result that he had to have it replaced . . . We spoke of Haldane McFall – her stepson. I asked if she had read his short biography of Irving. She had not known he wrote one. 'He was very brilliant, wasn't he?' I asked. She agreed. But he needed prodding she said; things came easily to him, he was a very good draughtsman. And she went on to speak of the other brother who had great charm, Irish charm.

Christmas Eve

I did up Darling's parcel and went out to buy her an azalea. Mother sent me up in a taxi to leave them.

CHAPTER XI

The Archie Tragedy: 1935-42

❦❧

I have two friends who often in my heart
With depth of cònfused love I've sought to blend,
Still undistinguishing which friend or friend
In their relation one, had largest part;
Indifferent to their difference, oft I'd start
Dismayed at its emergence to defend,
That each on other's likeness should depend,
And make no lasting schism in my heart.
But now I know their individual souls,
Like weather-prophets must divided live,
And in alternate coming teach at length,
From her the calm; in him what storms may give,
The moon's love her's and height of starry poles;
But his the sun when he laughs in his strength.[1]

In 1935 tragedy overtook Gladys. Considering the narrowness of her interests and outlook, the 'tragic mistake' over Archie assumed epic proportions and dominates the diaries of these years, proving more devastating for her than the declaration of the Second World War (which she later heard Mr Chamberlain announce on the wireless and only recorded because of the behaviour of her dog).

Gladys met Archie at Sion Hill Place in October 1934 when she was forty-five, and by the following June assumed that she was in love with him and that Sarah intended them to marry. (Archie was not consulted, but

appeared complaisant.) However, Gladys' assumption
that Sarah would approve an alliance between herself and
Archie was rudely shattered. Sarah's reaction shook
Gladys' faith in her and, if not ending their friendship,
drastically altered Glady's approach to it. Archie was an
attractive, flamboyant individual. His personality had a
vitality lacking in Gladys' enclosed world, a personality
which shows in the few letters he wrote her in his large and
generous hand – letters Gladys kept always. Archie blows
a welcome gale of life through the claustrophobic atmosphere that Gladys describes and one can well appreciate
his boisterous, selfish charm. (As Sarah observed, he was
'the opposite of [her] in every particular'.) Leaving aside
the symbolic reasons for Gladys' hopes for marriage with
him, he was certainly a character to sweep her up and out
of herself – probably the only forceful, amusing and
unattached male she had ever met. He was also passion-
ately interested in flowers and painting, an understandable
bond between them:

My dear GladAlice,
Having returned from the welcome relaxation of a
beautiful flower show I boiled the kettle, stirred
the tea-pot expertly with a teaspoon, and made
myself a nice cup o' tea.[2]

Did I tell you that your water colour of the calcareum
is very good indeed? When you know the
semperorium family in its varied branches as well as I
do, you will never worry about the shapes of the
rosettes, because you will find that the leaves open
and shut, and so greatly alter the shape of the plant,
according to the light, heat or damp that may be
prevailing at the time. In the warm evening,
especially, they open for the dew to soak into the heart
of the rosettes. Sorry to have no news, and so make a
dull letter – better luck next time I hope.[3]

Given Archie's charm, Gladys' obsession with his mother, and Sarah's professed interest in both Archie and Gladys, why did 'tragedy' strike? Perhaps Archie flirted with every woman he met, possibly he had inherited his father's desire for sexual relationships wherever his career took him; it is understandable that some of this information would come back to his mother, and reasonable to assume that Sarah would warn her friend of his unreliability. But Sarah did not simply warn Gladys. When Gladys confessed her hopes and plans, Sarah not only pounced on her with an uncharacteristic savagery, but she also seems to have exaggerated the facts of Archie's life, telling Gladys that Archie was twice married and once divorced. We do not know whether any of that is true but we can assume that if he had been married, he had not remarried. By 1937 Gladys had met and was freely mentioning a Miss Fabian in a letter to him, and that Miss Fabian was the sole beneficiary of Archie's will. (No other reference to a wife or divorce can be found.)

Three reasons could explain Sarah's ferocious reaction: that she considered Gladys ineligible to become a member of her family; that something far worse than divorce and remarriage lay in Archie's background, (possibly that she suspected congenital syphilis or that his way of life had been conducive to venereal disease); or she could have felt possessive jealousy that she would lose her hold over either or both of them. It is difficult to accept either the first or last excuse alone. However much she might have despised Gladys, Sarah would have assumed Archie's other, unknown, women to have been even less acceptable. And as for her feeling jealous of Gladys' avowed interest in her son, I feel that she must by then have been fully aware of her power over Gladys and that she was intelligent enough to appreciate her dominant role in their association. The possibility of Archie having congenital syphilis is unlikely – by the time they met he was over sixty and apparently in good health – and I doubt if Sarah, despite her earlier campaigning, was as hysterical as Christabel Pankhurst, who believed that 75 per cent of the male population was infected with the 'Great Scourge'.[4] We can only assume that she was taken by surprise, furious not to have been consulted, and quite churlishly bent on slapping Gladys down for her presumption. Gladys had to know her place – and that was not at Archie's side, any more than it was at Sion Hill Place, unless invited. Gladys was to come only when she was summoned, as Sarah had made quite plain early in their friendship, and not just when it suited her. Gladys may behave like a child and Sarah may treat her as a child, but son Archie was a grown man and such a combination was unthinkable. Sarah's reaction held no shred of feeling or compassion for Gladys. The whole idea was a personal affront to Madame Sarah Grand.

What led Gladys into this confusion of plans and assumptions is self-evident. Fate had presented her with the opportunity of falling in love with the son of the woman she adored. All her emotions could thus be wrapped tidily within one family. By marrying Archie she would have a closer link with Sarah: this must have crossed her mind when she first met him. It was such a perfect way to ensure Sarah's love and attention; such a cosy family they would be. And Archie unwittingly – not knowing how Gladys would interpret and misread every nuance and syllable – fuelled her passion with his friendly, easy-going approaches. He was, however, probably far more interested in the beautiful and dramatic Ina, whom he called Regina.

From those letters dated 1935 which Gladys kept (a note in the box announces 'several letters of this year which was the year of our upset about Archie, I destroyed'), we can see that Sarah recovered much more quickly than Gladys. Realising that she had harmed their friendship, and finding Gladys less eager to visit, Sarah wrote in September:

It seems as if I had seen you last ages ago in a far away land – the Sunday Afternoon Land, to which I must return to find you again. Keep me in your good recollection till then . . .

and in October she felt obliged to spell out her reaction to what she took as a rebuff from Gladys, for the first time finding it necessary to sweeten her response:

You were quite within your right, my dear, not to come and see me in the circumstances. I honour the convention or ignore it myself when it suits my convenience, or mood . . . The reason you gave for not coming this last time was [rather?] like a slap in the face. A shock. Why did you explain? . . . You had given the conventional excuse, and that would have been enough for me, as it would have been for a man. A man, in like case, would have answered his friend: 'All right, old chap, as you like,' and thought no more about it . . . There is wisdom in the maxim, 'Never explain'; but your explanation demands an answer from me. My attitude towards the whole question is the opposite of yours, as you will see. I must describe it to make you understand it. Differences can only be reconciled by understanding them, allowing for them, putting up with them, if you like. I repeat, you were quite within your right to honour an established convention. [Gladys had excused herself from visiting Sarah and Miss Tindall at Clan House because she could not return the hospitality.] The reason you honour it now, somewhat late in the day, I take it, is a change in yourself. It may or may not be a change of heart, but, any way, a change it is. I knew that that was inevitable. You have been in a state of upset for some time, on the move in every sense; at the end of one phase and not yet embarked on the next. Times of disorder are inevitable in the [---] of our individual pilgrimages; times when one doesn't know where one is or what one wants. To me your [unsettlement?] has plainly been working up to a crisis of late, and I have been concerned about you, but not afraid for you. There is always the promise: 'After darkest night / Comes, full of loving light, the laughing morning. / Hope on! Hope on!' Have faith in that as a promise; it won't fail you. And in the meantime, rely upon me to serve you to the best of my

ability in any way and at any time that I can. I shall keep your
welcome warm for you always in Sunday Afternoon Land,
and no one else shall ever be given the place there which
always has been and always will be reserved for you. I ask
you, furthermore to rely upon it that I am and shall be always
yours,

In change unchangeable
Sarah Grand
With my love.

And again, twice, in December:

. . . I am shy about expressing my feelings, but I do want you
to know that my heart is with you these difficult times, and
how deeply I am sympathising with you whatever the trouble,
how much I respect and admire your quiet restraint and the
courage with which you tackle the problems with which you
are faced. However sorely tried I am certain you are not nor
ever will be found wanting, and I am proud of you, my dear.
It tries me sorely not to be able to be of any real help to you.

Your parcels have always expressed the love I value, but this
year I feel something added to that – is it a better understanding? A greater tenderness? No, words don't express spiritual
values, and it is no use trying to find the one to describe what
I mean by the *something added* this year to all else that you have
ever put into your parcels that I am glad of and prize . . .
Dear one, I do love and appreciate and thank you for all you
do for me, the help you give me, and the pleasures. You have
made yourself very dear and precious to me, and I give you so
little in return . . .

By this time the Singers-Biggers' fortunes were low, and
early in 1936 they left for a more economical but unhappy
life in London – 'the technical end of my long and dear
association with my Darling friend'. However, Gladys
journeyed monthly to Bath to visit Sarah, and with that
distance between them the friendship revived. Sarah's
letters chatter on with memories and advice:

What a *Special Correspondent* you would make if only you could get into that [line?] on a good newspaper! A fine position with few women in it, and those few at the top of the tree. Women are better observers than men, no detail escapes them, and the few who master the art of [selection?] have an immense advantage over the majority of masculine observers. They know how to put in that finishing touch that converts a bald description into a picture and brings it to life . . . the *Spectator* I hear they give five guineas for the serial rights (mind you always stipulate so as to make them understand that it is only the *serial rights* you are selling them, otherwise you may lose your copyright).

. . . have been reading an interminable book – 1037 pages – a remarkable book. Perhaps you have read it: *Gone With The Wind*, by Margaret Mitchell, an American. It grips one and won't let one go. I wish it would for I don't want to be made either to think or to feel.[5]

The Victorians are coming into the news again now, and I was among them though not of them, it was before my time, a reformer and a prophet . . . and was so tenacious there was no ignoring me or casting me out. That was in the early nineties, and it was not till that Committee of some of the highest ranking ladies in the land sent one of their number to me in Tunbridge Wells with the message: 'Tell Sarah Grand that everything she said has proved true' (words to that effect . . .). And that was during the War. There is much substance for an article in that story which could easily be placed here and in the Colonies and America – those [critical?] times being the [theme?] and 'Sarah Grand Yesterday and Today' being used as a peg to hang it on . . .[6]

(Gladys has scribbled on the envelope of this letter:

'A review of her literary life hoping I might make use of the information to earn some needed cash for myself! She had forgotten that she had already told this story in the Preface to the new edition of *The Heavenly Twins*, 1927.'[7])

. . . Archie certainly enjoyed his birthday party, good man! They're so easy to please, men, worst and best of them. No sensible woman can fail to make them happy. She has only to

feed them and flatter them – the former well, the latter
discreetly.[8]

In London Gladys could pursue Archie with more ease.
The letters from him which survive are all dated 1936 and
1937 and show that he was unaware or unconcerned about
her 'tragic mistake'. He thanked her for photographs and
stamps, bemoaned the state of theatrical employment,
filled in details about Haldane and the McFalls' motto and
even attempted to console her:

I have just remembered that I have not answered your
burblings about my not having any possible conversational
subjects in common with you – that is sheer bunk! . . . I am
sure that, leaving aside the debating society battle royal we
could always enjoy about my relations, we should talk just as
fluently about dogs or house-keeping or perhaps gardens.[9]

But, as if the earlier upset and the foundering of Gladys'
dreams had not been enough, in November 1937, two
years later, Archie managed to cause far more trouble
between Gladys and Sarah. At this stage the letters hold
more than Gladys' Record, possibly because she had
learned to practise restraint in the diary, perhaps because
she cared less this time, and Sarah's fury had smaller effect.
As Sarah spells out in her letter, the trouble arose because
Gladys mistook Sarah's suggestion that she edit her
'literary remains' for a request that she act as literary
executor. Archie, an executor of Sarah's will, likewise
assumed that he would be literary executor. The letters
themselves explain the confusion. First came one from
Archie to Gladys mentioning his literary executorship of
Sarah's work and continuing:

But about a year ago, when I was in Bath, S.G. developed one
of her attacks of wanting to sell things, and talked of selling
her MSS – I begged her not to think of selling anything, as I
knew from personal experience that no one could get any
prices under present economic conditions – adding that people
were not buying necessities, let alone luxuries. Apparently

frustrated in her attempt to decide under which of these headings her MSS belonged, S.G. closed that subject – which I do now, I hope finally.

And later Gladys wrote to Sarah with her usual reckless-ness and incaution:

Darling,
I must ask you to relieve me of the post of Literary Executor with which you have honoured me – I told Archie about it and I find that the idea of acting conjointly with me – a point you did not reveal to me – is distasteful to him. Under the circum-stances it would be impossible for me to carry out your wishes, and I do not feel equal to envisaging even in prospect the dis-putes and bad feeling that would result from my taking part in what should be an entirely family affair. I am sorry that this letter contradicts the one I despatched to you last week, but then the present situation had not arisen.

Then Gladys wrote to Archie:

Dear Archie,
When I wrote to Madame that evening after receiving your letter, I said that I had told you about the Literary Executor-ship and that I found that the thought of working with me in that capacity was distasteful to you, . . . Madame has not replied yet, but I feel I would like to justify my action in your eyes if I can. You have not a very high opinion of women's loyalty as it is, and I fear I may by my unpremeditated words have lowered it still more. If Madame should make you acquainted with the contents of my letter, you may consider that I have been false to my friendship with you.

And she also kept the draft of another letter to Archie, dated 24 November, in which she refers to a Miss Fabian. We can assume that she is the Miss —— referred to by Gladys in the Record.

(Perhaps you will both hate me so much that it may draw you together! In which contingency I should be almost glad to be the scapegrace!) [deleted] But truly I cannot understand why Madame wished to put that onus and responsibility upon me,

without the stipulation I mentioned it might have succeeded.
She did not reveal the fact that you were to be the other
Executor – and if she had wished to make a breach between us
she would not have arranged it all so early in our acquaintance, as you say, in 1933–4. I did not refer in my first letter
to you, to the financial aspect – naturally all monies accruing
from the sale or publication of the MSS I was prepared to
regard as belonging exclusively to you – I felt all through the
interview that Mother's main wish was that you should benefit
from them. I may have been wrong in writing about our talk
as fully to you as I did but I told you my reasons for doing so,
but I wanted you to be possessed of the main points, so that
any possible intention of Madame's to break our friendship
would be counteracted, and so that you would not misjudge *my*
intentions in the event of your marriage to Miss Fabian. It's
all an unhappy muddle and I am more sorry than I can say
that it should have happened and that I have made it worse
and so [maimed?] beyond redress 2 such dear friends as her
and yourself. Yours, Gladalice.

P S Possibly I took it all too tragically and her instructions
which seemed to me of a nightmare quality then may have
been as unpremeditated and as open to argument and
alteration as the words of my own letters.

What (or whether) Sarah replied to Gladys in the meantime is not known until her letter dated 9 January 1938:[10]

My dear Gladys,
I have only just opened your letter of Dec 21st. I have been
too ill to attend to my Christmas letters until now, and even
now it is against the doctor's advice that I have begun to do
so. But I feel I must make an exception in yr. case or you will
be more unhappy than you need be made by my silence. You
seem to have misunderstood me when I sounded you
tentatively on the subject of my literary remains. I was only
enquiring if you would care to edit them and arrange them for
me after my death. It was a task for which you are well qualified and I hoped it would be congenial, I knew if you
undertook it it would be conscientiously and well done. I had
no idea of asking you to be my Literary Executor; you had no

qualifications for that part of the business, and I had not asked anyone else. In fact I had only just begun to consider what would be best to arrange about my literary remains, and you were the only person, so far as I recollect, to whom I had mentioned the subject at all. And that in a private interview. It is understood in my way of life that matters mentioned or discussed in private interviews are not to be repeated to anyone without permission. To do that is – well, it is not done. *Noblesse Oblige*. It was therefore a shock to hear that you had not only repeated this private conversation, but had repeated it – or the gist of it – to a member of my family. Like most other people, I do not intend to have my Will, or any clause in it, known until after my funeral, if possible. Nothing but mischief comes of premature knowledge of the contents of Wills.

Your acceptance did not settle the matter. There was a good deal more to be discussed, but before I had time to reply, you had written to Archie. Then you wrote to upbraid me for not having 'revealed' to you etc., etc. which was tantamount to accusing me of having tricked you into a false position by concealing a fact which it was essential that you should be told. After ten years close 'friendship', you could think that of me! It never occurred to you that there must be some mistake. Archie no doubt answered you on the assumption that, as an Executor, he would have the disposal of my lit. remains himself. A mistake. I can dispose of them myself by Will in any way I choose and I intend to, but, as I have said, I was only then considering how best. It was probably the first Archie had ever heard of literary remains and Executorships. I have not said a word to him about your [episode?], I do not intend to. And I beg that you will not say any more about it to him yourself. If it drops now, it will be forgotten . . . Any explanations with him would only keep the mischief going and reveal more of my business. You ask me to forgive. I don't presume to be in a position to forgive anybody anything. I am not resentful. I try to understand. That is the best [wisest?] thing to do in the circumstances. I am afraid this letter will not be any comfort to you. But it had to be written. And the writing has exhausted me for the present.

I wish you a happy New Year, and remain in change
unchangeably your faithful friend,
S.G.

P S The difficulty of writing at all, especially in bed, will I
hope be an excuse for the curtness.

In 1939 the Singers-Biggers sold 'some of our dear and
treasured pieces of furniture' to cover the cost of moving
back to Bath, and rented a small flat three doors away from
Sarah's house – a situation that earlier would have
delighted Gladys. Now, however, with her 'estrangement'
from Madame and Sarah's failing health and memory, it
meant very little to her. Her friendship with Archie had
petered out and ended in 1938; Sarah had been right about
the change in her friend, 'at the end of one phase and not
yet embarked on the next'.

As usual, Gladys moved house at the whim of her
mother. By 1941 they were back in London.

In March 1939 Nellie died of cancer and Sarah's reply to
Gladys' condolences lies in its envelope on which Gladys
had written 'A cruel letter':

Do try and understand the position here, dear one. My sister's
death added to the sorrow, has entailed the difficult business
on us of carrying out her last wishes, and settling her affairs.
We have neither of us time for sentimentality even if we had
the inclination. All this bother about 'feelings' is such school-
girlish stuff. We are neither of us whethercocks [sic] changing
about with the wind. I am not well enough to see anyone now
except people with whom I have to settle business matters, and
Archie has more than enough fully to occupy his time. I will
let you know when I can see you. Until then, please do not be
exacting.

In April 1942 Bath was bombed on two successive
nights, some 400 people died, hundreds of Bath homes and
historic Georgian buildings were destroyed, and Sarah was
forced to leave Sion Hill Place. She moved with her nurse
to Calne, a country town in Wiltshire about twenty miles to

the east of Bath, where she took a flat in the house of a Mrs
Harris at The Grange. Gladys returned to London to tend
her dying mother.

Bath 1935

January 6th (Sunday)

The weather turned much colder. I went to have tea with
Madame Sarah Grand at 7 Sion Hill Place.

I took the Victorian Dress which Miss Rawlins had lent me
and which I intended wearing as a character in Dickens at the
Dickens Fellowship New Year's Party. I slipped it on for
Madame over my own to show her and she entered into the spirit
of the fun and introduced me to Miss Clarke when she came in,
as a stranger.

'Go the light way home,' she said as I left. 'I am always afraid
you will encounter someone.' She was glad to read Winkie's
letter to me. Madame called Mrs Sonnenschein her 'G.A.'
('good angel') because she comes every morning to take Darling
for a walk. Madame says that sometimes she smokes a cigarette
at 4 a.m. when she can't sleep.

Madame having given me a book-token at Christmas on the
8th January, I bought H.V. Morton's book, *In the Steps of the
Master*[11], with it.

January 13th

. . . Mrs Sonnenschein came to tea and Miss Clarke also came
down. We talked of honey and cream and wine and the Bible,
and of capital punishment and of the decoration of rooms.
Darling Madame described my Christmas parcel and said she
did not open it for several days because she couldn't bear to spoil
it! Mrs Sonnenschein mentioned the return to favour of Morris
designs. Darling replied that she had suffered so much from
Morris papers (wallpapers) she could not think of his work apart
from them . . . 'I am glad that May Morris[12] is coming into her
own,' she said. 'She has lived for her father's memory.' Madame
recalled that she married her father's foreman. The marriage
turned out unhappily, said Mrs Sonnenschein, very early in the
experiment. She had put her father's socialistic theories into

practice and he had not approved. The man apparently disappeared.

'Did you know Holman Hunt?'[13] asked Madame casually as if it were quite a usual question. Mrs Sonnenschein answered as casually that she had met them at garden parties but did not know them well. 'She was a "deceased wife's sister",' said Madame, 'and she was made to pay for it socially.'

Before this they had discussed good manners (never put sugar and milk in the tea, but pass it, for example). Mrs Sonnenschein maintained that etiquette always struck her as insincere and hypocritical. Darling held that etiquette is the greatest blessing there is – social blessing. One knows one has done the right thing and there can be no jar. Mrs Sonnenschein was reading Morton's *In the Steps of the Master* and talked of the Temple. This led us to discuss the subject of sacrifice. Darling asserted that the revolt against human sacrifice was typified by Abraham's contemplated sacrifice of his son, and the substitution of animals by the appearance of the ram. The sacrifice (or the idea of the sacrifice) of Christ at the Crucifixion was, she held, atavistic but Miss Clarke and I held to the more orthodox belief that Abraham merely proved his obedience to God's commands, even to the last test of faith. 'That is not according to the latest critics,' Madame rejoined but Miss Clarke stoutly maintained that the authority of the Bible itself was worth all the critics . . . Upstairs Mrs Sonnenschein talked of her husband, the late Professor[14] . . . Madame spoke of his, the Professor's, works being popular. 'No, they were not so in England,' Mrs Sonnenschein replied. His scholarship was too precise, she thought. They were read for examinations. Internationally he was more popular in America and France and Germany. She referred to his book on Rhythm and told us how he believed that consciously or unconsciously English poetry was based on classical rhythms . . . This led us to Clough,[15] to Walt Whitman[16] and to modern Free Verse and its rhythm and how she believed a reaction would soon take place. We talked of the same trends in music and painting and how further licence would mean chaos . . .

Darling spoke well today, using literary words naturally with a keen grip of the subject under discussion, and I felt it to be a privilege to listen to such fine intelligence preserved despite age at a pitch of excellence that reflected the brilliance of a bygone era and to watch their sweet old faces smiling at and rallying one another as they smoked, and over all the luminosity of my Darling's shining star sapphire eyes. And yet 'Men were more exciting,' she said, talking of her preference for their conversation . . .

February 3rd

My Darling was in her violet dress and looking well. I had a little talk with her before Miss Clarke came down. Darling had opened the door to me and now, seeing Mrs Sonnenschein from the window, hastened to do the same for her. She had not told me that Mrs Sonnenschein was expected . . .

Darling joined in with an anecdote that when George Meredith lived at Box Hill he had a lovely view on which she commented thinking what an inspiration it must be. But he replied that the best view for a writer was to look out on a brick wall. At tea honey sandwiches brought the subject of honey and bees up for discussion. Mrs Sonnenschein said she hated bees because they were so cruel and had no individuality. They would never progress because they were socialists and she told how she found heaps of empty grub cases in her garden at times as they killed all those that were imperfect. Maeterlinck[17] and Virgil were spoken of. Mrs Sonnenschein said that Virgil did not know they were Queens, but called them King bees in his Georgic.

We talked of coincidences again. She told us how she had had an invalid in her house and how her maid had ordered a dozen oranges and she had remonstrated. The girl said she thought the quinine in them was so good for the invalid, whereat Mrs Sonnenschein went into a long dissertation as to how the real quinine was obtained from bark and how she thought the waters of Marah may have been embittered by such trees growing in the vicinity. Upstairs afterwards she was reading a League of Nations journal and found an article on the methods of procuring quinine from the bark of certain trees, in almost her own words. She instanced too the classical example of Adams' discovering Uranus at the same time as the Frenchman.[18] She had known Adams and had once looked through his telescope which moved as they used it so that they were able to keep the moon in view. He was a dear man. She went on to tell us of University etiquette and how particular they are at Cambridge about precedence. Two wives of newly-made Doctors were going out of a room and both drew back at the door uncertain which should go out first. So they enquired of each other at what hour their respective husbands had received the doctorate, and the wife of the one who had been honoured at 11.30 took precedence over the wife of the one who had not received it until noon. Darling said that as the wife of a senior officer, a surgeon colonel, she took precedence over women much older than herself and had not liked it as she was quite a girl at the time. Also, as Mayoress lately of course, she had had to go before Duchesses.

She had been reading *Gerald*,[19] the life of the actor Gerald du Maurier written by his daughter Daphne, and praised it, saying it was so real and unaffected. So often in biographies essential points were suppressed. I rather differed, saying I thought the girl should not have entitled it *Gerald*, and that I should not have called a book about my father, Hew. But Madame replied that they all called him that. Mrs Sonnenschein thought Madame was referring to the artist du Maurier, and this took them back to the Pre-Raphaelites 'Burne-Jones, etc.' and they were such good people, commented Mrs Sonnenschein in conclusion . . .

February 7th

As it was Dickens' birthday and the anniversary of the appearance of *The Heavenly Twins* I took some mauve tulips and a blue primula up to Darling to celebrate.

March 10th

To tea with Darling. She was not well and in a difficult mood. She had not liked the paper I had written for the Poetry Circle on Lord Houghton[20] and she did not care for the colour of my new dress. Miss Clarke said that Archie had enjoyed our mushroom soup! Discussed the play he had hoped to be in. I wrote to Madame next day and she misunderstood my intention in writing of her criticism of my Paper so that her answer hurt me cruelly. I thereupon replied as gently as I could. I bought some shamrock on the 16th and took it up with a little green mother-o'-pearl clip to Darling for St Patrick's day.

March 17th (St Patrick's day)

With Darling who was kind but distant. Something seems to have come between us or is it just my fancy and in myself? She was wearing the shell clasp I gave her. She told me of an Uncle who learned Hebrew at 96 and another relative who wondered why gardening tired her when past 90. Miss Clarke had provided blackberry jelly sandwiches saying that Archie had given them the jam. I enjoyed them . . .

March 24

My Darling kissed me of her own accord. Her hair had been newly washed and was white and fluffy. Her eyes with laughing imps in them and in a happy mood. At tea she told me why she had been unkind. Mrs Sonnenschein had left a book for me. Darling said that she had never felt like moulding her life on any one author. We talked of Richard Jefferies.[21] She had liked him in her youth. Mrs Warwick Hunt,[22] she related, had invited W.B. Yeats as a boy to stay with her. He used to roam lankly around the garden. Afterwards when she heard he had become a great poet, his hostess blamed her lack of perspicacity. Darling looked so like Archie at the door.

March 31st

I went to tea with Madame as usual. She was still happy and we kissed one another a second time on an impulse with laughter underlying it . . .

April 7th

With my Darling Madame. Mrs Sonnenschein there looking charming in a black dress . . . I asked Darling if she thought Archie would come in July to play the part of Dryden[23] in the Stuart Masque Ina had been asked to produce. She was non-committal . . . Bade me farewell with a light in her eyes and I loved her dearly.

April 14th

I went up rather nervously to my Darling. As I came round the Avenue bend I saw her at the drawing-room window. The sight of her took me right out of myself and my heart and soul flew up to her as to their home. She opened the door to me and kissed me. Oh, my own little mother. We talked for a while and I told her that Ina had written to Archie about the Dryden role . . . Mrs Sonnenschein sat on the floor, her face now noble, now gnomic, vital at 83. Mr sweet ate two cream cakes. She was in brown . . . Her kiss touched me like an angel's wing and I went from her purified and refined.

I bought her Easter flowers on the 18th, an Azalea, white roses and two arum lilies.

April 21st (Easter Sunday)

. . . When they discussed the marital disasters of actors I took part in the conversation somewhat too unreservedly under the circumstances, Archie being of the profession. Though I knew nothing then of his history beyond the fact that something had gone wrong in his domestic life. Darling opined that an actor's wife should not be on the stage and I agreed, and thereafter she smiled her secret smile, amusedly or seemed to, to my hyper-sensitive mood. I spoke of Mother as we rose to go upstairs and for a moment Madame paused on the word and looked at me. When Mrs Sonnenschein went Darling came back and asked if we had heard from Archie and we talked naturally of him. . . . A long, critical and amusing letter came from Archie next day, turning down the part of Mr Dryden. I wrote to Darling to tell her . . .

June 10th (Her [eighty-first] Birthday)

The flowers came in a motor and I called a taxi and took them and her presents up to her. Winkie had telephoned to say that Madame would call for me in a car this afternoon to go to tea at Miss Tindall's. The day was still after a stormy night, moist air and misty trees, waiting . . . They came, my beautiful in black face-cloth and beige blouse, Winkie, Mrs Sonnenschein and Miss Clarke . . . Winkie and Mrs Sonnenschein enlivened the party . . . When she got up to go she came to me saying, 'I must collect my family,' and raised her limpid flower eyes with what I, desiring a nearer kinship with her through Archie, took to be meaning, to my face, her hand on my arm. A shock of unexpec-ted joy went through me and left me filled with honoured and humble elation . . . We drove home together and were all happy. I asked Mrs Sonnenschein and Winkie to go with me to see the film of *Lorna Doone*.

Much of the pain and pleasure of mankind arises from the conjectures which everyone makes of the thoughts of others.[24]

June 13th

I come now to the most tragic mistake of my life – tragic to myself, but merely incredibly naïve in the opinion of others. At this distance of time it does seem unbelievable even to me that I could have deceived myself to such an extent. There are three factors to be remembered, I find, in looking back upon what led me to act as I did.

1. I thought that Madame wished me to take an interest in Archie and had suggested our meeting with that end in view.

2. I believed that she, and especially Miss Clarke, had already discovered the state of my feelings from a variety of delicate intimations which I imagined were plain to us both, intended and accepted as it were *sub rosa*. Indeed, one Sunday, the Sunday I asked if Archie would be likely to come for the Stuart Masque, Miss Clarke, who was laying out her cards for Patience, suddenly raised her eyes only less expressive than Madame's with a distinct question in them, which, taken off my guard, flustered as I was by giving voice to my longing for his return, I answered with mine involuntarily in the affirmative, acknowledging the correctness of her implied surmise. This look I thought Madame had intercepted and interpreted aright.

3. Having regard to all this silent interchange of underlying meanings, I gradually persuaded myself that I was encouraging a conclusion which I had no right to encourage. I was leading them to think that we had come to some definite understanding which was far from the truth and if I persisted in allowing it to remain uncontradicted I should be acting unfairly and placing Archie in a false position. But over and above all these considerations was the habit I had formed of telling Madame every smallest and most intimate matter that concerned me. I had no secrets from her, and I longed to impart to her this my loveliest secret of all, thinking it would make her as happy as it had made me. Therefore on June 13th I wrote to Darling and told her everything unreservedly, all my hopes and fears and joys and uncertainties, trusting her as my mother. Madame wrote afterwards that if I could have heard her exclamation of pain and

consternation on reading my letter I should not have thought her answer was heartless. But I did not hear it. Winkie brought me her reply and I had to sit through a nightmare afternoon at the cinema, through tea and the return with my guests after, before I was free to open the envelope. All that time it had lain in my bag on my lap, while my mind questioned and requestioned what its contents were likely to be. At last I took it on to the High Common and there seated on one of the benches where I had once been so happy, I opened it. The letter has long since been destroyed. Madame took for granted that I knew of Archie's divorce and said that as far as she knew he had remarried. From the opening words 'Your letter is soon answered' to the close, she softened no point that was calculated to wound my ill-advised attachment and sensitive self-esteem. She disavowed all knowledge of the network of confessional hints I had woven and had myself been caught in, saying they would have made her out but a vulgar match-maker and even suggested that I should console myself with someone whom she had thought more suitable in every way – who this hypothetical someone was I never discovered. But her repudiation of my dream was as nothing beside my realisation that she was not the mother I had thought her to be. How much of suffering on her own account, of disappointment, had gone to rob her of that tenderness I did not stop to ask. I was stunned by the finality of her reply and its coldness, and my pride was tremulous with indignation and sick from the blow she had struck it.

I wrote to her at once, not waiting for the night's counsel; when night came it held only the relief of tears. I did not go to her on the Sunday June 16th but I watched the white roses through the rain in our garden as speaking to me of her and what she had been to me. At night as I was sitting by the window in the drawing room a voice on the wireless sang 'Still as the Night – Deep as the Sea' and that exhortation to calm and constancy set me weeping again. I went to bed and was in misery all night for Darling. The next morning the white roses were an agony and a temptation to send to her, but I resisted the impulse. By the tea post on the 20th I had a letter from my Darling faithful, a conciliatory letter but one that again faced the truth and drew attention to my health as an excuse. I faced a mad suffering for a while, but finally wrote that I could not go to see her as she had asked. But the next day after an almost drugged sleep I woke to crying again for her, and at last I could bear my misery no longer and wrote begging her to see me and let us forget everything but our love and friendship for one another. I walked up to her house and dropped it in the letter box. The white rose petals were scattering the garden path when Winkie brought me another letter from Madame. She had returned to her unsympathetic attitude which not only confirmed me in my decision not to go to her but led me to confide the reason of my unhappiness to my own family. I wrote to tell Madame my determination to remain away from her for a time as the only way to save the remnant of our friendship.

The following days were taken up with the Stuart Masque in the Parade Gardens in aid of the Waifs and Strays. Miss Clarke and Winkie were at the opening performance, and came up after to speak to me. I think Miss Clarke understood that something had happened, but she did not mention it in any way and I was conscious only of restraint and hurt resentment. My sister produced the Masque most successfully.

On July 4th I woke to spasms of pain and Ina was just giving me some brandy and ginger when Winkie arrived with a letter from Darling. Ina told me and it seemed as if I heard through a dream without surprise. She asked me up on Sunday in her accustomed sweet way, promising to meet me at 3.45 by herself as I had requested in one of my notes. And so what could I do but cry my heart out with love and relief and write to say I would go, but I felt worn out with the long anxiety and could not think about what I should say when we met. After a wretched night dreaming of the day's ordeal I actually wrote a letter to say I could not go, but I tore it up. I put on my new blue linen dress and looked nice.

I went up to Madame's, therefore, on July 7th at 3.45. She explained later that her failure to meet me alone was due to an accident. Winkie opened the door to me and when Madame came in she gave me one worried anxious glance and kissed me warmly. But I could not then feel that all was well because she had not kept her promise. I understand now that it was natural for Winkie to run to the door as she was accustomed to do, and that it was impossible for Madame to stop her and explain why she wished to see me alone. Mrs Sonnenschein came, so that we never referred to all that had taken place. At tea Madame spoke of Henry James as 'a nice old woman'! We fitted the lampshade and upstairs listened to the wireless. I left early, hardening my heart against the drawing power of that little figure, against my impulse to enfold her in farewell, struggling as I was with the doubt of her sincerity. All through this time of trial it seems to me, on looking back, that it was Madame's loss I feared more poignantly than Archie's, the rupture of her friendship over-weighted every other consideration and yet the thought of his defection was not without its pain and bewilderment. I could not believe that he would have looked and acted so had he not been at liberty to claim my allegiance. (I was assured by him later that he was not married.)

Having taken Winkie one afternoon for an outing to the Hol-borne Museum, on the 13th July just a month after my ill starred letter to Madame, I wrote again to her to say *au revoir* as we were on the eve of leaving for the summer holidays, and to explain one little point, seeking a fuller reconciliation. On the 15th, the morning of our departure, I received a gentler and kindly explanatory letter from Darling accounting for not seeing me alone that Sunday. I made a dash for Sion Hill Place. She was walking on the lawn with Mrs Sonnenschein and Winkie. I gave her the schoolgirly embrace after all, making it all up, in fact two. 'I had to come,' I explained, 'in case something happened to me on the journey.' Madame with tender amusement in her eyes rejoined that something might happen to her in my absence, whereat I deprecated the possibility with emotion, nearly cried and left her hurriedly. I felt happy again and that evening we were in Lichfield – the immediate past absorbed in one more remote. From there we went to Matlock Bath whence I wrote to her and had her answer on the 22nd, and later I sent her a blue-john brooch and ring. She wrote me a sweet letter in return which brought tears to my eyes and which reached me in London where I bought her a transparent silvery grey toilet comb for her dear silver hair. Darling wrote me a letter of welcome on our return to Bath, August 1st.

A cold delayed my going to see her, and on August 9th I burned all the letters from Madame which had made us both so unhappy and the copies of two of my replies which I had kept. They looked like a black rose. One little fragment I saved; it had on it the word 'yours' still unburnt. The rest I intended to scatter on her field the coming Sunday. Winkie rang up to ask me up that afternoon. I owe it to Darling to record, as I have already said before, that in one of her letters, about the first she wrote to me at this period, she said that if I had heard the words spoken they would not have been or seemed too vehement; the tone of voice would have given her meaning. 'Oust it, my dear, as I have done. You will have no peace of mind until you do.' So she advised me, but her advice was too strong for me to follow at once. I had to work out my problem in all its aspects first, and it took me many sorrowful months, many a moment of ecstasy and of doubt and sadness before I could bring myself to acknowledge that she was right. I went for a walk on the Saturday with our little dog Jerry over Weston Fields. To the blue sky above I prayed to have my spirit liberated from all bitterness and selfishness, so that my Darling friend might be given back to me on the morrow. A blue butterfly rested on a thistle, the blue and purple so beautiful, exquisite beyond words.

August 11th

It was after four o'clock, her tea time, when I reached my Darling's avenue, but I paused to drop the flakes of the letters at the foot of one of the trees. They fell on a cobweb. She was waiting for me, the door opened by herself, and folded me to her gently and forgivingly. She was wearing all the trinkets I had sent her, witnessing so to the kindness of her feeling for me. Mrs Sonnenschein came in after Winkie had gone out, and then Miss Clarke in a new, red lace dress. We had a happy tea. Mrs Sonnenschein spoke of Joseph Chamberlain[25] and how some impractical women had turned him from his support of Women's Suffrage. Darling thought that it would have been a pity to stop them then as they would not have been as ready for the War as they were, had the advance been checked at that time. She was using my 'lighter' again and lit my cigarette from it. Winkie had sewn on the frill I had done for the lampshade. Upstairs Madame showed me my hydrangea still in flower. I thought, watching her, so compact and strong in spirit, that if she had shown herself as soft as I have wanted her to be on occasions she would never have accomplished her life-work. Miss Clarke kindly said that she was glad I had come back and I took her to mean the words in a double sense, and she asked me to help her choose a hat for herself in the town one day. When Mrs Sonnenschein went I showed my picture postcards to Darling and gave her the comb I had brought from London. She was pleased with it and sat clasping it. She was tired when I left and Miss Clarke saw me out, but all lingering bitterness and resentment had gone and I felt we were drawn more deeply and closely to one another than before. I kissed Miss Clarke at parting for the first time because I felt she understood and had been my advocate in spirit, if not actively, all through. I did not see Darling the next week but I took her up some flowers in a cut glass bowl, putting it on her table just inside her door and she wrote to thank me.

August 25th

Darling in her black cashmere and lace dress looked white at first and both she and Mrs Sonnenschein were depressed by the threats of war. Madame had stained her dress in some way and said forlornly, 'I see only that.' . . . Mrs Sonnenschein had two pairs of silk stockings on, one black and one white to obtain the desired effect of grey. 'It would never have occurred to me to do that,' Madame said, adding, 'but then I have no brains.' We talked of the Chippendale cabinets in the drawing room having belonged to only two people since their manufacture – of whom Madame herself was one – and of the wavy glass, 200 years old, in the fronts, one pane having been broken by a maid at Crowe Hall . . . Winkie, embroidering some *gros point* on a frame, suddenly informed me she had been given a Tennyson by Madame, and went to get it. It was an old 1871 American paper edition bound by a Chinese as it was given to Madame by a friend in China. It was illustrated, and at the end had the little poems 'The Window' or 'Songs of the Wren' with Sullivan's music. It was inscribed by Madame and a marker bore the verse about the soul of poetry consisting of remembering happier days . . . We spoke of our plans to leave Bath for London and she said a little wistfully, 'Are you anxious to be off?' But something was between us all the afternoon; it is an impossible situation fraught with pain for us both, and when she kissed me goodbye my heart throbbed to love her as of old and I could have wept it out but put a strong denial upon myself . . .

September 1st

. . . She told how at School she had shocked her teachers by saying she knew a man who had crossed the Red Sea on foot when
the tide was out. One could, she said, at a certain point . . . The
rain poured and the room was sweet with blush-pink roses almost
white. I remarked them thinking they came from Clan, but
Miss Clarke said they were some that Archie had pruned as he
knew how to do that. I held my breath but was glad to hear his
name. Darling looked so isolated and forlorn that my lingering
sense of antagonism, which still at times has tormented me,
vanished . . .

September 13th

I sent some roses with a little pink tumbler to put them in, to welcome Madame to Weston . . . She asked me to Clan on Sunday
but I refused and wrote explaining that I did not like to take hospitality from Miss Tindall which I could not return in any way.
On October 3rd, she replied. I had hurt her, but she ended up so
dearly that I spent most of the day on the verge of tears and sent
her some pink roses and carnations and wrote to her at night. But
she retreated again into her shell when she wrote next, making
me unhappy. (On October 10th we were in London and saw
what proved to be the new home destined for us in the New Year,
at 84A Philbeach Gardens.)

October 20th

I dressed early and walked up to my Darling. I composed no
speeches in advance, just went blindly, and then she opened the
door to me herself, standing with something – a flash of her old
gallant bearing, inviting, forgiving, and I looked at her, making
swift renewed discovery of her dearness and loveliness, and
threw myself into her arms, kissing her on a sob of surrender.
Oh, loved one! All was forgotten and healed in that moment, and
in my unpremeditated exclamation of how nice she looked. She
was in her black hat and costume, with her skunk fur . . . After
all our differences I rejoice to think that she remains so sure of me
and of my love for her.

October 23rd

. . . I spent the afternoon writing the journal of Darling's

Friendship (of which this is a later part), disintegrating the rainbow as it were, into component parts.

October 27th

As I came down the Avenue the west wind was making little jumping shadows of the leaves and branches as if they were a company of hobgoblins executing a dance of joy at our reunion. All is at peace between us and I thank God she has come back to me in all her early motherly tenderness and holy charm. She was wearing her violet velvet, and the pink shaded lights and her own better health gave her a soft colour. Her eyes were starry as they looked at me contemplatively or responsively in sympathy. We talked of the book I had been reading by George Meredith, *The Ordeal of Richard Feverel*.[26] Darling said Meredith was not a favourite of hers. She preferred more 'limpid' writing like George Eliot's. All she remembered of the story in question was 'the number of eggs they had eaten'. She was thinking of the breakfast on their honeymoon in the Isle of Wight. 'It was in his first manner – that was why I found it easy to read.' 'Yes, he knew the world,' she replied to one of my observations. 'And he knew how to write about women.' She thought I might like *The Egoist* . . . Also we discussed our new abode in London . . . She thought life would open out for me, though I did not feel it so myself. She would miss our Sundays together, she said, and we settled on Thursday as the day I should come to see her once a month. I said it had been so nice having her to myself today as I so seldom had had that pleasure lately. She held me close at parting and when I said we would make the most of this winter, she assured me I could come twice a week if I liked, and I warned her, smiling, that I might take her at her word . . .

November 10th (Sunday)

I went up to my Darling. She let me in but did not kiss me till we were in the dining room. Then of her own accord, as so rarely happens, she kissed me three or four times with unreserved sincerity saying they were for my letter which had touched her. Not, she added, for the presents, which it was against her principles to thank me for. She had nearly written and would have done so, but for that. I laughed, tears in my eyes, surprised that what I had said a thousand times, this once had reached her heart . . .

November 17th

. . . When Madame went down to see Mrs Sonnenschein, Miss Clarke suddenly spoke of Archie, that she had had a sympathetic letter from him about her illness and that he was still wearily going round the agents with no success, which was a great anxiety to him and to his mother, who helped him financially. 'I think he might do something else,' (than acting) Miss Clarke said, and I suggested 'writing' as once before I had done to Madame, as he writes such good letters. But Miss Clarke thought one had to be so new in the way one wrote nowadays . . .

December 15th

. . . Mrs Sonnenschein wanted to know what kind of a child Madame had been. She was always up to mischief she answered; would climb out of the window at School to play on the lawn and go down to the kitchen for the breakfast bread and butter and take it upstairs! (See *The Beth Book*.) 'But I was not expelled,' she announced in triumph. 'The headmistress only wrote to my mother that I should do better at another School – I was never expelled,' she repeated, smiling . . .

December 20th

My Darling's Christmas present to me arrived unexpectedly and was in nature as unexpected as its arrival. A pair of green Chinese beetle ear-rings set in gold.[27] They represented a happy period of her early life she wrote and I was deeply touched by her giving them to me. Her 'Heavenly Twin' beetles I called them in my letter of thanks.

December 22nd

. . . We discussed *Diana of the Crossways*[28] by George Meredith which I was reading. Miss Clarke said that Diana represented Mrs Norton,[29] and Dacier, Lord Melbourne;[30] that a friend of hers had recognised all the characters and was indignant. The incident of selling the political secret had really happened. Darling told me that Miss Harford was to be with her for Christmas Day and, she added, Archie. I made no comment beyond 'Oh' . . .

Christmas Eve

I took my parcels up to Darling and put in a card for Archie. Pouring with rain so I went up in a taxi.

December 29th

I dressed in a mood of uncertainty for tea with Darling, as Archie had made no sign over Christmas and though Madame had written me a lovely letter, one of her loveliest, on Dec. 27th, she had made no reference to his arrival. I had been in an inferno of doubt and suffering, wondering what caused their silence.

When I reached her dear house, she opened the door and in the gathering twilight as we entered the dining room to await tea, an extra plate was laid. Mrs Davis, on entering with the tea, asked if Mr Grand were coming down. Madame assented. And so I met him again. He came in rather nervously and I rose and shook hands saying merely that it was nice to see him again. It was almost dark in the room until the lamp over the table was turned on, giving a sense of intimacy to our little repast. I was quite calm and managed to take it all as a matter of course and naturally, and after the first strangeness, the same sense of relationship was established. I enjoyed tea with Darling and him in the quiet intimacy, and laughter and conversation were unforced. I was ideally happy, feeling both my dear friends in harmony, and wanted nothing more than their company, in the simplicity and cosiness of her familiar room. Upstairs Miss Clarke awaited us and she and Madame looked on while Archie and I talked together on the sofa. Once he looked at me, when putting on coals, in that peculiar kind of way he has, and I felt all my old responsiveness rise up to meet his glance. We talked of the Pyramid prophecies and the British Israelites,[31] among other things . . . She left me on the stairs when I took my leave and Archie helped me on with my coat, promising to come to tea before he returned to London and, opening the door, he said the old ladies liked him to read to them of an evening.

We stood a moment in the purity of the frosty air and I then hurried away. I felt happy and appeased as if some hunger had been satisfied. Archie came to tea with us on the last day of the year. I wrote to Darling . . .

Bath and London 1936

January 17th

I went up to Madame's for lunch as invited, but worn out with the last few days of strain, clearing out and packing up, sorting and dispensing with our unrequired belongings to dealers and charities, etc. I found the contrast of ultra quiet in her imperturbable surroundings a little trying. Madame told me at table that according to an old book on etiquette one should never use a spoon and fork to pudding unless absolutely necessary, but only a fork. As I was using both with Queens' Pudding I felt for a moment rebellious and rubbed the wrong way but I continued to wield them nevertheless, determined not to give in. I managed also to spill some coffee from a broken spout on to the polished table. They talked of Archie and of how he won't try for appointments they think he should make an effort to obtain. I took his part.

. . . After a rather touching little talk on reincarnation I left early and returned to give the dogs a walk, their last over Lansdown fields. Took belated snapshots which did not come out very well, the fiery winter sun low on the horizon and the mists spreading like an anticipation of the distance soon to be set between her and me.

January 19th

This day marked the technical end of my long and dear association with my Darling friend. Things were never the same thereafter . . . and try as I would to hold the beauty fresh and unfaded in my grasp, it receded gradually into the mists of the bygone. There were times when indeed the flower bloomed anew in my grasp and even now I have the petals which, if she could and if she would, might be breathed upon by her till they assumed their early contours in my heart, and I look beyond this life to that possibility when we may reach once more the perfect understanding of our earliest companionship. For though I have had other attachments, and one that eclipsed her for the moment, she has been my only lasting love 'in change unchangeable' forever.

After having had lunch with Mr and Mrs Bagshawe next door, I rested a while then I got ready to go to Darling, taking Bobbin the cat, my spinning wheel which she had promised to take care of for me, and the box containing the remainder of the booklets. My Darling looked so sweet and cosy and round in her dressing-gown of black satin. There was a silver mist outside which lighted the room to silver too, and rested softly on the silver tea things. Darling in the course of our conversation opined that painters as a race were more interesting than writers as they had more to say, having perhaps accustomed themselves to talking while working. Writers, on the other hand, observed more than they talked . . .

I tried vainly to thank her in adequate words for all she had done for me, all the meaning she had given to my life, the new values, the hours of happiness I owed her, and then I broke down. She helped me, saying gently that she did not like that I should think I owed her, and we talked of friendship and its significance, and made a day for meeting again. Miss Clarke came in and gave me some sweets. Outside it was raining, raining; I went along the Terrace to leave a little box with a string of beads for Mrs Sonnenschein, and then fearing to spoil my hat, I took it off and walked home crying with the rain, my face wet with mingled tears and rain drops like a creature from Bedlam in the dark, and I wrote to Darling at night. The following morning I sent flowers to my beloved friend and fruit to dear Miss Clarke and finally caught the 3.30 train to London with the two dogs, Barney and Jerry. Ina, my sister, met me and I joined her and Mother at the Van Dyke Hotel opposite the Natural History Museum, Brompton and Cromwell Road. King George V died that night and the national sorrow aggravated my personal sadness and cast a gloom over the initial days of our new life . . .

February 27th

I spent one of the happiest and holiest days of my life. After work I caught the 1.15 to Bath from Paddington to see Madame. Relief came directly the train began to move and my eyes to feast on the first green fields and cows in the sunshine. After the infinitude of trials and tribulations of settling in and getting accustomed to a totally new and entirely uncongenial mode of existence necessitated by our ever dwindling income, the prospect of a return to the pleasant scenes of a happier past was like 'balm to a hurt mind'. We were at Box Tunnel before I realised. Words fail me to describe the sweetness of alighting at Bath, finding it still there! I was radiant.

I stopped at the Bank and then drove on to my Paradise, to be clasped in my Darling's arms. Bobbin was at the door. Upstairs I threw myself on my knees before my dear and kissed her again in tears. 'Oh Mother,' I cried, 'I have been so miserable.' She comforted me quietly. Then, after, we talked and talked. She was in her brown and wearing her crystals. She agreed with me that happiness is not always found in living for others, unless one worshipped the other and then the worshipped one might not allow such self denial. Or, I chimed in, one might not have the opportunity. We went downstairs for tea and there were Christmas roses and Winter Jasmine on the table and a hot seedcake. Miss Clarke came in. Darling wondered who had ordained that the late King's funeral should be 'a walking funeral' – 5½ miles for those old Admirals, something of a joke!

. . . We stood together feeling the intense peace at the window. 'Almost tangible,' I said, and Darling looked up at me understandingly . . . Afterwards, she leaned her head restfully against the black cushion on the sofa and I watched the flames of the fire as so often before. Oh, it was so lovely to be there again! At last the car came for me and my loved one came out on the doorstep with a little gesture of farewell. I was a different creature when I left her. I sat in the train in a trance of uplifted thought and memory, on my heart's knees before the spiritual beauty of her individuality which no recital of items of conversation, nor descriptions of her manner or looks can give any idea of . . .

March 24th

. . . Bath looked a dream city basking in the sunshine and Oh it was wonderful to be with my Darling again. She was in the blue dress which she has had dyed black . . . I showed her a letter which Archie had written in the magazine *The Amateur Theatre* which we had cut out, about 'Ham' actors. 'Fancy Archie bestirring himself to write that,' she commented . . . The opalescent vase I had given her (the big creamy-white one) was filled with yellow forsythia beside the Mayor's portrait. With the light shining on her crystals, my very Darling looked all crystal clear hereself and luminous, like an angel lighting the room. I put my arm about her on the stairs and we almost promised to meet again for Easter. She gave me some tongue sandwiches to eat on the train going home. On my walk in Kensington Gardens next day I had a wonderful feeling of the eternal quality of my love and friendship for Darling. We shall never really be separated whatever happens . . .

April 12th

. . . She talked of her visit to America, how she really did not get to know the people because she went from one home of friends to another. She had many introductions given her but had not needed to use any. Madame stayed with Agnes Tobyn[32] [sic] at San Francisco. Some people said they liked her (Madame herself) but they did not like her lectures. She laughed good humouredly quoting this story against herself. Darling had visited Brynmar [sic],[33] the big School, and had lectured to the students. Afterwards one of them stood up and came forward to the platform carrying a bunch of chrysanthemums whose stalks were almost as tall as herself, and presented them saying, 'We want to give you these because we like you very much.' Darling said that that was one of the nicest things ever said to her, one she liked best to remember, and her eyes were suffused with happy tears as she recounted it . . .

On the 11th May Darling wrote using a word of endearment in her letter which she had never before given me. I had been very unhappy and depressed and this restored me to sanity and cheerfulness once more.

On the 13th I took our little dog Jerry for a walk to Holland Walk. The twilight was green beneath the trees and on the other side of the railings along the drive to Holland House, bluebells were growing, and just beyond, a miracle! a lacey wilderness of cow parsley. It was as if Darling, like an enchanted princess, had projected herself in flower form. I looked at them with tears and managed to gather some that had been thrown away by children as I did not want to steal the growing ones. I went home with charity at heart and wrote to her, sending her a spray . . .

On July 3rd I had a letter from Archie in which he gave me some good advice which alas, I foolishly ignored subsequently, to my regret. 'You say you wish to be friends with everybody – well that is a sentiment I heartily agree with and I sincerely hope you will not allow yourself to be drawn into controversies about anything with any one of us. From bitter personal experience I know it makes life very difficult.' . . .

September 15th

I walked up to Sion Hill Place. My Darling had been staying with
Miss Tindall but came home for the afternoon to welcome me.
There was a thunder storm while I was with her. We talked of
Winkie and of Archie . . . Dear Miss Clarke was very kind too,
and Madame kindly drove me back to the Hotel in the rain. It
was like old times to be sitting beside her in a car again. I jumped
out when we stopped and ran under cover, turning at the door to
wave to her, but she was not looking and the car moved on without her realising I had done so. I wrote a PC to Archie telling him
how I had found his mother . . .

November 2nd

. . . Darling took me into the morning room which is kept more
as a box room. I took off my coat and looked around. There was
her early portrait with the earnest eyes and Maltese lace collar in
its heavy black frame. I remarked upon it and Madame said it
was taken by a man at Warrington . . . Beneath it Darling
indicated a photo of her mother. 'This one?' I questioned. 'No,'
she replied laughing, 'that is George Eliot.' Below that again was
the one she referred to – not a face I cared for and not at all like
herself . . .

A reproduction of Lord Leighton's *Moon of Song* hung nearer
the window, Darling said that the artist had told her that he had
seen the two girls asleep in just those poses when he was in Libya
and the nightingale singing in the background. We studied the
draperies and the circle of the window and foliage, against which
the little bird is easily overlooked. Near by hung a photo of *The
Winged Victory*[34] – 'Such as it is,' Madame said – and below that
a smaller portrait of Beth as a child with bright eyes full of
mischief . . .

London and Bath 1937

January 20th

Archie came to tea with us and stayed to supper . . .

February 9th

Next day a letter from Archie made me very happy . . .

February 11th

I bought a Valentine for Darling and some little pearly hair pins like daisy petals to go with it. I arranged the parcel after tea and also read and sorted out some of her letters, such dear letters. I felt torn between her and Archie. Would that I could feel them one in sympathy and in my heart, as once I hoped. Wrote some verses for the Valentine next morning and then posted it.

. . . Archie sent me on the 22nd an Irish penny which he had been keeping for me, interpreting the design in a way that brought tears to my eyes and holiness to my heart. I wrote to thank him telling him all it meant to me . . .

March 3rd

I wrote to Archie last night to say I would not discuss Madame any further with him, owing to his answer to mine which had hurt me. I also wrote to Darling . . .

March 16th

Very unhappy interval as Archie did not write. I sent a shamrock handkerchief from the Irish linen shop and some shamrock to Madame for St Patrick's day and shawl to Miss Clarke . . .

March 27th

Bought Darling a very pretty padded cretonne tea cosy which Ina had found for Easter, with Easter cards. One for Archie, which I did not send . . .

May 7th

Wrote to Archie and PC to Madame.

May 10th

I had a letter from Archie, the most friendly he had written of late, sympathetic about Barney [who had been put to sleep] and dogs in general . . .

May 16th

Wrote to Archie.

May 20th

I wrote to Darling and sent her a booklet of Selfridge's Decorations [for the Coronation]. A letter from Archie who has been troubled with his eyes. He asked to come on the 30th . . .

May 30th

Archie came to tea and stayed to supper. He showed me his stamp collection. He told me he was born at Sandgate near Folkestone and the first flower he remembered was a gardenia . . .

June 9th

. . . We passed Bath and Bristol and then arrived at Weston. I drove to the Royal Hotel and, not seeing Madame anywhere, I was sent up to my room, No. 42, where I was too overcome with shyness to emerge for some time, so I wrote to mother and Ina until I should regain my composure and finally summoned up courage to go downstairs. I had been inclined to be a little hurt not having had a welcome, but I found my Darling waiting so faithfully and wistfully by the front door, having been told the wrong time of my train's arrival. She was so upset at missing me and said I ought to have asked for her. She had told them to tell her when I came and she was looking out of the glass doors so forlornly when I found her. The exciting thing was that Winkie was actually at Weston at the Convent for a while.

. . . On the way back to my room I met Miss Harford who was also on the same floor. She had been ill and had had to put off coming three times and that night she was going to bed for dinner so as to be up the following day. Such a sweet Great Dane came by carrying a child's spade. Madame came in when we were ready, to take me down to dinner . . . Madame asked me to sit at a table with her and Miss Clarke. We had a very good dinner with really nice duck, and junket for sweet. Madame was perfectly adorable to me and Clarkey went up to bed early. So I had my gracious friend to myself. Afterwards, in the drawing room, she confided many things to me, her plans for the future, etc. It was just like old times again. She told me lots of interesting things and was sympathetic and interested in all I said. She said that she used to stand up to write at one time, as writing for long at a time is such a sedentary occupation and she had thought it would do her good. She used to put her writing desk on a table and much of *The Heavenly Twins* was written that way.

She was wearing the black lace tea gown I had had lined for her from Elwoods. She looked very graceful in it, that pinky lilac under the black being very becoming to her. She was also wearing my white combs in her hair and was using my silk bag and a brooch of musical notes forming 'Dearest' with which I had once pinned on her white roses for her, and she was using, too, the roly poly case I had made her for her crochet cotton balls. Altogether everything was most harmonious. She asked me if I had told her all the excitements and I wondered if Clarkey had told her that Archie had been to see us. I replied, 'more or less I thought.' All through, I longed to tell her of that visit, but always on the verge of the confidence I hesitated to do so despite the pain it cost me to withhold anything from her, for fear of disturbing our graceful hour together. I bitterly regretted this later . . .

June 10th [Sarah's eighty-third birthday]

I sent Darling's present in to her and began my letter to Archie, which I continued at intervals all day. I had a nice breakfast by myself and after reading papers I went upstairs again to my room. Soon my beautiful called for me, her eyes full of tears, in thanks for my parcel and wishes. I rose a little guiltily from my occupation with my letter, and we kissed one another, I with a double love and deeply touched at her unconcealed emotion. Later I joined her downstairs and she gave orders about the table for tea . . . Miss Harford had come down for lunch wearing an orange band round her hat and a rose-coloured knitted blouse.

Madame was in her dark blue dress with a pink rose in her black hat. Winkie, I was told, now had leanings towards the stage. She was going to read for her exams and was to have a coach, giving herself two years in which to get through – but what the subject was I did not gather. I went up to dress after lunch for the party and then Winkie and a Miss Oliver from the Convent arrived. Soon Miss Tindall drove up in her car bringing Mrs Sonnenschein and Miss Kimball . . . Tea over we went out into the garden when I took a snapshot of the group, some standing and some sitting. [see illustration 11].

. . . Darling then went up to rest and I continued my letter to Archie, seeking to draw him into the festivities so that, in seeming at least, he could be one of us as he should have been in fact. I was very happy enshrining these two in my heart and told him all the details of the occasion, the company and the scene. I took the letter to the post, bought postcards and took a snapshot or two of

the Winter Gardens. We had a happy dinner together, but I felt
sad afterwards that I should be leaving on the morrow. Miss
Clarke played Patience and I looked at papers, lingering regret-
fully and reluctant to say goodnight.

June 11th

I finished my packing . . . I paid my bill £1.19.0 and . . . Darling
came with me down to the lawn where we sat talking sadly and
confidentially, mostly of her affection, nay, absorbing love for
Winkie . . . All too soon the time for my departure came and
they saw me into my taxi for the station. Darling kindly said that
I 'had been the making of the party' and I returned that 'I had
enjoyed every minute of it'. I had indeed, truly. She said she had
never seen me looking so well and nice as I had yesterday. I was
happy. I caught the 11.18 to London. There was the new plate-
glass window in my carriage. Bath the colour of pussy willows.
Reached London safely. Very hot by underground to Earls
Court whence I walked from tree shade to tree shade, home.
Mother opened the door, very sweet. She had bought me a
beautiful brown umbrella. Talked and talked to her and to Ina
later. I wrote to Darling. So ended three of the happiest days of
my life.

On the 14th Archie replied kindly to my letter but unrespon-
sively as to the party and critically of the surroundings. He asked
a question about Winkie's being at the Convent so I replied to it
. . . Madame reproached me for withholding the fact of Archie's
visit. I later wrote and told her all about it, explaining why I had
not done so before.

When Archie came to tea on the 21st July he told us that
Heinemann 'pirated' *The Heavenly Twins* in America and that
Madame was asked to write an appreciation of him at his
death, and because she refused has been ousted from their
advertisements . . .

On the 9th November I took the usual posy of carnations to
mark the Mayoral anniversary but her mood had changed and
not having herself remembered the date the attention had little
meaning for her. She spoke of appointing a Literary Executrix.
The interview upset me.

[Here there is a break of a year, caused by the misunderstanding
about Sarah's Literary Executors – see letters, pp. 295–99]

London and Bath 1938

October 23rd

I went to Bath for Miss Clarke's birthday and had a tender reconciliation with Madame who said I must never feel 'out of touch'
again. Miss Clarke very kind, and I returned happily.

November and December

I received a box of chrysanthemums, berries, ivy and jasmine
and some parsley from dear Miss Clarke. There was a tiny pink-
shelled snail amongst it which I put on a spray outside my
window. I wrote to thank her. I had started to crochet a shawl for
Madame's Christmas present.
    Posted Xmas card to Archie on 20th.
    Sent card to Miss ——— 35
    No letter from Madame, but Miss Clarke wrote and Miss ———
send card.
    On the 27th Ina brought me up a card from Archie, a lovely
little card of alpine flowers, beautifully coloured. I was tenderly
pleased with it. It was a snowy, severe Christmas. I made some
mincepies and packed them for Archie together with some slices
of plum pudding and a small flask of brandy. Also wrote to Miss
Clarke. I managed to finish Madame's shawl and packed it up on
the last day of the old year with a letter of good New Year wishes.

London and Bath 1939

I have torn out certain pages of this journal and burnt them
because I felt they were better forgotten. They referred chiefly to
my break with Archie. It was an unhappy time for us all and
Madame was not herself [*Addendum* 1951]

January 2nd

A dear letter from Madame but a postcard only from Archie
acknowledging my parcel. I was disappointed as I hoped for a
letter.

January 9th

I had another dear letter from Madame saying that Miss Clarke
was dangerously ill and telling me about Mrs Sonnenschein's flat
which she thought might do for me. It was sweet of her to think

of us midst her own anxiety. I wrote to her next day with thanks, but turned down the idea.

On the 13th, following more financial worries, we seriously contemplated Madame's suggestion and I wrote to her again. Next few days in suspense as to what Mrs Sonnenschein would say . . .

January 18th

I caught the 1.15 to Bath. Arrived in rain and drove up to Mrs Sonnenschein to see the flat. She was kindness itself and the flat, except for size and lack of running hot water (only a geyser) was promising. She thought this might be arranged. We had a happy tea and we talked in the dear Bath atmosphere I love. Then I ran in to see Madame. She looked stronger but was still very lethargic. I went up to see Miss Clarke who was brighter but sadly changed, her features sharpened . . . I tore up a lot of letters next day, all of Miss ——— 's, and felt better for having done so.

January 24th

A sweet but vague letter from Mrs Sonnenschein, and further money owing on our present flat, upset us. Having written to Miss Harford who was a former tenant of Mrs Sonnenschein's flat I heard from her on the 25th. She said she had left as Mrs Sonnenschein kept putting up the rent. Very worrying. I wrote to Madame, Mrs Sonnenschein and Miss Harford. Mother quite accepting the idea of Bath flat.

On February 4th my sister Ina and a friend, Esme Reid, motored to Bath to see the flat. Mother and I spent an anxious day wondering as to the verdict. They returned very favourably impressed, but mother seemed to think the move would be too expensive and disliked the idea of there being no hot water laid on. After another day's anxious wavering and discussion of the pros and cons we decided on the 6th to take Mrs Sonnenschein's flat at 4 Sion Hill Place, Bath. Wrote to her immediately and I also sent a postcard to Madame . . .

February 22nd

I wrote to Archie telling him of our decision to return to Bath and giving him the address . . .

March 22nd

I rang up Dando's about the gas and electricity and then went up to Sion Hill Place. Punctually the vans arrived, swinging up to the door like ships and then the fun began. I thoroughly enjoyed the excitement and felt very happy as the rooms took on habitable contours. Bright sunlight added to the joy. I came back to the Hotel and wrote to Mother and Ina and then walked up again to the flat. Things a bit crowded but felt it would all straighten out later . . .

March 27th

Ina went back to London as she is going on with her School of Acting, The Neilson Terry Guild. At dinner I was called to the phone. It was Spanswick, the butler for Madame, to tell me that Miss Clarke had passed away this evening. I went and wrote to Madame and walked up to Sion Hill Place, just dropping the letter in her box. I wrote and told Ina.

March 30th

The day of Miss Clarke's funeral. I walked to Lansdown Cemetery. The wind was rushing through the trees; there was sunlight and open spaces. I met Miss Lloyd and stood with her in the cold wind waiting for the cortège. Archie was in one of the cars. It was a simple service. Blue curtains, a lovely wreath of bunched primroses and violets at the foot of the coffin which had a cross carved on it. When the ceremony was over I turned and shook hands with Archie. He gave me a strong firm hand-clasp and I felt all questions cease in his ultimate strength, the masculine support I craved. I asked him later on if he were staying or going back. He replied that he was staying a few days. Dr Christie cast a bunch of heather into the grave. My wreath was a cross of daffodils. Miss Lloyd drove me back. The wind was in Archie's eyes which made them tearful, but not with tears. He and Commander Drake Clarke were rallying each other. At night I wrote to Madame to tell her my impressions and to him to ask him to come and have coffee with us tomorrow night.

March 31st

. . . Mother and I waited in vain for Archie after dinner. He did not turn up and sent no word . . .

[Sarah then wrote her 'cruel letter' to Gladys, see p. 299]

August 9th

Mrs Sonnenschein told me that Madame is suffering mentally and sees no one but Dr Christie, Miss Tindall and herself; also she said that Beth was now there.

August 12th

I was amazed to receive a letter from Beth with a box of souvenirs of poor Miss Clarke. Beth asked when I was coming in to see Madame and her. I wrote to Beth next day, telling her a little about the upset.

August 14th

A wonderfully kind and sincere letter from Beth broke down any remaining sense of resentment in me and I replied offering to go to see Madame one day this week, Archie being away temporarily . . .

August 16th

I had a nice letter from Beth asking me in any evening. I went in that evening but as Madame was unable to see me I had a nice talk with Beth. She was very sympathetic about my recital of woes and told me much of the circumstances Archie had had to contend with . . .

September 1st

We were surprised this morning by a visit from Madame's maid Lena to ask on Beth's behalf if we had heard over the wireless that the Germans had attacked Poland. We knew this meant war, but I was so taken up admiring Lena's beauty as of a frightened deer, that I did not take in the full impact of her news. Later we got rather nervy especially when we heard guns in the distance at lunch . . .

September 3rd

We listened in to Mr Chamberlain's speech at 11.15 a.m. declaring war on Germany. Deeply sorry for him. After 'God Save the King' our darling Jerry picked up his toy Panda and walked quietly out of the room, I nearly cried it was so pathetic.

October 23rd

The anniversary of poor dear Miss Clarke's Birthday. A year ago I came to Bath from London to see her. Today the beech leaves were falling with a sound as of gentle rain, gold against the green and gold of their parent trees, which were lifted grandly against the blue morning sky. After lunch I walked with Zami (my Aberdeen terrier) to Lansdown Cemetery, finding some berries on the way to put on her grave. I could not find it at first but asked the gardener and he pointed out the pathetic mound to me. It was grass grown and unmarked by stone or flowers. He said the space nearby had been bought also, and that 'then' (when it was occupied) the grass would be 'rüt'. 'Poor dear woman' I exclaimed to myself as I knelt to put my offering among the long grass. If I could have foreseen this last year. She was then wearing my blue shawl and so happy in her party . . .

November 5th

Beth came out and talked to Ina. She said that Archie likes a sirloin but that Madame has only toast and cheese at night for supper . . .

November 9th

Ina found out for me that the carnations I had ordered from Allwood's for Madame's Mayoress day had arrived.

November 10th

After feeling yesterday that most of my past life was just cancelled out by Madame's treatment of me, I had a note today from Beth suggesting once again that I should call and thanking me on Madame's behalf for the carnations.

November 11th

I wrote to Beth to ask her to tea, then met her and found she had a cold but I arranged to call to see Madame tomorrow.

November 12th

I saw Madame again after our long estrangement. It was a very misty day, the trees a lovely amber over a carpet of amber leaves with dark branches. I dressed after tea and went in to see Madame. Madame saw me at last, Beth kindly showing me upstairs. She was looking better than I had expected with a pretty colour and her little hands pink inside, her hair softly done. She was in bed and her hand held up to her mouth. I kissed her, though she said she was too 'sickly' to be kissed and at parting I kissed her hands, both of which she held out to me. She professed to have forgotten her last letter, thinking she had told me to come in any evening at 5.30. We talked generalities about the flat, the dogs, Mrs Sonnenschein and the Fetherstonehaughs, etc. She said that Beth was so good to her. I left when I thought her tired. She did not try to stop me. So things swing back to normal once more and I can see her again as usual. How simple things are when one can sink one's own sense of injustice and hurt. I went back and washed up and read a bit feeling well and strong again. I wrote to Darling next day . . .

November 18th

Beth rang up to say Madame had found a book on Arthritis for Mother and would I go in today or tomorrow. I said tomorrow as I wasn't feeling up to it today . . .

November 25th

My dear sister was very nearly gassed in the bathroom so we had an anxious week having only just saved her . . .

December 16th

Donald, Beth's little son, came out and I asked him how Madame was. He replied that she was 'a little well'. Winkie is coming on Tuesday . . .

December 22nd

A charming little Calendar came from Miss ——. I was glad she remembered me and still seems to like me, despite Archie's attitude.

December 24th

I did up Madame's parcel and wrote to her, taking them in on Christmas morning . . .

Bath 1940

The Hard Winter

Beth came in to wish us a Happy New Year. It was a terribly severe winter. On the 15th I took Madame a Calendar of jonquils and mauve tulips with a bunch of real flowers to go with it. But the suggestion of Spring was rather too previous! Ina saw Madame at her door one morning looking quite well; she seemed able to withstand the Arctic weather. I will set on record some of my observations.

. . . On the 28th January, the sky was raining needles of frost which made the pavements like glass with pieces sticking up in spikes as on a wall. Miss Michell[36] came in carrying a branch like a chandelier covered with icicles. Trees began falling. The telegraph wires were encased in tubes of ice and all the trees were clinking like bells. Large pieces of ice, like caskets of jewels. One yew tree had rounded icicles so that the branches looked like white glass grapes. The laurels were coated in frost with a long icicle hanging from the tip of every bright green leaf, which was stiff when moved. Clinking sounded whenever the breeze stirred. On the 31st the thaw began, and the ice falling continuously in crashes. A man said it was like a rain of bullets in the Avenue. When I went out on February 1st, I walked on fallen pencils of ice like gigantic pieces of coffee sugar.

Mother had a fainting attack, very similar to Ina's last November, and had to have several days in bed. I was tortured by chilblains and in a state of nervous tension. We saw Winkie and Donald and Beth at intervals.

We had more snow in mid-February and on the 17th there was a wonderful aquamarine sky making the snow covered branches and stars like a silver point etching against it – a holy night. Next evening there was a sudden thaw, everything dripping. A wonderful moonlight night on the 23rd with marbled clouds, their perspectives round the moon deepening to her glory like a picture from Dante's *Paradise*. Patches of damp on the pavement shone like moon silver.

On the 27th I spoke to Beth, asking after Madame. She said she was very 'wavering' . . . On March 8th I talked again to Beth, offering to go in to see Madame but she does not seem to want me . . . She says Madame's memory is very uncertain and that she forgets people have been there 10 minutes afterwards.

. . . Our beloved Mother was taken ill during this time and was operated upon at No. 10 St James's Square on the 15th and survived. But when I joined her there she looked so ill that I burst out crying and so did she. However we soon rejoiced at our reunion, and felt happy. I remained there next door to her for 3 weeks. Somewhere round about the 26th Ina cut Archie. He addressed her about me, but she passed him without speaking. He was at Sion Hill, but later we heard that Miss Tindall was putting him up.

. . . Later I began painting a card for Madame's birthday. I felt happier than I had done for five years.

Having gone up to the flat on June 6th, I went along to enquire after Madame and met Miss Tindall also on her way there. She did not recognise me at first. She said Madame might see me on Sunday. I had a glimpse of Archie later going up on Madame's doorstep. He asked something at the door and then went off without looking our way. It was fortunate that I missed him.

June 9th

I wrote to Darling for her [eighty-sixth] Birthday. Then after lunch I went up to the flat, and after collecting a few belongings I went in to see Madame.

She was looking so well and pretty with her hair softly done and a turquoise blue Shetland shawl, just a wisp of lacey wool, round her shoulders. She offered me tea and whisky and said, when I refused, that she wished she had something to give me to take away and she wished that I wasn't going (I had told her of my contemplated holiday at Torquay). I was so happy to see her again.

London 1941

My sister found my mother and me a flat in London and we moved to St Edmund's Terrace, Regents Park, near Primrose Hill.

. . . I wrote to Madame for the 7th [February], the anniversary of the publication of *The Heavenly Twins*, and on the 13th I observed my usual custom of sending her a Valentine, having bought a heart shaped vase and packed it in a box with shells I stuck on it, in approved Victorian fashion, with accompanying

Valentine card. Undiscouraged by no reply, I managed to get what purported to be shamrock for Madame on March 15th and painted the lid of a box with Mary's Tears and shamrock design to pack it in. It was successful and rather pretty . . .

. . . On Whit Sunday, June 1st, following my first night fire-watching, I wrote to Darling Madame telling her about it. The next few days I was planning her Birthday remembrances. A card I painted with many different flowers and a trinket box in white painted enamel with pink flower design with pink ribbon to tie it up. I posted her a paper too and made some crochet flowers. My idea in sending her things regularly was to assure her she was not forgotten by me and to provide her with little excitements. I did not look for nor expect answers every time. I wrote again for the 10th.

June 11th, Torquay

With Ina's letter came a Bath paper addressed as I thought in Miss Tylee's hand. I opened it in fear and trembling thinking it contained bad news of my Darling Madame and when I saw her portrait on the front page I nearly fainted with shock, for I made sure she had left me. The blank was so devastating, so bewildering that it left me in no doubt of what she still means to me. Despite the tests it has had to withstand, it has surmounted them all, our friendship. But when I found it was a birthday photograph and that the paper had been sent by Miss Gordon Gibson, relief and joy supervened and I rejoiced in the dear and lovely likeness. She had Bobbin, our cat, on her knees and her dear eyes were still expressive behind her owly glasses . . .

On the 19th I heard from Madame's nurse that she had been pleased with the Birthday presents I had sent and that her room was a bower of flowers. I left Torquay on the 16th and rejoined Mother and Ina in London.

I sent Madame the customary carnations for Mayoress Day November 9th and a plate painted with white roses. On the 11th I had a note from Nurse Rancombe[37] to say that the flowers and parcel had given Madame pleasure. She told me that Madame never remembers that she has heard from anyone but is well and happy.

Reading over my journals, the past seems so vivid that I almost persuade myself that I can go back to it and right the conduct of so much that went so sadly awry. I heard about now that

Winkie was to be married, and I wrote to her to wish her happiness. For Christmas I sent Madame some mittens I had knitted and a Calendar painted with clover and a white rose.

So ended 1941, during which I had kept the flickering light of our friendship alive by little remembrances which, like carefully placed twigs, I laid upon its sinking embers . . .

London 1942

March 24th

I felt much better and happier in a sunny morning and the mood was confirmed by my actually receiving one of my beloved Madame's rare little notes. *Madame asked if there were any chance of seeing me soon*, so I wrote at once to the York House Hotel, Bath, for a room.

At this time my dear Mother had become very ill, but she fluctuated from day to day and we had not given up hope of her recovery. My sister undertook to nurse her, sleeping in her room – or rather not sleeping since her nights were broken. I helped during the day and together we ran the flat, meals and shopping and housework and caring for the dogs. Miss Michell stepped in when I went to Bath on the 21st and was there until my return, following the two terrible air raids which terminated my stay in Bath. That God spared me and my beloved mother so that she recognised me on my return was a miracle and a mercy, for I should never have forgiven myself for leaving her at this time had she passed before I got back. But Madame had called me and she was still my ruling passion. I could not disregard the chance of renewed understanding, so I went. On arrival at Bath I rang up Mrs Rancombe and settled to go to see Madame on the following afternoon.

Notes kept of my visit to Madame Grand, April 22nd 1942

The day was grey and cloudy, the air soft . . . When I rang, the door that used to stand ajar in summer was unbolted and unchained and I was welcomed by Madame's nurse cheerfully, and from force of habit I turned into the now all too tidy dining room which has seen so many happy gatherings and which witnessed my first giving of allegiance to Archie, who seemed there to claim it . . .

Nurse let me go upstairs by myself. It was all as it used to be, every picture placed on the walls as I remembered them and the stair carpet patterned with little apples. Her door was open and as I asked if I might enter, the dearly remembered voice bade me, 'Come in,' and I said how lovely it was to be here again. But she herself, sitting up in bed, was different and yet the same. She had a blue flannel dressing gown on and a blue Shetland knitted shawl as scarf about her neck. We took stock of one another a little anxiously. She proclaimed that I had not changed, looked still the same. 'And neither have you,' I said, adding truthfully 'much', whereat she laughed a little ruefully. For she has changed – her face looks broader owing to the thinning of her hair upon her temples, and her eyes are strained with a return to the earlier process of collecting knowledge, the attainment of which had been set aside, washed away into a childlikeness by her years. Her mouth was more like herself and, when she looked down, it had the same little humorous twist as of old. It was the dear eyes that disconcerted me and made me feel her presence strange until I could accept her with the unchanging love I have for her, despite all alteration of age and appearance. The cat Bobby (Bobbin) was on her knee wrapped in my shawl which I had crocheted for her many seasons ago and he was content to stay there.

What did we talk of? Mother, Ina, the flat, the address of which she could not recall. Once or twice she asked to be set right, or to be reminded of things. Archie, it seems, 'holds the family together'. She said he manages all the financial side of their life, but when I asked if he were still in London, she told me to ask Nurse as she could not remember. Beth had vanished from her mind, but Winkie's marriage she recalled, though not the name of her husband's regiment.

Tea was brought in and I had it at a side table and we spoke of the hot 'seedy' cake of old which she was able to recollect. 'How long ago all that seems,' Madame said. 'But it is still there,' I replied, and to my asking whether she still smoked, she answered with conviction that she did. I saw there was a box of cigarettes by her bed and she took one out and lighted it with the lighter I had given her. 'You never smoked, did you?' she asked me. 'Only with you,' I replied. 'I gave it up later.' 'I corrupted you,' she said, with a return to her old chaff and fun.

We spoke of books. Madame still reads detective stories. I told her how we were reading Lockhart's *Life of Sir Walter Scott*[38]

and how much I liked so called 'escapist' literature, in the effort
to get away from this into another century. Darling sympathised
with this desire and talked intelligently of the war as if it were
some aberration that would pass. I told her of Lyndoe's prophecies[39] and she followed all I said of his probable Secret Service
status, but made little comment on his setting of August as the
month of termination. I changed my seat and went back to her
bedside. Once or twice she asked if the cat were there, glad that
he was drinking milk and pleased when I fondled him and put
him back on her bed. I now made a move to go, saying I did not
want to tire her, but she asked me to stay as it was a tonic to have
someone to talk to. She found it tiring lying there alone. I said
that Mother was not interested any longer in things. She replied
that she herself was interested in everything. I talked of her photo
taken on her last birthday. 'With the cat?' she questioned,
pleased, and I told her yes, and how I had it in a frame by my
bed, and she wanted to know which paper had published it. 'It
was very good of Bobby,' she said. 'It is nice to see you again,
Gladys,' she said wistfully and I wished aloud that I could live
near her and not in London . . .

At last I rose and kissed her dear hand, she held out both to me,
her finger with her wedding ring. And I asked her if she had had
her Easter flowers, but she answered no, and admonished me not
to spend too·much on flowers and the other things for her, just as
she used to do in the old days. I came round and stood on the
other side of her bed looking down at her and feeling very
tender, saying she was 'telling me off' as she used
to. And she smiled with a flash of her old humour again and
said, looking up, that she was what people called 'a great
age' – 'over 80' . . . And so I left her, having arranged to come
again on Sunday. 'Tell Nurse,' Darling had said in case she
herself forgot, but before I reached the door she asked me to let
her see how long my skirt was. She liked the coat and skirt, and
the length she approved as neither too long nor too short. I had
called her attention to the brooch she had given me which I was
wearing, the one I called 'the green diamond'. I said it brought
me luck. 'It is a mascot,' she said with an effort not to lisp, the
latter being now more pronounced. I told her how I always wore
it in an air raid and how frightened I was of them and of the guns
on Primrose Hill. 'Don't forget me,' I said as I kissed her hands.
'Oh no,' she answered in surprise, 'I won't forget you,' as if it
were an impossibility.

. . . On the night of the 25th we suffered the first of the Bath air raids.

April 26th

This was the Sunday following the first air raid on Bath . . . She had been up in the night throughout the blitz and on the pavement outside her house were neat stacks of her drawing-room window panes. She had risen to the occasion and had rather enjoyed the experience. She had a bottle of Champagne in the room ready, she told me, to drink the final peace when it came! I replied that I must come and share it! . . .

'I have a confession to make,' I announced in a pause, and I told her how Beth had given me back my own letters to herself. 'Oh,' she exclaimed, 'I am so glad – I am very glad you have them. They are valuable accounts of the times quite apart from their sentimental associations and they were written with no thought of publication.' I rejoiced that I might keep them, and that I had told her about them honourably. Madame also gave me permission to give some of her own letters to the Bath Library as accounts of the times, too . . . With many a murmured endearment and *au revoir* and backward look I took my slow leave, seeing her a little turquoise figure with rose face sitting up rather straightly against her pillows. That night the second Bath blitz took place.

[The following letter from Gladys to her mother and Ina is attached to Vol. VI.]
Darlings mine,
    I do hope and pray that you did not have a night such as we had here last night. I would get in for a blitz, wouldn't I? It was just after I had got back from a delightful talk with the Green-Armytages after dinner and had taken Ella out and settled her down for the night and had dipped into *The Marble Faun*[40] and was going on to have a good read in the Mason book when the sirens went. I didn't bother much as I thought it would be at Bristol but I heard a gun or two and then, my dears, a series of screaming bombs on top of the light going out and leaving us in pitch darkness . . . At last I managed to creep downstairs and asked, trembling, if there was a shelter. We were all conducted to the basement. A crowd of people, pretty packed, sitting on

crates and chairs which were brought in by candle and torch light. The noise was awful, what with coughs and the planes, guns, bombs and doors rattling. I was never more terrified except that night on the Common.

A woman next me, a very nice lady, had come from Exeter where they have had bad raids the last two nights (glass in Cathedral broken, etc.) for a rest! Her daughter had her little son on her lap and occasionally he set up a howl which nearly drove me dotty. Ella sat on my lap as good as gold while I kept my balance hanging on to the iron railing of the stone stairs. At long last the all clear went and we trooped up. I suppose that was just after midnight. But I didn't trust 'Priscilla Gordon'[41] and did not undress; fortunately, for in about half an hour, during which I could hear glass being swept up and fire engines tearing past, the siren went again. I hauled Ella off the bed and made a bee-line for the cellars once more. This one wasn't quite so bad and not so long. Well, we got upstairs again and I lay down dressed on my bed with the eiderdown over me and fell asleep. Suddenly I woke and lay listening, and then I'm blest if we didn't get another warning. It was 20 to 5, I was so sleepy I didn't know what to do, so got up and collected one or two treasures for my bag and stood thinking when a screamer descended and so did I but not screaming! 'Remember you're British.' It was pretty bad again and baby more fractious, but Ella a model of goodness and decorum. One woman was sick but swore it wasn't the raid. We could see flares or fire over a transom near and the machine gunning sounded very close . . . I was longing for tea, or your delectable cocoa, but no signs of refreshment. At last someone came down and said it was daylight and then in a little while the all-clear went.

. . . In the Lane there were several huge bricks scattered and an enormous one over the railings on the grass of the Park, but I couldn't see where it came from. I crossed over and could see the remains of the fires, one big one at the Rubber Works near the Gas Works, Weston way, still smoking and fire engine bells going at intervals. Several plate glass windows broken. There were rumours about the stations but I think they are all right . . .

April 26th [continued in new volume]
The following morning I determined to get home if possible. I

cannot account for the fact that I made no effort to ascertain whether Madame were safe or no. It seems to me that I accepted the notion that she would be impervious to attack. I went up to Talls in the effort to get a taxi, but the place was gutted and St Andrew's Church also. It looked majestic with shafts of sunlight pouring into the ruins. I decided then to leave my trunks and bags at the Hotel and to try to walk to Bathampton where I was told I should get a train to London. Therefore, carrying one small bag and leading Ella, I began my journey. Providentially I met Christian Carpenter the pianist as I was crossing the road, and she kindly offered to give me a lift in her friend's car as far as the Bathampton turning. The GWR[42] station had been put out of action during the night. I was therefore fortunate in finding a train ready to depart . . .

My Darling Mother was just able to recognise me and to rejoice with me at our reunion and safety. Having satisfied myself from the list of Bath casualties that Madame was unhurt, I wrote to her for May 6th. That day I had a letter from Nurse Rancombe to tell me she had taken Madame to Calne because her house had been rendered uninhabitable owing to broken windows, etc.

(The day after the last Blitz Nurse had borrowed a wheeled chair from Miss Tindall and put Madame in it. She refused to go without Bobby and Bobby was half mad. However they succeeded in catching him, gave him morphia and, with the cat on her lap, Madame started to be wheeled to Bathampton. Fortunately, they met an ARP[43] man who lent them a car and the journey to Calne was completed in comfort.)

During these days of anxiety and sorrow our darling Mother was passing slowly from us, and the end came early in the morning of May 13th. Among the expressions of sympathy we received was a telegram from Madame sent by Nurse. Mother was laid to rest with Dad in Tunbridge Wells Cemetery on May 18th. On Whit Sunday, May 24, I wrote to Darling Madame and suggested my going to Calne for her Birthday . . .

I must have had a favourable reply to my letter as on June 8th I began packing and on the 9th I travelled to Calne, taking a room at the Lansdowne Arms Hotel. That evening I explored the little town, my steps leading me to the Grange on the Chippenham Road where Madame had found a furnished flat in the home of

Mrs Harris. Afterwards I walked up Church Street . . . and then
. . . round the Church by the narrow paved path at the back,
leading to the little flight of steps which descend to Mill Street. It
was there, at the top of the steps, that I saw for the first time the
Archdeacon of Wilts, the Venerable J.W. Coulter. I did not
know who he was then . . . I was going on down the steps when it
was as if a hand had been laid on my shoulder and almost without
my own volition I turned about and followed him into the Parish
Church. There he welcomed me so kindly, shaking hands, and
drawing my attention to the Reredos, the Saxon remains and the
long black curtains which hid the higher windows . . . So I came
to the turning point of my spiritual life, for although I knew it
not then, it was to be through him that I was born again. So all
the former history led up to that, in its long train of cause and
effect.

(*Addendum:* In December 1944 I was confirmed into the Church
of England. Advent Sunday 3rd.)

June 10th

. . . After lunch I walked to The Grange where I had tea with
Darling Madame on her 88th birthday, her last birthday as it
proved to be.

I gathered hedge wild flowers as I walked along, tiny forget-
me-nots, bird's-eye, Our Lady's Bed-straw, Herb Robert,
daisies, and mixed them all together with the cow parsley I had
picked this morning. At the red brick pillared, wrought iron
gates, I turned up the drive. There were more daisies and a con-
stellation of pale yellow dandelions in a patch, and sycamore
wings overspread the roadway. The house is of the grandly rustic
style. It might be the apotheosis of a hunting lodge in the old
days, partly timbered and gables in red brick turrets overlooking
the gardens and the further downs. A covered porch had a bronze
bell, now tongueless, hanging in its recess, and I pulled another
of wrought iron which however did not ring.

. . . Nurse and I went up several flights of uncarpeted wooden
stairs passing their kitchen, a large light one, and finally through
a wooden gate across the stairs at the top. Two or more doors
opened from the gallery and the nearest was the entrance to
Madame's new dwelling. Her bed had its back (head) towards
me on the right with a screen round its head. I went in and

begged a kiss. She looked a little tremulously and appealingly up at me through her glasses and refused, saying that sick people were not nice to kiss. However I said she wasn't sick and insisted on a Birthday salute! I showed her the wild flowers, naming them, and Nurse remarked that the Church was sometimes decorated with cow parsley. I looked around. It was a large room with a high lattice window at one side . . . The walls were distempered with cream, with green paint, the floor black with vari-coloured rugs covering it. There was a spinet converted into a desk at one wall, that Madame agreed with me in deploring, though the golden brown of the case was not spoilt. The carnations I had sent were just right in colours blending with the rugs . . . The atmosphere was restful, and somehow fairy like, but in quality, not in lightness – a Mrs Molesworthian[44] room discovered within a tapestry house – and I was not surprised when they told me that this so called 'furnished flat' had been the nurseries of the main building in the old days. It still retained an over-soul of childish fancy, hovering vaguely and merging itself with the sadder child-likeness of old age.

Tea was daintily laid on a gate-legged table in the centre of the room. My Darling sat quietly, inertly . . . Bobby, on whom Madame now spends all the love of her heart, was hidden beneath the rose pink of the silk eiderdown. He came out and blinked at us, finally jumped down and to everyone's joy went and lapped his milk set for him in a corner. He was lifted up again by Nurse's sister and had an attack of coughing. Madame's anxiety about him made her fear that the touch had been rough and she said as much to herself but the sister being deaf did not hear . . . Bobby curled himself asleep at last on her lap and she lamented again that he was so much lighter than he used to be. It was heartrending to see the clinging love and fear with which she regarded him, her animal comfort, the last friend of all who courted her of old . . .

I showed her the brooch I was wearing, which I gave her long ago and which she had returned to me in 1936, and I recalled to her memory the white enamelled rose ring that accompanied it. She remembered that, in an uncertain flutter of recollection, and I thanked her for the note which she had put in the parcel which I had only opened the other day and so had never seen before then. It had been a poignant discovery to me, but the writing of it had gone from her mind . . . She seemed confused when I spoke of giving up the flat . . . Never until one speaks to the deaf or to the very old does life seem so complex in its variations or so full of twists calling for explanation which defeat one's every effort to simplify. She retained the thought that I should be far away, however, and said she would be lonely and wished I would be nearer and could come to see her. I promised her that I would come from the ends of the earth at any time if she needed me, if only she would tell Nurse to send for me . . . And at last I drew on my gloves reluctantly, tidied the side table for her and bade her farewell, kissing her with reiterated 'Happy Returns'. Once more she said she would be lonely without me and wished I were not going so far and how nice to have seen me. I felt deeply thankful that I had come and amply rewarded for the effort and time spent on the journey . . .

On June 13th I had a very kind letter from Miss Tindall asking me to be near Madame if possible and to keep her in touch with herself, as I was the only one of her friends now left who could reach her. The letter made me very happy . . .

. . . On July 29th I received a letter from Nurse Rancombe suggesting I might care to share a house with Madame at Calne. I sought Ina's advice.

. . . I wrote to Nurse Rancombe on the 26th August having decided not to share a house, but to go to the Hotel, at least to begin with.

August 31st

I left London for Calne, taking Ella with me.

. . . The next day I went to tea with Darling again and this brings my record up to that which I kept at Calne – the last months of Madame's life.

CHAPTER XII

Calne and Sarah's Death: 1942–43

◖◗

Chained to our hearts by many a loving deed;
Chained to our minds by words that cannot fade;
In bonds we hold thee, and by bonds you lead,
Mayoress of souls in God's own City made.[1]

The 'technical end of my long and dear friendship with my Darling friend' was, as we have seen, no end. Although the Bath blitz sent Sarah and her nurse to the safety of Calne, by September of that year Gladys had settled in a hotel room to be near her Darling Madame and to be with her until she died. Gladys was now fifty-three.

During these months the Record, which had flagged under their upsets and misunderstandings over Archie, returned to its earlier enthusiasm. Every detail of Sarah's room at The Grange and her daily deterioration were recorded, her repetitive questions, Gladys' encouraging monologues and attempts to interest her, the flowers, the sunsets, the symbolism. Isolated now from all her old friends and confined to her room, Sarah's world and interests telescoped to her nurses, her cat and Gladys. Distance, the war, old age and death prevented her friends from visiting and Gladys, ironically, became the link between Sarah and her friend Miss Tindall. Gladys was now not only necessary but a welcome correspondent; Miss Tindall's dislike or mistrust of her vanished and she wrote in 1942: 'You can't think what a difference it makes to me to hear an *educated* account of her state and one from a *lady*.'

And, after Sarah's death in 1943:

I shall always feel very specially united to you since your very kind watch over our dear Madame's last months. I am sure it made all the difference to her as it most certainly did to me.

As late as 1951, she was still writing to Gladys: 'Some of our beautiful lilies-of-the-valley are on her grave today – and all looks nice and well cared for.' And Gladys took to sending Valentines to her as proxy for, and the final link with, her friend.

As Sarah sank physically and mentally, Gladys found a substitute for her in religion. She left Christian Science – which had never truly satisfied her – and turned to the Anglican Church, taking her first communion shortly before Sarah died. The ritual of the Church and thoughts of a Hereafter were to sustain and console her in her bereavement and the void was filled, the transference completed, before Sarah left her.

Calne 1942

September 1st

'I promised I would come,' I greeted her. 'And here I am.' 'Yes, you did,' she acquiesced. Madame was looking rather pale and her face seemed thinner than when I was last with her in June. She looked more like herself as a result.

Nurse Rancombe had done her hair very smoothly and well on top, and it suited her, being so neat. She was wearing Mother's powder blue *crêpe de chine* dressing jacket I had sent her with a soft white muslin collar, and I noticed that it did not make her look sallow, owing to the paleness of her dear face against the pillows. Her eyes had a very sweet expression almost matching in hue the blue silk. She was occupied with her nails and was wearing dark woollen knitted mittens which later she removed as being too hot. Over her knees was Miss Tindall's small blanket in a deeper blue, the embroidered name of Bobby (the cat) in one corner and bound with ribbon . . . She ate sparingly of tea and lighted a cigarette, anxious that she had not exceeded her allowance, only to put it out almost immediately, saying she did not like it. I took her *Country Life* from Ina and she was pleased and told me that I must thank Ina.

I talked of my sojourn in Scotland which interested her for a time. When we were left alone she said somewhat restlessly that she wished she could be up and doing. 'But,' I comforted her 'you do get up and sit in your room sometimes.' She agreed that she did but that it made her feel sick at first. I noticed a little peculiar shade pass over her face as I was talking, and guessed from it that she was tired so I did not prolong my stay but promised to come to see her again soon, saying I had some p. cards to show her. 'Yes,' she answered 'when I am fresher.'

I must not forget to record that as we were speaking of the war, when Nurse was in the room, at tea, I happened to say that Ina had met a spiritualist during her holiday on Dartmoor who had prophesied that we should all wake up some morning and find the War over, that he had had messages to that effect and that it would be sooner than we expected, Germany would crumple. 'That's just what Madame says,' exclaimed Nurse. I turned to Madame and she confirmed it with 'Yes I do,' looking at us with authoritative acquiescence, as if possessed of an inner knowledge and assurance. Apparently she has won to a complete indifference to the almost constant din of planes, night and day. One night Nurse said they had bomb practice here till 2 a.m. and Madame did not seem at all affected. Once or twice she asked anxiously, 'Where's Bobby?' and smiled fondly and contentedly at him when he appeared and sat down, regarding her aloofly from the middle of the room.

As I put on my coat she said it was a nice one and I told her it was one of Mother's . . . I kissed her forehead gently in farewell. She had said when I first went in that I looked tired out. I certainly felt so . . . I had a long talk with Nurse after. She was very anxious about Madame's furniture and the expense of running the two places, wondering what was best to do: 7 Sion Hill Place and this flat. The Doctor had asked whether Madame had any relatives and Nurse had told him, 'Yes but they never come to see her.' He answered, 'They should come.' Winkie did come once since her marriage but did not introduce her husband. Nurse said that if Madame were moved, she would have to go by car or ambulance. And again Nurse said how fond she had grown of Madame and how she hopes it may not be her duty to close her eyes. 'I do hope I shan't be the one to close her eyes,' she repeated tears filling her own as she spoke.

September 3rd

I took some sunset coloured dahlias to my Darling. She was looking smaller and thinner with grey shadows and poignantly like my mother, looking at me with contemplative tenderness in her half shut eyes . . . She was reading *The Laird of Glenfernlie*[2] by Mary Johnstone. I read her part of Ina's letter about our projected cottage.[3] Nurse had been reading *The Heavenly Twins* and thought it beautiful with such helpful thoughts. 'To think she has written all that, it is right that she should be treated with consideration and taken care of properly.'

September 4th

I met Nurse in the town, who said that Madame was brighter with the brighter day and making jokes. She told me that Darling's decline was due to arterial sclerosis, like Mother.

September 6th

The siren went just as I started to Madame, so I turned back to look after Ella. When the all-clear went in about an hour, I started off again and arrived at The Grange to find that neither Madame nor Nurse had heard the alert, and thought I was ill . . . I took out Miss Tindall's letter and read her some of it where she sent her love, and asked for a message. 'Oh, please tell her I am so glad to have her message.' That little sentence came so spontaneously and I wrote it down at once . . .

September 20th

. . . Madame asked me, 'Where are you now?' 'Calne,' said I. 'Yes, but where?' So I told her about the Hotel, and the Trust Houses which she wanted elucidated. When I went to speak to Nurse before leaving, she told me that yesterday, September 19, Madame signed the paper relinquishing her right to her home in Bath, 7 Sion Hill Place, Lansdown. Nurse advised her to think carefully before doing so and to decide whether or no she wanted to return, but Madame said she did not wish to go back and had signed the document without delay.

September 23rd

Madame had begun tea when I entered, and was sitting up looking quite bright. She had had a visit from Archdeacon Coulter,
but he would not stay to tea. I had met him coming away and
guessed he had been to see her. In answer to our chaff, she smiled
saying that 'It broke the monotony'. A little later she asked
rather wistfully, 'Did I say the right thing to him, Nurse?' 'You
always say the right things,' we assured her and Nurse added, 'I
wouldn't have you any different from what you are in any particular' – to which speech Madame responded quite seriously
'That is a great compliment.' I wanted to quote the saying of a
man seldom being a hero to his valet, but refrained, fearing to
hurt Nurse's feelings. The Archdeacon talked of books,
mentioning *The Thirty-Nine Steps*.[4] 'Priestly,' I murmured, confusing it with *Riceyman Steps*.[5] 'No, Buchan,' Madame corrected
me . . . 'It is nice to see you, Gladys,' she said as I made ready to
go, and: 'Have you had any tea?' 'Yes, Darling,' I replied. 'I've
been stuffing,' which pleased her. She fills up her hiatuses of
memory with kindly intentions and polite enquiry, a phantom
hostess drawing round her the now fragile folds of ceremony to
shield her from the void. 'I wish we could do something for you,'
she reiterated. Like closing harmonies she speaks these phrases
every time, and every time they touch me with the same
poignancies . . .

October 14th

. . . Isabel had made a new kind of cake and asked if Madame
liked it. Madame voted it 'not very interesting' and was told that
it contained vitamins. 'They sound like some kind of objectionable insect,' she replied, at which we all laughed. I took some hot
tea. 'You have no feeling for your tissues,' Darling remarked as
often before, 'that tea is scalding.' . . . She recalled, as she
looked at the walking length of my skirt, the ridicule that Lady
Harburton[6] had brought down on herself in advocating skirts of
the kind in earlier days and wished she had lived to see these
skirts . . .

October 18th

Madame's lovely eyes were like pools of twilight. She looked at
me critically and then said, 'Doesn't she look a poor thing,

Nurse?' I suppose I may have seemed a bit washed out as I was tired after having been much moved by the morning service and sermon . . .

October 20th

Madame did not talk much to begin with today. Nurse was combing her fringe when I went in. I told her of an article on George Moore in *The Sunday Times*,[7] thinking it might interest her as she used to know him, but she had not the slightest recollection of him. This was strange, as she did remember the gardener, and an interesting comment on the relative value of fame and honest worth as reflected in her mind which now unconsciously, as hitherto consciously, showed itself discriminating as ever . . . Before I went Nurse showed me the yards of beautiful crochet work [an altar cloth Sarah had made], a wide border patterned in morning glories, and I recalled Madame having shown it at its commencement to me years ago at Sion Hill Place. There was also a little insertion with a design of leaves. Nurse had been entrusted with the work by Archie and it was in a work bag. 'She hasn't wasted *her* time,' Nurse remarked approvingly . . .

October 25th

. . . 'I had something I wanted to say to you but I can't remember it,' she told me when we were left alone after tea. Then gently, with hesitant sweetness as if it were something fresh though I felt she had really recalled what she professed to have forgotten, she said, 'I am so glad you come, that there is someone who takes an interest in me, that I am not left entirely to my attendants. Do go on coming.' I was greatly touched and said I would for as long as I could and that I thought of her even when I was not with her. 'Your thoughts come to me,' she assured me . . .

November 9th

. . . I thought they were telegrams of greeting to Madame on the date, but no one remembered. None out of the crowd her long service in the Mayoralty benefited had the grace to recall it or to thank her in this the twilight of her life. Dear heart did not know nor care much about the date. 'Is it December?' she enquired, but she liked the yellow and white chrysanthemums I took her in the morning and the geraniums tied with purple. I sought to make them regal. She was sitting up in bed. 'It's Mayoress' Day, Darling,' I said and I told her I regretted that I could not get her any carnations . . . Nurse called out, 'Something from the *Tales of Hoffman* won't depress you,' and she put on the *Barcarolle*.[8] I wondered if Madame would remember and she did for, as before, the melody held its poignant appeal for her and as before her dear face softened and grew sensitive under the influence of the past enshrined in that music. 'I am very fond of this,' she said as if the words were wrung from her. After it was over I told her how I had heard it in a theatre at Edinburgh last summer and how it had made me feel I must get back to her at any cost. 'How nice of you,' she answered gently. She hummed a little of the *Barcarolle* after it was over. She said that she had always wanted a voice, that she felt she could have expressed herself in singing, the only way she could have done so. 'How can you say that,' I laughed, 'when you have written all those books?' But Darling merely smiled . . .

November 16th

I took Darling some purply brown leaves and berries which I thought might be myrtle. I was feeling dull myself and unable to rouse her. I arranged the berries with the golden chrysanthemums and she thought the latter were asters. The leaves I told her were lovely in the sunshine, like pebbles are when wet, but were dull in the room as stones when dry . . .

November 19th

. . . Darling . . . made a general reflection, 'I don't know what happens, I go to sleep and forget. It is like a dream when I wake and I ask myself if it has happened or not.' In a pause I asked Darling if she had ever taken Holy Communion. 'I'm a Quaker,' she answered, and again spoke of Penn.[9] She replied to my questioning whether I ought to or not, that no one would question my doing so. Then to further scruples she suggested, 'Why don't you ask the parson?' I demurred and she sympathised with my reluctance. I said I should be nervous taking it. 'Self conscious?' she questioned. 'Yes,' I answered . . .

December 19th

This morning, as Ina was with me on a visit, we both went to see Madame. She replied in answer to Ina's enquiry about her health, 'Oh, I'm first rate.' To Ina's telling her of the girl porters at the station wearing trousers, Madame remarked 'How sensible.' . . .

Calne 1943

February 28th

I saw dear Madame again this morning after I had been to Church. I asked downstairs first of all before going up, and the cook said she thought Madame was a little better. When I went up Nurse said the same, but when I saw Madame herself I thought her sadly changed from Friday. Then she had been able to answer me and there was still a light in her eyes, but this morning her head was bowed on her breast and her eyes seemed lifeless, except for an occasional glimmer. I think she knew me after a minute or two, but did not rouse herself, looking down or past me with a set and stern expression about her mouth and a grey shadow upon her face . . . She has lost interest in Bobby, Nurse says, but she is still taking food.

March 5th

Her eyes were limpid green this morning and herself much better though depressed. She spoke of Bobby. I gave her a message from Miss Tindall to which she replied, 'Oh, thank you.' Also she remarked I had a cold and took notice of the hunting crop I was carrying to ward dogs away from Ella . . .

March 8th

I went to Darling Madame this morning. She was asleep so I sat with her until she wakened, recognising me with a loving smile and looking at me with lingering sweetness. Bobby sat on the bed and gave me a glance full of knowing understanding. I suggested Madame might sleep better without her glasses, but it seems she never takes them off even at night . . . Nurse says she does not speak unless spoken to.

March 17th

After lunch a box of shamrock (so called!) came from Ina and I walked up with it to Madame . . . When I arrived my Darling sweet flower was sitting up looking like a wild rose. Her little white hands in dark mittens were trembling. I put the shamrock on the coverlet above her breast . . . Her mind seemed clearer today and followed more easily what was said . . .

March 23rd

Yesterday morning I thought her changed very much in the few days I had been absent. Though her mind still retains its improvement when she hears, her dear face had lost all colour and had become dull and greatly aged. Her hair was not so silvery, her poor nose curved towards the still sweet mouth, her eyes drained of the willow leaf green, fading, fading and only faintly resembling their normal beauty and expression . . .

April 5th

The morning was warm and sunny. Spring had come. I took Ella to a little lane running along beside the churchyard and there I happened to see a white violet on the ground. I stooped and picked it up. It was almost perfect but for a slight bruise on one petal. I then went up to see my Darling Madame. She was asleep when I went in . . . Nurse had removed Madame's spectacles and she looked more like herself of old. Her eyes so deeply sad were yet of their original blue grey and a pearly pink overspread her features which were only slightly swollen as if with tears. Her head bent forward on her breast, her mouth shut firmly in closely folded lines. I gave the little white flower into her white hand with its cream coloured mitten, scarcely more white than itself. White shawls wrapped her round. She carried the violet slowly, with infinite effort and patience to her face to inhale its sweetness and looked at it attentively and long, with a heart-rending wistfulness . . . I told her that the cow parsley was out but she had forgotten about it. I told her I was taking Holy Communion next Sunday and she understood, seeming to question, but made no comment. I gave her Rachel Mary [Tindall's] love, and I asked her if there was anything I could do for her, write to anyone? 'No,' she said quietly and finally, 'There is nothing.' . . .

April 8th

. . . When I returned to the Hotel that evening I found a box of
white violets had arrived from Miss Tindall with the request that
I take them up to Madame. I had told Miss Tindall how lovely
Madame had been over the violet I had picked up. It was too late
then to go again so I undid the flowers and put them in water over
night . . .

April 17th

I went to Madame as a refuge from my anxiety about the Archdeacon as he had just told me of his impending operation. I sat
beside her, trying to get over the shock and praying for him. She
was sound asleep and breathing heavily, a blue shawl about her. I
sat for some time but she did not wake . . .

May 5th

. . . Nurse gave her her tea and I sat talking on, loath to leave the
region of such perfect peace, for there is great and untold peace
about her. She is passing very beautifully, just like a white
flower, as she has lived. I kissed her forehead and her little white
hand and for the first time she did not make the instinctive withdrawal characteristic of her. I felt I should not be able to leave her
and Calne on the 18th as I had planned. When I returned to the
Hotel I wrote to Archie, her son, to urge him to come and to say I
would not try to renew our friendship if he did . . .

May 12th

This morning after breakfast Isabel (Nurse's sister) came to tell
me that my dear Madame had passed away this morning, about
20 minutes to 3 a.m. I felt very shaken and came upstairs to finish
my letter to Ina . . . Nurse came in later. They both said that
after I had gone last evening Madame had given a very beautiful
smile with her eyes wide open and lovely . . . I went to see her
after lunch. On my way I gathered blue speedwells and cow
parsley. When I went in Nurse lifted the handkerchief from her
dear face and turned down the sheet. 'Oh,' I said, 'doesn't she
look lovely.' She might have been sleeping, as Our Lord said.
There was no shock for the beholder and I felt no fear. In her little
mittened hands Nurse had placed my card with the Heavenly
Twins kittens. You're not going to leave that there? I asked.
'Why not?' Nurse responded, 'She has fingered it often

enough.' I felt infinitely touched. Darling was wearing Mother's bed jacket of padded blue silk with the white muslin lace collar I had sewn on when I sent it to her as a present after our own Mother's death, and a white flowered nightgown tied with blue ribbon at the throat. Her neck looked soft above it and her eyes tightly sealed as if faintly bruised, the vestige of palest pink still in her lips and an ivory sheen on her skin beside which her hair looked darker. Her wedding ring was still on her finger. I did not touch her but knelt down and through my tears I talked to her, for Nurse closed the door. She might have been breathing. I stayed some time. My White Rose, my Little Flower, my Little Love, so infinitely dear, so heart rendingly helpless and pure and remote . . .

. . . Thank God I have no regrets. All the difficult time about Archie was healed and no bitterness remained . . . I had an extraordinary sense of unreality, as if Darling's body was there and yet not there when I knelt beside her. When I came back and took Ella out, a piece of cow parsley lay in my path on the hill, like a message . . .

May 14th

I took the 10.30 bus to Bath, leaving Ella with the Manageress, kind Mrs Greene. Nurse was in the bus so we talked all the way over. The way was like the road to Paradise, an avenue of white May trees over one stretch which will be lovely for Madame's progress tomorrow. On arrival I went to the York House Hotel then walked across Victoria Park to Coles' Nursery in Weston Road. There I ordered a heart-shaped wreath of flowers from the nice sympathetic man and talked to him of Madame. In the evening a telephone message came from Miss Woolsey. The funeral was fixed for 12 noon tomorrow and I was to meet the cortège at Dr Christie's house in the Paragon and bring my own flowers. I telephoned Coles to send them to the Hotel.

May 15th, The Day of Madame Sarah Grand's funeral

I went out early and chose a sheaf of flowers from Ina. Blue iris and poets' narcissi. I walked, with my own wreath too, to 35 The Paragon. It was a gusty morning, but sunshiny. I rang and Dr Christie asked me to wait in the dining room, where, after a while, I was joined by Miss Woolsey. Soon the funeral car drove up and we went out. I walked to the back of the car and handed

in my wreath which was laid on the heart of the coffin. I had
bought three white roses, carrying two and wearing one. I then
got into Nurse's car. Archie, who has grown very thin and looks
taller than I remembered him, inspected the coffin and flowers as
they were being arranged in the funeral car. Then he got in his
car with Miss Woolsey, who was representing Miss Tindall, and
Father Cooper. Dr Christie was in a third car. Nurse had put a
bunch of forget-me-nots on the coffin as from Bobby. We drove
in silence up Lansdown Hill – up the hill where one morning she
and I had been in a bus together, passing her turning almost
unobserved save for those who raised their hats in respect for the
unknown dead. So she came to her own and her own knew her
not and we turned into the gates of Lansdown Cemetery.

At the Chapel the occupants of the first car got out. Archie was
standing beside ours as we drew up. I alighted without looking at
him, remembering what I had said in my letter. He made no
advance and I felt nothing much, he might just as well have not
been there. Father Cooper was wearing a beretta and cloak. We
entered the Chapel. It was hung with drapery of Mary blue, a
lovely sky blue, and only Miss Tindall's wreath of bay leaves and
yellow iris was on the coffin. The 90th Psalm was said and the
Epistle read with 'Our Father'. There was no music, no
memorial booklets. Then it was over and she was carried some
distance along the path to the grave beside Miss Clarke. As we
neared it, a thrush burst into song and other birds answered.
The sun continued to shine and a fresh breeze was blowing.

The coffin was lowered very gently. It was of boxwood, with
oxodised silver handles and a large silver plate which had on it the
name *Sarah Grand aged 88* in large letters. The forget-me-nots
were still there. Miss Woolsey dropped white lilac into the grave,
and I knelt and cast in two white roses. One fell beside the forget-
me-nots on her breast, the other between the earth the coffin side,
its head uppermost as if growing or held by her hand. I knelt,
gazing and thinking of her and of our long friendship. I talked to
the Spanswicks[10] who used to serve Madame at 7 Sion Hill Place.
He showed me a telegram he had received from Beth Robbins
asking them to go as she was unable to come from Aberdeen,
Scotland. Lena, his wife, was in tears. I then looked at the
flowers. There was a wreath from the Corporation of red and
yellow tulips and iris, a lovely bunch of lilies-of-the-valley from
Miss Ross, and Miss Lloyd's was pink and mauve pink roses and

iris, etc. Other wreaths were multi-coloured but I thought mine suited her best because it was like Belleek china – white lilac, white single stocks and valley lilies, studded with white roses; it could not have been lovelier. At last we turned and left her – I had not cried at all. They asked me to take refreshment but I declined and was put out at College Road. Thence I walked by Sion Road to the seat where we had twice sat together and I walked up her 'Riviera' where it seemed as if she were beside me, and I went and stood on her doorstep now so shabby and deserted, remembering how often in joy and trepidation I had waited there, and I walked down the Avenue, and she came with me and tears filled my eyes at last. There were buttercups and cow parsley in her field and the tree at whose foot I had thrown the ashes of the letters which had hurt us – all now dreams, for 'Here we have no continuing City'. Bath lay bathed in mist and sunshine and as I came out on Cavendish Road a gramophone played 'You Are My Sunshine, My Only Sunshine' and I turned in thought to the sacred love which God has given me to make up for the loss of my darling Madame.

As I sat on the terrace of the Roman Baths that afternoon I thought of the time she and I had stood there together during a Mayoral Reception – a memory greets me at every corner in Bath and nearly all are memories of her.

I caught the 5 p.m. back to Calne, and from the train watched the white May trees as they glided past with a million million white tiny roses: wedding, spring and snow time all, in honour of my White Flower.

The next day, Sunday, Nurse came in for a talk after Church to tell little incidents that had taken place after the funeral and the following morning she brought me one or two souvenirs, little things I had given Madame, among them the little model cat she liked so much and the silver plated miniature entrée dish for cigarettes and the hand bell which used to stand beside her bed. This bell I sent to Miss Lloyd who had it converted into a paperweight. I did not see Nurse again, they took charge of Bobby the cat.

On July 8th 1944 I heard from Miss M.J. Lloyd that poor Archie had been killed in a London air raid, a flying bomb. The following day, Sunday, I went to Holy Communion at the Abbey, Bath, 8 a.m. and prayed for him.

> *Sic transit gloria mundi*,
> but the other world remains.

CHAPTER XIII

Finale

❧❧

I bring you the eyes of the field
The Blue Sweet eyes of the Day,
Because your own flower-eyes are sealed
To which I used to pray.

These have a country name 'Speedwell',
Along life's many roads –
And now o'er paths we cannot tell
Towards the blest abodes.[1]

Sarah Grand died a month before her eighty-ninth birth-day, and fifty years after gaining notoriety as the author of *The Heavenly Twins*. Her obituarists on both sides of the Atlantic could scarcely remember her. Many related her to Cedric Chivers, as his wife or sister-in-law, to account for her more recent fame as Mayoress. The *New York Times*[2] called her, 'Woman Suffrage Leader Who Served as Mayor of Bath Six Times . . . One of England's most outspoken suffragists'. Laetitia Fairfield[3] wrote to the *Manchester Guardian*: 'She was the real pioneer of public enlightenment on venereal disease. Participants in the Ministry of Health's campaign today can only guess dimly how much courage this took fifty years ago.' Yes, courage: she lived and died a courageous woman.

In 1939 she had redrafted her will appointing Archie and Beth as executors. She left all published works, manuscripts and copyrights, trinkets, jewellery and personal effects in equal shares to Beth and Beth's daughter Felicitas (Winkie). Archie received only her gold Albert chain with locket, gold watch and an annual income of £52 until his death – which occurred, as reported by Gladys, in an air raid the following year – £2000 then reverting to Beth and the rest in trust to be invested '(but not in Ireland)' for Winkie. Her estate amounted to £4632 6s 6d.

Gladys, for all her devotion and expense on Sarah's behalf over sixteen years, and for all Sarah's later protestations of gratitude, sympathy and desire to help her, received no mention. She joined the funeral cortège low in priority – Sarah's local obituary lists 'other mourners were Miss Woolsey (who represented Miss Tindall, her greatest friend), Dr J. Veronica Christie, Miss Gladys Singers-Bigger'.[4] Despite her love and dedication, the part she played at the end of Sarah's life was never acknowledged.

What became of Gladys? She first moved to the cottage at Dittersham, Devon, she had long planned to share with Ina and Ina's rich friend Miss Michell. From there she arranged the planting of a white rose tree on Sarah's grave and tried once more to build interest in *The Sarah Grand Miscellany*. Charles Whitby, author of 'The Woman and Her Work', the appreciation, in the *Miscellany*, wrote to Gladys:

I have a very high regard for Mme Sarah Grand and her work, and wd. gladly do all I cd. to revive interest in both. The fact has to be faced that, for the present, the GP [general public] seems oblivious to both: even here, where she did so much for us and the City, her death passed almost unheeded. I don't feel a bit hopeful about my own chance of being able to awaken public interest in this high-minded woman and her fascinating novels . . . Anything like a re-writing of the whole thing, or a campaign of soliciting callous publishers, I really could *not* face . . .[5]

After their few years at Dittersham, the three women moved to Miss Michell's home, The Grange, Kenninghall, near Norwich, where Ina died quite suddenly of coronary thrombosis in 1960. 'What a lovely way to go,' Gladys told a friend. 'She came home from a concert in London, had a hot drink, went to bed and died.' She was buried in their parents' grave at Tunbridge Wells.

No such easy way out lay in store for Gladys. Without Ina as catalyst, she quarrelled (about keeping dogs) with Miss Michell, who treated her like a servant and made her scrub the stone floors. And she returned to Bath where she lived in increasing poverty. Anyone who remembers her remarks on her extreme independence and stubbornness. When she could no longer move about easily she discouraged the visits of old friends and stopped seeing most of them. She lived in one dark room on the ground floor of 2 Darlington Street near the Sidney Gardens, overlooking St Mary's Church. Her room was divided in two by a curtain, and contained gas fires she was only allowed to use during certain hours of the day and which she could not reach to light herself. Increasingly crippled with arthritis, and partially blind, she relied on her landlady to bring her a meal each day and to shop for her. Towards the end she existed mainly on bread and tea and an occasional half packet of fish fingers.

The landlady complained that she was difficult, and her few friends, concerned about how she was living and how little food and heat she could afford, began arrangements for her to move to a Royal United Kingdom Benevolent Association Home. The Assistant Curate at Bath Abbey, who visited her frequently, describes her as 'a very fine Christian, a gentle woman. She talked nothing about her family, wanted spiritual help, assurance. I saw the spirit working in her; what Communion meant to a committed woman.'[6]

At Christmas 1969 a friend found her alone in the empty house with nothing but some Christmas cake. On

5 January the same friend helped her to pack to leave Bath for the RUKBA Home at Camberley. That night, the coldest of the year, the landlady turned off the gas at eight o'clock.

The inquest held on 13 January made headlines in the local papers:

WOMAN (81) DIES FROM COLD
I'M SHOCKED SAYS BATH'S CORONER

An 81-year-old woman living within half-a-mile of the centre of Bath died from cold a Bath inquest was told last night.

And the Bath Coroner . . . recording an open verdict, said he was shocked that the woman could become so exposed as to die within three days . . . 2½ hours after Miss Gladys Singers-Bigger was admitted to the hospital her temperature was below 85 degrees. Normal temperature is 98.4.[7]

Her death was recorded as from broncho-pneumonia after suffering from hypothermia. She had been discovered in the morning, lying on her bed partially dressed and completely uncovered.

And so Gladys died alone 'with nothing left but her pride' – and £1300 which she left to a godson in Canada who had sent her money during the previous year 'to keep warm' – and on the eve of departure for an easier life. But perhaps she would have preferred it that way, perhaps she preferred to die in the city she knew so well and which held so many memories.

Amongst her papers was found a letter dated a couple of months earlier referring to a gardener who required 25s. per year for the next ten years to maintain the grave of Madame Sarah Grand.

Notes

❦

Chapter I: The New Woman

1   Lock hospitals: see note 4.
2   Grand, S., 'The Woman's Question', *The Humanitarian*, March 1896.
3   Grand, S., 'Marriage Questions in Fiction – the standpoint of a typical modern woman', *Fortnightly Review*, 69: 378–389, 1898.
4   Three Contagious Diseases Acts were passed, in 1864, 1866 and 1868, and were designed to check the epidemic spread of syphilis in the armed forces. The Acts provided for the forcible surgical examination of any woman suspected of being a prostitute, in any of the garrison towns and seaports included in the Acts, and her detention in a government-certified (Lock) hospital if she were found to be infected. Despite much agitation and a Royal Commission in 1871, the Acts were not repealed until 1886.
5   Mill, J.S., *On the Subjection of Women*, London, 1869.
6   Acts of Parliament that changed the legal status and independence of a woman include: The Infants Custody Act, 1839 (giving her responsibility for her child up to the age of seven and leading to the equal guardianship of children, 1925); the Married Woman's Property Acts, 1870 and 1882; physical force against a wife denied, 1891; and equal grounds for divorce, 1923.
7   Quoted by Crow, D., *The Victorian Woman*, Allen & Unwin, London, 1971.
8   Ellis, Mrs S., *Wives of England*, London, 1843.
9   Acton, Dr W., *The Functions and Disorders of the Reproductive Organs in Childhood, Youth, Adult Age and Advanced Life, Considered in their Physiological, Social and Moral Relations*, 1857, quoted by Marcus, S., in *The Other Victorians, A Study of Sexuality and Pornography in Mid-Nineteenth-Century England*, Weidenfeld & Nicolson, London, 1966.
10 Stutfield, H.E.M., 'The Psychology of Feminism', *Blackwood's Magazine*, January 1897.

11   Ibsen, H., *A Doll's House*, 1879, and *Ghosts*, 1881, first performed in London in 1889.

12   Archer, W., in the preface to the 1900 edition of *Ghosts*.

13   Stutfield, H.E.M., *op. cit.*

14   Marholm, L., 'The Psychology of Woman', Grant Richards, 1899, translated by Etchison, G.A.

15   Fairfield, L., letter to *Manchester Guardian*, 19 May 1943.

Chapter II: Early Life in Ireland and Yorkshire

Note: All quotations not enumerated here and in subsequent chapters are from *The Beth Book*.

1   Frances changed her name to Sarah Grand after she left her husband in 1890.

2   Her baptism form puts the date as 16 June, but all other references mark it as 10 June.

3   Dunn, M.J., letter to her sister Charlotte, 30 January 1840.

4   McFall, H., letter to Mrs Ayre, 17 March 1903, and Grand, S., *The Beth Book*.

5   'My stepmother tells me there was a legend amongst the country people that "the blood of the bees put in the same vessel with the blood of the ravens would never mingle". She says it was always supposed to have come true in the unhappy marriage of George Henry Sherwood and Margaret Bell. I cannot see the point. Do you know anything of it?' Letter from Haldane to Mrs Ayre (see note 4 above) – courtesy of Mrs Barbara Dando, Johannesburg.

6   McFall, C.H., 'Madame Sarah Grand', *The Biographist & Review*, J.S.A. Ridout & Co., Gillingham, Dorset, July 1902.

7   Grand, S., speech to Oldfield Park Wesleyan Sunday School, Bath, May 1923.

8   Grand, S., letter to Singers-Bigger, G., April 1932.

9   Grand, S., letter to Singers-Bigger, G., 29 April 1931.

10   Grand, S., 'Some Recollections of My School Days', *The Lady's Magazine*, January 1901.

11   Butler, J.,: see Petrie, G., *A Singular Iniquity – The Campaigns of Josephine Butler*, London, 1971; and Crow, D., *The Victorian Woman*, Allen & Unwin, 1971.

12   Interview with Grand, S., *Bath Daily Chronicle*, 19 June 1928.

13   Singers-Bigger, G., Diary, Volume V, November 1935.

Chapter III: Marriage and the Far East

1   Maitland, W.H. *History of Magherafelt*, no further details.

2   Thornton, J.H., CB, MB, BA (MRCS 1855) Deputy Surgeon-

General Indian Medical Service (retd), *Memories of Seven Campaigns – a record of thirty-five years' service in the Indian Medical Department in India, China, Egypt and the Sudan*, Constable, 1895.

3   Grand, S., 'Some Recollections of My School Days', *The Lady's Magazine*, January 1901.

4   Grand, S., 'The Baby's Tragedy', *The Lady's Realm*, 1890; and in *Emotional Moments*, a collection of her stories, Heinemann, 1908.

5   Grand, S., *Two Dear Little Feet*, Jarrold & Sons, 1873.

6   Singers-Bigger, G., Diary, Volume II, February 1930.

7   Singers-Bigger, G., Diary, Volume V, January 1935.

8   Grand, S., *Ideala: A Study from Life*, published in Warrington, 1888, then by Bentley, then by Heinemann.

9   Grand, S., 'Ah Man, A Study from Life', *The Woman at Home*, October 1893; and in *Our Manifold Nature*, a collection of her stories, Heinemann, 1894.

10   Grand, S., 'The Great Typhoon', *Aunt Judy's Magazine for Young People*, April 1881.

11   Singers-Bigger, G., Diary, Volume III, December 1932.

12   'Ah Man', *op. cit.*

13   'The Great Typhoon', *op. cit.*

14   Grand, S., letter to Richard Bentley, 31 January 1889 in the Department of Special Collections, University of California Library, Los Angeles.

15   Unsigned article in untitled newspaper, 3 May 1901.

16   *Ideala, op. cit.*

17   Cruse, A., *After the Victorians*, Allen and Unwin, 1938.

18   Twain, M., annotations to *The Heavenly Twins* in the Berg Collection of the New York Public Library.

Chapter IV: Disillusion in Warrington

1   Grand, S., 'Mama's Music Lessons', June and July 1878, 'School Revisited', June and July 1880, 'The Great Typhoon', April 1881, all published in *Aunt Judy's Magazine for Young People*.

2   Grand, S., *Ideala: A Study from Life*, published anonymously by E.W. Allen of Ave Maria Lane, 1888 (printed at the Guardian Office, Warrington); later by Bentley, 1889, and Heinemann, 1894.

3   Grand, S., *Sarah Grand Miscellany*, unpublished, Bath Reference Library.

4   Grand, S., *A Domestic Experiment* (by the Author of Ideala: A Study from Life), William Blackwood & Sons, 1891.

5   Grand, S., *Singularly Deluded*, first serialised in *Blackwood's Edinburgh Magazine*, August–December 1892; and Blackwood, 1893.

6 Grand, S., 'Eugenia' in *Our Manifold Nature*, Heinemann, 1894.
7 Grand, S., 'An Emotional Moment' in *Emotional Moments*, Heinemann, 1908, and in *The Beth Book*, 1897.
8 Grand, S., *The Beth Book*, Heinemann, 1897.
9 Regimental Headquarters Records, The Queen's Lancashire Regiment, Warrington.
10 Warrington Borough Council Minutes, 30 May 1883.
11 Vicinus, M. (ed.), *Suffer and Be Still*, Methuen, 1972, quoting correspondence in *Western Daily Press* on the Contagious Diseases Acts.
12 Grand, S., *The Heavenly Twins*, Heinemann, 1893.
13 Brooke, E.F., *A Superfluous Woman*, Heinemann, 1894.
14 Grand, S., letter to Fisher, F.H., Editor of the *Literary World*, 22 March 1894, in Department of Special Collections, University of California Library, Los Angeles.
15 Grand, S., interviewed by Tooley, S., 'The Woman's Question', *Humanitarian*, March 1896, and in *Review of Reviews*, April 1896.
16 *Sarah Grand Miscellany*, *op. cit.*
17 Unsigned article in untitled newspaper, 3 May 1901.
18 Murray, Q., *Battleton Rectory*, John Heywood, 1885.
19 *A Domestic Experiment*, *op. cit.*
20 *ibid.*
21 Grand, S., 'Janey, A Humble Administrator', *Temple Bar*, October 1891; and in *Our Manifold Nature*, Heinemann, 1894.
22 Grand, S., 'Kane, A Soldier Servant', *Temple Bar*, July 1891; and in *Our Manifold Nature*, Heinemann, 1894.
23 Grand, S., 'The Rector's Bane', in *Emotional Moments*, Heinemann, 1908.
24 *Ideala*, *op. cit.*
25 Grand, S., letter to Fisher, F.H., editor of the *Literary World*, 10 May 1898, in Department of Special Collections, University of California Library, Los Angeles.
26 Ruskin, J., 'Of Queens' Gardens', *Sesame and Lilies*, Dent, 1865.
27 Grand, S., letter to Singers-Bigger, G., April 1936.
28 'Madame Sarah Grand', *Cassell's Universal Portrait Gallery*, 1894.
29 Caird, M., *The Morality of Marriage and other Essays on the Status of Women*, George Redway, 1897.
30 *ibid.* 'Married Life, Present and Future'.
31 Caird, M., Phases of Human Development, 'Suppression of Varient Types', *The Morality of Marriage*, *op. cit.*
32 Grand, S., Foreword to 1923 edition of *The Heavenly Twins*, Heinemann.
33 *ibid.* and in 'Some Women Novelists', *The Woman at Home*, 1896.
34 *ibid.*

35 Grand, S., letter to Singers-Bigger, G., February 1932.
36 Grand, S., letter to William Blackwood & Sons, 27 July 1890, in National Library of Scotland.
37 See p. 100 for details of Haldane's career.
38 Grand, S., dedication on presentation copy of *The Heavenly Twins*, in Department of Special Collections, University of California Library, Los Angeles.

Chapter V: Success in London

1 Grand, S., letter to Fisher, F.H., Editor of the *Literary World*, 10 May 1898, in Department of Special Collections, University of California Library, Los Angeles.
2 Tooley, S., 'Some Women Novelists', *The Woman at Home*, 1896.
3 Interview in *Chicago Tribune*, 1901.
4 Singers-Bigger, G., Diary, Volume III, December 1932.
5 Cotton, J.J., 'Madame Sarah Grand', *Macmillan's Magazine*, September 1900; Bernard, J.F., *Talleyrand: A Biography*, Collins, 1973.
6 Sir Frederick Pollock, a famous and active London lawyer; died 1937.
7 See note 4.
8 Grand, S., 'Janey, A Humble Administrator' and 'Kane, A Soldier Servant' in *Temple Bar*, 1891, and also in *Our Manifold Nature*, Heinemann, 1894.
9 Grand, S., 'Josepha Recounts a Remarkable Experience' in *Variety*, Heinemann, 1922.
10 Grand, S., Foreword to 1923 edition of *The Heavenly Twins*.
11 *ibid.*
12 The National Union of Women's Suffrage Societies was formed by Millicent Fawcett in 1897, the Women's Social and Political Union by Emmeline Pankhurst in 1903.
13 Grand, S., 'The Duty of Looking Nice', *Review of Reviews*, August 1893.
14 *The Heavenly Twins*, Foreword to 1923 edition.
15 Ellis, S.M., *George Meredith, His Life and Friends in Relation to His Work*, Grant Richards, 1919.
16 Twain, M., annotated copy of *The Heavenly Twins*, p. 149, in the Berg Collection, New York Public Library.
17 *The Heavenly Twins*, 1923 Foreward.
18 Grand, S., letter to Fisher, F.H., 23 March 1894, in Department of Special Collections, University of California Library, Los Angeles.
19 *The Heavenly Twins*, 1923 Foreword.

20 Mott, F.L., *Golden Multitudes, The Story of Best-Sellers in the United States*, Macmillan, 1947.

21 'The Strike of a Sex', *The Quarterly Review*, Vol. 179, July and October 1894.

22 Ellis, S.M., *op. cit.*

23 *The Heavenly Twins*, 1923 Foreword.

24 Whyte, F. *William Heinemann – A Memoir*, Jonathan Cape, 1928.

25 Cruse, A., *After the Victorians*, Allen and Unwin, 1938.

26 Obituary, *Manchester Guardian*, 1943.

27 Whyte, F., *op. cit.*

28 Cunningham, A.V., 'The New Woman Fiction of the 1890s', *Victorian Studies*, December 1973.

29 Mott, F.L., *op. cit.*

30 Review in the *Athenaeum*, 18 March 1893.

31 Hardy, T., *One Rare, Fair Woman, Thomas Hardy's Letters to Florence Henniker, 1893–1922*, (ed.) Hardy, E. & Pinion, F.B., Macmillan, 1972.

32 *ibid.*

33 Shaw, G.B., letter to R. Golding Bright, 19 November 1894; *G.B. Shaw Collected Letters 1874–1897*, (ed.) Laurence, D.H., Reinhardt, 1965.

Chapter VI: Fame and Freedom in France and England

1 Whitby, C., *Sarah Grand, The Woman and Her Work* (unpublished).

2 Quoted in 'The Strike of a Sex', *The Quarterly Review*, July and October 1894.

3 Grand, S., 'The New Aspect of the Woman Question', *The North American Review*, March 1894.

4 Linton, E.L., 'The Girl of the Period', *The Saturday Review*, 14 March 1868 (published anonymously).

5 Quoted by Caird, M., 'A Defence of the "Wild Women" ', *The Morality of Marriage*, George Redway, 1897.

6 Layard, G.S., *Mrs Lynn Linton, Her Life, Letters and Opinions*, Methuen, 1901.

7 *ibid.*

8 'The Tree of Knowledge – on the subject of education and marriage of women', *The New Review*, June 1894.

9 Corelli, M., 'Motherhood', *Windsor Magazine*, December 1899.

10 *The Quarterly Review*, *op. cit.*

11 Black, H.C., *Pen, Pencil, Baton & Mask*, Spottiswoode, 1896.

12   'A Chat with Mme Sarah Grand – Women of Note in the Cycling World', *The Hub*, 17 October 1896.

13   *ibid.*

14   Singers-Bigger, G., Diary, Volume II, September 1928.

15   Grand, S., quoted in *Review of Reviews*, August 1893.

16   Black, H.C., *op. cit.*

17   Grand, S., 'Josepha Recounts a Remarkable Experience' in *Variety*, Heinemann, 1922.

18   *Bath & Wilts Chronicle*, April 1925.

19   Grand, S., 'The Undefinable' in *Emotional Moments*, Heinemann, 1908.

20   Grand, S., 'She Was Silent' in *Emotional Moments*, Heinemann, 1908.

21   Grand, S., 'Eugenia' in *Our Manifold Nature*, Heinemann, 1894.

22   *ibid.*

23   Macarthur, J., 'Notes of a Bookman', *Harper's Weekly*, 2 November 1901.

24   Grand, S., *The Human Quest, being some thoughts in contribution to the subject of the art of happiness*, Heinemann, 1900.

25   *The Quarterly Review*, *op. cit.*

26   Grand, S., letter to Fisher, F.H., 26 August 1894, in Department of Special Collections, University of California Library, Los Angeles.

27   Grand, S., letter to Fisher F.H., 11 November 1894, *ibid.* Mrs Humphry Ward (1851–1920), granddaughter of Thomas Arnold, headmaster of Rugby, and niece of Matthew Arnold. Most famous for *Robert Elsmere* (1888), *The History of David Grieve* (1892) and *Marcella* (1894). An anti-suffragist, she became President of the Anti-Suffrage League in 1909. For many years she reviewed books for *The Times* where her husband was art critic.

28   This could be Lockhart and Wilson, editors at *Blackwood's Magazine*, who attacked the literary establishment – Coleridge, Leigh Hunt, Wordsworth and Keats – and were involved in libel actions.

29   Grand, S., letter to Fisher, F.H., 23 November 1894 Department of Special Collections, University of California Library, Los Angeles.

30   Grand, S., letter to Fisher, F.H., 3 April 1895, *ibid.*

31   Grand, S., letter to Fräulein Langrecht, Edgbaston, 1894.

32   Grand, S., letter to Fräulein Langrecht, February 1895.

33   Grand, S., letter to Terry, E., undated, in Department of Special Collections, University of California Library, Los Angeles.

34   Grand, S., letter to Fisher, F.H., 3 April 1895.

35   Allen, G., *The Woman Who Did*, John Lane, 1895.

36   Information from Mr Gordon McFall.

37   Grand, S., 'The Woman's Question', *The Humanitarian*, March 1896.

38 Grand, S., letter to Fisher, F.H., 24 March 1895, in Department of Special Collections, University of California Library, Los Angeles.

39 *The Hub*, *op. cit.*

40 *ibid*.

41 *The Humanitarian*, *op. cit.*

42 *Bath Daily Chronicle*, 31 January 1933.

43 Grand, S., letter to Singers-Bigger, G., October 1937.

44 Grand, S., letter to Singers-Bigger, G., October 1937.

45 Ellis, S.M., *George Meredith, His Life and Friends*, Grant Richards, 1919.

46 *ibid*.

47 Inscription inside back cover of *The Heavenly Twins* in Department of Special Collections, University of California Library, Los Angeles.

48 Singers-Bigger, G., Diary, Volume V, February 1935.

49 Ellis, S.M., *op. cit.*

50 Singers-Bigger, G., Diary, Volume II, March 1930.

51 Grand, S., letter to Singers-Bigger, G., October 1937.

52 Camden Pratt, A.T., *People of the Period*, Neville Beeman, 1897.

53 Singers-Bigger, G., Diary, Volume IV, September 1934.

54 Untitled, undated news cutting, Bath Reference Library.

55 Singers-Bigger, G., Diary, Volume III, December 1932.

56 'Some Women Novelists', *The Women at Home*, 1897.

57 Grand, S., Preface to *Our Manifold Nature*, Heinemann, 1894.

58 'Clear, C., *The British Weekly*, 2 December 1897.

59 The *Athenaeum*, 27 November 1897.

60 Clear, C., *op. cit.*

61 Danby, F. and Harris, F., *Saturday Review*, 20 November 1897.

62 *ibid*.

63 Grand, S., letter to Fisher, F.H., 4 December 1897, in Department of Special Collections, University of California Library, Los Angeles.

64 Grand, S., letter to Lucus, D., 16 November 1897, *ibid*.

65 Grand, S., letter to the Editor, *Daily Telegraph*, 22 November 1897.

66 Grand, S., letter to Fräulein Langrecht, July 1898.

67 *ibid*.

Chapter VII: Suffrage and America

1 Grand, A.C., letter to Singers-Bigger, G., 1936.

2 Dawson, C., stationed in Tunbridge Wells with the East Surrey

(Territorial) Regiment, 1915, was told by Beth that she had seven Christian names.

3   Grand, A.C., letter to Singers-Bigger, G., 1936.

4   The committee of a borough council which deals with all matters of policing and lighting the borough.

5   Grand, S., 'The New Woman and the Old', *The Lady's Realm*, 1898.

6   Grand, S., *The Modern Man and Maid*, Horace Marshall & Son, London, 1898.

7   Grand, S., 'Marriage Questions in Fiction – The Standpoint of a Typical Modern Woman', *The Fortnightly Review*, 69, 1898.

8   *ibid*.

9   Grand, S., letter to the Editor, *The Morning Leader*, London, 5 February 1900.

10 Grand, S., 'The Saving Grace' in *Variety*, Heinemann, 1922.

11 Forbes, A., 'My Impressions of Sarah Grand', *The Lady's World*, June 1900.

12 *ibid*.

13 Singers-Bigger, G., Diaries, September 1928 and March 1931.

14 Grand, S., letter to Singers-Bigger, G., September 1931.

15 Singers-Bigger, G., Diary, Volume III, June 1931.

16 *ibid*.

17 Forbes, A., *op. cit*.

18 *Critic*, New York, 39, 1901.

19 Mott, F.L., *Golden Multitudes: The Story of Best Sellers in the United States*, Macmillan, 1947

20 *Ellen Terry's Memoirs*, (ed.) Craig, E., St. John, C., Gollancz, 1933.

21 Singers-Bigger, G., Diary, Volume I, September 1928.

22 Singers-Bigger, G., Diary, Volume V, February 1936.

23 See note 21. Bryn Mawr deny her having been there.

24 Singers-Bigger, G., Diary, Volume 1V, July 1933.

25 *Ellen Terry's Memoirs*, *op. cit*.

26 Foreword to the 1923 edition of *The Heavenly Twins*.

27 Rowlette, R.O., 'Mark Twain's *Pudd'nhead Wilson*: Its Themes and Their Development', Butler University, Indianapolis.

28 *Bath Daily Chronicle*, October 1923.

29 Macarthur, J., 'Notes of a Bookman', *Harper's Weekly*, 2 November 1901.

30 Grand, S., letter to Mr Christy, her literary agent, 24 April 1903, in Department of Special Collections, University of California Library, Los Angeles.

31 Kingsmill, H., *Frank Harris*, Lehmann, 1949. 'In the three or four years before the First World War, Dan Rider's bookshop, off St

Martin's Lane, used to be a meeting-place for a number of writers, painters and journalists: Joseph Simpson, Lovat Fraser, Middleton Murry, Haldane Macfall, Holbrook Jackson, and others.' See also *Enid Bagnold's Autobiography*, Heinemann, 1969.

32　McFall, H., letter to Mrs Ayre, 17 March 1903.

33　The Weir-Mitchell rest cure was a fashionable therapy to relieve nervous disorders and restore nervous capital by separating the patient from all mental effort. It was commonly described as 'milk, monotony and massage'.

34　Grand, S., letter to Fisher, F.H., 1 January 1907, in Department of Special Collections, University of California Library, Los Angeles.

35　Grand, S., letter to Singers-Bigger, G., June 1931.

36　Linklater, A., *An Unhusbanded Life*, Hutchinson, 1980.

37　Prospectus of Women Writers' Suffrage League, quoted in Showalter, E., *A Literature of Their Own*, Virago Press, 1978.

38　Grand, S., letter to Bertha Newcombe, January 1909, in Fawcett Library.

39　*New York Times*, 13 May 1943.

40　*The Common Cause*, 8 May 1913.

41　NUWSS Kentish Federation First Annual Report, 1913, in Fawcett Library.

42　Grand, S., letter to Fawcett, M., August 1914, in Bath Reference Library.

43　Tynan, K. (Mrs. H.A. Hinkson), *The Middle Years*, Constable, 1916.

44　Tynan, K., *The Star*, 1 November 1922.

45　*ibid*.

46　Grand, S., letter to Fisher, F.H., 1 January 1907.

47　Whitby, C., 'Sarah Grand, The Woman and Her Work' (unpublished).

48　Grand, S., *Adnam's Orchard*, Heinemann, 1912.

49　Strachey, R., *The Cause*, Virago Press, 1978.

50　*ibid*.

51　Singers-Bigger, G., Diary, Volume 1, June 1928.

52　Tindall, R.M., letter to Singers-Bigger, G., April 1949; and Grand, S., letter to Singers-Bigger, G., October 1932.

53　See note 2.

54　*ibid*.

55　Grand, S., 'Exquisite Bath – Impressions of a Newcomer', *Bath & Wilts Chronicle*, 27 May 1922.

56　*Bath & Wilts Chronicle*, 20 October 1922.

Chapter VIII: Bath – Enter Gladys

1 Wood, J., *An Essay towards a Description of Bath*, 1742.
2 *Bristol Sports News*, 28 October 1922.
3 *Glasgow Herald*, 3 January 1923.
4 *Bath & Wilts Chronicle*, 20 October 1922.
5 *ibid.*, 27 May 1922.
6 See note 4.
7 The talented niece of Ellen Terry.
8 Recollections of Mrs D. Radcliffe, Mrs K. Doyle and Miss E. Russ.
9 *ibid.*
10 Singers-Bigger, G., *The Animals' Gospel*, eight poems, no date.
11 Singers-Bigger, G., Diary, 7 February 1925.
12 *ibid.*
13 *ibid.*, July 1925.
14 *Evening Standard*, 3 October 1927.
15 *Bath & Wilts Chronicle*, 23 January 1926.
16 Recollections of Mrs Edna Davis.
17 Viscount Richard Burdon Haldane (1856–1928) statesman, lawyer and philosopher. Published *The Philosophy of Humanism* (1922) and *Human Experience* (1926); greatly admired by Gladys.
18 Singers-Bigger, G., Diary, February 1926.
19 British Empire Shakespeare Society of which Ina Singers-Bigger was President and 'Rita' Vice-President.
20 'Rita': Mrs Desmond Humphreys, see note 11, Chapter IX.

Chapter IX: The Lesser Boswell

1 Singers-Bigger, G., 'Two Impressions', *Lilies of the Hill*, a booklet of unpublished poems written for Sarah, in Bath Reference Library.
2 As the Post Office delivered almost with the speed of a private messenger, it was more usual to write a letter than to make a telephone call.
3 Grand, S., letter to Singers-Bigger, G., December 1927.
4 *The Times*, 27 July 1928.
5 Spender, E.H., *The Fire of Life*, Hodder & Stoughton, 1926.
6 Ninon de l'Enclos (1620–1705), renowned for her wit and beauty, kept a celebrated salon.
7 Harrison tablet: Frederic Harrison (1831–1923), philosopher, historian, lawyer, lived latterly and died at 10 Royal Crescent, Bath.
8 Viscount Richard Burdon Haldane (1856–1928), statesman, lawyer and philosopher, published, *inter alia*, *The Philosophy of*

Humanism (1922) and *Human Experience* (1926) which greatly impressed Gladys.

9   Geoffrey Fyson: schoolmaster and poet, son of George Fyson, founder of the Bath printers.

10   Fresh Air Fund: holiday fund for poor children of the city.

11   Rita: Mrs Desmond Humphreys a prolific romantic novelist, contemporary of Sarah and friend and frequent guest of Mrs Singers-Bigger, both of whom she describes in her *Recollections of a Literary Life*, Andrew Melrose, 1936.

12   Edna, her maid, says that Sarah never made her own bed; Edna and Mrs Taylor did so for her.

13   Caroline Spurgeon (1869–1942): first woman professor at an English university, first President of the International Federation of University Women, authority on Chaucer and Shakespeare.

14   G. K. Chesterton (1874–1936): essayist and novelist, twice visited Bath to stay with Cedric Chivers, unveiled a plaque to Dr Johnson.

15   Marie Corelli (Mary Mackay, 1855–1924): popular romantic novelist, best known for *A Romance of Two Worlds*; she kept a gondola (and a gondolier) at Stratford-on-Avon.

16   Herbert Gustave Schmalz (1856–1935): painter of genre and biblical subjects and later of flowers which he signed 'Angelico'.

17   Alexandra day: the selling of rose shaped flags in June, instigated by Queen Alexandra, to raise funds for hospitals.

18   Sir Harry Hatt: Mayor of Bath 1915–16, Chairman of Electric Light & Sewage Disposal Committee.

19   'Bally Castle in Co. Mayo' and mention that Sarah had 'step daughters': inaccurate, probably misheard by Gladys.

20   'Ah Man': a short story by Sarah where the Chinese butler, Ah Man, is crushed to death while rescuing the narrator's 'wretched writings' from a house collapsing in an earthquake.

21   Ferdinand, enchanted by Miranda, in *The Tempest*, Act I, scene ii: '. . . My prime request,
Which I do last pronounce, is, O you wonder!
If you be maid or no?'

22   Lord Terry de Beach: character in *The Winged Victory*.

23   Sarah presided at a meeting at the Guildhall in support of the Quaker appeal for funds to feed starving Germans in the Ruhr, in February 1924. A hostile audience of ex-servicemen broke up the meeting in disorder.

24   The Mayor's Officer: carries the city sword and precedes the Mayor at official functions.

25   General Booth: founder of the Salvation Army in 1878.

26   Gibran, K. (Jabran Khalil Jabran), *The Prophet*, Heinemann, 1926.

27 Ellen Terry (1848–1928) was 'confused' and poor sighted for seven years before her death.
28 Sarah Siddons (1755–1831) began her career in Sheridan's *The Rivals* in 1778 in Bath and lived at 33 The Paragon where Ellen Terry unveiled the plaque.
29 William Heinemann died in 1920.
30 John Walter Cross married George Eliot in 1880, seven months before her death. He died in 1924.

Chapter X: Sunday Afternoon Land

1 Singers-Bigger, G., 'Wings in Our Eyes', *Lilies of the Hill*, unpublished poems in Bath Reference Library.
2 Singers-Bigger, G., letter to Grand, S., 14 December 1929.
3 Singers-Bigger, G., letter to Grand, S., 17 December 1929.
4 Grand, S., letter to Singers-Bigger, G., May 1932.
5 Grand, S., letter to Singers-Bigger, G., 5 July 1931.
6 Whitby, C., 'Sarah Grand: The Woman and her Work', unpublished MS.
7 An endorsement by local aristocracy was bound to help sales of the book. The Duke of Beaufort's estate, Badminton, lies near Bath, and the Dowager Duchess must have been a contemporary of Sarah.
8 Grand, S., letter to Singers-Bigger, G., 16 August 1931. Grant Richards had published Haldane McFall's *The Wooings of Jezebel Pettyfer* and *Ibsen*. As Haldane had recently died, Beth could have been in correspondence with him about her father's work.
9 Grand S., letter to Singers-Bigger, G., 15 December 1931.
10 Singers-Bigger, G., letter to Grand, S., March 1928.
11 Singers-Bigger, G., letter to Grand, S., July 1929.
12 Grand, S., letter to Singers-Bigger, G., 1 January 1931.
13 Grand, S., letters to Singers-Bigger, G., 7, 8 and 25 November 1934.
14 *Bath Weekly Chronicle & Herald*, 15 May 1943.
15 *ibid.*
16 Grand, A.C., letter to Singers-Bigger, G., April 1936.
17 *ibid.*
18 Grand, A.C., letter to Singers-Bigger, G., February 1937.
19 Grand, S., letter to Singers-Bigger, G., 24 October 1931. Nigel Playfair: actor-manager at the Lyric Theatre, 1918–32.
20 Lord Rosebery (1847–1929): Liberal Prime Minister 1894–5; stayed at 5 The Circus, received the freedom of the city and unveiled memorials to Chatham and Pitt.
21 Grand, S., letter to Singers-Bigger, G., 28 October 1934.

22 Grand, S., letter to Singers-Bigger, G., November 1934.

23 Arnold Ridley, born Bath, 1896, later TV and radio actor.

24 Grand, S., letter to Singers-Bigger, G., December 1934.

25 Mother Mary Gabriel, who knew and taught Winkie in 1934.

26 Grand, S., letter to Singers-Bigger, G., December 1939.

27 La Retraite du Sacre Coeur: the Catholic convent at Weston-super-Mare where Felicitas Robbins ('Winkie') was educated and where Sarah spent holidays.

28 Mrs Sonnenschein: widow of Professor William Swan Sonnenschein, Editor of *The Best Books*, 1st edn 1887, Routledge.

29 Bret Harte (1836–1902): American novelist, lived in London from 1885.

30 Lady Henry Somerset: 1890 President of British and World Women's Temperance Association, also important suffrage worker.

31 Lady Jackson: untraceable.

32 Eliot, G., *Middlemarch*, Dent, 1930.

33 Gibbs, Sir P.H., *The Hidden City*, Hutchinson, 1929.

34 Rea, L., *The Six Mrs Greenes*, Heinemann, 1929.

35 Anthony Hope (Sir Anthony Hope Hawkins, 1863–1933): author of *The Prisoner of Zenda* (1894), *Rupert of Hentzau* and other 'sword and cloak' novels.

36 Portrait by Alfed Praga, London society portrait painter; signed and dated 1896; presented to the City of Bath by Archibald Carlaw Grand in 1943. See illustration 3.

37 Alice Meynell: poet and essayist and friend of George Meredith.

38 This passage was marked by Sarah: 'Incorrect – Delete'.

39 Sir Edmond Gosse (1849–1928): critic, essayist, biographer and great friend of William Heinemann; chose and introduced Heinemann's International Library.

40 Roy Campbell (1901–1957): South African poet, converted Roman Catholic; most famous for *The Flaming Terrapin*.

41 Andrew Lang (1844–1912): Scottish man of letters.

42 Sir Henry Seagrave in 1927 broke the speed record on land; died 1930.

43 Amy Johnson in 1930 became first woman to fly solo from Croydon to Australia.

44 Sir Edward Ball: untraceable. (But Gladys could have misheard – Sir Robert Ball (1840–1913): Irish astronomer and mathematician.)

45 Marie Corelli (see Chapter IX, note 15).

46 *The Ninth Vibration* by Adams Beck: neither traceable.

47 Mrs Tynan: Katharine Tynan, journalist and author, contemporary and acquaintance of Sarah in Tunbridge Wells about 1910.

48 Coventry Patmore (1823–1896): poet, wrote in celebration of married love 'The Angel in the House'; converted Roman Catholic and later wrote on religious subjects.

49 Francis Thompson (1859–1907): poet; in 1885 was destitute in London, prey to opium; taken up by Alice Meynell and her husband; most famous for 'The Hound of Heaven'.

50 Widcombe Lodge where Henry Fielding wrote *Tom Jones*.

51 Sarah had shares in the Central Argentines and in LNE Railways, but in 1932 they failed to pay dividends, thereby affecting her income. (Letter to Gladys, October 1933.)

52 Mrs Massingberd: temperance leader and anti-vivisectionist; founded the Pioneer Club in 1892 for the political and moral advancement of women.

53 Dane, C., *Will Shakespeare*, 'an invention in four Acts', Shaftsbury Theatre, 1921.

54 Besier, R., *The Barretts of Wimpole Street*, Gollancz, 1930.

55 Robert Buchanan (1841–1901): poet and novelist, started writing plays in 1880.

56 William Archer (1856–1924): Scottish drama critic, dramatist and apostle of Ibsen.

57 The General Election of 1931 resulted in a National Government formed by Ramsay MacDonald.

58 Ouida (Marie Louise de la Ramée, 1839–1908): flamboyant novelist who wrote romances of fashionable life; died in poverty in Italy.

59 Young, E.H., *Miss Mole*, Cape, 1930.

60 Clara Codd: untraceable.

61 J. Krishnamurti: intended Messiah of the Theosophists, a young Hindu discovered by Annie Besant.

62 Sylvia Pankhurst's book: *The Suffragette Movement*, Longmans, 1931; Virago Press, 1977. (Sarah is mentioned on p. 284.)

63 Life of Edmund Gosse with photographs: not traceable.

64 Not in the *Sunday Times* index.

65 Arthur Waugh (1866–1943): publisher, editor and critic; father of Evelyn and Alec.

66 Algernon Swinburne, 'By the North Sea' from *Studies in Song*, Penguin, 1961.

67 Tomas, G., *A Tenement in Soho*, Cape, 1929.

68 Leslie Stephen (1832–1904): editor of *Dictionary of National Biography*, father of Virginia Woolf and Vanessa Bell.

69 Borden, M., *A Woman with White Eyes*, Heinemann, 1930.

70 Morgan, C., *The Fountain*, Macmillan, 1932.

71 Housmann, A.E., *The Shropshire Lad*, 1898.

72 Untraceable.

73 Sir Arthur Carlton, theatre proprietor, four times Mayor of Worcester, lived in Bath, 1922–3.

74 The year 1932 was the bi-centenery of the trial of Warren Hastings. Circa 1787 dozens of books, pamphlets, debates were printed about Hastings' 'impeachment by the House of Commons for high crimes and misdemeanours'. This could refer to *Trial of Warren Hastings Esq.* in 24 volumes collected by Hastings.

75 Mark Rutherford (William Hale White) wrote *Revolution in Tanners Lane*, 1887. Langton and Groombridge: villages in Kent near Tunbridge Wells.

76 Mrs Frederic Harrison: wife of Comtist philosopher (see Chapter IX, note 7); early unofficial leader of anti-suffragists, friend of Mrs Humphry Ward.

77 Walter Theodore Watts Dunton (1832–1914): novelist and critic, and friend and patron of Swinburne who dedicated 'By the North Sea' to him.

78 *Mädchen in Uniform* (Young Girls in Uniform) by Christa Winsloe, 1932, play about girls' boarding school, with lesbian undertones.

79 Henry Austin Dobson (1840–1921): poet, solicitor, critic for the *Athenaeum*, guardian of Swinburne.

80 William Heinemann had two Siamese cats in 1917, called Peter and Paul.

81 *Kennst du das Land?* by Goethe.

82 Sarah was President of the Bath branch of the National Council of Women, but records of dates were lost in the war.

83 Lord Crawford: Conservative Member of Parliament, Cabinet Minister in 1916 and 1922.

84 Ramsay MacDonald: Labour Prime Minister in 1924 and 1929 and leader of the National Government in 1931.

85 Grand, S., 'The Modern Girl', *Temple Magazine*, February 1898.

86 Harriet Martineau (1802–1876): political economist, historian, novelist.

87 Sibyl Ruskin, a friend of Gladys and Ina.

88 Arthur Hugh Clough (1819–61): poet.
 'Say not the struggle nought availeth,
 The labour and the wounds are vain,
 The enemy faints not, nor faileth,
 And as things have been they remain.'
 (*Penguin Book of English Verse*, 1956)

89 Bram Stoker: Henry Irving's business manager and author of *Dracula*, 1897.

90   Gladys had written in 1925 of a teaparty with Rita: 'We spoke of
      Mme Grand . . . they say she is divorced and that her grand daughter
      is also seeking a divorce at the present moment, all of which goes to
      account for the sadness of her expression.' Sarah was protesting
      against the stigma of divorce being applied to her; she was not *divorced*
      from her husband. Her annoyance that Rita had suggested it would
      account for her over-compensation about her relationship with her
      husband.

91   'Madame Sarah Grand and Women's Emancipation', *The Vote*,
      August 1933.

92   *Saturday Review*, 20 November 1897.

93   Ella Hepworth Dixon: an early Heinemann authoress; wrote *The
      Story of a Modern Woman*.

94   Mrs Walters: John Walter III was proprietor of *The Times*,
      1847–1894, succeeded by his son.

95   Logan Pearsall-Smith's mother was Hannah Whitall, American
      Quaker and writer who brought her family across the Atlantic in 1888
      and died in England in 1911.

96   *Cavalcade*: a play by Noel Coward tracing a family from the Boer
      War to 1933, recently filmed.

97   Marquise St. Evrémonde: a character in *A Tale of Two Cities*.

98   *The Camberwell Miracle*: untraceable.

99   Thirkell, A., *High Rising*, Hamish Hamilton, 1933.

100   Siegfried Sassoon married Hester Gatty in December 1933; lived
      near Warminster, Wiltshire.

101   Daisy Ross: an old friend of Sarah from her Tunbridge Wells
      days.

102   W.T. Stead: influential editor of the *Pall Mall Gazette*, who
      championed Josephine Butler's campaign against the Contagious
      Diseases Acts.

103   I can only assume that this refers to Beth's alleged divorce. Such
      upheaval could have made it practical for Winkie to spend Christmas
      alone with Sarah, and could explain a peremptory telegram.

104   See note 51.

105   Mrs Baker Eddy: founder of Christian Science in 1879.

106   Positivism: from c. 1840, based on Comte's philosophy that
      physical sciences must be the basis of knowledge and also of moral
      values. Frederic Harrison and his wife (see note 76) were both
      Positivists.

107   Baroness Burdett Coutts (1814–1906): banking heiress and
      philanthropist.

108   Oxford Movement: started in 1926 by a Lutheran pastor, F.N.
      Buchman, changed its title to Moral Rearmament Group in 1930s.

109   Brooke, R., *Selected Poems*, Sidgwick & Jackson, 1927.

110 'Singularly Deluded', first published in *Blackwood's Magazine*, August-December 1892.

111 Herbert Beerbohm Tree (1853–1917): actor-manager who built and ran Her Majesty's Theatre.

112 Julia Nielson Terry, actress niece of Ellen Terry, with whom Ina had performed in South Africa.

113 Reid, T.W., *The life, letters, and friendships of Richard Monckton Milnes, first Lord Houghton*, Cassell, 1890.

114 *Kingdom Come* by Hugh Redwood: untraceable.

115 Gladys was converted to the Anglican Church the year before Sarah died.

116 *The Moon of Bath*: untraceable.

117 The engagement of Prince George, Duke of Kent, to Princess Marina of Greece.

118 Bjornstjerne Bjornson (1832–1910): Norwegian poet, dramatist, novelist and political and social leader; in 1903 won Nobel Prize for literature.

119 Probably *Mr* Wharton. Edith Wharton (1862–1937), one of America's most distinguished novelists, won the Pulitzer Prize for *The Age of Innocence* in 1921. Her husband became mentally ill and she eventually divorced him in 1913.

120 Gertrude Atherton (1857–1948): American novelist, noted for *Patience Sparhawk and her Times* first published in 1897. *The Heavenly Twins* was published in 1893 – Gladys got both dates wrong. Atherton's memoirs were probably *Adventures of a Novelist* (autobiographical reminiscences), Cape, 1932.

121 Charlotte Boynton from Burton Agnes Hall married Sarah's uncle, William Sherwood.

Chapter XI: The Archie Tragedy

1 Singers-Bigger, G., 'Two Friends', *Lilies of the Hill*, unpublished poems in Bath Reference Library.

2 Grand, A.C., letter to Singers-Bigger, G., June 1937.

3 Grand, A.C., letter to Singers-Bigger, G., October 1937.

4 Pankhurst, C., a series of articles in *The Suffragette*, 1912.

5 Grand, S., letter to Singers-Bigger, G., May 1937.

6 Grand, S., letter to Singers-Bigger, G., July 1937.

7 The last edition of *The Heavenly Twins* published by Heinemann contained a Foreword by Sarah dated: Crowe Hall, Bath, January 1923.

8 Grand, S., letter to Singers-Bigger, G., October 1937.

9 Grand, A.C., letter to Singers-Bigger, G., February 1937.

10 Usually Sarah's letters to Gladys have no introduction.

11   Morton, H.C.V., *In the Steps of the Master*, Rich & Cowan, 1934.

12   May Morris (1863? – 1938): daughter of William Morris, poet, artist, manufacturer and socialist; she was an embroiderer and lecturer on embroidery and jewellery, and edited her father's works.

13   William Holman Hunt (1827–1910): leading Pre-Raphaelite painter, married Fanny Waugh in 1865 who died the next year; he then married her sister Edith in 1875 despite the Table of Affinities forbidding such marriage. (This ruling was not overcome until the passing of the Deceased Wife's Sister's Marriage Act in 1907.)

14   Professor William Swan Sonnenschein (see Chapter X, note 28): his widow lived at 4 Sion Hill Place; his book on Rhythm is untraceable.

15   Arthur Hugh Clough (see Chapter X, note 88).

16   Walt Whitman (1819–91): American poet who celebrated modern life in his verse.

17   Maeterlinck, M., *The Life of the Bee*, Allen & Unwin, 1901.

18   John Couch Adams discovered Neptune at the same time as Urbain Leverrier, a Frenchman, and confirmed by a German astronomer Johann Galle in 1846. Uranus was discovered by Sir William Herschel (astronomer to George III) in 1781 at Bath, in his back garden at 19 New King Street.

19   Du Maurier, D., *Gerald*, Gollancz, 1934.

20   Lord Houghton: the politician Monkton Milnes (see Chapter X, note 113).

21   Richard Jeffries (1848–87): naturalist and novelist.

22   Mrs Warwick Hunt: untraceable.

23   John Dryden (1631–1700): English Restoration poet and dramatist.

24   From *The Last Idler* by Samuel Johnson.

25   Joseph Chamberlain (1836–1914): Liberal Secretary of State for the Colonies during the Boer War; father of Neville; possibly influenced by Beatrice Webb, social reformer but anti-suffrage.

26   Meredith, G., *The Ordeal of Richard Feverel*, Chapman & Hall, 1859; *The Egoist*, Kegan Paul, 1880.

27   These beetle ear-rings are now in the possession of Victoria Art Gallery, Bath City Council, and are referred to by Rita in her *Recollections of a Literary Life*: 'I didn't . . . sport long green ear-rings and beetle wing ornaments as another novelist had done. She, at all events, has made a mark on time and occasion, and never been out of the public eye.'

28   Meredith, G., *Diana of the Crossways*, Chapman & Hall, 1885.

29   Caroline Norton (1808–77): English author, granddaughter of Sheridan; her own marital troubles led her to write pamphlets and address to the Queen to reform the divorce laws. And see p. 55.

30   Lord Melbourne (1779–1848): political adviser to Queen Victoria;
    husband of Lady Caroline Lamb, novelist, notorious for her
    infatuation with Lord Byron.
31   There was a theory, apparently substantiated by the pyramid
    prophecies, that the British were the lost tribe of Israel.
32   Agnes Tobin: American poet; friend of Sarah in Paris.
33   Bryn Mawr College, Pennsylvania.
34   The Winged Victory: a statue in the Louvre, Paris, and title of one
    of Sarah's novels.
35   Miss — : Miss Fabian, Archie's friend in London, to whom he
    bequeathed his Estate.
36   Miss Michell: Ina's rich friend with whom she and Gladys lived
    after their mother and Sarah died.
37   Nurse Annie Rancombe and her sister Isabel cared for Sarah from
    1941.
38   Lockhart, J.G., *Memoirs of the Life of Sir Walter Scott* (7 vols.,
    Edinburgh, 1837) A. & C. Black, 1909.
39   Lyndoe, E., *Complete Practical Astrology*, Putnam, 1938. He
    drew the birth charts of the French Republic and the German Empire
    showing why they were antipathetic. In a copy of the book presented
    anonymously to Bath Reference Library in 1951 – possibly by
    Gladys – there is a pencil calculation on p. 312 showing the chart for
    the French Republic: '. . . sextile Mars rad. coming on May 9
    1945 – German surrender date.'
40   Hawthorne, N., *The Marble Faun or the Romance of Monte Beni*,
    Kegan Paul, 1889.
41   Priscilla Gordon: close friend of Ina in Bath – in this context it
    must be a family joke.
42   Great Western Railway.
43   Air Raid Precautions.
44   Mrs Mary Louisa Molesworth (1839–1921): Scottish fiction writer
    best known for her children's books.

Chapter XII: Calne and Sarah's Death

1   Singers-Bigger, G., 'God's Own City', *Lilies of the Hill*,
    unpublished poems in Bath Reference Library.
2   *The Laird of Glenfernlie* by Mary Johnstone: untraceable.
3   Now that their mother was dead, Gladys and Ina planned to share a
    cottage with Ina's friend Miss Michell at Dittersham, Devon.
4   Buchan, J., *The Thirty-Nine Steps*, Longmans, 1938.
5   *Riceyman Steps* was not by J.B. Priestley but by Arnold Bennett.

6 Lady Harburton founded the Rational Dress Society in 1887.
7 Article on George Moore: untraceable.
8 *Barcarolle* from *Tales of Hoffman* had been played in a Bath tea room on 6 December 1928 with similar response (see p. 207).
9 William Penn (1644–1718): founder of the colony of Pennsylvania, USA, joined the Society of Friends (Quakers); preached and wrote as a Friend; imprisoned for nonconformity.
10 Sarah's butler and maid at Sion Hill Place.

Chapter XIII: Finale

1 Singers-Bigger, G., 'Speedwell Farewell', *Lilies of the Hill*, unpublished poems in Bath Reference Library.
2 *New York Times*, 13 May 1943.
3 Fairfield, Laetitia: letter to *Manchester Guardian*, *op. cit*. She was Rebecca West's sister.
4 *Bath Weekly Chronicle & Herald*, 15 May 1943.
5 Whitby, C., letter to Singers-Bigger, G., 30 June 1943, courtesy of Elaine Showalter.
6 The Reverend Gordon Stringer.
7 Bath & Wilts Evening Chronicle, 14 January 1970.

Bibliography

Books by Sarah Grand

Two Dear Little Feet (by Frances Elizabeth McFall), Jarrolds, 1873.
Ideala: A Study From Life, E. W. Allen, 1888; Bentley, 1889; Heinemann, 1893.
A Domestic Experiment, Blackwood's, 1891.
The Heavenly Twins, Heinemann, 1893.
Singularly Deluded, Blackwood's, 1893.
Our Manifold Nature (collection of stories), Heinemann, 1894.
The Beth Book, Heinemann, 1897, Virago Press 1979.
The Modern Man And Maid, Horace Marshall, 1898.
The Tenor And The Boy, Heinemann, 1899.
The Human Quest: Being some thoughts in contribution to the subject of the art of Happiness, Heinemann, 1900.
Babs The Impossible, Hutchinson, 1901.
Emotional Moments (collection of stories), Hurst & Blackett, 1908.
Adnam's Orchard, Heinemann, 1912.
The Winged Victory, Heinemann, 1916.
Variety (collection of stories), Heinemann, 1922.
The Breath of Life (quotations from work by Sarah Grand), privately printed, 1933.

Short Stories and Articles by Sarah Grand

'Mama's Music Lessons', *Aunt Judy's Magazine For Young People*, June and July 1878.
'The Baby's Tragedy', *The Lady's Realm*, 1880.
'School Revisited', *Aunt Judy's Magazine For Young People*, June and July 1880.
'The Great Typhoon', *Aunt Judy's Magazine For Young People*, April 1881.

'Janey, A Humble Administrator', *Temple Bar*, October 1891.

'Kane, A Soldier Servant', *Temple Bar*, July 1891.

'Boomellen: A Study From Life', *Temple Bar*, March 1892.

'Singularly Deluded', *Blackwood's Edinburgh Magazine*, August – December 1892.

'The Morals of Manner and Appearance', *The Humanitarian*, August 1893.

'The Duty Of Looking Nice', *The Review of Reviews*, August 1893.

'Ah Man: A Study From Life', *The Woman At Home*, October 1893.

'The New Aspect Of The Woman Question', *The North American Review*, March 1894.

'The Man Of The Moment', *The North American Review*, May 1894.

'The Modern Girl', *The North American Review*, June 1894.

'The Tree Of Knowledge – on the subject of education and marriage of women – with Mme Adam, The Rev. H. Adler chief Rabbi, Walter Besant, Bjornstjerne Bjornson, Hall Caine, Mrs Edmund Gosse, Thomas Hardy, Mrs L. Linton and others, *The New Review*, June 1894.

'Should Irascible Old Gentlemen Be Taught To Knit?' *Phil May's Winter Annual*, 1894.

'A Page Of Confessions', *Woman At Home*, October 1894.

'The Condemned Cell', *Norfolk Daily Standard*, 22 December 1894.

'The Woman's Question', *The Humanitarian*, March 1896.

'Fragment of a letter by Sarah Grand', *The Lady's Realm*, Vol. 1, 1896.

'When The Door Opened', *The Idler*, January 1898.

'The Modern Girl', *Temple Magazine*, February 1898.

'The New Woman And The Old', *The Lady's Realm*, August 1898.

'The Modern Young Man', *Temple Magazine*, September 1898.

'On The Choice Of a Husband', *The Young Woman*, October 1898.

'Marriage Questions In Fiction – the standpoint of a typical modern woman', *Fortnightly Review*, 1898.

'Does Marriage Hinder A Woman's Self-Development? (A discussion by Sarah Grand, Hon. Mabel Vereker, Gertrude Atherton, Lady Troubridge, Mona Caird, Lady Hamilton, Mrs Wynne)', *The Lady's Realm*, V, November 1898 – April 1899.

'At What Age Should Girls Marry?', *The Young Woman*, February 1899.

'Should Married Women Follow Professions?', *The Young Woman*, April 1899.

Letter to the Editor, *The Daily Telegraph*, 22 November 1897.

Letter to the Editor, *The Morning Leader*, 5 February 1900.

'Babs The Impossible', *The Lady's Realm*, 1900–1901.

'Some Recollections Of My School Days', *The Lady's Magazine*, January 1901.

'The Man In The Scented Coat', *The Lady's World*, June 1904.

Preface to Bartholomew's 'As They Are', 1908.

'One of The Olden Time', *The Pall Mall Magazine*, July 1911.

'The Case Of The Modern Married Woman', *The Pall Mall Magazine*, February 1913.

Mid Victorian Memories by M. B. Betham-Edwards 'with a personal sketch by Sarah Grand', John Murray, 1919.

'Exquisite Bath – Impressions Of a Newcomer', *Bath & Wilts Chronicle*, 27 May 1922.

'Bath Today', *The Graphic*, 3 December 1921 and *The Bath Anthology*, 1928.

Articles about Sarah Grand

'Sarah Grand', *The Gentlewoman*, 23 December 1893.

'Madame Sarah Grand', *Cassell's Universal Portrait Gallery*, 1894.

'The Strike Of Sex', *The Quarterly Review*, July and October 1894.

Black, Helen C., *Pen, Pencil, Baton, Mask: Biographical Sketches*, 1896.

Tooley, Sarah, 'The Woman's Question', *The Humanitarian*, March 1896.

'Sarah Grand On Men And Women', *Review of Reviews*, April 1896.

'Women Of Note In The Cycling World – A Chat With Sarah Grand', *The Hub*, October 1896.

Caird, M., *The Morality Of Marriage And Other Essays On The Status And Destiny Of Woman*, George Redway, 1897.

Stutfield, H.E.M., 'The Psychology Of Feminism', *Blackwood's Magazine*, January 1897.

Tooley, Sarah, 'Some Women Novelists', *The Woman At Home*, 1897.

Camden Pratt, A.T. (ed.), *People Of The Period*, Neville Beeman, 1897.

Forbes, Athol, 'Impressions Of Sarah Grand', *The Lady's World*, June 1900.

'Novelists Of Today – Madame Sarah Grand', *Warrington Press*, 3 May 1901.

Layard, G.S., *Mrs Lynn Linton, Her Life, Letters And Opinions*, Methuen, 1901.

Macarthur, J., 'Notes Of A Bookman', *Harper's Weekly*, 2 November 1901.

McFall, Haldane, 'Sarah Grand', *The Biographist & Review*, 1902.

Black, Helen C., *Notable Women Authors Of The Day*, Maclaren, 1906.

Foerster, E, 'Die Frauenfrage in den Romanen von George Egerton, Mona Caird und Sarah Grand', *Marburg*, 1907.

Tynan, K., *The Middle Years*, Constable, 1916.

Ellis, S.M., *George Meredith: His Life and Friends in Relation to his Work*, Grant Richards, 1920.

Whyte, F., *William Heinemann: A Memoir*, Cape, 1928.

Priestley McCracken, L.A.M., 'Madame Sarah Grand And Women's Emancipation', *Minerva* and *The Vote*, August 1933.

'Rita' (Mrs Desmond Humphreys), *Recollections Of A Literary Life*, Melrose, 1936.

Cruse, A., *After The Victorians*, Allen & Unwin, 1938.

Mott, F.L., *Golden Multitudes: The Story Of Best Sellers In The United States* Macmillan, New York, 1947.

Laurence, D.H. (ed.), *G.B. Shaw: Collected Letters 1874–1897*, Max Reinhardt, 1965.

Hardy, E. and Pinion, F.B. (ed.), *One Rare Fair Woman – Thomas Hardy's Letters to Florence Henniker 1893–1922*, Macmillan, 1972.

Cunningham, A.R., 'The New Woman Fiction Of The 1890's, *Victorian Studies*, 1973.

Showalter, E., *A Literature of Their Own*, Virago Press, 1977.

Lister, S.P., *Sarah Grand And The Late Victorian Feminist Novel*, MS, Manchester Polytechnic, 1977.

Cunningham, G., *The New Woman And The Victorian Novel*, Macmillan, 1978.

Huddleston, J., *Sarah Grand, A Bibliography*, University of Queensland, 1979.

General Bibliography

Allen, G., *The Woman Who Did*, John Lane, 1895.

Bagnold, E., *Autobiography*, Heinemann, 1969.

Bellows, W., *Edmund Gosse: Some Memories*, Cobden-Sanderson, 1929.

Bernard, J.F., *Talleyrand: A Biography*, Collins, 1973.

Brendon, P., *Eminent Edwardians*, Secker & Warburg, 1979.

Brooke, E.F., *A Superfluous Woman*, Heinemann, 1894.

Caffyn, K.M. ('Iota'), *A Yellow Aster*, Hutchinson, 1894.

Chappell, J., *Noble Work By Noble Women*, S.W. Partridge, 1900.

Craig, E. and St John, C. (ed.), *Ellen Terry's Memoirs*, Gollancz, 1933.

Crow, D., *The Victorian Woman*, Allen & Unwin, 1971.

Cockshut, A.O.J., *Truth to Life: The Art of Biography in the Nineteenth Century*, Collins, 1974.

Colby, V., *The Singular Anomaly – Women Novelists of the Nine-*

teenth Century, University of London Press, 1970.

Dangerfield, G., *The Strange Death of Liberal England*, Macgibbon & Kee, 1966.

Davidoff, L., *Class and Gender in Victorian England*, MS, University of Essex, 1978.

Egerton, G., *Keynotes*, Elkin Mathews & John Lane, 1894, Virago Press, 1983.

First, R. and Scott, A., *Olive Schreiner*, André Deutsch, 1980.

Fulford, R., *Votes for Women*, White Lion, 1976.

Gardiner, L., 'A Cheapened Paradise', *Westminster Review*, 1888.

Gawsworth, J., *Ten Contemporaries*, Ernest Benn, 1932.

Gissing, G., *The Odd Women*, Anthony Blond, 1968, Virago Press, 1980.

Harris, W.J., 'Egerton, Forgotten Realist', *Victorian Newsletter*, 1968.

Harrison, F., *The Dark Angel: Aspects of Victorian Sexuality*, Sheldon Press, 1977.

Healey, E., *Lady Unknown: The Life of Angela Burdett-Coutts*, Sidgwick Jackson, 1978.

Hogarth, J.E., 'The Monstrous Regiment of Women', *Fortnightly Review*, December 1897.

Holman-Hunt, D., *My Grandfather, His Wives and Loves*, Hamish Hamilton, 1969.

Hudson, D., *Munby: Man of Two Worlds*, John Murray, 1972.

Huws Jones, E., *Mrs Humphry Ward*, Heinemann, 1973.

Johnson, D., *Lesser Lives*, Heinemann, 1973.

Johnston, J., *The Life, Manners and Travels of Fanny Trollope*, Constable, 1979

Kingsmill, H., *Frank Harris*, John Lehmann, 1932.

Laski, M., *George Eliot and Her World*, Thames & Hudson, 1973.

Liddington, J. and Norris, J., *One Hand Tied Behind Us*, Virago Press, 1978.

Linklater, A., *An Unhusbanded Life: Charlotte Despard – Suffragette, Socialist and Sinn Feiner*, Hutchinson, 1980.

Linton, Mrs Lynn, *My Literary Life*, Hodder & Stoughton, 1899.

Marcus, S., *The Other Victorians: A Study of Sexuality and Pornography in Mid-Nineteenth-Century England*, Weidenfeld & Nicholson, 1966.

Marholm, L. (trans. Etchison, G.A.), *The Psychology of Woman*, Grant Richards, 1899.

Mavor, E., *The Ladies of Llangollen*, Michael Joseph, 1971.

Menzies, Mrs, *Memories Discreet and Indiscreet: A Woman of No Importance*, Herbert Jenkins, 1917.

Mill, J.S., *On the Subjection of Women*, 1869.

Mitchell, J. and Oakley, A., *The Rights and Wrongs of Women*, Penguin, 1976.

Nethercot, A.H., *The Last Four Lives of Annie Besant*, Hart-Davis, 1963.

Petrie, G., *A Singular Iniquity: The Campaigns of Josephine Butler*, Macmillan, 1972.

Pankhurst, E., *My Own Story*, Virago Press, 1979.

Pankhurst, S., *The Suffragette Movement*, Longmans, 1931, Virago Press, 1977.

Raeburn, A., *The Suffragette View*, David & Charles, 1976.

Rowbotham, S., *Hidden from History*, Pluto Press, 1977.

Rowell, G., *The Victorian Theatre*, Cambridge University Press, 1978.

Rossi, A., *The Feminist Papers*, Bantam, 1974.

Ruskin, J., *Sesame and Lilies*, Dent, 1895.

Scott, W.S., *Marie Corelli: The Story of a Friendship*, Hutchinson, 1955.

Simon, L., *The Biography of Alice B. Toklas*, Peter Owen, 1978.

Strachey, B., *Remarkable Relations*, Gollancz, 1980.

Strachey, L., *Eminent Victorians*, Chatto & Windus, 1918.

Strachey, R., *The Cause*, Virago Press, 1978.

Thompson, P., *The Edwardians*, Weidenfeld & Nicolson, 1975.

Thornton, Sir J.H., *Memoirs of Seven Campaigns*, Constable, 1895.

Tims, M., *Mary Wollstonecraft: A Social Pioneer*, Millington, 1976.

Vicinus, M. (ed.), *Suffer and Be Still*, Indiana University Press, 1972.

Wardle, R.M. (ed.), *Collected Letters of Mary Wollstonecraft*, Cornell, 1979.

White, T. de V., *A Leaf from the Yellow Book: The Correspondence of George Egerton*, The Richards Press, 1958.

Wollstonecraft, M., *A Vindication of the Rights of Women*, Dent, 1929.

Woolf, V., *A Room of One's Own*, Hogarth Press, 1929.

[Note: Any book that mentions Sarah appears in the previous section.]